Praise for *The Los...*

Also by Vaseem Khan

The Malabar House series
Midnight at Malabar House
The Dying Day

The Baby Ganesh Agency series
The Unexpected Inheritance of Inspector Chopra
The Perplexing Theft of the Jewel in the Crown
The Strange Disappearance of a Bollywood Star
Inspector Chopra and the Million Dollar Motor Car
(Quick Read)
Murder at the Grand Raj Palace
Bad Day at the Vulture Club

The Lost Man
of Bombay

Vaseem Khan

HODDER

First published in Great Britain in 2022 by Hodder & Stoughton
An Hachette UK company

This paperback edition published in 2023

3

Maps by Rosie Collins

A CIP catalogue record for this title is available from the British Library

Paperback ISBN 978 1 529 34114 0

Typeset in Adobe Caslon by Hewer Text UK Ltd, Edinburgh
Printed and bound in Great Britain by Clays Ltd, Elcograf S.p.A.

Hodder & Stoughton policy is to use papers that are natural, renewable
and recyclable products and made from wood grown in sustainable
forests. The logging and manufacturing processes are expected to
conform to the environmental regulations of the country of origin.

Hodder & Stoughton Ltd
Carmelite House
50 Victoria Embankment
London EC4Y 0DZ

www.hodder.co.uk

To Prem Kumar Badhwar, my father-in-law, who passed away this year, a man of great integrity, wisdom, and, when the mood took him, a wry sense of humour.

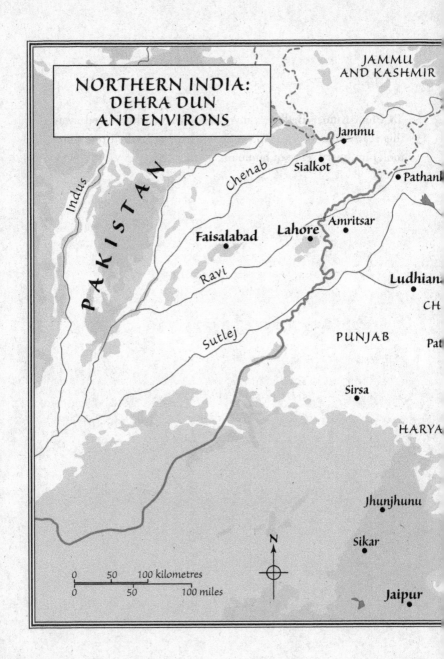

NORTHERN INDIA:
DEHRA DUN
AND ENVIRONS

JAMMU
AND KASHMIR

Indus

PAKISTAN

Chenab

Jammu

Sialkot

Pathank

Faisalabad

Lahore

Amritsar

Ravi

Ludhian

CH

Sutlej

PUNJAB

Pat

Sirsa

HARYA

Jhunjhunu

Sikar

Jaipur

N

0   50   100 kilometres
0   50   100 miles

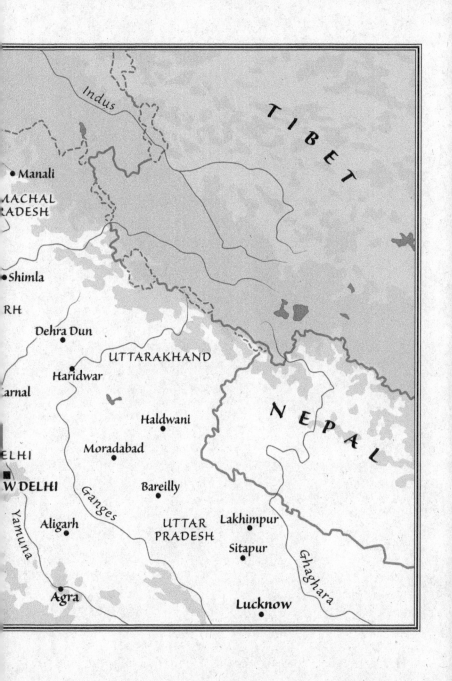

I

March, 1950 – Tsangchokla Pass, Himalayan foothills

'Have you lost your mind?'

It was almost impossible to understand what Martel was saying above the rising wind.

Peter Reynolds blinked the snow out of his eyes. The blizzard was coming in hard and fast; soon they'd have to break camp and wait it out.

But he couldn't let go of what he'd seen. Or, at least, what he'd *thought* he'd seen.

'I think there's someone up there.'

Martel's cadaverous face registered a moment's confusion, then twisted into anger. Peter sensed another argument.

When they had left to begin their adventure, just three weeks earlier, they'd departed as colleagues, having met eight months prior in New Delhi, a city undergoing a slow and painful transformation under Nehru's fractious new government.

A friendship had developed, of sorts. Two Europeans – traditional foes, an Englishman and a Frenchman – navigating the bureaucratic jungle of the nation's capital. Not that that was how the Indians saw themselves. Dealing with the pompous new breed of civil servant had become the bane of Peter's life. Independence had brought freedom to the country, but with it had come opportunists settling into the vacuum left by the departing British. If Delhi had been a city of forts and mendicants before, it now served as a bastion of political cutthroats and blowhards with the moral scruples of rutting goats.

The paperwork alone was enough to make a man blow his brains out.

The trek had been a welcome break. Martel, an experienced climber, had proposed the expedition, had even picked a route suited to Peter's level of skill.

Or so he'd said at the time.

They'd taken the *Himalayan Queen* up from Delhi, then hired a jeep to ferry them to the village of Yamunotri, nestled in the foothills of the Garhwal Himalayas. From here they'd set off on foot, nothing but the packs on their backs, making their way up through the Dhumdhar Kandi Pass, an experience Peter would not soon forget.

The scenery, as Martel had promised, was enough to take a man's breath away: vivid mountainscapes, crystal clear night skies, the occasional snow leopard. What he'd neglected to mention was the cold and the danger. The high mountain passes were no place for an unseasoned climber, weak-limbed by the first stirrings of mountain sickness.

It didn't help that he was in the company of a man whose recklessness would have made a drunk sapper seem sober by comparison.

Not that the Frenchman had shown any remorse. He had that peculiar temperament oblivious to anything but its own inverted logic.

Sociopath. That was the word.

Having barely survived the Dhumdhar Kandi Pass, Peter had made up his mind to quit. But somehow, Martel had beguiled him. The simple fact was that they had planned a two-man expedition. Even Martel wasn't foolhardy enough to continue on his own.

Guilt. That, and the fear of ridicule in the eyes of a Frenchman.

Quitting was simply not an option.

They'd trekked down from the pass to the hamlet of Dharali, then turned up to Nelang. From here, they'd headed northwards to the Tsangchokla Pass, leading into Tibet, their ultimate destination.

'It will make a fine story,' Martel had told him. *'Imagine la tête que feront tes enfants!'*

Well, he was certainly imagining the faces of his children now. Imagining them gathered around his casket at the old church in Hampstead with his wife, Amanda, dressed in black and cursing her fool of a husband.

Martel's growl cut across his thoughts. 'No one could be alive up there.'

Peter hesitated. How sure was he of what he'd seen?

They'd been trekking through the high pass, knee-deep in snow, a stiff wind lacerating their faces. The valley snarled around them, sharp granite ridges covered in their winter blankets.

Martel had told him the route was often employed by Buddhist pilgrims.

What he hadn't bothered to point out was that even fanatics rarely ventured here in the depths of winter.

And then the worst had happened.

A roar above and behind him. He'd turned to see a section of the nearest ridge shear away, come tumbling down in great slabs of snow and ice. Crying out in terror, he'd flapped and cursed his way out of the torrent's path.

When the snow had settled, he'd looked back and seen . . . a narrow cave opening high up on the ridge's flank. And in the mouth of the cave, what looked like the shape of a man.

He'd used his binoculars, but couldn't be certain.

He'd caught up with Martel, who'd been a hundred yards ahead and had missed the minor avalanche entirely.

3

Convincing him to go back was never going to be straightforward.

'Out of the question. If anyone *is* there, then he is dead.'

'All the more reason to check. His family would wish to know.'

'It is not our responsibility.'

'I can't see anyone else out here.' Peter squared up to the Frenchman. He was sick of Martel's condescending attitude. 'I'm not moving on until we take a look.'

Martel must have seen something in the set of his shoulders.

'Merd!' he shouted and then turned and began trudging back the way they'd come.

Peter smiled under his hood, gripped his walking poles, and followed.

It took some time to find a safe route up to the cave.

Martel led, cursing all the while. On more than one occasion the unsettled snow shifted under them, almost making Peter question his obstinacy.

Finally, they slipped into the opening. The cave mouth was small and shadowed in darkness. Outside, dusk was falling.

He stared down at the shape he thought he'd seen.

A wash of relief as he realised his eyes hadn't deceived him.

The dead man was splayed against the inner wall of the cave mouth. Rocks had piled up behind him, where the roof had collapsed, packed in with ice and snow. It seemed obvious that he must have been further in, and the avalanche had nudged his body towards the opening. Without that movement, he might have remained hidden, Peter thought. In the summer months, no one would bother to climb up here simply to explore a narrow opening in the rock face.

With a sharp bite of horror, he noted that the man's face was all but gone, crushed by falling rocks.

Martel had dropped to his knees and was examining the body closely, running a torch over it. 'He's a white man,' he eventually concluded.

Peter knew that many western climbers had perished in and around the Himalayas, lost in the high passes or attempting reckless mountain exploits.

He shuddered. *There but for the grace of God . . .*

Martel had begun searching the man's pockets.

'What are you doing?'

'Looking for identification.' He patted down the man's thin shirt and trousers. The outfit was completely unsuited to the cold.

How had he ended up here in this remote cave?

Martel pulled something from an inner pocket.

A book.

Slipping off a bulky glove, he blew warmth on to his fingers, then flipped open the book and trained the torch on the flyleaf.

Peter resisted the urge to snatch the volume from the Frenchman's hands.

A gust of wind blew into the cave, howled around them.

Finally, Martel looked up at him. The torchlight gave his sallow cheeks a skeletal aspect.

'Bombay,' he said, simply.

2

'What can you tell me about him?'

'I can tell you he's the most famous man in the country about now.'

Persis scowled. Standing in the Grant Medical College autopsy room, the pungent smell of formaldehyde stinging her nostrils, she was in no mood for Bhoomi's macabre brand of humour.

The newspapers had had a field day.

An unidentified white man found dead in a cave up in the Himalayan foothills.

A man of mystery.

The Ice Man.

Who was he? How long had he been there? What had he been doing there?

The only clue: a book discovered on his person, a book that had led, for a reason she hadn't yet ascertained, to his body being sent to Bombay.

As the clamour grew to unravel the Ice Man's fate, the case had been shunted from one government office to another until it had landed at Malabar House, the runt of Bombay's constabulary, a station where those in ill favour were sent – some as a penance, others because there was nowhere else to put them.

Persis, as the first – and to date, only – female inspector to have qualified for the Indian Police Service, had found herself in the latter category.

In her short time at the station, she'd been tasked with several politically sensitive cases, the kind that no one else wanted – no

6

one in their right mind, at any rate. Her efforts had thrust her into the national spotlight, an uncomfortable place to be at the best of times.

It seemed not to occur to her detractors that their objections were at odds with the ideals of the new India. Hadn't women fought the same fight, shed the same blood? Why should they be denied the right to participate in Nehru's bright new dawn?

She shook the thought aside and focused on the Ice Man.

Roshan Seth, her commanding officer, had drily explained the situation that morning.

'The Ice Man has become a cause célèbre, Persis. This makes him a headache for our superiors. No one wants to be seen to fail. And so, they've handed the job to us. And now I'm handing it to you. Congratulations.'

She stood back as Bhoomi went through his routine, occasionally barking at his assistant, a small wiry man named Kemal Butt, who had set up a camera so that the body could be photographed.

The pathologist carefully cut away the dead man's clothing, revealing a pale corpse – middle-aged, if she had to guess – with sandy hair and strangely blackened hands, ears and throat.

'Did *you* remove his shoes?' she asked.

'Well spotted,' said Bhoomi, as his assistant photographed the naked body, the flash popping brightly in the low-ceilinged suite. 'No. He came in without any shoes. Or gloves, for that matter.'

Bhoomi picked up a foot, took a closer look, as if examining a marrow at the market. He noticed her staring.

'Do you know what happens to the human body in extreme cold?' He didn't wait for an answer. 'Our bodies react by reducing blood flow to our hands and feet to preserve our core temperature. It's a process called vasoconstriction. But in doing so, we lose heat in our extremities. As fluid in our tissues begins to freeze, our cell walls break down, leading to necrosis.'

'Frostbite.'

'Yes. And that is precisely what is missing here.'

She waited for him to expand.

'This man did not die because of the cold. There is evidence of damage to the body caused *by* cold, but I believe that to have occurred post-mortem, a result of the icy conditions in which he was preserved.'

'Why is he wearing such thin clothes? Where are his shoes and gloves?'

Bhoomi lowered the foot. 'Have you heard of a phenomenon called "paradoxical undressing"?'

She shook her head.

'In the final stages of hypothermia, the mind begins to play tricks. Sometimes, it convinces us that we're warming up – possibly because of damage to the vasomotor centre. Climbers who succumb to the cold are often found in a state of undress.'

'You're suggesting he might have been wearing more clothes?'

'It would be a strange man who went up into the mountains dressed as our friend here.'

He said no more and bent once again to his work. She watched as he took measurements of the body, and then carried out a fingertip search, leaning over the corpse and noting his observations in a leather-bound journal.

Once done, he gestured at Butt to help him turn the body over, the pallid flesh slapping wetly on the autopsy table.

The sound didn't bother her, nor the sight of the mutilated corpse.

Death had never fazed her – not in the autopsy suite of the police training college at Mount Abu, and not in the streets of Bombay during the worst of the Partition rioting, when fly-covered bodies lay out in the open for days.

She waited while Bhoomi finished his examination. The pathologist took extra care with the wounds to the crushed face. Pausing midway, he picked up a swab and ran it around the inner whorl of the right ear. 'Strange,' he muttered.

'What is?'

'The ear is blackened. Initially I thought it was frostbite, but we've determined that it's not that. Neither is it due to routine post-mortem discolouration of the skin – note how the colour here is much darker than the feet. This is some sort of . . . substance. It's also smeared on his hands and throat. Quite possibly his face too, though there's not much left of that to be certain. I'm not sure what it is.' He continued to stare at the swab, then deposited it into a bag. 'I'll have to send it away for testing.'

He returned to his bank of instruments, picked up a small saw, and bent to the business of opening up the body.

She looked on as he extracted and weighed the organs, then placed a body block under the dead man's head, before making an incision across the fractured crown and peeling back the scalp. In short order, he had exposed the brain, scooped it out, weighed it, then set it down on a steel tray.

Next, he pulled back the face and began a detailed examination of the skull.

When he finally stepped away, he looked perturbed.

'Here is what I *can* tell you . . . by my estimation, our victim was a man in his early forties. I can't be sure, but if I had to guess, he's been up in that cave for some time. Years. Five, maybe ten. It's impossible to be certain. Human bodies can be preserved almost perfectly by very cold conditions, certainly over the period we're talking about.'

'How did he die?'

'My working hypothesis is that he died from blunt force trauma to the cranium and face. The morphology of his wounds is consistent with him being struck by rocks. One possible scenario might be that our friend here lost his mind in the grip of incipient hypothermia, tore off most of his clothes, then climbed up into that cave where a rock fall killed him. That would explain the absence of pronounced frostbite. Once he was dead, and in that cave, tissue damage from the cold would have slowed.'

There was something in his tone.

'You sound unconvinced by your own scenario.'

He clicked his tongue. 'The fact that his wounds are so precisely centred around his face and skull makes me wonder . . .'

She waited.

'Look, there's no way for me to be certain, but . . . it almost seems as if his face was deliberately caved in. The number of blows, the damage inflicted, the impact pattern of the strikes . . . they all indicate a force that I find hard to believe could have been generated by falling rocks, in what, if the report accompanying the body is to be believed, is a very small cave. What I mean is – the rocks would have had to have been either incredibly dense or fallen from a great height to make this sort of mess. The cranium is incredibly robust,' he added.

She understood instantly. 'You're suggesting he was murdered?'

He shrugged. 'I'm suggesting it's a strong possibility.'

3

'Murdered?' said Seth, bleakly.

'Yes.'

He closed his eyes and breathed in aggressively through his nostrils. Under normal circumstances she'd have expected him to reach for the bottle of whisky in the top drawer of his desk, but she knew he'd made a conscious effort over the past weeks to curb the habit.

Roshan Seth, Superintendent of Police, and her commanding officer, had once been a leading light in the Bombay police, before the advent of independence had fired his career out of a cannon into the side of a barn. The changing of the guard had provided his rivals with the opportunity to settle old scores. Though never directly accused, rumours had poured into the ears of those that had taken over the running of the Imperial Police Force, whispers that suggested Seth had pursued his duty with excessive zeal during the Raj.

In the new India, such an accusation was tantamount to a death sentence.

In truth, she knew that Seth might well have preferred the hangman's rope to the living death he now experienced, relegated to Malabar House, placed in charge of a group of misfits and undesirables, his career as dead as the Ice Man. A shrewd officer, once fastidious, he had succumbed to the lure of the bottle. His days were now spent lurking in his basement office like a giant bat with a jaundiced liver and a terminal case of cynicism.

'Do we have any leads as to his identity?' he now asked.

'He was a white man in his forties. That's about all we can say. His face is crushed beyond all recognition. It would be pointless to release a photograph.'

'There can't be many foreigners who've gone missing up there.'

'You'd be surprised. I spoke to a Himalayan mountain guide earlier today – he runs a rescue service up near where the Ice Man was found. Apparently, dozens of climbers go missing in that region every year. Most are still up there. Recovery is difficult and expensive. Often, they don't even bother to log their planned routes with the local authorities.'

Seth tapped the desk. Without a glass in his hand, he seemed oddly naked.

'So what *do* we know?'

'Very little. The only thing we have to go on is the book that was found on him. I've brought it back from the morgue. I was about to examine it before you hauled me in here.'

He gave her a sour look. 'Heaven forbid you should keep your commanding officer in the loop. What's the book?'

'I don't know. I haven't looked at it yet.' She allowed a trace of impatience to enter her voice.

He raised his hands in surrender. 'Fine. Fine. Just let me know as soon as you have something. Shukla is making my life miserable. Delhi is holding his feet to the fire on this one.'

She knew, from past experience, that Additional Deputy Commissioner of Police Shukla was a political animal, with the smile of a crocodile and the temperament to match. 'Why does Delhi care?'

'Because we live in an enlightened era, Persis. India is now a member of the global fraternity. The Ice Man is all over the airwaves. Everyone wants to know who our mysterious white friend was.'

'It's funny. Hundreds of thousands of Indians died during the Raj and no one gave a damn.'

He waved her words away as if swatting a fly. Old grievances. Pointless to dwell on the past now. India was steaming ahead, forging an identity that would define her place in the world in the decades to come. Nehru was remaking the country in his own image, penning a national fairy tale to rival the myth-making of the Hindu pantheon. A lingering hangover from the colonial era might have dulled her political senses, but India was now awake, seven millennia of tradition and history reasserting itself.

There was no time to play the victim.

'How do you plan to proceed?' Seth asked.

'I'll have a look at the book, see if it points me anywhere. In the meantime, let's hope someone remembers a white man who went trekking up in that region and never came back.'

He leaned back, folded his hands over his stomach, then unfolded them.

'There's something else.' He paused, suddenly agitated. His eyes slid away. 'Have you heard of the Bombay Slum Rehabilitation Programme?'

'No.'

'An idea dreamed up by someone in the state legislature with too much time on their hands. The aim is to pan for gold in the murkiest pools of our fair city. Seek out the best and brightest in Bombay's slums and give them a leg up. That sort of thing.'

'Why are you telling *me*?'

He took a deep breath. 'Because, Persis, it has been decided that *you* will take on a mentee as part of this shiny new initiative.'

She stared at him, stony-faced. 'I don't think so.'

His moustache twitched. 'You seem to be under the illusion that you have a choice in the matter.' He leaned forward, set his elbows on the desk. 'It's simple. They assign you a mentee. You meet the mentee. You talk to the mentee. You impart *wisdom*.'

'If it's so simple, why don't you do it? Sir.'

'I'm afraid *you* have been specifically requested.'

'By who?'

'By the mentee. By those running the programme. By God, for all I know.'

'And if I refuse?'

His lips curled back in a parody of a smile, but he said nothing. There was no need.

She turned and walked stiffly to the door, then looked back. 'I think I liked you better when you were drinking.'

Back in the office, she weaved her way to her desk and slumped into her seat. Slipping off her cap, she set it down and leaned back. The ceiling fan ruffled a sheaf of papers, congealing the sweat on her brow.

Even in early March the temperature was sweltering.

In other nations, spring announced a time of rebirth and renewal, serenaded by the mellifluous descant of nightingales, and the heady fragrance of cherry blossom and freshly cut grass. In Bombay, by contrast, spring heralded the onset of a torrid heat that curdled the open sewers and mounds of rotting vegetation dotted about the city like decorative flourishes, feasted upon by pie dogs and feral pigs who couldn't quite believe their luck.

The open-plan office, a jumble of desks and battered steel filing cabinets, was all but deserted. Of her fellow inspector, Hemant Oberoi, there was no sign. Neither was Sub-Inspector George Fernandes present. She knew that Fernandes was still recovering from the bullet wound he'd sustained during their last investigation.

Her thoughts were interrupted by the arrival of Sub-Inspectors Birla and Haq, clattering into the basement space like a brass band into a lift.

Haq, a large man with a lantern-shaped head and cauliflower ears, collapsed into his seat, wiped a fleshy forearm across his brow, then bellowed at the office peon to fetch him a glass of water.

Gopal, dozing on a stool in the corner, leaped up as if lashed by a whip, and scuttled from the room.

Birla made his way over. 'How goes it with our frozen friend?'

Of all those banished to Malabar House, Birla had been the one to show her the most civility or, at any rate, the least disrespect. A slender man in his late forties, with a savage crew-cut and a small, neat moustache, his career in the service had been distinguished by mediocrity. He'd found himself consigned to the station following a slight against a senior officer. The fact that the slight had been committed by his daughter – a refusal to entertain the advances of the officer in question – had been neither here nor there.

He wouldn't be the first father to pay for the sins of a head-strong daughter.

She quickly brought him up to speed.

Birla was her designated second on the investigation, though he had other duties that were occupying his time. Malabar House's recent notoriety – partly thanks to her own efforts – had resulted in a sudden glut of cases. The other stations in the city appeared to have agreed among themselves that anything of a quirky nature, anything politically charged and with little hope of resolution, might justifiably be shunted to Bombay's smallest police outpost.

In effect, they'd become a dumping ground for cases no one else wanted.

In a way, it made sense.

The station was already a dumping ground for officers no one else wanted to work with.

Malabar House, a four-storey Edwardian building located on John Adams Street and built in the grand British tradition, complete with gargoyles, balconied windows, a sandstone façade and an arcaded front entrance, was owned and operated by one of the country's leading business houses, the basement leased to Bombay's smallest and most unwanted police station, ostensibly the base of operations for a branch of the CID – the Criminal Investigation Department – tasked to investigate sensitive cases.

The reality put the lie to this convenient fiction.

The only cases that landed there were the ones with a tendency to explode in the faces of their investigators.

'Mystifies me why anyone cares,' expounded Birla. 'I mean, if you choose to climb mountains, you shouldn't be surprised if you end up freezing to death in a cave.'

After he'd wandered back to his desk, she picked up the evidence bag that Bhoomi had vouchsafed to her at the morgue. From inside, she slipped out the book found in the Ice Man's possession.

It was a notebook, pocket-sized and bound in pebbled brown leather, the edges scuffed, the leather faded.

She opened it to the flyleaf and immediately saw why the Ice Man had been sent to Bombay.

On the blank page was a stamp: BOMBAY PRESS, 1943.

She supposed the person who'd made the decision hadn't realised that the stamp meant nothing. The Bombay Press was, indeed, based in the city, but the notebook itself might have been sold anywhere in the country.

1943. She now had an upper limit for the length of time the Ice Man had been up in his mountain cave.

Seven years.

She continued flicking through the notebook.

The first section was taken up by various maps of India – she noted that they were all maps from the pre-Partition era, some stretching back to the beginning of the colonial period, India still labelled as *Hindoostan*. Others had legends setting out the map's provenance, for instance: *STANFORD'S MAP OF INDIA: BASED ON THE SURVEYS EXECUTED BY ORDER OF THE HONOURABLE THE EAST INDIA COMPANY, SPECIAL MAPS OF THE SURVEYOR GENERAL AND OTHER AUTHORITIES, SHOWING THE LATEST TERRITORIAL ACQUISITIONS OF THE BRITISH EMPIRE.*

She wondered briefly if the Ice Man had been a cartographer.

Perhaps he'd been exploring the high passes with the intention of mapping them?

But if that were the case, where was his equipment? Why did he have no identification on him? Had those items been lost too when he'd discarded his clothes – as Bhoomi supposed – in the throes of his death madness?

The maps were followed by ruled pages, mostly blank, a few scribbled with notes, mostly incomprehensible. The Ice Man's handwriting – if indeed it was his – was cramped, cursive, and looped into an ineligible morass. The few notes she could make out were bland observations, mainly of the weather, or odd comments such as '*P – 65 paces to corner*' or '*X – cigarette at 3.14 p.m. Panamas*'.

There seemed to be nothing about what he had been doing up in the mountains.

At the very end of the book, she found something odd.

Three missing pages, torn out. And then a fourth page, containing two lines.

The first line was a message, presumably written by the Ice Man: *'In the event of my death, please ensure that this journal reaches my wife.'*

There was nothing else. No name or address. Nothing to indicate precisely who the author had meant. Yet the line told her something: somewhere out there was a woman waiting for her husband to return. And that might mean that, somewhere, a missing persons report had been filed.

White men didn't just vanish in India without someone kicking up an almighty fuss.

Below this was another line, written in the same hand:

Caesar's Triumph holds the key

An enigmatic statement ... What could it possibly mean?

4

She was still pondering the question as she parked the jeep in the alley that ran by the side of the bookshop.

Getting out, she made her way to the front, where a string bean of a man in ragged shorts and a white vest boasting more holes than cloth was perched above the lintel, sanding down one of a pair of stone vultures perched on a plinth above the glass façade.

The Wadia Book Emporium had been passed down from her grandfather to her father, and had survived rioting, fire, and war. The shop enjoyed a loyal fan base, and this, in concert with her father's legendary bloody-mindedness, had carried it through the worst years of the Quit India movement when mobs routinely rampaged through the streets searching for symbols of the British Empire to push against the wall of history and beat to kingdom come.

A bookstore frequented by many of Bombay's white residents had proved a lamentably seductive target.

Peering into the shop, she was surprised to discover the lights had been dimmed. Her father invariably worked late, though opening and closing times were often at the mercy of his moods.

She walked in through the front door. It was never locked – if there was one thing Bombay's thieves seemed disinclined to pilfer, it was books. This was a continual source of amazement to her, given that the city's legendary pickpockets would steal the air from a drowning man's lungs if given the chance.

She walked to the rear of the shop, threading her way past *Accounting, Literary Incunabula*, and *Zoology*, skirting the battered old Chesterfield her father kept at the back, then up a flight of stairs to their apartment.

Upon entering, she found herself in the living room, where Sam and his long-time friend Dr Aziz were drinking by the grand piano.

She stared at them in astonishment.

Both men were resplendent in tuxedos. Though she'd seen Aziz in evening dress before, she'd never yet caught her father in anything so refined.

He noted her gaze and stared belligerently back at her from his wheelchair.

'What are you wearing?' she said.

'Good evening, Persis,' said Aziz, straightening from the piano and tilting his tumbler at her.

'What is he wearing?' she repeated, turning to the doctor.

'You can perfectly well see what I'm wearing,' said Sam tetchily.

'Yes,' she said. 'The question is *why* are you wearing—' She stopped. Her nostrils twitched.

Striding across the room, she lowered her nose to his neck.

'Is there a reason you're sniffing at me as if I were an old carpet?'

'You're wearing cologne!' she said accusingly.

'Is that a crime now?'

'No. I mean, it's just—'

'If you must know, I've been out. With Aziz. To the opera.'

'The opera?' Her tone could not have been more disbelieving if he'd told her the pair of them had returned from the moon.

A moment's silence thickened around them, and then she said, 'Papa, where have you *really* been?'

He stared at her, his thick grey moustache twitching in irritation. 'I don't have to stand here and be insulted by my own daughter.'

'You *can't* stand,' said Aziz helpfully. 'You're in a wheelchair.'

Sam glared at the man, then trundled out of the room, the door banging shut behind him.

Persis turned to the doctor. 'Uncle Aziz, what's going on?'

Aziz looked down into his glass. 'It's as your father says. We disported ourselves at the opera.'

'My father hates the opera. He once told me he'd rather pour boiling oil into his ears than listen to fat white men singing baritone.'

'Suffice to say that his views on the matter have changed.'

'Papa? Change?' Her incredulity could have scoured the paintwork.

'Persis, your father is simply . . . *awakening*.'

'Awakening? To what?'

Aziz smiled mysteriously. 'To possibilities.' He swung his forearm up to check his watch. 'I'm afraid I must fly. Mr Flaherty is expecting me at nine to inspect his . . . his watering can. Poor chap has a frightful problem with nocturnal emissions. I suspect an infection!'

After Aziz had left, she stood there a moment, looking at Akbar, her grey Persian tomcat, perched atop the piano, licking his paws.

Akbar refused to meet her eyes.

Something had to be very wrong if even the cat looked guilty.

She went to her bedroom, stripped off her uniform, and walked into the shower.

Undoing her single plait, she unfurled her long black hair and spent a moment gazing at herself in the mirror.

Aunt Nussie had told Persis many times that she was the spitting image of her mother, Sanaz, a society beauty in her day. Born to wealth, Sanaz had broken her father's heart by eloping with Sam Wadia, a man of limited means, prospects, and temper.

The marriage had been happy, but short-lived.

Sanaz had died in a motorcar accident when Persis was just seven.

It would be two decades before Persis would learn that Sam had been at the wheel of the car in question.

What would her mother make of her father's mysterious behaviour?

What would she make of Persis's own circumstances? A woman with few friends, a loner – and unmarried, in spite of Aunt Nussie's best efforts.

Of course, she wasn't entirely alone.

There were the handful of friends she'd clung on to from her college years: Dinaz, Jaya. And then there was Archie Blackfinch, the English criminalist she'd worked with on her past two cases. A man who'd somehow managed to disturb the simple equilibrium of her life, slipping, almost unnoticed, into the narrow space she'd left between her personal desires and the ambitions that drove her.

Thoughts of Blackfinch brought with them an unwelcome swirl of emotion. She shook the feelings aside. What good did it do to dwell on the matter?

She showered, put on a silk kimono imprinted with Japanese calligraphy, then returned to the living room where Krishna – the houseboy – was serving dinner. Her father had also returned, having divested himself of his evening dress, and was hunkered over the dining table in a cotton shirt and shorts.

She took a seat opposite and helped herself to chicken with saffron rice.

Krishna beamed a gap-toothed smile at her.

Her father's geriatric driver and manservant had once doubled as her nanny. He'd been as proficient in that role as he was in the kitchen, but, over the years, they'd become acclimatised to his cooking, like hostages during an extended siege.

Avoiding the topic of her father's recent interest in the arts, she instead told him about her day, and her progress – or rather lack of it – with the Ice Man investigation.

'They're all lunatics,' pronounced Sam. 'What's the point of climbing a mountain anyway? What have you really achieved? Does the mountain care?'

'If we didn't climb mountains, we'd never achieve anything,' she said mildly.

'It's that sort of thinking that leads men to start wars. Trying to prove their own greatness.'

She ignored him. Men – and women – climbed mountains because they spoke to something inside the human soul. In the grand scheme of things, humans were so insignificant that, occasionally, they needed to reassure themselves that they still mattered.

'You're too young to remember the German expedition that was lost on Nanga Parbat in 1934,' Sam continued. 'Nine men dead. It was led by a fool named Willy Merkl. Well, he was in Bombay earlier that year. Came into the shop. Stood there in his shiny suit smoking a cigarillo, spouting Hegel and all sorts of guff about the triumph of the human spirit. What rot! What has he got to show for his triumph of the human spirit now? A grinning skeleton, with ice in his eye sockets, that's what.'

She changed the subject. 'Why is there a man sanding down Achilles and Hector?'

Achilles and Hector: the childhood names she'd given to the stone vultures above the shopfront.

Her father's gaze dropped to his plate. The overhead light glinted from his bald dome. 'I thought the shop could use a few repairs.'

She set down her spoon and fixed him with a *look*. 'Papa. What's going on?'

'What do you mean?'

'First, you go to the opera. Now, you tell me you're redecorating—'

'It's hardly redecorating.'

She stared at him, but he refused to meet her eyes.

'Nothing's going on. If I were you, I'd save my energy for the Ice Man. You're going to need it.'

5

Her father's words proved prophetic.

The pathologist's opinion that the Ice Man had been murdered exploded on to the front pages on the second day.

She'd arrived at Malabar House to find Seth agitatedly pacing the lobby of the grand old building, smoking a cigarette.

She hadn't realised that he indulged.

'I've given up drinking,' he explained. 'I thought I'd try these instead. They're supposed to be better for you.'

He coughed like a stalled carburettor, bending over double and almost hacking his lungs out on to the terrazzo. Lurching his way to the marble counter, behind which the building's receptionist – a young woman in a mango-coloured sari – observed him with alarm, he snatched up a folded copy of the *Indian Chronicle* and thrust it at Persis.

'I suppose you've seen this?' he wheezed.

She examined the front page.

ICE MAN MURDERED!
ENIGMATIC MOUNTAIN MAN
VICTIM OF FOUL PLAY

The journalist, Aalam Channa, had somehow procured a photograph of the Ice Man's crushed face.

'That place is leakier than a burst pipe,' observed Seth.

It was an accusation often levelled at Raj Bhoomi's mortuary. Then again, she knew that Channa was a journalist with few scruples, a man who'd sell his own soul if it meant a good headline.

His recent attempts to undermine her own reputation still burned in her memory.

'This doesn't change anything.'

'Try telling that to Shukla,' countered Seth morosely. He examined the burning tip of his cigarette, then threw it on to the floor before crushing it savagely underfoot.

The day passed at a speed that would have seemed indecent were it not for the fact that she managed to accomplish next to nothing.

The garish headlines instigated a deluge of crank calls.

In the space of a few short hours, the Ice Man was identified as a native of no less than a dozen countries, with a roll call of backgrounds so extravagant as to embarrass a coven of professional spies. A noted sadhu from the port town of Pondicherry promised to reveal the Ice Man's fate if suitable financial recompense could be agreed upon for the perils he would face in communing with the departed.

She tasked Birla to follow up on the various leads, a labour he accepted grudgingly, bending to his telephone with a sigh.

Meanwhile, she began calling the other stations in the city, seeking missing persons reports that corresponded to the rough physical description of the victim.

The process was laborious and dispiriting. Record-keeping across the city's eighty odd stations was fragmented, largely dependent on who had been in charge, and how often the station had been burned down during the Quit India riots.

They made little progress during the course of the day, turning over nothing that helped in identifying their victim or understanding what he may have been doing up in the mountains.

By the time she headed home, late in the evening, she'd begun to understand exactly why no one had wanted the case. She could already smell the stink of future failure, a rancid odour that clung to the station like a Delhi fog.

6

Persis had often heard her father complain that a day in Bombay was equivalent to at least three anywhere else on the subcontinent. The sense of events moving at an ever-increasing pace, like a speeded-up film, was never far from her mind, more so in the past year since her arrival on the force.

On the third day, she arrived at the station to find Roshan Seth waiting to usher her into his office, where she discovered Hemant Oberoi sitting slackly in a chair, legs akimbo, as if he'd just returned from a hunt with his hounds.

Oberoi, the senior inspector assigned to Malabar House, had earned her ire early on with his vocal insistence that women had no place on the force. Tall, handsome, wealthy, and prone to rashness, he had landed at Malabar House following an ill-judged affair with the sister of a high-ranking government martinet. His time at the station had been marked by seething resentment at the hand fate had dealt him, manifesting in a surly attitude towards his colleagues.

As Seth made his way to the far side of the desk, Oberoi got to his feet with deliberate slowness.

'Why is *she* here?' he said, not bothering to look at Persis.

'She's here because I want her here,' replied Seth curtly.

He tore a sheet from a notepad on his desk and threw it at Oberoi.

'There's been a double murder over in Fort. A couple by the name of Renzi. I want you to take Persis and head over there.' He held up a hand. 'Before you object: Persis has shown herself to be a very capable investigator. I trust her. If you don't like it, you can hand me your badge and quit.'

The ride over to the Renzi residence could not have been more uncomfortable if she'd found herself in a tank with live eels. Oberoi made little secret of his displeasure at being forced to work with her; the feeling was mutual.

Having parked the jeep outside the Renzis' substantial bunga- low, he turned to her and said, 'Let's get one thing straight. I don't give a damn what Seth says. This is *my* case. I don't need your help or your opinion. You can tag along if he says so, but you don't open your mouth.'

Not waiting for her to reply, he crashed out of the jeep and began barking at the guard seated by the gate.

She sat there a moment, seething, then composed herself and followed him out.

They approached the two-storey, sandblasted mansion, painted in duck-egg blue, over a gravelled drive. To one side, parked under a coloured awning, she could see a small fleet of cars.

Clearly, the Renzis were an affluent couple and not afraid of showing it.

She recalled Seth's parting words. 'There's a reason the case has been sent to us. The wife is a Bombayite, from a political family – and by political, I mean her father is a long-standing thorn in Nehru's side. Tread carefully.'

They were met in the lobby by a well-dressed older man, hair greying at the temples, peppered beard trimmed neatly to the chin, dark features lined with sorrow. Introducing himself as Arthur De Mello, he explained that he was Stephen Renzi's busi- ness manager.

'Tell me about him,' said Oberoi brusquely.

De Mello blinked. 'Stephen was Italian but he'd lived in India for several years. He married . . .' He paused, overcome.

'Yes?' said Oberoi testily.

'I'm sorry. It's still hard to believe they're dead.'

'Dead is dead,' said Oberoi, unsympathetically.

De Mello seemed shocked. Persis bit down on her tongue.

'His wife is – was – Leela Sinha. The daughter of Pramod Sinha, the politician.'

'Show me the bodies.'

They followed De Mello as he led them up a flight of stairs to a carpeted landing. They walked along a corridor, before stopping outside a half-open door, where several house servants were gathered, clutching each other and weeping.

De Mello took a deep breath, then bade them enter.

The walls were papered with floral pinks and pale yellows, the marbled floor covered with a scattering of thin rugs. A chandelier shimmered above a four-poster bed, gauzy white mosquito nets hanging between the posts. To one side of the room stood a pair of stout mahogany wardrobes. On the other was a mirrored dresser with a padded stool, a skirt of gold tassels running around the bottom. A vase of dried flowers perched on one corner of the dresser, looking as if it might fall to the floor at any moment. Beside it was an ornamental wooden doll staring unseeingly out into the room.

De Mello approached the bed, then stopped. He waved at it helplessly, then turned away.

Oberoi stepped forward and savagely yanked back the net curtain from between the nearest posts.

Persis peered past him.

A flutter in her stomach like the beat of a raven's wing.

Two bodies lay on the bed, a man and a woman, dark halos of blood soaked into the pillows and bed linen around their heads.

The pair were dressed in their underclothes, the man in a vest and silk shorts, the woman in a short white nightgown that was startling against her dark skin.

'Well, they're certainly dead,' muttered Oberoi.

Persis moved closer.

The man – a white man – was unrecognisable. His face had been smashed in, nose crushed flat, the jaw hanging loose, teeth pulped into the mess. The sight was sickening, but she found a centre of calm inside her; a cold current beneath the surface of a lake.

She continued her examination.

Stephen Renzi was tall, with a good build, the belly slighting seeding to fat. His legs and arms were covered in fine dark hair, as was his head, now matted with blood.

On his left hand, he wore a wedding band. She noted that a watch lay on the nightstand. It looked expensive.

The woman beside him had been spared the brutal death her husband had suffered.

Her face was intact – unblemished skin, delicate eyebrows, a thin nose, full lips.

Leela Renzi had been a beautiful woman, and remained so in death.

'He slit her throat,' she murmured.

'What?' Oberoi turned his head. 'What did you say?'

'I said he slit her throat. The killer. But he battered the husband's face in. Why?'

'Why what?'

'Why kill the wife one way and the husband another?'

'What difference does it make? They're both dead, aren't they?'

Oberoi turned to De Mello, who was standing by the window, framed in light, dabbing at his eyes with a handkerchief.

'Who found the bodies?'

'The cook. Stephen and Leela didn't come down for breakfast, so she came up to see if they wished for breakfast in bed.'

'What time was that?'

'Around nine. She found the bodies and called me.'

'Why you and not the police?'

'Because she was in a panic. She wanted to speak to a familiar voice. I'm sure you can understand.'

'What did you do when she called you?'

'I told her not to touch anything, then rushed over to the house – I only live ten minutes away. I was praying that, somehow, she'd made a mistake, or that she was playing a horrible trick on me. I was wrong.'

The door opened behind them and a small, portly man bustled in. Sweat sparkled in his untidy grey moustache.

Persis recognised the medical examiner, Sengupta.

They waited as Sengupta bent to the bodies and quickly certified death. Never a talkative man, he checked his watch to confirm the time, filled out the necessary paperwork, and handed it to Oberoi without bothering to acknowledge Persis's presence.

'Can you estimate time of death?' asked Oberoi.

Sengupta blinked his turbot eyes. 'Based on temperature readings and the fact that rigor mortis has just begun to set in, I'd say they were killed maybe five to seven hours ago. That would put time of death between three and five a.m.'

'Dead of night,' muttered Oberoi.

'Yes, very droll,' said Sengupta drily.

'What?'

'What?'

The two men stared at each other.

'He thought you were making a pun,' said Persis, eventually.

Oberoi shot her a look.

Sengupta sighed, peeled off his gloves, picked up his bag, and departed the room without a backwards glance.

Oberoi turned to De Mello. 'I want to talk to everyone who was in the house last night.'

Fifteen minutes later, De Mello had assembled the house staff in Stephen Renzi's study.

The room was airy, with a drizzle of honey-coloured light flooding in from a bay window, pinewood bookcases, and an uncluttered writing bureau. The walls were a testament to a man who enjoyed the hunt: the stuffed heads of a menagerie of beasts looked down on them accusingly: a tiger, a deer, and the tusked skull of a bull elephant.

On one wall hung a pair of crossed rifles.

Oberoi walked up and down the parade as if conducting an inspection. Persis knew that he was fully aware of the intimidating figure he cut, especially to a group of servants caught in the eye of suspicion. It was another aspect of his personality that grated on her, the dismissive manner with which he treated those born to lower rank.

De Mello introduced the staff: Safiya Mirza, the elderly cook; Mary Gracias, the Goan cleaner; Vishal Deo, the eighteen-year-old houseboy; and Manas Ojah, the Renzis' driver.

'What about the security guard?' asked Oberoi.

'I sent him home,' said De Mello. 'He came in last evening to cover for the regular man. He was at the gate all night.'

'You can vouch for that?'

De Mello's brow furrowed. 'Well. No. Of course not.'

'Where *is* the regular man?'

'He went on leave. To his village.'

Oberoi's face slackened. He said nothing, but Persis could see his mind ticking over in the silence. Finally, he spoke. 'I want his details. This guard who just happens to vanish on the very night his employers are murdered.'

'His name is Ismail Siraj,' said De Mello, stiffly. 'But he has nothing to do with this. He's been with the Renzis for years.'

'Why don't you leave the police work to me?' said Oberoi bluntly.

Persis dug her fingernails into her palm as her colleague proceeded with his interrogation, which largely consisted of firing accusations at his cowed audience. The man had the investigative instincts of a boulder rolling downhill.

By the end of his efforts, he'd determined very little.

None of the servants lived on the premises. At the end of their respective duties, they had all returned to their own homes – all lived in the vicinity, all claimed to have been fast asleep in their beds at the time of the murders.

The last to leave had been the houseboy, Vishal Deo, who'd departed at around nine, after dinner had been cleared.

The cook, Mirza, had had to rush off quickly, and had left him to clean up.

'What were the Renzis doing when you left?' asked Oberoi, looming over the boy.

'Mr Renzi was listening to the radio in the downstairs parlour. Mrs Renzi had just returned. She said she was tired and went up to bathe.'

'Returned?'

De Mello answered for him. 'Leela was due to travel to Jaipur for a week of sightseeing with her friends. They had an overnight sleeper booked. Their plans were cancelled at the last minute when one of their party fell ill at the station.'

'Who knew about this trip?' asked Persis.

Oberoi shot her a warning glance. She ignored him.

De Mello rocked back and forth on his feet. 'What does it matter who knew?'

Oberoi leaned in towards the young Deo. 'She was very beautiful, wasn't she?'

Deo seemed confused. 'Yes. Madam was very beautiful. Like a film star.'

'You liked her, yes?'

'She was very kind to me.'

'But it wasn't kindness you wanted from her, was it? Not a young man like you. You wanted more.'

Deo's eyes rounded as he finally grasped where Oberoi was going. 'No! I – I didn't have anything to do with this.'

'I'll find out, you know,' said Oberoi calmly. 'I always do. And then they'll hang you. Just like they hanged Godse.'

Godse. Gandhi's assassin. Persis knew the mere mention of the man's much publicised execution would be enough to evoke terror in the young Deo.

'Did you know that when a man hangs, his bowels empty themselves?' Oberoi continued. '*That* will be your legacy. Dying in your own shit and piss with a rope around your neck.'

Deo whimpered.

'What about enemies?' interrupted Persis.

'Stephen was a businessman,' replied De Mello. 'Renzi Motor Parts and Engineering. Business has been booming these past few years. That sort of success attracts competitors. But none that would do something like *this*.'

'I'll be the judge of that,' said Oberoi. 'I want a list of all his business rivals.'

De Mello nodded.

'Is anything missing from the house?'

'I don't believe so. I mean, I can't be certain, but none of the servants have reported anything.'

'His watch,' said Persis.

They turned to her.

'His watch was on the table by his bed. They were still wearing their wedding bands. This was no burglary gone wrong. This was personal.'

'I told you not to speak.'

They were back in the corridor, alone.

'I don't need your permission to state a fact.'

'The only fact you need to consider is that *I'm* in charge. You do what I tell you.'

His irritation raised her hackles. They stared at each other, neither willing to take a step back.

'Um. Hello?'

They turned to find a young man hovering at the bottom of the stairs. He was tall and thin, with a mound of glistening hair balanced atop his head like a roosting bird. A black leather bag dangled from one hand, while the handle of a wheeled trunk was grasped in the other.

Persis recognised Mohammed Akram from the city's forensic science unit.

Under normal circumstances, the unit's chief, Archie Blackfinch, a Metropolitan Police criminologist currently deputed to the Bombay force, would have been in attendance, but she knew that Blackfinch was out of the city, in Delhi. Akram was the brightest of the students he was training up to replace him.

Personally, she'd always thought he looked like someone's terrified nephew.

'Who are you?' said Oberoi. 'What are you doing here?'

Akram's knees knocked together. His Adam's apple bobbed up and down.

'He's with the forensic unit,' said Persis. 'You'd know that if you ever did any real police work.'

She turned and beckoned Akram up the stairs. He ascended at

the speed of a geriatric chimpanzee, trundling his trunk behind him, wheels banging on the wooden steps.

Leaving Oberoi to stew, she led Akram to the Renzis' bedroom.

Once inside, Akram stood for a moment appraising the scene. As his eyes alighted on the bodies, he flinched, but, realising she was watching him, he recovered himself and said, gruffly, 'Murder. A nasty business.'

'You don't have to try and impress me. Just do your job well.'

He blanched, then nodded and set to work.

She watched him as he removed a tripod and camera from his trunk, set it up, then photographed the scene and the bodies.

When he'd finished, he pulled on gloves and began his examination of the environment.

'The killer probably came in through the window,' he said.

She'd already surmised as much.

The window looked down on to a rear courtyard, bounded by a brick wall about six feet in height. A relatively simple obstacle to negotiate. The climb up to the Renzis' bedroom would have taken greater effort, but a cast-iron drainpipe passing just feet from the window provided an access route for a nimble and determined killer.

The window hadn't been forced. It was a safe bet that, with the prevailing heat, the Renzis had left it open at night.

The door creaked open behind them and Oberoi strode in.

He watched Akram for a while, then said, 'What are you doing now?'

'I'm dusting for fingerprints,' said Akram, bent over the windowsill. 'I'll need to take prints from the house staff, so I can exclude them.'

'Exclude them?'

'Well, yes,' said Akram. 'What I mean is they may have left prints here in the past. We will learn nothing if I match their prints to ones I now find. On the other hand, if we discover a foreign set of prints, then it makes sense to compare them to our records.'

'What makes you think it *wasn't* one of the house staff?'

Akram's lower lip curled. 'If that's the case, prints won't tell us much. Unless we find the murder weapons. Of course ...' He stopped.

'Of course what?' prompted Oberoi.

'I was just thinking that the killer may have worn gloves.'

'I doubt it. This wasn't the work of a criminal mastermind. I'd bet on a crime of passion. The houseboy, maybe. Driven mad by lust. Sneaks back in during the night. Bashes in Renzi. Tries to have his way with the wife. She refuses, so he slits her throat. Or our missing security guard, perhaps.'

'And *his* motive?' said Persis.

'Who knows? Maybe he was just fed up taking orders. Fed up of not having the fine things his employers had. You know the type.'

'Why don't you enlighten me?'

Oberoi said nothing. There was no need.

When Akram had finished dusting the scene for prints, they searched the room together, going through the wardrobes and the dresser.

There was little to find.

From a drawer in Leela Renzi's dresser, Persis picked up a bottle of sleeping tablets.

She examined the bottle, then handed it to Akram to add to his log of evidence.

Next, she returned to the study and went through Stephen Renzi's desk.

Aside from yellowing business papers, a sheaf of invoices, a tailoring receipt, and a half-empty box of matches, there was nothing remotely of relevance.

Downstairs, she found De Mello sitting in the parlour with a glass in his hand.

'I'm sorry,' he said, noting her gaze. 'I needed something to – to—'

'You don't have to apologise.'

He remained seated; a tired, aging man, hollow-eyed with grief. 'He was like a son to me,' he said eventually. 'We built this business together. But it was *his* enterprise that made it tick, his persona our clients warmed to.'

'Did they have children?'

'No. Leela wanted them, but Stephen was always too busy. Next year, he would tell her. Always next year.'

'What made him come out to India?'

'He said he wanted to get away from Italy. It wasn't a great place to be after the war.'

'Why India?' she persisted.

De Mello smiled sadly. 'He said he loved the people.'

'Do you have any photographs of him?'

'Of course,' he murmured, instantly realising the meaning of her words. In Stephen's current state, the policewoman could have no idea what he'd looked like.

He struggled up from the sofa, then walked to a side unit. Opening a drawer, he took out a photo album and handed it to her.

She flicked through the album – wedding pictures of Stephen and Leela Renzi.

He wasn't a handsome man, but there was a charm to him, that much was obvious. Big shoulders, a rugged, clean-shaven face with a crooked nose and warm eyes, and thick black hair, swept back.

She slipped one of the photographs out of its sleeve. 'I'll need to keep this.'

De Mello nodded.

'I found sleeping tablets in Leela's drawer?' Her tone was quizzical.

'Yes. She had trouble sleeping. She was an insomniac.'

Persis thought it might have been a blessing. The tablets had probably ensured that Leela Renzi hadn't woken when her killer had slit her throat.

'How did Stephen spend that last day? I mean, did he do anything out of the ordinary? Meet with anyone unfamiliar?'

'No. He was at the office all day. He seemed preoccupied, but then we're going through a busy period. The business is growing.'

Oberoi came crashing into the room.

His gaze dropped to the photograph in her hand. He strode forward and, before she understood his intent, plucked it from her.

'Our victim, I presume.'

She stared at him coldly.

'I'll hold on to this.'

He turned and marched out.

She watched him leave, then bent back to the album.

7

She returned to the station late into the afternoon.

Her head sang. The murderous heat, the killings, Oberoi's attitude.

The trick to living, her father had once explained, was to decide early on what you liked and what you didn't, and then pitch yourself headlong into the things you disliked anyway. Because if you didn't, fate would notice, and nail you to the cross of your worst fears.

She'd learned long ago that her worst fear – her *only* fear – was failure.

'Persis, do you have a minute?'

She turned to find Seth beckoning her into his office. She supposed he wanted an update on the Renzi murder. Perhaps she should leave it to Oberoi ... Anger flared at her temples. Oberoi wouldn't know how to read a crime scene if it kicked him in his behind.

She lifted herself from her seat and followed him in.

To her surprise, she found that he wasn't alone.

Seated before his desk, blinking owlishly from behind horn-rimmed spectacles, was a small woman in a plain kurta and loose drawstring trousers.

Not a woman, she corrected herself. A girl. Dark-skinned, uncommonly thin, with a square face and an uncertain air.

Persis looked inquisitively at Seth, who had flopped back into his seat.

'Persis, I want you to meet Seema Desai. She's your new mentee.'

*　　*　　*

'How old are you?'

They were back in the main office, Seema standing to attention as Persis looked up at her from her chair.

'I'm eighteen, madam.'

'You don't look eighteen.'

The girl blinked. 'Would you like to see my ration card?'

'No . . . Where do you live?'

'Dharavi, madam.'

Dharavi. One of Bombay's oldest slums, a fixture in the city's southern zone for more than half a century. Once a mangrove swamp, the slum had seen intermittent growth spurts, first as Bombay's colonial rulers had expelled tanneries from the peninsular districts, and, most recently, with the influx of refugees following Partition.

'Schooling?'

'Yes, madam.'

'I meant what schooling do you have?'

Her eyes grew cautious. 'I – I have basic schooling, madam.'

'Do you have your matriculation certificate?'

'No.'

'You failed your exams?'

She stared straight ahead, her cheeks flushing. 'No.'

'Then why don't you have your certificate?'

'I was unable to take the exams.'

'Why not?'

'I was working, madam.'

Persis frowned. She noticed that the girl's spectacles were held together with tape. 'What were you working as?'

Another flush. 'I – I was – I am – a cleaner.'

'Cleaner? What were you cleaning?'

Her jaw tightened. 'Railway latrines.'

Persis exhaled a bitter laugh, then said, 'Who put you up to this?'

'Madam?'

'Who asked you to apply to this programme?'

'No one asked me, madam. I wanted to join.'

'You've been cleaning latrines and now you think you're qualified to become my mentee?'

Something flashed deep in the girl's eyes. She ground her jaw but said nothing.

Persis stood. 'Wait here.'

She stormed back into Seth's office.

He waved his hands in the air as if to ward off an evil spirit. 'I know what you're going to say.'

'Good. Then you'll save me from having to say it.'

'Give her a chance!'

'She was cleaning latrines!'

'What has that got to do with anything?' He snatched up a pack of cigarettes on his desk and lit one, took a pull, then erupted in a bout of violent coughing that levitated him a good six inches off his seat. He stared at the glowing tip of his cigarette. 'The girl's sharper than she looks.'

'Really? Can she even read?'

'As a matter of fact, she can.'

'How? She didn't take her matriculation exams.'

'She taught *herself*, Persis.'

This gave her pause. 'She can't possibly be the best candidate.'

He flashed a wolfish grin. 'She's the *only* candidate.'

She hesitated. 'I'm not against a woman wanting to better herself. How could I be? But I don't have the time to take anyone under my wing. Besides, I—' She struggled to frame her thoughts. 'I don't have the temperament for this sort of thing.'

'I have every faith that you will rise to the occasion. If it's any consolation, imagine how *I* felt when they sent you to me.' He grinned mirthlessly. 'Resilience thrives in the strangest places, Persis. Give her a chance. That's all I ask.'

The door opened behind them and Hemant Oberoi walked in. He took off his cap and ran a hand through his hair, squinting suspiciously at Persis.

'I hope you're not briefing him on the Renzi case.'

'No,' said Seth. 'We were discussing a different matter. Why don't *you* fill me in?'

Oberoi needed no second invitation. 'We've talked to the staff, checked out their alibis. They all have family at home who say they came back that evening and didn't leave till the morning. Of course, that doesn't mean to say one of them didn't sneak off during the night, or that their nearest and dearest aren't covering for them.'

'Did the Renzis employ a security guard?'

'The guard on the front gate swears he didn't see or hear anything.'

'He was probably asleep,' said Persis. 'Besides, the killer likely entered the compound via the rear wall.'

Oberoi ignored her. 'What's interesting is that the *regular* guard left that same evening to visit his family. They live in a village just outside Indapur, about three hundred kilometres east of the city.'

'You have reason to doubt his story?' said Seth.

'I don't believe in coincidences.'

Seth looked at Persis. 'What do you think?'

'I think it's too early to conclude anything.'

She sensed Oberoi twitching beside her.

She turned to him. 'What's his motive? Nothing was stolen. He's been working there for years. No one had a bad word to say about him.'

'People change,' said Oberoi.

'No,' she shot back. 'People *never* change. Not fundamentally. A fool will always be a fool.'

He flushed, his lips twisting into a snarl.

'Have the families been informed?' interrupted Seth hurriedly.

Oberoi continued glaring at her, then turned away. 'The woman's family have. Renzi has no family. At least none he mentioned to anyone.'

'Doesn't that strike you as strange?'

Oberoi shrugged. 'Apparently, he was very private about his past.'

Seth grimaced. 'I suppose I would be too if I'd lived under Mussolini. Like all those ordinary Germans who colluded with the Nazis, pretending they had no idea what was going on ... How did the woman – Leela, isn't it? – how did her father take it?'

'I haven't spoken to him. He was notified by Renzi's business manager.'

Seth blinked from behind a cloud of smoke. 'They say he's a holy terror. Pramod Sinha. He's been a vocal Nehru critic for years. Has quite a power base in the Fort region. Instigates rioting at the drop of a hat.' He sighed. 'One of you will have to pay him a visit. Keep him abreast of the investigation. Make the right noises. We have leads; we're optimistic about catching the culprit.'

'It's too early to make such a claim,' said Persis.

'Yes. But it's not too early for him to make my life a living hell.' He waved his cigarette at Oberoi. 'Go and see him.'

Oberoi paled. 'I – I think that's a job for Persis. I have leads to follow up.'

Seth managed to keep a straight face. Cowardice in the face of politics was something he was well acquainted with. 'Congratulations, Persis. Try not to upset him any more than he already is.'

*　　*　　*

Back at her desk, she spoke briefly with Seema Desai, and then sent her home, telling her that she would be in touch.

Next, she dragged forward her typewriter and began completing the paperwork for the Renzi investigation. She knew Oberoi's notes would be useless, if he'd bothered to make any at all. She could hear him on the phone, boasting about the big case he was heading up, no doubt to one of the round-eyed women who seemed to follow him around like dazed sheep.

An hour later, he left, departing with a final, 'Don't forget to go and see Leela Renzi's parents tomorrow. I'll want a report.'

He charged out before she could respond.

By the time she'd finished her notes, she was alone in the office, the only sound the squeaking of the lone mouse who'd made the basement his home.

Stumpy.

She'd christened him that because of his stunted tail, lost in some long ago skirmish. Like a reclusive film star, he only came out on rare occasions, usually in the depths of the evening.

She went to the steel filing cupboard that served as the station's evidence cabinet and retrieved the notebook found with the Ice Man's body.

Flicking through it, she once again stopped at the enigmatic entry: *Caesar's Triumph holds the key.*

Reaching into her desk, she took out the books she'd brought over from her father's shop over the past two days. Some were about the Roman Empire, others about Caesar himself. She'd been steadily making her way through them, searching for a clue, anything that might shine a light on the riddle posed by the Ice Man.

She took up where she'd left off in a translation of Suetonius's *The Twelve Caesars.*

Written in AD 121, the book, penned by Emperor Hadrian's personal secretary, Gaius Suetonius Tranquillus, served as an important primary source about life in ancient Rome, as well as offering a bawdy portrait of the first twelve Roman emperors, including the likes of Caesar, Caligula, and Nero.

Suetonius began by dissecting Caesar's military conquests, his victories in Gaul, and his civil war against his arch-rival, Pompey. He harped on Caesar's extraordinary ability to inspire loyalty in his men.

As she read, she made notes, scanning for anything that might be considered a 'triumph' for the legendary general and statesman.

The problem was that the word could be interpreted in many ways.

First, there were Caesar's numerous military victories: a decisive battle at Alesia in Gaul, campaigns in Greece and Egypt – where he subsequently set Cleopatra on the throne – followed by later victories in Africa and Hispania.

Next, there were his many achievements as a statesman, particularly the years he'd served as Roman dictator, transitioning the Roman Republic into the Roman Empire.

She found a third meaning in her research.

In ancient Rome, a 'triumph' also referred to the highest honour bestowed upon a victorious general – a procession through the city, paid for by the Senate, winding from the Triumphal Gate to the Temple of Jupiter. Captured prisoners would be marched along in chains, to be slain at the end of the procession to wild applause from the local citizenry.

What the prisoners thought of this rousing finale was left unrecorded.

Caesar received an unprecedented four triumphs, over a two-week period in 46 BC, celebrating each of his victorious campaigns.

She sat back.

Caesar's Triumph holds the key.

The key to what? Why was she even bothering with this? Her efforts had thrown up nothing. Without context, it was a pointless exercise.

The lack of forward momentum on the case made her palms itch. She could feel the net tightening around her; the clamour for progress. How long could she hold them off? How long before the demand for a result, any result, became unbearable?

The phone rang, startling her.

She stared at it a moment, then picked it up.

'Still in the office? Why am I not surprised?'

Blackfinch.

She stilled the instinctive gladness that bloomed inside her.

She'd only known the Englishman a short while, but it already felt as if they'd worked alongside one another for years. And not just work. A strange tension had crept between them; why deny it? A shared understanding, a way of looking at the world. Moments of intimacy that had escaped their control.

Matters had become complicated, and she'd quickly put a stop to it.

There was no future in pursuing a – a *feeling*. A relationship with a man like Archie Blackfinch was unthinkable. Career suicide.

Besides, her father might forgive many things, but a romantic liaison with the old enemy was beyond the pale.

It had almost come as a relief when Blackfinch had announced that he'd been summoned to the nation's capital for a few days.

'How are you, Archie?'

'They should give you a warning before you set foot in the city. *Abandon hope, all ye who enter here.* If the bureaucracy doesn't kill you, the boredom will.'

She smiled. 'When will you be back?'

'I'm not sure. The politico I've come to see has already kept me waiting two days. Punctuality seems to be something that happens to other people out here. Not much I can do about it. I'll probably have to kowtow till my knees bleed. I hope he appreciates the *gift* I'm taking him.'

'Gift? Is that what they're calling it these days?'

He grimaced. 'I don't like it any more than you do. But when in Rome . . . The boys in Bombay told me it had to be done. Do you know there's an establishment here that actually specialises in that sort of thing? "Gifts" for that very special occasion.' He gave a hollow laugh.

She could well believe it.

Since the numinous hour of independence, many of the revolution's earnest ideals had fallen by the wayside. Nehru had inaugurated the new nation in an ecstasy of sanctimony, but the backdrop of Partition and the riots that had left a million dead was proving a poor platform from which to set out a mantra of unity and universal brotherhood. Corruption, sectarian violence, and the tumult of a thousand factions pulling in a thousand different directions had put the lie to Gandhi's vision of a post-colonial utopia.

The new India often seemed a country where not only were few singing from the same song sheet, but where the song sheet had been torn to shreds, and the pieces set alight, along with the song's composer.

'So, what have you been up to while I've been away?'

She brought Blackfinch up to speed on the Ice Man and Renzi cases. 'Perhaps we should talk when you return?' she said. 'I could use a second opinion.'

'Over dinner?'

She hesitated, disconcerted by his hopeful tone. That was not what she'd meant. 'How about a working lunch?'

'You just want me for my intellect.'

She gave a fast laugh, diffusing the knot of tension that had crept into the conversation. For a man with as many peculiar mannerisms as the Englishman, he also possessed a surprising sense of humour. It was one of the many things she liked about him. It didn't hurt that he was uncommonly handsome, tall and dark-haired, with green eyes, spectacles, badly knotted ties, and perennially scuffed shoes.

By the time she left the office, her mood had lifted.

Pausing at the door, she listened to the mouse squeaking gently in the darkness, then turned out the lights.

8

The interior of the chapel was bathed in flickering candlelight.

Father Francis Rebeiro paused by the door. For a moment, he listened to the sounds of the night, noises drifting over from the adjacent slum, a raised voice, the blare of a radio.

The sweet rot of garbage, carried on a warm breeze, twitched his nostrils.

Behind him, he heard Grunewald shift before the altar.

The tall European knelt before the Cross, praying in that odd way he had, lips moving silently, eyes closed, an intensity writhing over his austere features that Rebeiro had rarely encountered. The man was an enigma, as close to an old-school missionary as the Goan had ever met.

In the years he'd known him, he'd found Grunewald sincere, conscientious, hard-working, and unfathomable. Faith wasn't a matter of simple piety with him. He grasped at belief in the way a drowning man grasped at a lifebelt.

In many ways, he was the perfect man to preside over this unloved little chapel perched on the edge of a moral wasteland, which was how Rebeiro had always viewed the slum. Populated by Hindus, and a small but vocal contingent of Muslims, he'd found his own patience stretched to breaking point over the years.

How many times had he caught them defecating in the narrow alley behind the chapel, sometimes brazenly urinating against the crumbling stones of the exterior wall? They'd leave goats tied up outside; they'd stand in the courtyard during Mass shouting at each other at the top of their lungs, spraying betel nut juice on to the palm planters.

In the monsoon, the open sewer became an excremental horror, the tide seeping through invisible openings and washing over the flagstones.

But Grunewald took it all in his stride.

He lacked the scholastic background of many of Rebeiro's colleagues, the years of theology, the rigorous philosophical skills sharpened in a seminary of repute. He made up for the lack with sheer, wild-eyed fervour. More than any man Rebeiro had known, Grunewald could 'find God in all things', drawing directly from Ignatius's *Spiritual Exercises*. For the big German, the contemplation of God's divinity was indistinguishable from the act of pursuing God's will on earth or the ineffable mysteries of transubstantiation.

He was the bluntest of instruments, but, perhaps, in these turbulent times, that was no bad thing.

'Don't forget to lock up.'

Grunewald gave no indication that he had heard.

Rebeiro considered repeating himself, but then decided against it. Grunewald had seemed distracted since the previous morning, troubled by matters he was either unwilling or unable to share. Perhaps, in due course, he'd hold forth with whatever it was that ailed him.

But Rebeiro doubted it.

The elder man grunted and shuffled off into the night. A warm meal awaited him, and a glass of port. Maybe he'd have time to read a few more pages of *Lady Chatterley's Lover*. The book was banned in the country, but a friend, a French priest from Bayeux, had smuggled a copy in.

It was already proving eye-opening.

For ten minutes, nothing moved in the chapel.

Finally, Grunewald, a tall, angular man, dressed in a white cassock, rose to his feet. His hair was cut short to the scalp, and was of a blondness so pale it was almost white. That ethereal presence had caused Rebeiro to remark, only partly in jest, that Grunewald was either a ghost or filled with the unspeakable radiance of God.

He entered the tiny vestry at the rear, checked that the small shuttered window was closed and securely fastened.

A sound turned his head. It had come from the main chapel.

He stepped back outside, saw a shape in the shadows.

'Is someone there? May I help you?'

The shape detached itself from the darkness, and began to move towards him.

At first Grunewald merely waited. Visitors sometimes strayed in here, late at night, floating in on a tide of distress, sadness, loneliness, the range of human malaise for which the only prescribed cure was solace in God.

And then recognition bloomed, like a struck match flaring in darkness.

His eyes widened; his knees buckled, and he stretched a hand to the altar, bracing himself against it, as his breathing became ragged and the past reached out to engulf him.

9

'It's the silly season.'

Seth's eyes were looking increasingly bloodshot, Persis thought. Perhaps giving up the whisky hadn't been such a good idea. Her father had long ago told her that accepting the reality of the human condition meant accepting Man's inherent weaknesses.

Then again, her father said a lot of things after he'd been at the Black Dog.

Nevertheless, Seth seemed to be wasting away, a vanishing act that she almost felt was deliberate ... She watched him now as he sucked furiously on a cigarette. There was something almost hunted in his aspect.

It didn't help that progress in the Ice Man case had stalled.

The incendiary headlines had failed to elicit any tangible leads as to the victim's identity. Nor had they turned up a missing persons report for anyone remotely matching the Ice Man's physical build.

But that wasn't why the SP had dragged her into his office.

'There's been another murder,' he continued. 'Another foreigner. Some priest. Someone wandered into his chapel late last night and caved his skull in.'

'I'm already busy with the Ice Man and Renzi cases.'

'The Renzi case belongs to Oberoi. Let him deal with it.'

'That's like leaving an infant alone with a loaded gun.'

'Be that as it may ... I need you to go and see to this. Those wretched Catholics are liable to kick up a fuss if we don't show some intent.'

She thought about arguing, then thought better of it. What was the point? With Fernandes away, the station was short-handed. There was no one else to send, and she was damned if she was going to let Oberoi lead another investigation.

'Fine. Give me the address.'

The chapel sat on the very edge of a small slum.

On the other side was the Crawford Market, where you could buy anything from piranhas to working chronometers.

She parked the jeep on the road. Clouds of flies rose from the carcass of a langur, Birla flapping at them as he exited from the far side.

The heat hit them like a cricket bat to the back of the skull.

A blind beggar drew a creaky melody from a sitar set in his lap. She doubted that the sound of a cat being strangled was conducive to eliciting alms. Her eyes lingered on him – the spectral presence, the birdlike bones of his face, the way poverty gripped him in its claws. The sight was becoming more common by the day as the city's population surged, refugees and migrants drawn in from all corners of the country.

To Bombay: city of dreams.

Outsiders who spent any length of time in the city often arrived at the erroneous conclusion that Bombay was an ancient metropolis. The rundown, hangdog look that characterised much of the mashed-together architecture, and the pervasive creep of the slums, gave the impression of a place that had been around the block a few times, like an ageing courtesan with rattling teeth and a bad case of halitosis.

The Portuguese, the first of the city's foreign arrivals, had left behind a legacy of crumbling churches and a Catholicism so virulent it was said the Pope himself now glanced eastwards before delivering Holy Communion. Subsequent Muslim invaders had dotted the city's byzantine enclaves with mosques and minarets, adding the lilt of muezzins' calls to the general cacophony that bludgeoned new arrivals like cannon fire.

Latterly, the East India Company had transformed Bombay with its piratical sense of enterprise, furnishing the city with railways, law courts, and a skyline of grand Gothic edifices intended to endure a thousand years, but which, like pretty much everything else in the tropics, had wilted beneath the twin onslaughts of sun and monsoon.

If nothing else, the Raj had achieved a minor miracle: by silting in the marshes, the city had transformed from a collection of soggy islands into a single landmass. To the bemusement of the city's original inhabitants, the Kohli fisherfolk, Bombay's new masters had flung open the gates to invite settlers from the furthest reaches of the Empire.

The problems of a population that continued to grow, post-independence, were only now becoming apparent.

Threading her way through a narrow opening, she proceeded along an alleyway smelling of urine and sewage, and into a lane darkened by overhead cables.

At the top of the lane stood the chapel.

A constable was ostensibly guarding the scene, passing the time with locals. Slum dwellers. On a bench inside the courtyard, a portly priest in a white cassock sat mopping his bald skull with a handkerchief.

The constable observed her approach, confusion gathering in his eyes.

She was used to it by now, the cognitive dissonance generated by seeing a woman in an inspector's uniform for the first time. She was amazed her presence didn't incite nosebleeds.

A wolf whistle turned her head.

A grinning man in shorts and a sweaty white shirt winked at her and made a lewd gesture. His friends laughed.

She pulled out her revolver and walked towards him.

The grin vanished. One by one his companions melted away until he stood in a circle of empty air.

'Did you say something?'

He gave her a queasy look. 'No.'

'Do you live in the slum?'

Silence.

She cocked the revolver.

'Yes . . . madam.'

'Did you know the murdered man?'

'No, madam.'

'Are you sure?'

'Yes, madam.' A fresh film of sweat had oozed out on to his face. His moustache was wringing wet.

'Where were you last night?'

He blinked. 'Last night?'

'When the priest was murdered.'

'I – I was at home.'

'Can anyone vouch for that?'

He said nothing, seemed on the verge of fainting.

She turned and walked away.

The body lay in front of the altar. The medical examiner, Sengupta, had arrived, dropping to his haunches to complete his investigation. It was cooler inside the chapel, but the priest continued to sweat, wiping his brow in agitation every few seconds, all the while muttering under his breath.

She noted that there were few windows, lending the chapel a gloomy aspect. Of the succession of ogival openings built high into the walls, at least two were boarded up.

The victim, a tall white man in a cassock, lay on his back, one arm outstretched as if imitating the Sistine Chapel's Adam, the other bent by his side.

Seth had been right. His face was a bloody mess, smashed to a pulp.

A jolt of electricity ran through her, earthing itself in the flagstones beneath her feet.

The similarities between this man's injuries and Stephen Renzi's were impossible to ignore.

She turned to the priest. 'You knew him?'

The man's gaze lingered on the corpse. A shudder passed through him, and then he seemed to collect himself. 'Yes. My name is Father Francis Rebeiro and this is my diocese. Peter was my ward.'

'Your ward?'

'He came to us a few years back. I mentored him. I posted him here to this chapel.'

'Were you the one who found the body?'

'Yes. Myself and Matthew.'

'Matthew?'

'The altar boy.'

'Where is he?'

'I sent him home. This is no place for a child.'

She kept her expression neutral. 'How did he end up here?' She waved at the body. 'In Bombay, I mean.'

'I'm not sure. He's German, by birth, but he'd been living abroad. He never really spoke about his past. He came to India at the beginning of 1947 and joined our order.'

'When was the last time you saw him?'

'Last night. Around eleven. I left him to lock up.'

'Does he usually lock up?'

'Yes. First one in, last one out.'

'Was he here all day yesterday?'

'Yes.'

Her gaze drifted around the austere interior of the chapel.

'It's an outpost.' Rebeiro sounded apologetic. 'We're hoping to grow the congregation.'

'You mean you want to convert the slum dwellers,' interjected Birla, suddenly.

'Not at all,' said Rebeiro hurriedly. 'We don't proselytise. People come to Christ of their own choosing.'

'Tell that to all those you burned at the stake in Goa.'

Persis flashed her deputy a look. Birla subsided.

Rebeiro, chastened, mopped furiously at his brow.

'Tell me about him.'

The priest seemed relieved at the change in tack. 'He was a strange man. Closed off. Driven. He didn't talk much, but when he did you sensed his earnestness.'

'Did he have family here? Friends?'

'No one. He wasn't the type to cultivate friends. He lived for the Church.'

'You don't think of *yourself* as his friend?'

The question seemed to surprise him. 'No. Not really. I knew him better than anyone else, which is to say I didn't know him at all. The only subject he was ever willing to engage with me in was religion. Don't get me wrong – part of my role *was* to mentor his religious progress – but life is about more than just the Church. It's not heresy to say that.'

'But Grunewald disagreed?'

'Not exactly disagreed. He simply took his vows – poverty, chastity, obedience – as articles of faith. Frankly, his ardour bordered on the fanatical.'

'In what way?'

He hesitated. 'Well, he was the only Catholic I knew who still practised mortification of the flesh. Do you know what I mean by that?'

Persis nodded.

'Bodily penance died out in the Church long ago,' continued Rebeiro. 'But Grunewald seemed intent on punishing himself. He had a braided whip that he used to flagellate himself with until his back bled. I admit, the first time I walked in on him doing it, I was disturbed. I tried to talk to him about it, but he argued that he was simply following in the footsteps of the saints.'

'How did he spend his time here?'

'Well, he conducted the prayer services, of course. Ministered to those who came to see him.'

'Ministered?'

'He'd sit and listen. Take confession where it was offered. People find solace in faith, Inspector. But sometimes solace needs a human face.'

'Did he keep a register of the people who came to see him?'

'That's not how it works.'

'Perhaps he mentioned someone in particular?' she persisted. 'Someone who came to him for guidance, and who may have left disappointed. Or someone who poured their sins into his ear, and then decided they had been injudicious.'

'Perhaps I've given you the wrong impression of him. Peter wasn't a wild-eyed zealot. He was softly spoken, a gentle man. In all the time I've known him, he never gave anyone cause to dislike him. In truth, he never allowed anyone to get close enough to do so.'

'Where did he live?'

'He had a room at the seminary. St Pius X College in Parel.'

She sensed someone behind her.

Sengupta was holding out a piece of paper. 'I've certified death. Time of death: approximately between eleven p.m. and one a.m. last night. Identification of the victim was made by the priest here. You may wish to confirm it. The damage to the face means that a direct identification is impossible. But I suspect there aren't that many six-foot-six blond white men wandering about the slums in a cassock.'

She took the paper from him, scanned it, then folded it into her pocket.

'You were at the Renzi scene yesterday. Stephen Renzi was killed in an identical manner. Do you think it was the same killer?'

His expression remained impassive. 'It's not my job to speculate.' Without a further word, he departed, a brief flare of light entering the church as he opened and closed the door behind him.

'Do you have a telephone here?'

Rebeiro shook his head.

She turned to Birla. 'Go back to the main road. Find a telephone. Call Akram and tell him to get down here.'

The sub-inspector nodded. 'I've had a quick look around the place. No sign of the murder weapon.'

She turned back to the body, stretched out between the front row of pews and the altar.

Blood made a halo around the head; some had seeped into the cracks between the flagstones. The crushed and bloodied aspect of Peter Grunewald's face might have seemed horrific to some, but to her, it excited only a quickening of her instincts.

Could a killer be loose in the city? Preying on white men?

She looked up at the altar, a simple wooden affair with a series of alcoves housing statues of the Virgin and various saints. From the centre rose a Cross, upon which a loinclothed Christ was splayed, eyes rolled towards heaven.

The irony did not escape her. The murder had taken place in the presence of history's most famous martyr. Would Peter Grunewald's congregation elevate him to a similar rank?

Religion had never played much of a part in her own upbringing.

As Parsees, she and Sam were members of Bombay's smallest religious community, their faith tenuous since her mother's passing. The only thing she could say for sure was that *her* mortal remains would be fought over by the vultures that flocked to Bombay's Towers of Silence.

The thought filled her with a perverse satisfaction.

'Do you have a photograph of him?'

Rebeiro considered the question. 'I'm not sure. He was notoriously shy about that sort of thing. I'll take a look when I return to the seminary.'

An hour later, Mohammed Akram arrived.

He nodded at her nervously as he set down his trunk.

She waved at the body. 'Does anything look familiar to you?'

He peered at the victim. 'The damage to the face,' he said immediately. 'Stephen Renzi?'

She nodded. 'That's why I need you to be thorough and precise. Can you do that?'

His Adam's apple pistoned up and down. 'Yes, madam.'

She left him to his work and stepped back out into the sun, the priest following in her wake.

The crowd had thinned as the morning had worn on. The initial flare of excitement had tailed away. There were jobs to hurry to, errands to run, school. Even here, the pace of life – a frenzied, headlong rush into the unknown – rarely changed.

Bombay's ever-growing slums were cities within cities. Choking, maze-like warrens of kutcha houses, hotspots of disease and hardship that the municipal authorities left to sink or swim.

Might there be a killer somewhere in here?

Motive. It all boiled down to motive.

What reason could anyone have had to bludgeon Peter Grunewald to death? Or Stephen Renzi, for that matter?

Thinking of the Renzi murders reminded her that she was due to visit Leela Renzi's parents that afternoon. But before that, she had an appointment with Raj Bhoomi at the Grant Medical College for the autopsies.

'Tell me,' she said, 'did you notice anything unusual in Grunewald's behaviour recently?'

Rebeiro seemed to meditate on the question. 'He was agitated. Something had upset him. I have no idea what that might have been, but his prayers had taken on an even greater intensity. And if you knew Peter, you'd know that *that*, in itself, was alarming.'

By the time she stepped into the autopsy suite, the bodies had been prepped, undressed, photographed, and Bhoomi's initial fingertip investigation conducted.

He was in a sombre mood, she was glad to note.

She supposed that at some point death became meaningless to a man accustomed to grappling with corpses on a daily basis. Yet, occasionally, the profanity of a particular passing might strike an unexpected note of melancholia. The murder of a husband and wife in their own bed was far enough outside of the usual to sober even a man like Bhoomi.

She waited impatiently as he went to his bank of instruments, returned with a saw, and began the process of cutting open Stephen Renzi's body.

Her gaze lingered on Leela Renzi, stretched out beneath a white sheet, only her head visible. Her expression seemed beatific in the washed-out light of the autopsy suite, the only indication of her violent end the grisly line visible across her throat.

She recalled De Mello's words – in particular, that Leela had been due to leave the city that evening. Only a last-minute change of plan had led to her being in the home that night.

On such random casts of the die could a person's fate turn.

By the time Bhoomi finished, it was late into the afternoon. He washed his hands, then asked her to follow him.

She was surprised when he led her not just out of the suite, but all the way up two flights of stairs and into the college's courtyard.

'I'm sorry,' he explained. 'I needed to see the sun.'

She waited as he took a battered tin from his pocket and rolled himself a bidi. 'Do you smoke?'

'No.'

'Good. It's a filthy habit.'

He lit the thin cheroot and took a deep lungful. Blowing out a cloud of smoke, he seemed to contemplate the passing throngs of chattering students hurrying to classrooms.

'Tell me about them.'

'*He* was murdered with a hammer. Or a weapon with a profile very similar to one. Blunt force trauma. At least twenty blows, to the front of the cranium and the face. I found round depressive fractures in the frontal bone and the zygomatic arches. The facial structure was completely destroyed – nasal, maxilla, the mandible.' He shuddered. 'The level of violence was unusual. This was a crime of anger. Of rage.'

'And yet the wife wasn't treated the same way.'

He knuckled the side of his nose. 'No. A single, deep, incised neck injury on the front of the neck, starting from just under the right ear, and severing the carotid artery. In other words, her throat was cut. The attacker was right-handed.'

'Is that conclusion or conjecture?'

'With the evidence to hand: conjecture. If the killer had been behind her, I would have said he was left-handed, because of the way the knife was drawn across the throat. From her right side to left. But, based on my examination of the crime scene photographs and the position of her body, I don't think this was the case. I think he leaned over her as she slept and simply slit her throat. The deep tailing off of the wound on the left side of her neck indicates that he was right-handed. If he had been left-handed, it would have been an unnatural angle to maintain pressure all the way to the end.'

They stood in silence for a moment, absorbing the horror of it. The idea that you could fall asleep one day and never wake again, murdered as you were lost in dreams.

'After he killed her, he walked around to the other side of the bed and murdered the husband. I think he woke him first. Or he woke of his own accord.'

She waited for him to explain.

'Defensive injuries. He raised his hands to ward off hammer blows. Several carpal bones in his right hand are broken as well as the ulna of his left hand.'

She pondered this, then said, 'There'll be another body coming in soon. A foreign priest by the name of Peter Grunewald. His injuries are almost identical to Renzi's.'

He looked at her sharply. 'You think it was the same killer?'

'I don't know. But it seems an incredible coincidence. A day after an Italian is bludgeoned to death, a German is murdered in the same manner?'

'Perhaps it's a copycat.'

'Renzi's murder hasn't made it into the papers yet.' She glanced at him. 'I suppose it won't be long now that his body's here.'

He stiffened. 'What's that supposed to mean?'

She didn't bother to reply.

'Look. I can't be here every minute of the day. Plenty of others have access to the morgue.' His voice had risen to a whine. 'I can't be held responsible if someone decides to let reporters in the back door.'

'I thought being in charge meant that you *were* responsible.'

He seemed about to argue, but then thought better of it.

'I want you to expedite the Grunewald autopsy.'

'Fine,' he said sullenly, turning his back to her.

She realised that she'd offended him, though in truth, she'd merely stated a fact.

Tact. Somehow it had always escaped her. She recalled Archie Blackfinch's words from an earlier investigation, to the effect that if she wanted others to help her, she'd have to make them feel wanted.

'You're doing a fine job,' she said, then realised that she meant it.

His shoulders twitched. He nodded, accepting the compliment, then dropped the roll-up to the floor and crushed it under his heel.

'I'll let you know when I've scheduled Grunewald. I've got a backlog, but I'll jump him to the top of the queue.'

'Thank you.'

On that note, they parted, walking stiffly off in opposite directions like duellists.

II

Fort. The area had taken its name from the old fort, built by the British, the ruins of which could still be found down by the docks. Until the mid-nineteenth century, to speak of Bombay was essentially to speak of the area circumscribed by the fort's walls.

Over time, other buildings had been erected in the surrounding environs, to the greater glory of the empire. The Bombay High Court, the Rajabai Clock Tower, the Victoria Terminus railway station, the Asiatic Society, Elphinstone College. As one commentator had drily observed, there was more architectural heritage packed into the pugnacious little enclave than the rest of the city put together.

Persis recalled that in olden times, the walled city had refused entry to anyone arriving after sunset, forcing latecomers to spend the night outside the city walls, at the mercy of brigands and passing leopards.

Today, the Fort district was one of the most vibrant in Bombay, home to expensive restaurants, art galleries, museums, and the stock exchange.

Only the very wealthy could afford to live here.

Then again, had things been any different during the Raj? The only change she could discern was that where once the familiar strains of 'God Save the King' had drifted from ballrooms and drawing rooms, now it was Rabindranath Tagore's 'Jana Mana Gana' that the wealthy played to evince their patriotic bona fides.

The Sinhas maintained a luxurious five-storey mansion on British Hotel Lane that looked more like an office block than a home. It had once served as the British Hotel, the establishment from which the winding alley took its name. The hotel had shut its doors a century earlier, auctioning off its fixtures and fittings, down to the monogrammed plates in its kitchen.

Persis was let in via ornate gates, and met in the lobby by an enormous Sikh. The man resembled the Colossus of Rhodes, if the Colossus had been persuaded off his pedestal and bundled into a double-breasted grey suit and a mustard-coloured turban.

He introduced himself as Aman Singh, Sinha's aide, and asked her to follow him up a flight of marbled steps.

'The lift is out of order,' he rumbled.

They walked up five flights. On each floor, doors branched off into the interior of the house. A door on the third floor gaped open; a woman stood framed inside the throat of a narrow corridor. The sound of wailing could be heard within.

The desperate keening brought home to Persis the fact that she was visiting with grieving parents, not just a politician whose fearsome reputation preceded him.

They continued upwards. The fifth floor served as Sinha's offices, explained Singh, doubling up as campaign headquarters during election season.

She was led through an anteroom in which a battery of typists flailed away at Remingtons and Godrej Primas.

Behind them, a large red banner depicted a yellow hammer and sickle.

She followed Singh through into the private office of Pramod Sinha, an expansive space with wood panelling, bay windows, art deco floor tiles, and a marble-topped desk centred on a heavy Kashmiri rug. On the wall behind the desk was a blown-up photograph of Gandhi, Nehru, and Subhas Chandra Bose. A smaller print showed a much younger Sinha sitting at the Mahatma's feet, looking up in callow adoration at a loinclothed Gandhi threading cotton on to his spinning wheel.

Sinha was sitting behind the desk, telephone in hand, barking into the receiver.

A striking man, was her immediate impression.

A square, dark face, set off by the brilliant whiteness of his kurta, below a cap of dyed black hair that fitted the top of his head like a welded plate. Above his upper lip bounced a black moustache, as shaggy and full of life as a Scottish terrier.

Sinha completed his call and thumped the receiver back into its cradle. His face grew still, as he registered her presence. She introduced herself.

'Please. Sit.'

She folded herself into one of the high-backed Regency chairs, then waited as Sinha sprang up out of his own seat, trotted to a sideboard, and poured himself a drink. He tilted the bottle in her direction, but she declined.

He fell into his seat again, took a large gulp, then fixed her with a steady, bloodshot gaze.

She'd never met the man, but was acutely aware of his reputation. Sinha was one of those unscrupulous politicians that India seemed to have summoned forth in multitudes following independence. The kind who'd sell their grandmothers for an electoral seat, and throw in a couple of aunts for good measure.

His political career had seen early success with the Congress Party, only foundering when he'd adopted a contrary stance on Nehru's planned social reforms, taking issue with the Prime Minister's attempts to bring greater representation for Dalits – the Untouchables – into government.

Sinha's ideals, like many in the new India, did not stretch to the lowest rungs of society. Men like Pramod Sinha had found it easy to abandon the tenets of constitutionalism, to live by their own rules, claiming a sort of noble madness as they navigated the political morass of post-colonialism.

He'd left the Congress in a huff, and immediately joined the Peasants and Workers Party of India, a Marxist outfit founded a year after independence.

It explained the bust of Karl Marx Persis could see nestled in an alcove behind the man's desk.

She wondered, briefly, *why* Sinha was at his desk a day after his daughter's killing. According to Stephen Renzi's business manager, Arthur De Mello, the man had doted on her.

As if sensing her thoughts, Sinha said, 'De Mello tells me you wish to speak with me about Leela's murder?' His manner was brusque, impatient. She detected a seam of anger.

She'd seen it in others, men rarely touched by the vicissitudes of fate, unmanned by circumstance, lashing out in blind fury.

'Yes, sir.'

'Are *you* heading up the investigation?'

She hesitated. 'No. My colleague, Inspector Hemant Oberoi, is in charge.'

'Then why is he not here himself?'

'I – He's following up a lead. Sir.'

Sinha's moustache twitched. 'You have a suspect?'

She took a deep breath. 'No,' she said, firmly. 'But we have avenues of investigation that we are pursuing.'

He grimaced. 'When you've been a politician for as long as I have, you learn to recognise the art of saying something without saying anything at all.' He lifted his tumbler to his lips, took another large swallow. 'I've heard of you, of course. The famous policewoman. Perhaps you *should* be leading the investigation.'

She coloured. It was surprising to hear a man like Sinha suggest such a thing. She'd received scant credit in the newspapers for her work on recent cases, the plaudits handed to the men who'd been tangentially involved. But Sinha's comment implied that he knew more.

'I've made enquiries,' he said, as if reading her mind. 'Your colleagues at Malabar House enjoy a miserable reputation. In an ideal world, my daughter's murder wouldn't have been assigned there. But I seem to have lost my ability to influence matters.' He gave a bray of self-pity. 'Would you believe me if I told you that your commissioner once waited on me like a Kamathipura courtesan? Now he won't even return my calls.'

She found words in her mouth. 'Your daughter was murdered in her sleep. It's an indefensible crime.'

Tears welled unexpectedly in his eyes. He blinked them back, coughing to reassert his composure.

'What do you want to know?'

'With a case like this, it's important to establish motive. I don't believe anything was stolen from your daughter's home. I'm looking for something ... personal.'

'Leela was the sweetest soul. People used to ask me why we had no more children, why I didn't have sons. The truth was I didn't need another child. Leela was everything to me.' He seemed on the verge of breaking down. 'I can't believe anyone would want to harm her.'

'I'm not certain that they did. She wasn't meant to be in the house that night.'

He instantly grasped her meaning. 'The killer came for Stephen?'

'It's a theory. Of course, if this were a crime of passion ...' She hesitated.

'Go on.'

'Well, if Leela had become romantically involved with someone else, or if another man had become infatuated with her, it might explain why nothing was stolen, why Stephen was bludgeoned with such seeming rage, and why she was killed in the way that she was.'

Sinha's eyes fell to the desk as he relived the horror of his daughter's final moments. 'No. Leela was faithful to Stephen. She loved him dearly. I can't say whether another man had become enamoured of her – but it wouldn't surprise me. She was beautiful and gregarious. She trusted too easily. I'd warned her. God forgive me, but my daughter was a fool.'

'Tell me about Stephen . . . How did they meet?'

'I'm not certain. Leela said it was at a function, here in Bombay. This was back in 1946. Stephen hadn't been long in the city. He was running a motor parts shop. Of course, I immediately told her to stop seeing him. A foreigner, an Italian, and an unsuccessful one at that! Hardly a suitable match.'

Persis flushed as a sudden image of Archie Blackfinch flashed in front of her eyes. Sinha's words might have come from her aunt.

'But I've always been a fool where my daughter is concerned. When she made it clear that they would marry with or without my permission, I gave in.'

'What did you make of him?'

He considered his reply. 'He surprised me. I'll give him that. He was a likeable man. Big, boisterous, like a bear. He had a sense of humour. He liked to drink. I'd heard Italians were lazy, easily distracted, but he was a hard-working man. I loaned him the money to grow his motor parts business, used my connections to land him his first big contract. But he did the rest himself. He gave Leela a good life.'

'They were happy?'

'As far as I could make out. Yes.'

'Do you know of any recent business dealings that might have soured? Anyone he may have upset?'

Sinha thrust himself backwards in his chair. 'Stephen had that rare quality of being able to maintain goodwill even when you disagreed with him.'

'What do you know about his past?'

'Very little. That was the one thing he rarely talked about. He was an only child, and both his parents had passed away. With no family connections left back in Italy, he decided to move abroad.'

She paused. 'I'd like to speak to your wife, too, if I may.'

He seemed dismayed by the request. For an instant, he floundered. 'She's inconsolable. I should be with her. The reason you find me at my desk is because work is the only way I can bury my grief. If I wasn't here, I'd go mad.' He waved at his aide, standing silently in the corner like a statue. 'Singh will take you down.'

It was immediately evident that Leela Renzi had inherited her good looks from her mother.

In her mid-forties, Priya Sinha retained the aspect of a much younger woman.

Persis had been led down to the third floor, along a corridor, and into a drawing room packed with women. A pall of grief hung in the air. This room was the source of the piteous wailing she had heard earlier, she realised. They'd stopped crying, but she had the sense that it wouldn't take much to set them off again.

Priya Sinha sat on a boxy sofa, a woman close on either side like a pair of bodyguards. Or jailors.

She was dressed in a drab brown sari; most of the women wore muted colours.

A woman who had lost her husband wore white, but there was no designated colour for a parent who'd just lost a child, just as there was no word for one.

She'd always found that strange. Widow. Widower. Orphan. Yet no word for a mother who'd lost her daughter. Perhaps it was a happenstance so abhorrent to nature that even lexicographers had failed to find a way to capture it.

Her arrival, dressed in her khaki uniform, caused a stir of interest.

They knew who she was, of course. Anonymity had vanished with her first case, the murder of a senior British diplomat, an investigation that had made national headlines. In the wake of that case, and the one immediately after, she'd received a deluge of mail, the majority of it hate-filled, aghast at her attempts to single-handedly dismantle Indian society, to poison the minds of a generation of young women with her ungodly ambition. There had been calls for her to resign, to throw herself into the Arabian Sea, to pour petrol over herself and light a match.

In among the madmen – and not a few women – there'd been the odd message of encouragement.

We're proud of you. Keep going. Don't let them stop you.

Her thoughts flickered briefly to Seema Desai. Had it been Persis's own example that had inspired the young woman to want to follow in her footsteps?

She introduced herself, and asked if she might speak to Sinha alone.

A moment of confusion, and then the woman nodded, rose from the sofa, and led her out to a small parlour, closing the door behind her. The curiosity of her fellow mourners snuffled at the bottom of the door like a hound on the scent.

'Would you like tea?'

'No,' said Persis, then added: 'Thank you.'

Priya settled by the window, silhouetted by late afternoon light flowing through sheer curtains. An unbearable sadness communicated itself in her posture.

'How can I help you, Inspector?'

Persis apprised her of the investigation. After a few moments, she got the impression that the woman had stopped listening. She tapered off.

A silence settled in the room, as thick and choking as ash.

She waited, stifling the urge to force the conversation along.

Finally, the older woman spoke. 'She was my closest friend. I know it's strange for a mother to say that about her daughter, but it was always that way, ever since she was a girl.' She stopped. 'Finding her killer won't bring her back. It won't change anything for me.'

'But it may save another life.' She wasn't sure if she believed that, not yet. The idea of a serial killer loose in Bombay was such a novelty that she couldn't quite commit to it.

She explained her theory that the murders had been motivated by passion.

'Leela was not ... involved with another man, if that's what you're asking. I would have known. Nor did she mention anyone who'd approached her or acted in such a manner towards her.'

'What about Stephen? Can you think of anyone who may have held a grudge against him?'

'He was a good man. Not the man I would have chosen for her, but he made her happy. They loved each other dearly. It's a shame—' She stopped again. Her cheeks trembled. 'Each year, I'd think, *this* is the year. This is when Leela finally gives me a grand-child. I couldn't understand it. What was she waiting for? She kept saying the time wasn't right. If they'd had a child, I'd have something to—' She lapsed into a tortured silence.

'Is there anything you can tell me, anything at all? Anything out of the ordinary?'

She was silent for so long that Persis thought the woman had become catatonic. Finally, she stirred. 'Wait here.' She left the room.

Persis waited impatiently, her eyes wandering around the space. The pastel colours, the geometrically shaped furniture, the terrapin tank. A modern Bombay home.

When Priya returned, she held out a sealed package. 'Shortly after they were married, Leela gave this to me. She asked me to keep it locked in my safe. I found that strange. They had a safe in their own home.'

'Did she tell you what was in it?'

'No. Only that it belonged to Stephen.'

'You've never opened it?'

'No.'

'Your husband?'

'He doesn't know about it. Leela never mentioned it again.'

Persis weighed the envelope in her palm. 'Don't you want to open it?'

A look of infinite sadness passed over her features. 'What could possibly be in there that will give me solace, Inspector?'

12

Malabar House was deserted.

She sent the peon for lime water, then sat down at her desk. Taking off her cap, she flapped her shirt collar, then turned her face up to the ceiling fan.

Gopal returned with a glass. She drained it, then sent him out to the nearby Chinese restaurant, The Dancing Stomach, for something to eat.

She watched him scurry out, then took the package Priya Sinha had given her and opened it.

Inside, wrapped in a white cloth, she found a long, heavy brass key, and a square of card on which was written:

100

She held the card between her fingers. What could it mean? *100*. There was something portentous about the number being set out in this way, no explanation, no context.

She picked up the brass key.

The shaft ended in a complicated series of geometrically tooled ridges. It looked too complex for a house key . . . A key to a safe, perhaps? But if the safe was in the Renzi home, why had Stephen Renzi asked his wife to secrete the key with his in-laws?

She picked up her notebook, leafed through it, and found the number for Arthur De Mello, Renzi's aide. A quick conversation determined that he knew nothing about the key.

He confirmed that it couldn't be the key to the safe in the Renzis' home. He had a copy of that and it looked nothing like the key Persis had described.

The peon returned with her order. Noodles.

She ate quickly, shovelling the greasy fare into her mouth with the bamboo chopsticks that had come with the dish. Halfway through, one of the chopsticks snapped. She was forced to break the other one to level them off and then use the mutilated halves to finish her meal.

The phone rang.

She wiped her mouth with a handkerchief, and picked up the receiver.

Francis Rebeiro seemed agitated. 'Can you meet me at the seminary? I've found a photograph of Peter, as you requested.'

'Why don't you have it sent to the station?'

He cleared his throat, an anxious sound. 'There's something else . . . It's easier if I show you.'

It took her thirty minutes to drive from Malabar House to Parel, where the St Pius X College had been an institution for over fifteen years, under the patronage of the Jesuit and Franciscan Orders. The two groups had been fixtures on the subcontinent for centuries, engaged in missionary pursuits, with varying degrees of success. They'd often been at loggerheads: the Jesuits – the intellectuals of the Church – professing to follow in the footsteps of Ignatius of Loyola, founder of the Society of Jesus, while Franciscans pointed to the example of their own spiritual guide, Francis of Assisi, a man who had, allegedly, kissed and washed the sores of lepers.

Persis had never quite believed the stories.

There were plenty of lepers in Bombay. In her experience, both Franciscans and Jesuits – and just about every other sane person in the city – tended to give them a wide berth.

Still, in a country where religion served a similar function for its citizens as water did for fish, the Catholics had managed to stay clear of controversy in recent years. The Partition rioting – pitting Muslim against Hindu and Sikh – had passed them by.

At least, that was the case in the northern half of the country. It was a different matter elsewhere.

The Portuguese continued to exert control over Goa, as they had done for four centuries, but the clamour to bring the territory into the national fold was growing. It was only a matter of time before the Centre acted.

She was met at the gate by Rebeiro.

She followed the priest across a wide lawn towards the central St Pius building, a monument in white sandstone that looked like a five-star hotel, with a flat roof and a Grecian portico. Having attended an Anglo school run by Catholics, she'd long known of St Pius X College, Bombay's principal seminary, but had never set foot inside.

They entered a red-tiled entrance hall with a high, vaulted ceiling, from which hung an enormous wooden wheel studded with candles. On the walls around them were portraits of senior bishops of the Archdiocese of Bombay, together with a portrait of the Pope.

A marble statue of a cassocked priest, one arm outstretched, was prominent in the centre of the space. On a brass plaque at the foot of the statue were the words: *Bishop Savio Ferra, First Father Rector – Gone to be with our Lord.* Beside the late bishop knelt a statue of the Virgin, cradling the infant Jesus, a coquettish smile on her lips.

A trick of perspective made it appear to Persis as if the bishop was holding his hand over Mary's head, in benediction.

As they made their way into the interior of the college, priests and young men in the robes of novitiates hurried by them, glancing curiously in her direction. She supposed few women ever set foot here, least of all women dressed as police officers.

Rebeiro led her into the dormitory wing.

They passed an open doorway. Turning her head, she saw young men engaged in the time-honoured biblical pursuit of ping-pong, hopping around in their robes and thrashing at a white ball with wooden racquets.

They tracked down a long corridor.

At the far end, Rebeiro stopped outside a wooden door. Grasping the doorknob, he said, 'This was Peter's room.'

'Room' was an exaggeration, she soon discovered. She found herself in a narrow cubicle, with whitewashed walls, a tiny cot, a roughly hewn wooden wardrobe, a single fluorescent light bulb with exposed wiring, a galvanised bucket in one corner, and a small sink above which hung a cracked mirror. On the edge of the sink was a razor and a bar of soap.

On the wall above the bed hung a cross, below it a wooden plaque inscribed with the words: *Ad maiorem Dei gloriam.* She retained enough Latin from her schooldays to recall its meaning: For the greater glory of God.

'The bed was too small for him,' remarked Rebeiro sadly. 'But he never complained.'

'Is this all he had?'

'It was by choice,' said the priest, defensively. 'We don't place restrictions on a few home comforts. Many of the younger men have novels, film posters, photographs of loved ones, music. We teach them to live a life informed in Christ, but, ultimately, their pastoral mission lies out in the real world.'

'But Grunewald wasn't like that?'

'No. He arrived with a – a sense of tortured morality. That's the best way I can describe it.'

She noticed a small pile of ash beside the bed. A burned-down mosquito coil.

'Did he explain why?'

Rebeiro shook his head. 'I guessed something had happened in his past. But he was unwilling to discuss it. Not even in the confessional.'

She heard a bell ringing from somewhere within the complex.

'Vespers,' explained Rebeiro. 'The evening prayer.'

She spent the next ten minutes searching the room.

There was little to find. A spare cassock and some underclothes in the wardrobe, together with a brace of liturgical texts: *The Autobiography of St Ignatius* and *Return to God Through Prayer*. At the bottom of the wardrobe she found the corded whip Rebeiro had mentioned. The dark leather was stained darker in places.

Grunewald's blood, she guessed.

She wondered at the maniacal fervour that could lead a man to castigate himself so cruelly. She remembered a refrain by one of her teachers at the Cathedral Girls School: *We are helpless without the grace and power of God.*

If a man truly believed that, then nothing was out of bounds.

'He came to India for repentance,' she said eventually. 'The question is: what was he repenting *for*?'

Rebeiro closed his eyes and muttered something unintelligible, then said, 'Come with me.'

He led her back through the college to a chapel where young men had gathered for the evening prayer service. 'Wait here.'

More youths brushed by her as she hovered impatiently in the doorway, her gaze following Rebeiro as he entered the chapel and weaved his way to a boy lighting candles by the altar.

A brief exchange.

The boy looked startled, and then meekly followed the priest back out.

'This is Matthew,' said Rebeiro. 'He was Brother Peter's altar boy.'

Matthew refused to meet her eyes. She judged him to be no more than thirteen or fourteen, a thin, short boy with a feminine sleekness accentuated by a clear complexion and large eyes.

'Come,' said Rebeiro.

He led them onwards to his office, a room with bare flagstones and a glowing painting of a blond-haired, blue-eyed Christ set high behind a small desk smelling of furniture polish.

Rebeiro rummaged in his drawer, then took out a sheaf of photographs and a small parcel wrapped in a plain white handkerchief. He set the parcel on the desk and handed her the photographs. They were a series of shots taken of a line-up of priests in white cassocks – four Indians, and a white man towering over them.

Peter Grunewald was startlingly blond, with deep-set eyes, wide lips, and a blank, unsmiling expression.

'Matthew, please tell the inspector what you told me earlier today.'

The boy looked terrified, eyes rooted to the floor.

'Speak up.' She allowed a trace of harshness to enter her tone.

Finally, his voice creaked into motion. 'This morning, I went with Father Francis' – he glanced at Rebeiro – 'to the church for the Terce service. That's when we found Brother Peter.'

'Would you usually go with ... Brother Peter?'

'No. He always goes ahead, at around six, to open the chapel for the Lauds prayer. I have classes in the morning.'

'What about last night? Didn't anyone notice that he wasn't back in the dormitory?'

'Peter kept to himself,' interjected Rebeiro. 'He rarely dined with the rest of us. As I mentioned before, he was a solitary animal.'

A thought occurred to her. 'How did he fit in here? Was he well liked? Did he upset anyone?'

Rebeiro looked shocked at the implication. 'We're a family here, Inspector. Christ's family. Peter was one of us.'

She swallowed an automatic retort, instead turning back to the boy. 'Please carry on.'

'When we entered the chapel, we – we found Brother Peter by the altar.' A shadow passed over his face. 'Father Francis went outside to raise the alarm. While he was gone, I noticed something on the altar.' He stopped, then plunged on. 'An object I'd never seen there before. I picked it up and hid it inside my cassock.'

'Why?'

'I don't know. I think – I think it was because I didn't want it to be associated with Brother Peter. I didn't want him to be remembered in that way.'

'In what way?'

Confusion entered his eyes, and he turned helplessly to Rebeiro. 'Where is it?' she said.

Rebeiro picked up the object on his desk and handed it to her. She unwrapped it and held it up to the light, her brow furrowing.

She looked at Rebeiro. 'What is this?'

'That's just it, Inspector. We don't know.'

13

Arriving back at Malabar House, she went immediately to see Seth.

By the time she'd finished telling him her theory that the Renzi and Grunewald murders might be linked, the work of a single killer, he'd slumped down so far into his chair that his head was practically level with the desk.

'I don't suppose you have any evidence for such a claim?' he asked, wearily.

'Aside from the timing and the manner in which they were killed? And the fact that both are white men?'

'So the answer is no. May I suggest you keep your theory to yourself?'

'What if I'm right?'

'What if you're not?' he shot back. 'Have you thought about the consequences of spreading such a story?'

Her nostrils flared. 'I haven't *spread* anything.'

He eyed her morosely, then shakily poured out a whisky.

'I thought you quit.'

'So did I.' He took a gulp, then: 'How did you get on with Sinha?'

'He seemed subdued.'

'Most unlike him.'

'He's just lost a daughter,' she reminded him.

'What about Oberoi? I haven't seen him around today.'

'I'm not his minder.'

'I thought you were the one who didn't want him left alone in charge of the investigation?'

She glared at him. 'I have no idea where he is.'

He tapped the side of his glass. 'Any movement on the Ice Man case?'

She shook her head.

Back out in the office, she found Birla readying to leave.

'I want you to do something tomorrow,' she said, handing him the brass key that Leela Renzi's mother had given her. 'Go to a locksmith or, better yet, a locksmith's association, and find out what sort of key that is.'

Birla nodded and pocketed the key.

'By the way, do you know where Oberoi is?'

'No. Haq's been away all day too. Something stinks.'

Moments later, they found out exactly what that was when Oberoi barrelled into the office.

He stood before her, legs planted wide, grinning ferociously, as if he'd just returned from vanquishing an army.

She heard Seth lock his office and walk up behind her. 'What's going on?'

'I've solved the case,' announced Oberoi, imperiously.

It transpired that the reason he had been absent all day was because he and Haq had driven out to Ismail Siraj's village. Siraj was the security guard who'd taken leave the evening of the Renzi murders. They'd tracked him down, arrested him, and hauled him back to Bombay, where he'd been charged and deposited at the Arthur Road Jail.

Persis rose slowly to her feet. 'On what evidence did you charge him?'

'My instincts say he's guilty.'

'Your instincts are what got you sent *here*.'

He coloured, losing some of his Napoleonic bearing.

Seth broke in. 'I'm not asking for mountains of evidence. But a small *foothill* might prove useful in court . . .'

Oberoi's thin moustache twitched.

She turned to Seth. 'He has no idea what he's doing.'

A growl escaped Oberoi's lips. 'And I suppose *you* do? Don't confuse a headline or two with experience.'

She flushed. 'I have a cat. He's the sort of cat who couldn't catch a mouse if it crawled into his mouth and died there.'

It was Oberoi's turn to redden.

'Why *did* you charge him?' interrupted Seth, hurriedly.

Oberoi's furious gaze lingered on her, and then he turned back to the SP, a grimace of triumph turning up the corners of his mouth. 'I charged him because he confessed.'

'You seem to have lost your appetite.'

She looked up at her father, then back down at her plate. Krishna's attempts at a Hyderabadi biryani left much to be desired.

Her father, she noted, had no problems shovelling down the half-cooked rice. Sam had the stomach of a Mongolian warlord and the liver of a Cossack.

He set down his fork, picked up a napkin, wiped his moustache, then settled on to his elbows. 'What's wrong?'

'Oberoi's being a jackass.'

Sam grunted. 'So what's new?'

She'd mentioned her colleague on frequent occasion. It was helpful sometimes to alleviate her darker moods by talking over Oberoi's wrong-headedness.

'He's arrested the wrong man.'

'How do you know it's the wrong man?'

'I—' she faltered.

'Are you sure it isn't just because you don't like him?'

'No. I mean . . . No. The investigation has barely begun and he's already made up his mind.'

'Doesn't mean he's wrong.'

She glared at him. 'Whose side are you on anyway?'

'Ah,' he said, leaning back. 'You want sympathy. Perhaps you should spill your troubles into Akbar's ears, instead of mine.' He glanced at the cat, sitting at the head of the table, licking his paws.

The phone rang before she could retort. She answered it with her back turned to him.

It was Jaya. 'Do you remember I told you Dinaz was going to be in town? . . . Well, she's here. Do you want to meet us for drinks?'

'Now?'

'I suppose you have something better to do? Let me guess, another enchanting evening with your father?'

She stiffened. 'Fine. Where are you?' Noting down the address, she put down the phone, and turned back to her father. 'I'm going out.'

Usually, Sam would grumble out a protest. *It's late. You've been away all day.* But today he merely nodded. 'Will you be out till late?'

'I expect so.'

14

They met in a restaurant in Kala Ghode, an establishment once run by an Englishman who'd upped sticks and fled back to the home country once the Quit India movement began to collapse beneath the weight of its non-violent ideals.

The place was now owned by an Indian, who'd kept much of the original décor, including the row of portraits of British monarchs along the back wall, lovingly brought into focus by soft lighting.

Dinaz and Jaya were already on to their third cocktails.

They made a strange triumvirate, Persis thought. Jaya, the elegant housewife, and mother of two; Dinaz, a tall, thick-shouldered woman who looked as if she should be charging downfield with a rugby ball under her arm; and Persis herself, now in a long-sleeved swing dress in black plaid, a picture of understated femininity quite at odds with her workaday appearance.

They embraced quickly, then Dinaz batted her down into her seat.

'Thought for a minute you weren't going to show up. Would have had to track you down like one of my tigers.'

For the past few years, Dinaz had been in Calcutta, working with the Sundarbans Forest Management Division. Like Persis, she'd put career before hearth and home, and appeared to have profited by it. She certainly seemed in fine spirits, as robust as a galleon under full sail. She'd always lacked the social polish of a Jaya, but didn't seem to give a damn.

Persis ordered a whisky and they chatted for a while, performing the stilted catch-up ritual of old friends who'd once been close and now saw each other too infrequently for that to remain the case.

'Saw your picture in the papers,' grunted Dinaz. 'Nearly fell off my perch. Here's to you, old girl.' She raised her tumbler and knocked it back before barking at a hovering waiter for another.

The youth sprinted away at such a pace he left scorch marks on the floor.

Persis suspected he'd already suffered the lash of Dinaz's acid tongue.

'What about you? How are things out in the forest?'

'It's less a forest and more a swamp. If the tigers don't get you, the crocodiles will. Still, I wouldn't be anywhere else.'

They talked about old times, growing up in Bombay, their fondly remembered days together at the Cathedral Girls School.

'Not quite the same without her, is it?' said Dinaz wistfully.

She meant Emily, of course. Emily St Charles, the last of their quartet, and once Persis's closest friend. Growing up as a motherless, insular child, Persis had always been an outsider, friendless at school, largely ostracised, until Emily had befriended her, dragging Dinaz and Jaya along in her wake.

Those had been good years.

They'd made a tight-knit group, weathering together the trials of adolescence, and later standing shoulder to shoulder as the independence struggle had engulfed the nation. For the first time, Persis had understood what others meant by the notion of camaraderie. Without these women, she sometimes felt she'd have ended up in a cave living the life of a hermit.

Emily had left the country once the violence began to spiral out of control, despite Gandhi's best intentions.

Persis had felt her absence like the ringing silence after a bell that has tolled for hours suddenly stops. A hollow in an interior part of herself. That they'd fallen out of touch only added to the feeling of melancholy that occasionally caught her unawares.

Dinaz was on fine form, a font of ribald jokes and scurrilous stories about Calcuttans who she deemed small, round, and supremely enamoured of their own erudition.

'Guess who I bumped into last week?' she said, her cheeks inflamed with whisky. 'Your betrothed.'

Persis frowned.

'Cousin Darius. Handsome devil. Cuts quite a figure these days. Looked as if he'd swallowed a live cobra when he spotted me.'

Dinaz was teasing, of course.

For the past five years, her cousin had been climbing the ladder at a prominent managing agency in the Bengal capital. The fact that he was over a thousand miles away had done little to curb her aunt's enthusiasm for hurling her only child at Persis as a prospective marriage partner. Batting away those advances had taken up more energy than she'd have admitted to, and it was only recently that Nussie had finally begun to accept that Persis's future might lie somewhere other than in her own home.

'He asked about you,' Dinaz continued, clearly enjoying herself. 'I told him you'd written to me telling me how much you missed him; what a terrible mistake you'd made turning him down.'

'Leave the poor girl alone,' tutted Jaya. 'Besides, she's already spoken for.'

Dinaz raised an eyebrow. 'Do tell.'

'Persis here has a secret admirer. An Englishman.'

'You mucky devil!' breathed Dinaz. 'Well, who is he then? Spill the beans.'

'No one,' said Persis, her cheeks burning. 'Jaya's mistaken.'

Jaya gave her an odd look, but said nothing more. She turned to Dinaz instead. 'What about you?'

'Me? I've been keeping those Bengali babus on their toes. I'm currently the mistress of the district engineer, if you can believe that. He's a head shorter than me and utterly hideous. But he happens to love the Sundarbans. Likes to get lost in the swamp every couple of weeks to get away from his wife.'

'Dinaz!'

'A girl like me can't be picky,' she said. 'I haven't got your looks or – or whatever it is Persis has. Dusky allure. Naked aggression. Some men like that, you know.'

She stood up and braced the waiter again. 'Where's the powder room?'

'Please follow me, madam.'

They watched her barrel after him. Jaya set down her glass. 'So . . . what's really going on with your Englishman?'

'A misunderstanding. Besides, it wasn't as if it could have led anywhere.'

Jaya stared at her suspiciously, then shrugged and changed the topic, chattering on about her young children, the film she'd seen earlier that week, her life of glamour and ease.

Dinaz returned. She crooked a finger at Persis. 'Come with me.'

'What is it?'

'Come on!'

Mystified, Persis scraped back her chair and followed Dinaz around the curve of the restaurant, to a secluded section at the rear. Peering from behind a bamboo trellis, Dinaz pointed to a table on the far side of the space.

At first she didn't see it, and then the image burst into focus.

It was her father.

Sam, dressed in a smart jacket and tie, was seated at an angle to her, his wheelchair drawn up to the table. Opposite him was a well-dressed woman, thick dark hair bundled above her head, with bright earrings and lustrous skin. It was impossible to be sure of her age from this distance, but Persis guessed late middle-aged.

What the hell was Sam doing here? And was he ... *laughing*?

Shock enfolded her, such that, for a moment, she was lost for words.

'Looks like your father's out painting the town red while you're pretending to be a vestal virgin.'

She continued to stare at Sam, not quite believing it was him.

What was he doing here? He should have been at home, tucked up in bed by now or stretched out on the sofa like a corpse, snoring away with Akbar curled up on his stomach, waiting for her to return.

She continued staring, unable to look away ... Sam actually appeared to be *enjoying* himself.

She couldn't fathom it.

15

She was still worrying over the matter the next morning when she arrived at the Arthur Road Jail near Jacob Circle.

Bombay's oldest and largest place of incarceration had long been the subject of heated political debate in the state legislature. The prison, originally built for eight hundred, was ill equipped for the sudden swell in numbers that followed the influx of refugees to the city and the subsequent escalation in criminal activity. The place was so overcrowded and the conditions so filthy even the rats had been heard to complain.

Persis signed in at the guardhouse and asked for Ismail Siraj to be brought to an interview room, a flagstoned cell with a single barred window, a wooden desk bolted to the floor, and a pair of steel chairs.

When Siraj arrived, the guard pushed him into a seat and shackled him to the desk, then retreated to the corner.

She examined the man before her, not sure what she had expected.

Siraj was older than she'd guessed, in his late fifties, with short, wiry grey hair, a beard that wouldn't have looked out of place on a swami, and the dazed look of a horse that had run into a wall. He was a small man, with sloping shoulders and a cowed demeanour.

The bruises on his face told their own story.

She introduced herself, then, 'I'm investigating the murder of Stephen and Leela Renzi. I need you to answer some questions for me. Can you do that?'

He continued to stare into space.

'How long have you worked for them?'

Silence.

'What happened to you?'

Nothing.

She looked at the guard. 'What happened?'

'I don't know what you mean, madam.' He looked supremely disinterested.

'His face,' she said, raising her voice. 'What happened to his face?'

He flashed an indulgent smile that made her want to get up and bang his head against the wall. 'Perhaps he had an accident.'

'Get out.'

The guard looked confused.

'I said get out!'

She watched him leave, still protesting, then turned back to Siraj.

'Yesterday you were arrested by my colleague, Inspector Oberoi. I'm guessing that your confession was made as a result of his interrogation ... I'm not Oberoi. I don't think you killed the Renzis. But I can't help you if you won't speak to me.'

For the first time, animation returned to his face. His eyes met hers. Could she be telling the truth? Hope flared.

'I didn't kill them. I've known Leela since she was a child. I used to work for her father. When she married Stephen, and moved home, she took me with her. She called me Uncle. How could anyone think—' He stopped, overcome.

'Why did you confess?'

'It wasn't because he beat me,' he said. 'He threatened my family. Said he would arrest my son as an accomplice. See him hang.'

'And you believed him?'

'My son's nineteen. He lives with me. He's studying at Bombay University. Leela Madam pays – paid – his fees. I can't allow this to affect his future.'

She leaned forward. 'Your son is safe.'

He looked at her sadly. 'You're young. You don't know the way things work. A man like Oberoi can do anything he wants. Who am I? No one. I have no voice. Someone has to pay for Leela's death. Your colleague has decided it must be me. I'll not trade the noose with my son.'

She realised it was futile arguing. 'Is there anything you can tell me about that day?'

He shook his head. 'I left the house early in the evening. I was nowhere near Bombay when the— When it happened.'

'Anything else that strikes you now? Anything that was different or unusual about the Renzis?'

He considered this. 'Leela was her usual self. She was looking forward to the holiday she had planned with her friends.' He shook his head morosely. The designs of fate. 'Stephen Sahib – I think something was bothering him. He seemed agitated that morning.'

'Why?'

'I don't know. It was just an impression. He was curt when he left the house. Most unlike him. He was a jovial man. Loud. Always had something to say. But that day he was silent. I sensed he was worried about something.'

16

In Bombay, it wasn't so much a case of he who casts the first stone, as cast the first stone before it is cast at thee.

She arrived at Malabar House to find Oberoi champing at the bit. He'd received a call from Arthur Road Jail. She didn't have to guess what it had been about.

Standing stiffly in Seth's office, she listened to him rant, practically frothing at the mouth as he accused her of undermining his case. To hear him speak, one would have thought the whole edifice of justice on the subcontinent had been laid low. Hands balled into fists by her side, it took every ounce of restraint for her not to respond in kind.

Seth weathered the storm from somewhere under his desk.

When he was sure it was over, he emerged cautiously, like a crab after the tide.

Oberoi had left, banging the door behind him, trailing dire threats if Persis went anywhere near Siraj again.

Seth took a newspaper out from his drawer and set it on the desk. It was the *Indian Chronicle* and it had gone to town on the Renzi double murder. The lurid headline read:

ITALIAN-INDIAN COUPLE MURDERED BY FIEND. SERVANT ARRESTED.

She didn't have to guess where Aalam Channa, the journalist responsible, had obtained his information.

Her heart sank. Siraj's chances of acquittal had fallen dramatic-ally. Channa had all but convicted the man, baying for an early trial, followed by summary execution. He was the kind of man who'd ask Siraj to strike a pose for the front page while ascending the gallows.

In a place like Bombay, the concept of innocent until proven guilty only applied to those with wealth, power, or influence.

With Channa stoking the fire, and a confession on record, Siraj was all but doomed.

The one saving grace was that there was no mention yet of the Grunewald killing.

'Tell me,' he said, 'did you go there just to antagonise Oberoi or because you genuinely think he has the wrong man?'

'Siraj was nowhere near Bombay at the time of the killings.'

'Oberoi says he has no credible alibi. He drove a motorbike out of the Renzi house. Alone. He could have easily doubled back.'

'The man has no motive.'

'What you mean is you haven't found one yet.'

She glared at him.

'There's no point looking at me like that,' he said, mildly. 'If you really don't think he did it, go and find out who did. In the mean-time, Siraj stays exactly where he is.'

The smell of fried samosas hung in the air.

Birla and Haq were sharing a lunchtime snack. Birla caught the look in her eye and stood up smartly, hastily dabbing at his mouth with a handkerchief. Haq ignored her, his heavy shoulders hunched over a steel plate.

She spoke to his back. 'You went with Oberoi yesterday to arrest Ismail Siraj.' It was an accusation, rather than a question.

Haq said nothing. He was cut from a different cloth to Birla, she knew. A born foot-soldier, the type of man who rarely thought for himself when others could make the effort instead.

'I suppose you were the one who helped him decide he was a murderer.'

Haq's hand froze halfway to his mouth.

She stepped closer. 'Is that what you call police work? Beating a confession out of an old man?'

He set down his samosa, pushed away his plate, then stood up. Towering over her, his thick brow furrowed with distaste. 'Do you have an actual question for me? *Madam.*'

'According to his confession, Siraj left the Renzi home at around six, but doubled back later. Did you ask his family what time he arrived in their village?'

Haq blinked. He had the face of a camel, an expressionless sculpture kicked out of granite with steel-toed boots.

His lips twitched, but he said nothing.

'Siraj is a Muslim,' said Birla, softly.

For the first time, Haq became animated, glowering at his colleague, his lips curling into a sullen pout. Birla's words had found their mark.

The shadow of Partition still lay over the country, the communal violence unleashed during those terrible years, lingering in the memory like a dark dream. If a fractious peace reigned, it was merely the embodiment of Nehru's will; sporadic bouts of violence continued to shatter the notional unity. Birla and Haq, Hindu and Muslim, had found a way to work together – not by choice, but through necessity.

By reminding Haq where his allegiances might lie, Birla had tapped into the very emotions that had underpinned the troubles. A dangerous gambit.

Seconds passed.

Finally, sensing that Haq was not about to risk undermining Oberoi, she turned away, registering her disgust with a dismissive wave of her hand.

'His father said he'd arrived just after midnight.'

She stopped, turned back. 'If that's the case, Siraj couldn't have been in Bombay at the time of the murders. He couldn't have got back here by three a.m. It's a good six hours to his village.'

'Oberoi says his father is lying to protect him.'

'What do *you* think?'

His eyes became round at the idea that anyone should care about *his* opinion. He glanced at Birla, licked his lips, then turned, swept up his cap, and left.

'Well,' said Birla, drily, 'that was impressive. It's not often he's so communicative.'

He reached into his pocket and handed her the key she'd given him the day before.

'There is no locksmiths' association in Bombay, just a lot of locksmiths. I took it to Trivedi's in Colaba. They've been in the same spot since my grandfather was in shorts. They say this is the key to a safety deposit box. The kind used by big banks.'

'Which bank?'

'They don't know.'

She grew thoughtful. 'Stephen Renzi was a foreigner. Chances are he'd have picked one of the big international banks. That should narrow things down.'

The banking sector had been transformed in recent decades, primarily by the swadeshi movement – the call for self-rule and self-reliance – a banner taken up by Gandhi during the Quit India years. Private banks run by Indians *for* Indians had mushroomed around the country, loosening the stranglehold of the Imperial Bank of India, bastard love child of the British-chartered presidency banks of Calcutta, Bombay, and Madras.

Foreign banks had been slower to establish themselves.

With Nehru's government threatening additional controls over the sector, the environment had become decidedly hostile to new ventures. As a consequence, there were only a handful of established international banks in the city.

She held the key out to Birla, who sighed, swiped it from her, picked up his cap, and left.

She returned to her desk.

Opening a drawer, she took out the package that Francis Rebeiro had handed to her at the seminary. In all that had happened since, she'd barely had time to examine it.

Unwrapping it, she set it down carefully on the desk.

The small wooden figure, no more than six inches in height, had been expertly fashioned, whittled out of a dark wood – teak or rosewood, if she had to guess.

He wore a distinctive high-collared tunic with large square breast pockets and a wide sashed belt, above loose-fitting trousers dropping to boots. A slouched hat rested atop a nondescript, clean-shaven face. In the figure's hand was a menacing, recurved knife, held across the chest.

She recalled now the words of Matthew, Peter Grunewald's altar boy.

The boy had found the figure on the morning of Grunewald's death, placed on the chapel's altar. He claimed that he'd taken it because he didn't want anyone to think that Grunewald had introduced a pagan idol to the altar.

Pagan. It was a strange word, harsh on the tongue, redolent of infraction.

Rebeiro had reassured the boy that the idol did not represent an alien god, that Grunewald hadn't endangered his immortal soul.

She was sure the priest was correct. There was a distinctively human cast to the wooden doll. It looked more like a boy's toy – a soldier, perhaps, or a policeman from another time and place.

The thought touched off a memory, or the shape of one. She grasped at it, but couldn't quite—

The phone rang. It was Bhoomi from the morgue, calling to tell her that he'd scheduled the Grunewald autopsy for one o'clock. It was the only slot he had free.

She checked her watch.

Thirty minutes.

If she left now, she had just enough time to make it.

As she approached her jeep, parked in an alley behind Malabar House, she sensed a presence at her shoulder.

Oberoi's face was uglier than she had ever known it, puffed up by rage.

'If you go near my prisoner again, I'll—'

'You'll what? What will you do?'

Some of the air went out of his tyres. He seemed taken aback.

She stepped forward, forcing him to backpedal. 'If you had even an ounce of sense, I wouldn't have had to talk to him. We both know he didn't kill the Renzis.'

A hard edge crept back into his eyes. 'He's a liar. And you're a fool for believing him. People like that ... they can't be trusted.'

And there it was. The unspoken prejudice that convicted men like Siraj before they set foot inside a courtroom. The fear that stalked the homes of India's wealthy, that one day, the servant, the driver, the security guard, would slit their throats while they slept, would rise up – in anger, in greed, in hate – to claim their due.

Blood hummed in her ears. 'You don't deserve to wear that uniform.'

His eyes narrowed ... and then he was stepping towards her again, fist raised, cheeks bulging with fury. Instead of stepping back, she moved into him, grabbed his arm, pivoted on one leg, and used his forward momentum to flip him over her hip and on to the floor.

He hit the concrete with a thud, the breath knocked audibly out of him. His eyes crossed and he stared dazedly up at the narrow ribbon of sky above the alley.

She backed away towards her jeep, hand on her revolver. 'I'm glad we had this talk.'

She waited until he'd recovered himself enough to struggle to his feet. He stared at her with undisguised loathing, his hatred a tangible thing, squirting from him in pungent whiffs as he turned and walked stiffly away. A warning Sam had given her when she'd first joined the force rang in her ears. Her male colleagues might learn to tolerate her presence as a necessary evil, but they'd never accept her as an equal.

She closed her eyes and leaned bonelessly against the jeep, allowing the tension to drain from her.

Finally, she turned back to the jeep.

A hand on her shoulder.

Without thinking, she spun around and lashed out with a fist, catching him square on the jaw.

He fell back, hitting the canvas with a thud, a puff of dust rising around his tall frame.

She stared down in horror and confusion.

'Christ,' mumbled a dazed Archie Blackfinch, clutching his jaw. 'It's nice to see you too, Persis.'

17

'I can see why you'd think he and Stephen Renzi were killed in the same way,' said Bhoomi.

They were standing in the autopsy suite, waiting for the pathologist's assistant to finish photographing the body. Grunewald's pulped features were turned up towards the whitewashed ceiling. A sense of horror engulfed her as she realised she could make out one of his eyeballs in the bloody mess that was all that remained of his face.

For want of a distraction, she reached into her pocket and took out the photograph Rebeiro had given her.

Bhoomi stared at it. 'He looks very . . . German.'

When he finally bent to his work, she stepped back into the shadows, allowing her thoughts to return, momentarily, to Archie Blackfinch.

'I thought I'd surprise you,' he'd said ruefully, standing up and dusting himself off. 'You invited me to lunch, remember?'

She'd struggled to rein in her emotions. A gladness welled inside her at his return, but with it came no small measure of confusion. She was in no mood to deal with the uncertainty that the Englishman's presence incited in her. As a result, she'd been curter with him than perhaps he deserved.

'You should have called ahead.'

'It wouldn't have been much of a surprise if I had.'

'I don't like surprises.'

'No,' he said, wincing as he rubbed his jaw. 'I can see that.'

An awkward silence.

'You know, some people entertain the ridiculous notion that an apology might be in order after punching a friend in the face.'

She coloured. 'It was an accident. You shouldn't have snuck up on me.'

He'd looked at her closely. 'Are you okay? You seem ... flustered.'

Flustered. How she hated that word. She'd heard it often enough at the academy, used as a way of demeaning her, of characterising her as easily upset, emotionally unreliable.

Nothing could have been further from the truth.

Her ability to remain grounded in the midst of chaos had always been her defining characteristic.

'I have to go. I have work to do.'

'Of course.' He seemed nonplussed. This wasn't the reception he'd been expecting.

Her thoughts fastened on a recent memory, the two of them in her jeep, late one evening after a difficult day, her lips on his, his hand moving up her waist ... A moment of madness. She could understand his confusion. It mirrored her own.

But she'd made the right decision. There was no going back.

He straightened his shoulders. 'Do you still want to discuss the cases you're working on?'

She nodded automatically, far from certain.

Sunlight glinted off his spectacles. 'Perhaps we can meet later, then?' The note of hope in his voice touched off an inexpressible sadness, spreading inside her like ink thrown into a bowl of water.

She took a deep breath. 'Yes, that would be fine.'

'Please sign for these, madam.'

She was back in the autopsy suite, Bhoomi's assistant, Kemal Butt, standing before her, holding out a cloth bag. 'The victim's personal effects.'

She took the bag, signed for it, then walked out into the ante-room that served as Bhoomi's office.

Reaching into the bag, she placed the objects on Bhoomi's cluttered desk, piled with teetering pyramids of manila folders and random scraps of paper, seemingly tossed aside and forgotten. The mess reminded her of the desk's owner. It was strange, she thought, how a man so meticulous in his work could be so slovenly outside of it.

There were only three items in the bag.

A wallet containing thirty-eight rupees in crumpled notes, a cheap watch with a scuffed leather band and an art deco dial, and a crucifix.

She picked up the crucifix.

It was heavier than she'd imagined, six inches tall, made of solid metal – possibly copper, slightly oxidised, the original gold finish all but eroded away – and strung on a chain. The arms of the cross were solid, perhaps three-quarters of an inch on a side. An unusually large crucifix to wear around one's neck. But then, Peter Grunewald had been an unusually large man, a veritable giant by the standards of the subcontinent.

A Christ was etched on to both sides of the crucifix, rail-thin, lank-haired, arms splayed, clad only in a loincloth. On one side his gaze was fixed downwards; on the other, up towards heaven. On both sides the letters INRI had been inscribed just above his head. She knew, from Bible class at school, that they represented the Latin inscription that Pontius Pilate had ordered etched into Christ's cross – a final insult, ironic and provocative: *Iesus Nazarenus, Rex Iudaeorum* – Jesus the Nazarene, King of the Jews.

Below the feet was a skull and crossed bones, a reference to Golgotha, the hill of his crucifixion, known to the Romans as the 'place of the skull'.

Something about the crucifix unnerved her. It seemed to possess a weight beyond the material, a darkness that leached warmth from her hand ... How had Grunewald worn this, every hour of every day?

The phone rang, startling her.

She couldn't locate it at first, and then realised that it was buried beneath a drift of paper. She looked around, but Bhoomi's assistant was nowhere to be seen.

Cursing, she picked up the receiver. Like her father, she was one of those people unable to abide a ringing telephone.

'Yes? This is the morgue.'

A silence. 'Persis? Is that you?'

She recognised Birla's voice. 'Yes. What do you want?'

'I was trying to reach *you*, as a matter of fact. I've managed to track down the safety deposit box for that key. Unfortunately, they won't let me take a look at it. Protocol.'

'Where are you?'

She took down the address, then checked her watch. 'I'll be there as soon as the autopsy is done.'

An hour later, Bhoomi joined her in the anteroom to offer his conclusions.

'First things first. He was killed by blunt force trauma. Repeated blows from a hammer or hammer-like weapon. At least twenty-eight strikes to the cranium and the face. Similar injuries to Stephen Renzi. Perhaps even more frenzied.' He stopped, pulled off his spectacles and wiped them on his coat. 'You're going to ask me if it was the same weapon, the same killer. The answer is: quite possibly. The wound profiles look very similar, but there's no way to be certain. I found no other evidence to link the two killings.'

She swallowed a curse. What had she been expecting? That Bhoomi would corroborate her theory? Something she could take to Seth, convince him that the two cases were one, to allow her to stop this madman before he killed again?

'There's something else. He sustained a blow directly to the apex of the parietal bone.' He tapped the top of his head.

For a moment, she looked at him in confusion . . . and then, like a thunderclap, she understood what it was that he was trying to tell her . . . *How could a man as tall as Grunewald have been struck in that way?*

The answer came to her instantly. 'He was kneeling.'

'Either that or his killer was eight feet tall. I think we can safely rule out the latter.'

'How did someone sneak up on him in a deserted chapel late in the evening?' The question wasn't aimed at Bhoomi. She was merely articulating her own thoughts. The pathologist chose to answer anyway.

'Perhaps he was so deep in prayer that he didn't notice.'

The explanation was unconvincing.

'By the way, the test came back on that substance I found smeared on the Ice Man's ears.' He paused, a magician heightening suspense before whisking away the tablecloth. 'It's a mixture of brown paint and grease. It seems as if our friend rubbed it on to his ears, his hands, and possibly over his face too, though there isn't enough of *that* left to be certain.' He shook his head. 'Strange, isn't it? Three men, three destroyed faces. The last time I saw anything like that was when I attended to the victims of a mine collapse, down in Mysore.'

'Three? You don't seriously think the Ice Man has anything to do with Renzi and Grunewald?'

'No, of course not. I was merely pointing out the strangeness of it.'

'Why would he smear paint and grease on his face?'

'I have absolutely no idea, Inspector.'

She was still puzzling over it as she left the autopsy suite and climbed her way back upstairs to her jeep.

18

As she approached Flora Fountain along Mahatma Gandhi Road, the Chartered Bank loomed on the left-hand side. She'd passed it numerous times over the years, an elegant, buff-coloured building with a basalt façade, completed at the turn of the century in the neo-Classical style popularised by Victorian architects and draughtsmen.

A riot of cupolas, mouldings, and cornices, the four-storey edifice was crowned by a statue of a trident-wielding Britannia. The bank's shield, carved into the tympanum, spoke to its origins, a medley of images representing Britain, China, India and Australia, once the most significant of the British Empire's far-flung dominions. The bank's full name, she now recalled, was the Chartered Bank of India, Australia and China, and it had once played a significant role in supporting the Far East opium trade that had made such lavish fortunes for enterprising Englishmen.

Inside the bank, she walked into a large hall with a domed ceiling reminiscent of a cathedral, designed, no doubt, to impress upon visitors the grandeur of the colonial era.

Electric fans whirled softly from the walls. Sweat prickled the nape of her neck.

She found Birla wearing a hole in the Minton tiles in one of the many bays that made up the hall.

Beside him was a thick-set Indian with a pompous jaw, a heavy moustache, and the expression of a man who had decided to lay down his life for a cause. His name was Sharma, and the cause, she soon discovered, was an impassioned defence of the bank's virtue.

'I'm afraid it's out of the question.'

'The man is dead,' said Persis, grinding her jaw. 'Murdered.'

'Be that as it may. Without the proper paperwork, I cannot possibly allow you to investigate the contents of his box.'

'What paperwork would you like from a corpse?'

He pulled a monogrammed handkerchief from his pocket and dabbed at his forehead. 'There are official channels for such requests. I'd be happy to point you in the right direction.'

She resisted the urge to haul him up by the collar. An image flashed before her eyes: setting her revolver under his chin and daring him to recite from his banking regulations *one more time*.

Instead, she paused to think the problem through.

Birla, having visited no fewer than eight banks that day, had discovered that the brass key Stephen Renzi had asked his wife to hide in her parents' home belonged to a safety deposit box that he had opened at the Fort branch of the Chartered Bank. Stephen had opened the box under his own name. The fact that he was now dead, murdered in his bed, had proved insufficient cause for the bank to allow the authorities to access the box.

'Do you have a telephone I can use?'

'Certainly.'

He gestured towards his desk, a slab of mahogany on which was set a two-toned phone in black and glistening chrome. She took out her notebook, flipped through to the number she was seeking, picked up the receiver, and dialled.

Minutes later, she was speaking with Pramod Sinha, Stephen Renzi's father-in-law.

She quickly explained the situation, then handed the phone to Sharma, whose anxiety had increased in the preceding minutes from righteous indignation to existential angst. He held the receiver to his ear as if it might explode. Dabbing furiously at his forehead with his handkerchief, he replied to Sinha's one-sided harangue with a succession of *yes, sirs*, visibly wilting until it seemed he might vanish inside his own suit.

Persis could only guess what Sinha was saying to the man.

She had gambled on Sinha's notoriety and the fact that he was a local. He may have lost friends in high places following his departure from the Congress Party, but he still had enough clout to scare the socks off a man like Sharma.

She regretted having to reveal the existence of the safety deposit box to the politician, but Sinha seemed disinterested in the contents. She guessed he was still preoccupied with the grim business of coming to terms with his daughter's death.

Having set down the phone, Sharma took a moment to compose himself, then led them stiffly down a flight of steps, through a locked door, and into the safety deposit box section of the bank.

She knew, from the card that Renzi had left behind, that they were after box number 100.

Sharma brought the box out to a viewing cubicle and placed it on a desk. 'I shall be outside,' he said, and glided away as if on castors.

Birla hovered on her shoulder as she set the brass key into the lock and turned.

Clutching the lid, she flipped it open and looked inside.

19

It was past six by the time she returned to Malabar House.

On the way, she'd driven around the curve of the Back Bay, glad of the breeze spiralling in off the water. Birla had been restless beside her, keen to get away.

A young man was due to visit the Birla residence, en famille. A potential match for Birla's daughter. The thought had brought the usually taciturn sub-inspector out in a cold sweat. His pockmarked face, beneath its close-trimmed beard, looked glassily out to sea, fearing the worst. His daughter was a firebrand, a woman who not only knew her own mind, but was keen on ensuring everyone else knew it too.

Birla suspected a grim evening was in store for the young swain should his charms prove less than endearing.

'We need more background on Renzi,' said Persis. 'Grunewald, too, for that matter.'

Birla muttered something non-committal.

'Are you listening?' she said sharply.

He puffed out his cheeks. 'Yes.'

'I want you to visit the Italian and German consulates. See if you can dig up anything. Try the Foreigner's Registration Office, too.'

'They call it the Federal Foreign Office.'

She glanced at him quizzically.

'The German consulate. Officially, it's called the Federal Foreign Office. My daughter once applied to work there. She speaks

German. They refused her. When the war started, she asked me if it would be fine to torch the place.'

Having dropped Birla off outside Malabar House, she parked the jeep, then went back out on to the main road. She stopped at Afzal's tea stall, bought a chutney sandwich, and then walked back to Malabar House and down into the basement.

She was glad to discover that Oberoi and Haq were nowhere to be seen. Nor was Seth.

The relative quiet, after a tumultuous day, brought with it a sense of relief.

She set down her cap, leaned back in her chair, and chewed on the sandwich.

Her thoughts meandered, scrabbling over the three investigations that now preoccupied her. She tried to impose some sense of order on all that she had so far discovered, but there seemed only dead ends.

The Ice Man had been murdered at some point in the past seven years, his body found in an unmarked cave in the Himalayan foothills. He'd smeared brown paint and grease on to his face and hands. In his pocket was a notebook with an enigmatic inscription: *Caesar's Triumph holds the key.* Who he was remained a mystery.

Stephen and Leela Renzi had been brutally murdered while they slept, with differing weapons. Stephen, an Italian, had run a successful business. But he had no obvious enemies. Similarly, there was no visible motive for anyone to wish his wife harm. The worst of it was that Oberoi had arrested a man for the killings whom Persis believed to be innocent. A convenient scapegoat.

As an additional puzzle, Stephen had, for years, kept a safety deposit box at a local bank. What she had discovered inside made no sense to her.

As for Peter Grunewald . . . In theory, there was little to connect him to the Renzi slayings. A German priest, murdered in a nondescript chapel on the edge of a slum. Yet the method of murder was too similar and the timing too close for her to dismiss it as coincidence.

But what possible motive could anyone have had to kill the big German?

The thought prompted her to take out the wooden doll that had been found in the chapel. The altar boy, Matthew, swore it hadn't been there the day before. Could Grunewald have placed it there? She didn't think so. The man was devout, bordering on maniacal. To have placed a non-saintly figure such as this on the altar would have been sacrilegious.

Which meant that someone else had put it there. Who? The killer? If so, why?

Once again, thinking about the doll touched off a memory . . . There was something about it that felt tantalisingly familiar . . . She closed her eyes, tried to still her mind, allow the memory to surface of its own accor—

Her eyes snapped open.

She stood up so abruptly that her chair fell back, clattering on the floor.

Ignoring it, she strode to the evidence cabinet, turned the key in the lock, and took out the envelope containing the set of photographs Mohammed Akram had taken of the Renzi crime scene.

Returning to her desk, she spread them out, then began feverishly going through them.

She knew what she was looking for . . . it had to be here . . .

She held up the photo, a large black and white shot of Leela Renzi's dresser . . . A mirror. A jumble of perfumes and beauty accessories. A vase of dried flowers . . . and an ornamental wooden doll.

20

The shop was dark.

She checked her watch. For the second time in a week she found herself disconcerted. Sam had been a creature of habit for so long that the smallest perturbation in his badger-like routine seemed cause enough for, if not alarm, then the beginnings of concern. And then there was the strange incident from the previous evening.

Who had her father been having dinner with? Why had he not told her about it?

She'd waited for him to explain himself at breakfast, but he'd simply stuck his nose in the *Times of India* and pretended as if nothing had happened.

Of course, he hadn't actually *seen* her there.

Perhaps she should have confronted him? She'd chosen not to do so, held back, in part by Dinaz, but also by a strange reluctance to intrude upon what appeared to be an intimate occasion. She'd expected that he'd say something of his own accord, offer some innocent enough reason for his presence at the restaurant, and they'd laugh at the coincidence.

But he'd returned so late that she'd already fallen into an anxious, dream-ridden sleep.

A mewling sound broke into her thoughts.

Akbar broke from the shadows at the base of the shop's door and padded over.

She bent down and scratched him under the chin, wondering what he was doing down here. It was most unlike him to be out after dark. The Persian tom's indolence would have put a pasha to shame.

She stood and looked along the street.

Midges roiled around the heads of lamp posts. A bicycle weaved its way between a handful of evening strollers. A woman called shrilly from an upstairs balcony to the street below.

The bookshop was stationed halfway along a street of Victorian-era residential dwellings, narrow, two-storey homes sandwiched between whitewashed art deco apartment towers. The haphazard nature of the street's architecture was common to the city. Bombay, perhaps more than any place on the subcontinent, had served as a testing ground for every conceivable fetish plaguing the draughts-men of its various colonisers. The city was like a woman who'd lived through a succession of fraught marriages, each husband demanding that she dress to please his whims.

The only other shopfronts along the winding road were Motilal's General Store and Apeni Khaplang's Apothecary.

The apothecary had been a fixture on the street since Persis's childhood, Apeni herself an émigré from the north-eastern province of Nagaland. Her father claimed that she was the descendant of a Naga chieftain, and that somewhere, hidden among her shelves of herbs and tinctures, lurked a gallery of shrunken heads.

For her own part, Persis had found Apeni to be a gentle and considerate woman, with a penchant for plain speaking. Sam's words were symptomatic of the prejudice often aimed at the various peoples of the north-east.

A memory bobbed to the surface, erupting from the haze of her teenage years.

Rumours of an unspoken closeness between her father and Apeni. The thought brought with it discomfort and self-doubt. How well could anyone really know the interior life of another human being? Their innermost thoughts and desires?

She'd always believed she understood Sam; there was a simplicity and steadfastness to him as obvious as a great tree. Yet, in the past days, he had become an altogether different being, a man of buried secrets and hidden whims.

Entering the apartment, she slipped off her cap and swiped a forearm over her grimy forehead, holding the door open behind her so that Akbar could slip inside.

She turned, stepped into the room . . . and froze.

Her father was in his wheelchair, at the piano. Seated beside him was the woman from the restaurant.

Shock ran in waves up and down her spine. For a moment, she simply stood there, paralysed by emotions she could not easily have named. It hadn't escaped her attention that Sam and the woman had quickly drawn apart upon registering her presence.

Finally, the woman stood.

She was a vision of elegance, taller than she had seemed in the restaurant. Older too. Her hair was thick, a heavy black mixed in with deep browns, and piled atop her head in the Greek fashion, a few lines of grey threaded through the mass. The crow's feet at her eyes, in concert with telltale grooves around her mouth, suggested an age range anywhere from late forties to mid-fifties. Her most arresting feature: a pair of lake-green eyes, the kind common in Kashmir.

She wore an embroidered *kantha* gown, hand-stitched in reds and greens, with a pattern of intersecting butterfly wings floating down the front.

Sam broke the spell. 'Persis, I'd like you to meet Meherzad Umrigar. She's . . . an old friend. She's been coming to the store for years.'

Persis knew that she should say something, but her jaw had frozen shut.

Meherzad stepped forward. 'It's lovely to meet you, Persis. Please call me Meher.'

Her voice held a musical quality, and a sense of breeding so strong you could have put a saddle on it.

Persis opened her mouth, but nothing emerged. Her throat was caught in a strangler's grip.

The woman's smile flickered.

Sam seemed stricken, squirming in his wheelchair as if he were sitting on a bed of nails.

She took a deep breath and forced out a reply: 'I need a shower.'

She stayed in her room for as long as she could.

Standing in the shower, she'd left the tap on cold, shivering under the cascade until her emotions had flattened out. Not that it helped.

By the time she'd dressed – in an elegant sleeveless red spotty pinafore dress and comfortable sandals – her pulse was racing again. Akbar had followed her in and was looking at her warily from his position of relative safety under the bed.

She knew that she was being childish.

In the two decades since her mother had passed, her father had never brought a woman home, nor raised the topic of remarrying. Years had been lost in self-pity and self-recrimination, Sam blaming himself for his wife's death, carrying that guilt in the way that others carried a torch to light their way through the dark. She suspected, from the odd hint that Aunt Nussie had dropped, that he had occasionally dallied with members of the opposite sex – but if he'd done so, he'd been unfailingly discreet. Or perhaps she'd simply closed her mind to the idea that her father was wracked by the needs of any other man.

Seeing Sam and his fancy woman together, at the Steinway, had brought back memories of her mother. Sanaz had been musically inclined, a trained pianist and a mezzo-soprano. From her, Persis had inherited her love of Chopin, of Bach, of Schubert. Sanaz had attempted to teach Persis the piano, but she'd never truly been able to master the keys. Impatience had made her a poor apprentice.

She retained few memories of her mother now, but the scraps that remained she held on to all the more tightly, a mosaic of fragmented images and incandescent memories, capable of reducing her emotions to ash.

She braced herself, then returned to the living room.

Krishna had set out dinner. Sam and Meher had waited for her, sitting on one side of the walnut-topped dining table like the members of a jury.

She walked to the far side and lowered herself into a chair.

'I'm Persis. I'm sorry about . . . earlier.'

'It's lovely to meet you, Persis. Your father has told me so much about you.'

'He's told me nothing about *you*.' The words burst out of her like a molten hiccup.

Sam frowned, but, before he could reply, Meher placed a hand on his arm. The proprietary nature of the gesture didn't escape Persis.

The woman turned to her. 'I understand that this must be quite disconcerting for you—'

'What do you mean by *this*? What exactly is *this*?'

Her expression wavered. 'Well, the fact that your father has a . . . a friend.'

'My father already has friends. Dr Aziz is his friend. Krishna is his friend. *I'm* his friend.'

'Persis—' growled Sam.

'It's fine, Sam,' said Meher, her expression neutral. She examined the younger woman with an evaluating gaze. 'Perhaps we should eat?'

They ate in silence, punctuated by staccato bursts of chatter initiated by Meher.

Persis listened with her head down, fork attacking her plate of pasta as if she harboured a personal grudge against the Italian race. The woman went on about how she'd known Sam for years, how the Wadia Book Emporium was the only bookshop that stocked her favourite French writers, how she was a patron of innumerable art galleries and museums, a one-woman cultural committee.

'It must be incredibly exciting,' she said, smiling brightly. 'Being India's first police*woman*?'

'I've been abused, attacked, and shot at. My reputation has been torn to shreds in the newspapers. I rarely receive credit for my efforts. Oh, and I've shot dead two men.'

'Persis, you're being rude,' said Sam. He'd been uncharacteristically subdued, picking his way carefully through the conversation like a horse trotting through a minefield.

She took a deep breath, then faced Meher. 'I apologise. It's just – I've been caught unawares.'

'I completely understand.'

'It's not that I have anything against my father . . . finding a friend. It's just that . . .' She tailed off.

'You've both been alone for so long.' Meher smiled.

She nodded. 'Something like that.' She struggled to find the words to express her feelings. In truth, she felt embarrassed by her behaviour. Meher seemed perfectly pleasant, an intelligent and thoughtful woman. But she seemed oblivious to the upheaval that her irruption into their lives would bring in its wake. It had been Sam and Persis against the world for more years than she cared to dwell on.

It was no easy task reimagining that life.

Why hadn't Sam mentioned her before? Why hadn't he discussed it with her first?

'If it makes you feel any better,' said Meher, 'this is no easier for me. I've been alone a long time too, Persis.'

The telephone rang behind them. Krishna scampered to answer it. 'It's for you,' he said, pointing the receiver at Persis.

She stood, walked to the sideboard, took the receiver from his hand. 'Yes?'

'Hello, Persis. It's me. Archie. I was wondering if you had time for that meeting now?'

21

It wasn't often you saw a waiter in Bombay who looked as if he'd just been dug up from his own grave.

Persis stared at the man over the top of her menu card, wondering if he might crumble to dust at any moment. His name was Sethna and she knew he was an old retainer at Leopold's, the sort of colonial relic who was a part of the furniture at many of Bombay's Irani restaurants, a lackey who, in the glory days of the Raj, would scurry to appease the whims of a foreigner, but turn away a hungry beggar with a stout boot and a disapproving glare.

She'd eaten here many times with her father, and lately, with Archie Blackfinch.

The place was only a mile from her home and she'd chosen to walk.

She'd felt guilty leaving the meal with her father and Meher, but she needed the air, needed to clear her head.

In the end, all she'd done was work up a sweat, which soon permeated her thin dress. She arrived feeling bedraggled and malodorous.

Not that Blackfinch had seemed to notice. He'd greeted her with his customary hound-like enthusiasm. Then again, the man had a tendency to charge straight through emotional barriers like an elephant with toothache.

She had enough self-awareness to acknowledge that the Englishman's lack of savoir-faire was matched only by her own. The difference was that Blackfinch, bewilderingly, rarely seemed to cause upset. Indeed, he was positively well liked. His awkwardness and innate ability to say the wrong thing at the wrong time only seemed to endear him to others, whereas her own forthright manner had left her alienated and mistrusted.

'I'll have a White Horse,' she told the waiter.

Sethna collected their menus, bowed at the waist with an audible creak, then turned and walked stiffly away like a clockwork soldier.

'You look lovely,' said Blackfinch. He was wearing a cream jacket over a white shirt and an indigo tie with a gold tiepin in the shape of a peacock. Overdressed for a place like Leopold's, she thought, with its open frontage, red-checked tables, and distinctly canteen-like air.

She pushed back a straggle of hair that had escaped her customary bun. 'How was Delhi?'

'An experience. And not one I'd like to repeat. I'd rather spend a week in a nest of vipers. At least *they'd* have some sense of decency.' His thick dark hair had been Brylcreemed back and his cheeks shone with good cheer. His green eyes flashed behind his spectacles.

'Was your mission successful?'

'I'm hopeful. The final tranche of funding should be signed off soon. After that … well, the sky's the limit. A lab in every city. That's the goal anyway.' He bared his teeth. 'But you know what they say. Many a slip twixt cup and lip.'

'And what will *your* role be in this mighty expansion?'

'I suppose they'll ask me to shepherd the other labs along.'

'So you'll be leaving Bombay soon?'

He blinked as if the thought hadn't occurred to him. The conversation ground to a halt. He reached up and loosened his tie, took a large gulp from his tumbler.

'Persis—'

'Let's talk about something else.' She gave him no chance to interrupt. Her emotions were already raw from the encounter with Meher Umrigar. She felt incapable of trying to assess the status of her relationship with the Englishman.

That was the problem with needing someone. As soon as you allowed another person into your life, you also gave them power over you, including the power to hurt.

Did Blackfinch have any idea how she felt? The anxieties that she hid beneath a façade of stone? Did he even understand his own feelings?

She turned away from such thoughts, instead laying out the details of the trinity of cases she was working on.

He listened without interrupting, though she could sense his mind was lingering on her earlier comment. 'I can't add much to your Ice Man case,' he said, when she'd finished. 'But I did get a chance to talk to Mohammed about the Renzi murders. The lack of forensic evidence suggests to me it was either a well-planned job – which doesn't make sense given that nothing appears to have been taken – or the culprit was someone from within the household. Hence the lack of foreign fingerprints or forensic artefacts.'

'We've already established alibis for the staff.'

'Not everyone. Mohammed tells me the security guard, the man Oberoi arrested, has only a shaky family alibi to vouch for him.'

The skin around her eyes tightened in anger. 'You believe Oberoi?'

He shrugged. 'All I'm saying is that it would be wrong to discount the possibility just because you don't like Oberoi.'

'Siraj was miles from Bombay when the murders took place.'

He fiddled with the cutlery before him, lining it up against the table edge. An odd habit she'd become accustomed to.

'You said Siraj had worked for them a while. Ergo, he knew their routines, their habits. He would have known they left their bedroom window unlatched, especially in the heat . . . Let's say, for the sake of argument, that he leaves that evening, makes a song and a dance about heading out of town. But he doesn't go far. Doubles back, hides out, and then, later that night, he climbs back over the rear wall, in through the window, and does the deed.'

'And the testimony from Siraj's father?'

He brushed a speck of imaginary fluff from the tablecloth. 'We both know the lengths to which parents will go to protect a child.'

She forced her temper down. 'There's no motive. No earthly reason that Siraj would have wanted to kill them.'

'Motives are like submerged bodies, Persis. They tend to float to the surface sooner or later.'

She turned away a moment, considering his words.

The restaurant was thronged, a mix of foreigners and locals. It was one of the reasons she and Blackfinch frequented the place. An Indian woman sharing a meal with an Englishman here was less cause for raised eyebrows. 'What would you say if I told you the Renzi and Grunewald cases are connected?'

'I'd ask if you had more than just a similar modus operandi.'

She quickly explained about the wooden dolls.

On the way home from the station, she'd stopped at the Renzi residence and retrieved the doll from Leela Renzi's dresser. It was identical, in every respect, to the one found by the altar boy at the scene of Peter Grunewald's death.

She took them out of her bag now, and set them on the table.

Blackfinch picked them up and examined them. 'The Steadfast Tin Soldier.'

She looked at him curiously.

'It's a Hans Christian Anderson tale. About a toy soldier, with one leg. Comes to a sticky end.' He flashed an opaque smile.

'They're beautifully crafted. Clearly, they hold some meaning for our killer. Assuming they *were* left by him.'

'What other explanation can there be?'

They mused on the problem a little longer, before surrendering.

'There's something else,' she said, digging back into her handbag. 'Shortly after he was married, Stephen Renzi asked his wife to stash a package at the home of his in-laws. Inside was a key to a safety deposit box. *This* was inside the box.'

She handed him an envelope.

He took it from her, opened it, and slipped out the piece of folded paper inside, smoothing it out on to the tablecloth.

It had clearly been ripped from a notebook, but that was as much as she had been able to ascertain.

The paper was marked with a series of letters from the alphabet, unconnected, unexplained.

NIWMQ YA SICSMO

Blackfinch tapped the sheet with a finger. 'You say this has been in a safety deposit box for years?'

'Three years, to be precise.'

'A lot of trouble to go to just to keep a jumble of random characters safe.'

'The note was important to him. It's a code.'

'Possibly.'

Her previous case had seen her tackle a series of cryptic clues left behind by the curator of the Bombay Asiatic Society, an Englishman who'd walked out of the place with one of the country's most valuable historical treasures, a six-hundred-year-old copy of Dante's *The Divine Comedy*.

Along the way, she'd been forced to hone her knowledge of codes and ciphers.

She put the folded sheet and wooden dolls away. 'I should get back.'

'I was thinking of taking a stroll by the harbour.'

Her thoughts returned to Sam and Meher. Were they waiting for her to return? Would Meher still be there? She couldn't stomach the idea of facing them again, not until she'd had a chance to work through her own feelings. 'Yes. That would be fine.'

They walked the five hundred yards from Leopold's to the Gateway of India, winding their way behind the Taj Palace Hotel and past the Victorian bulk of the Royal Bombay Yacht Club. The club had been under fire for years, its refusal to admit Indians a running sore that had only festered since independence.

She'd been in there once, with Emily, many years ago, called upon to deliver books from her father's store for the club's reading room. Sam had always refused to set foot – or wheel – in the place (though he wasn't averse to taking the club's money), but both she and Emily had felt an inordinate excitement at the prospect of entering a hidden world.

She'd never seen so many Englishmen in one place before, starched uniforms and cotton shirts, drinking Scotch and soda as they boasted to each other of treks to the Himalayas and tiger hunts in Bengal.

At the time, as an impressionable teenager, it had all seemed impossibly thrilling.

It was only later, when the independence struggle had dug its way under her skin, that the inherent perversity of the club's refusal to entertain the people of the country in which it stood became obvious to her.

She remembered Aziz eloquently explaining for her the British mentality.

'Did you ever read *Robinson Crusoe*? The British still in India are very much like our shipwrecked mariner. They find themselves marooned in a land of bounty, but a bounty that can only be harvested through great trial and tribulation. It's a shock to them when they discover that the natives – we poor Man Fridays – might wish to share in that bounty, and not go about our lives solely upon their sufferance.'

The plaza in front of the Gateway buzzed with late evening activity – a riot of taxis, tongas, hawkers, beggars, dragomen, and pedestrians taking in the soupy night air, leavened by a breeze coming in off the harbour, where a line of boats bobbed on the chop, mast-lanterns glowing in the dark. The smells of the waterfront – spice, fish, and that inescapable odour that was everywhere in Bombay: the cloying miasma of humanity.

As they walked along the Strand, she saw a line of homeless huddled under the promenade wall. In the morning, a gang of stick-wielding hawaldars, in concert with porters from the various hotels along the promenade, would move them on. Until then, they had this small refuge. They had each other.

'What's bothering you?'

He continued to surprise her. Blackfinch's antennae were usually as useless as a windsock in a high storm. But, of late, he seemed narrowly attuned to her moods.

She hesitated, uncertain if she should reveal the cause of her anxieties – not least of which was her own feeling of ambivalence towards *him*.

There was no denying her attraction. But what use was attraction when it came at such a price? Did Blackfinch not understand what it would mean for her to openly accept him as a partner? A white man? An Englishman? What would the newspapers make of that?

In the end, she said nothing, leaving his question hanging in the air.

Sinking his hands into the pockets of his trousers, he whistled tunelessly as they walked on towards the Bombay Presidency Radio Club. She knew that this stretch of the promenade had once housed some of the wealthiest families in the country: British and European merchants and high-ranking civil servants. The few Indians permitted to stay here had been those of value to the Raj, members of India's ruling princely families, dynasties bought and paid for.

'How's your brother?' she asked, for want of something to say.

'Thad? He's well. It's lambing season, so he's got his hands full. Literally.' She knew that his brother, Pythagoras, lived on a farm in England with his wife and two young daughters. Blackfinch called him Thad – Blackfinch's own given name was Archimedes – and the pair seemed to share a close relationship, writing to each other regularly. 'Did I tell you Susan came to see him?'

Susan. Blackfinch's ex-wife. A wrong turn into a maze that had taken six years to find his way out of.

'Why?' They'd stopped at the end of the promenade. He became fascinated by his shoes. 'She wanted to know where she could write to me.'

She waited for him to continue, her heart buzzing like a swarm of bees on a summer's day.

'She has the strangest notion we should get back together.' He grinned savagely. 'I'd rather stick my head in a crocodile's mouth. I'd rather spend another week in Delhi.'

She looked at him as if seeing him for the first time. His handsome face, his perennial expression of mild bewilderment, the sense he always gave her of being hastily assembled by a god with other things on his mind. He'd become such a fixture in her life over the past months that the idea of him one day not being there seemed altogether implausible.

The night air pressed heavily on her shoulders. Inchoate feelings of dread and desire threatened to overwhelm her.

'It's late,' she said, and turned away, hailing a passing tonga.

He could only watch stupidly as she climbed into the cab and ordered the driver homewards.

She leaned back, expecting him to call out, and was inexplicably disappointed when he simply watched her vanish back along the way they'd come.

22

Her first port of call the following morning was the Renzi home. She'd called De Mello, Stephen Renzi's business manager, and asked him to assemble the staff.

They were waiting for her in the parlour, a nervous gaggle, still visibly upset from the traumatic events that had taken place in the home, and the revelation that one of their own, Ismail Siraj, had been arrested for the crime.

She pulled De Mello aside. 'I'd like to interview them now. One by one.'

De Mello frowned. 'Why? Your colleague has already spoken to them. They have nothing to do with the killings.'

She refrained from explaining how little she thought of Oberoi's efforts at interrogation. 'Perhaps not. But new information has come to light and I'd like to discuss it with each of them.'

She showed him the sheet that Stephen Renzi had kept hidden in a safety deposit box, explaining how she had come by it. 'Have you any idea what this might be?'

He looked quizzically at the jumble of letters on the page. 'It's meaningless. What could this possibly have to do with the murders?'

'Perhaps nothing,' she muttered, folding the sheet away. De Mello stared at her, dark circles framing his eyes. Clearly, he was sleeping badly.

His expression of stern confusion reminded her of her father; she stamped down quickly on the thought.

She'd returned home the previous night after her dinner with Blackfinch and found, to her relief, that Sam was out. By the time he'd returned, she'd already fallen into a fitful sleep.

That morning she'd slipped out while he was still in the bathroom readying himself for breakfast.

A part of her knew that she should have sat and talked through her feelings with him, but each time she considered doing so, she found her mother's shade at her shoulder, whispering in her ear. To fully acknowledge Sam's new companion would be tantamount to betraying Sanaz, and how could she live with herself if she did *that*?

One by one, the staff were let into the room.

She showed them a photograph of Peter Grunewald and asked if they'd seen him at the house or in the Renzis' company. At first, none could recall any such individual. And then the cook, Safiya Mirza, said, 'Yes, I've seen him here, at the house. It was late last year. He knocked on the door. I thought he was begging for alms – they do that, you know, these priests. But then he asked for Stephen Sahib. I told him he wasn't at home. He left a message which I passed on.'

'What was the message?'

'Just that Stephen Sahib should come and see him.'

'How did Stephen react when you told him?'

She considered the question. 'He seemed displeased. But he never mentioned it again and I never thought of it.' Her eyes widened. 'Is this man the murderer?'

Persis deflected the query with a question of her own. 'What happens to you now? The staff, I mean?'

'De Mello has agreed to keep us on for another month until we can find other work.'

'And if you can't?'

She smiled obliquely. 'They were good employers. Considerate. Generous. It will be difficult for a woman of my age to find another couple as accommodating.'

Persis asked her about the possibility of Leela Renzi having a lover or a jilted would-be paramour. Mirza shook her head. 'Madam wasn't the straying kind. She loved Stephen, idolised him.'

Mary Gracias confirmed the same, in between breaking down into coarse sobs that wracked her slender frame. She also launched into a passionate defence of Ismail Siraj, suggesting that whoever could believe that a man like Siraj might be guilty of such a heinous crime needed their head examined.

Persis took the opportunity to ask the cleaner whether she had ever seen the wooden doll on Leela's dresser prior to her murder. The woman looked confused, and then shook her head. 'No.'

This lent weight to Persis' belief that the doll had been left there by the killer.

Gracias's words in defence of Siraj were echoed by Manas Ojah, the driver, a narrow-faced man in his late thirties, a native of Assam, with a patchy beard that seemed as if it was dying of some rare disease. 'Ismail is an honest man, a peaceful man. He could not have committed this crime,' he intoned mournfully. 'It's simply not in him.'

'Is there anything else you can tell me, anything at all?'

He hesitated, then said, 'A week before he was killed, Stephen Sahib was involved in a disagreement.'

'What sort of disagreement?'

'It was nothing. A small misunderstanding, I think. I was driving him and a business associate to the Opera House. Stephen Sahib loved the opera. Halfway through the journey they began arguing. Then Stephen Sahib asked me to stop the car. His friend got out and left.'

'What were they fighting about?'

'I'm afraid they were speaking in English and it was too fast for me to follow. I think it was a business matter.'

'Who was this friend?'

'I believe his name is Marlowe Sahib.'

The last of her interviewees, the young boy, Vishal Deo, seemed overawed. His experience with Oberoi had left him shell-shocked and fearful. Though she knew he was eighteen, he had the guileless look of a child. Yet, he was the only one of the staff who had witnessed Leela Renzi unexpectedly return to the house that evening.

The boy swore that he'd been at his home throughout the night. He slept in the same room as four younger siblings. It would have been virtually impossible for him to leave without waking at least one of them.

This reminded her that she needed to confirm their alibis. She was loath to trust Oberoi's thoroughness in such a vital matter.

Over the course of the following two hours, she drove to each of their homes – none lived more than a twenty-minute walk from the Renzi house – accompanied by De Mello, and quickly confirmed their whereabouts on the night of the murder.

Safiya Mirza was a widow and lived with her daughter – they slept in the same bed. Mary Gracias had been in bed with her husband, and Manas Ojah in bed with his wife. Deo's siblings confirmed that not only had he been in their shared room all night, but that he was a noisy sleeper, and had kept them awake mumbling in his dreams.

Finally, she asked De Mello about Marlowe.

'Trent Marlowe,' he replied. 'He's an American. A business acquaintance of Stephen's. Why?'

She recounted Ojah's statement, that the pair had had an argument.

De Mello frowned. 'That's unusual. Stephen wasn't the kind to air his grievances so openly.'

'Do you know Marlowe?'

'Only in passing.'

'Where can I find him?'

'I don't know. But I can find out.'

23

Trent Marlowe, it turned out, was one of the new breed of Americans sniffing around the country since the arrival of independence, looking for an angle.

Marlowe had found it in the automotive sector, and in Nehru's ambitious notions of economic reform. According to Arthur De Mello, the American had slipped into bed with the Indian government; the ugly child of their union was a half-baked plan to build Indian-made luxury sedans. He'd even convinced some state apparatchik to grant him a plot of land at the city's southern tip, where he might raise his automotive Xanadu.

She found the plant down by the United Services Club – known locally as the US Club – ironic, given that there were no Americans stationed on the premises. The club acted as a base for the three Indian services – army, navy and air force. Plenty of American officers *had* been inside, of course, during the war years, invited in to thrash away a few languid hours on the club's par-seventy golf course.

She parked in the lot, then made her way to the reception, where a smartly dressed young Indian picked up the phone to make a call, then led her up three flights of stairs to Marlowe's office.

The office was large enough to house two tennis courts side-by-side, with brilliant white marble floors, art deco mirrors on the walls, and a mahogany desk the size of a billiards table. One wall was taken up by a gallery of windows overlooking what she presumed was the factory floor, though it was hard to tell, as it was still under construction. An army of labourers, welders, bricklayers, engineers, and foremen hurled themselves around the place in a frenzy. The chaos resembled a war with fifteen different factions and constantly shifting allegiances.

Marlowe was standing by the bank of windows looking down on to the scene.

He was shorter than she'd expected, a slim man wearing trousers, a crisp white shirt, and braces. His hair was dark, slicked back, and his expression lugubrious, with sallow cheeks and hangdog eyes. A rumpled face like an unmade bed.

Marlowe was a good name for him, she thought.

He looked a lot like Bogart, but without the charm.

He waved at the view. 'Empire of the ants.'

The comment hung there, apropos of nothing.

She introduced herself, and he asked her to take a seat. Falling into his own chair, he reached into the breast pocket of his shirt, excavated a crumpled packet of Capstans, tapped out a cigarette, and lit it with a lighter in the shape of a racehorse.

He waved the pack at her. She declined.

'How can I help you, Inspector?'

She quickly explained her involvement in the Renzi case.

He tilted his head back and blew a cloud of smoke into the air. 'Helluva thing. I couldn't believe it when I heard.'

'I'm told that you were friends.'

'We were. Or at least, we were business acquaintances who occasionally stepped out together.'

'What *was* your business with him?'

He jerked his head over his shoulder. 'My business is out *there*, Inspector. I build cars. Technically speaking, it's my father's business. After I came back from the war, he handed it to me, then promptly retired to play golf. When Gandhi threw the Brits out,

I thought there might be a gap in the market. What I hadn't real-ised is that to get to Cinderella I'd have to marry her ugly sisters first. This "licence Raj" you guys have got going is a pretty sweet gig.'

She looked at him coldly. 'You haven't answered my question.'

He bared his teeth. 'Stephen sold motor parts. I'm building a factory that makes cars. You work it out.'

'Was the relationship amicable?'

'Sure.'

'No hiccups along the way?'

'Is there a point you're trying to make?'

'My understanding is that you and Stephen had a disagreement a week ago. While driving to the opera. He threw you out of his car.'

He started out of his seat, eyes blazing. '*Threw* me out? What the hell do you mean by that? Sure, we had a little spat but *I* chose to get out of that car. Me.'

'What was this spat about?'

His jaw turned pugnacious. 'I made him an offer. For his busi-ness. Said I'd buy him out. A generous offer, mind. He flew into a rage. As if I'd asked to sleep with his wife, for Pete's sake.'

She imagined the scene. Marlowe making a derisory offer for a business Renzi had built with his own hands. To Stephen Renzi, it probably *was* as insulting as if the American had made a pass at his wife.

'Now that he's gone, I suppose the path is clear for you to close the deal.'

He stared at her then stubbed the cigarette out on his desk, not bothering to reach for the ashtray. 'Now you listen here, lady. I had nothing to do with Stephen's death. I read what the killer did to him, to them both. What kinda man do you take me for?' His anger rushed out in a torrent. 'I've killed before. In the war. We both did. You think it's easy? Even when you take out a guy from fifty yards away, it's a helluva thing. Whoever did *that* to Stephen . . . he was a madman.'

She was silent a moment, working out what it was about his outburst that had snagged in her mind . . . Her brow furrowed. '"We *both* did"?'

He fell back, the anger dropping out of his face. 'I guess it doesn't matter who knows. Not now . . . Stephen was a soldier, once upon a time.'

'He told you that?'

'He didn't have to. I guessed it right away. You can always tell. He was pretty close-mouthed about it. Hated bringing it up. So would I, I suppose, if I'd fought on the wrong side of history.'

24

She was still turning this fact over in her mind when she returned to Malabar House.

She stopped off in the ladies' washroom on the ground floor, wetting a handkerchief and wiping down her face and the back of her neck. Her reflection stared at her from the gilt-edged mirror. She felt strangely energised, but her face seemed anxious, drawn.

Perhaps the evening with Blackfinch had been ill-judged. His presence made her palms itch, left her with a swirl of emotions that chipped away at her resolve.

Work. She always felt better when she could distract herself in her work.

Back at her desk, she inserted a clean carbon sheet into her typewriter, and began to type, putting on to paper the threads of her various investigatory efforts.

An hour passed in a flash.

And then, abruptly, the paper stopped feeding into the machine.

Cursing, she bent to check that the paper release wasn't engaged. Then she checked the feed rollers for flat spots.

Nothing.

Finally, with an impending sense of dread, she examined the platen.

She saw straight away that it had cracked. It would have to be replaced. Until then, the machine was useless.

Seth chose that moment to walk in, chatting to someone eclipsed by his narrow frame. He reached her desk and moved quickly to the side, like a matador whisking away his cape, revealing Seema Desai, the young woman assigned to Persis as a mentee.

Desai stared at her with something approaching belligerence. 'Good afternoon, madam.'

Persis frowned. 'What are you doing here?'

'You haven't sent for me,' explained the girl. 'I'm waiting for an assignment.'

Seth began to back away. 'I'll leave you both to it. I have an urgent call to make.' He turned tail and fled for his office as if pursued by lions.

Persis stood, towering over the girl. 'I'm extremely busy at the moment. I'll get back to you when I have something for you to do.'

'May I watch you work?'

'Well . . . no.'

'Then may I wait here?'

'Wait here? What for?'

'To learn how to become a policewoman.'

Persis looked at her as if seeing her for the first time. 'A policewoman? You?'

The girl blinked behind her cracked spectacles. 'Why not?'

She saw that Birla, standing nearby, was smirking. 'Haven't you got something to do?' she snapped.

His smile slipped and he scurried back to his desk.

She turned back to the girl. 'Look, it isn't that simple. Becoming a policewoman takes years. Training. Study. Physical tests.'

'What makes you think I can't do those things?'

'It's not as easy as that.'

'Why not? *You* did it, didn't you?'

She opened her mouth, but words failed her. She heard Birla snort, and reddened.

'Look. Don't misunderstand me. It's not that I don't want to help you, it's just that I don't have the time. I'm investigating several cases.'

The girl stared at her, then turned and began to walk away. She stopped after a few paces, turned back, and said, 'If I had money, connections – if I didn't come from the slums – would you have the time for me then?'

There was bitterness in her voice. Anger, too.

And a sense of futility that lingered with Persis long after the girl had gone.

'That was harsh,' observed Birla.

'I didn't mean it the way it sounded.' She wanted to explain, but what would be the point? Birla couldn't understand. She'd never had the knack of getting along, of making others feel at ease. Besides, she was still finding her own way in the service; sometimes it felt as if she was swimming in a sea full of sharks. How could she possibly prepare an eighteen-year-old girl from the slums to face *that*?

'Did you find out anything about Renzi or Grunewald?'

'Nothing from their respective embassies. They made a few calls on my behalf, but all they found were dead ends. I scratched out a few details about Renzi from the Foreigners Registration Office. He's listed there. They dug up the forms he'd filled out. Arrived in December 1945. He gave his home town as Atrani, a coastal village in southern Italy, barely a thousand people. I went back to the Italian embassy, and asked them to call the town's municipal office. Told them it was official business related to the war. They had the mayor's secretary go through the electoral rolls, birth records. It took hours. Not that it did much good. Stephen

Renzi isn't listed there. Never has been. No one by that name was ever born there or lived there.'

'He lied?'

Birla nodded. 'Yes. My guess is that Renzi isn't his real name.'

'And Grunewald?'

'Grunewald is a ghost. And I don't mean because he's dead. He never registered with the FRO, at all. There's no record of him anywhere, and no place to start looking.'

It was at that moment that Oberoi came clattering into the office. He took one look at Persis, blanched – no doubt recalling the way she'd thrown him to the ground the day before – recovered himself, and charged past them both to Seth's office.

She sensed something was up. She rose to follow him, then stopped. 'By the way, my typewriter has stopped working. See if you can find me a replacement.'

'Don't worry about thanking me,' muttered Birla, to her retreating back.

Inside Seth's office, she found the SP on the phone, Oberoi prowling the space before his desk as impatiently as a tiger with a boil on its backside.

Seth's chorus of *yes, sirs* finally ended, and he put the phone down, his shoulders sagging.

'That man will be the death of me,' he muttered. He looked up at them. 'That was Shukla. He wants to know what the devil we're doing about the Ice Man.'

'Who cares about the Ice Man?' exploded Oberoi. 'What's happening with Ismail Siraj? When will they set a court date?'

Persis turned to face him. 'The investigation is still ongoing.'

He squared up to her. '*I'm* the lead, and I say we have our man.'

She stepped towards him, instinctively. He flinched, but made no move to back away.

'Enough!' Seth stood up, and looked directly at Persis. 'Where *are* we with the Ice Man?'

She hesitated. 'No further forward. There's no new evidence to examine, no new leads. Unless we get lucky, the Ice Man's identity is going to remain a mystery.'

'Lucky? Is that what you want me to go back to Shukla with?'

She weathered his anger with a shrug. 'Those are the facts.'

He collapsed back into his seat. 'Why are you still chasing the Renzi case?'

She held up a finger. 'Wait here.' As she turned, she heard him mutter, 'Where else would I go? It's *my* office.'

She jogged to her desk, took out the wooden dolls, and returned to Seth's office. She set them down on the SP's desk. 'One of these was left in the Renzis' bedroom following their murder. The other was left at the scene of Peter Grunewald's killing.'

Oberoi frowned. 'Who is Peter Grunewald?'

Seth answered. 'A German priest murdered the day after the Renzis.' He picked up the wooden dolls and examined them.

'What are you talking about?' Oberoi's composure, loosely worn at the best of times, was slipping. 'What's going on here?'

Seth sighed. 'What Persis is trying to tell us is that we might have a serial killer on our hands.'

'A what?'

'A serial killer. A man intent on murdering foreigners, by the look of things.' He put down the dolls.

'So what now?' The question was directed at Persis.

'Well, firstly, this means that Siraj can't be the killer. By the time Grunewald was murdered, he was almost certainly out of Bombay. Don't forget that Oberoi arrested him in his village.

Others saw him there the following evening, when Grunewald was killed. It's not just his father alibiing him this time.'

'You may be right,' he said, grudgingly. 'But we'll need more than a pair of wooden dolls to convince a judge to release him. What else have you got?'

She hesitated. 'We need to find out why the killer targeted Renzi and Grunewald.'

'What possible connection could there be between them?'

'One of Renzi's staff remembers Grunewald coming by the home some months ago. The two men knew each other.'

'That's hardly conclusive. Have you considered the possibility that these murders might be entirely random? That we have a madman out there? Perhaps he's simply picking them because they're foreigners.' A shadow passed across his brow. 'We should probably sound the alarm.'

'If you do that, you'll alert our killer. If he has any sense, he'll vanish.'

'If he had any sense, he wouldn't be wandering around the city braining innocent civilians, now, would he?' Seth glowered at her. 'What happens if we say nothing and he kills again?'

'What if he gets away? Resurfaces somewhere else? How many will he kill then?'

Oberoi had been listening to the exchange in agitated silence. Now he stepped forward and swiped up one of the dolls. He examined it, then said, 'There are probably a thousand dolls like this in the city. It's pure coincidence they were found at the scenes.'

'Don't be a fool.'

'I have another theory. I say *you* planted these. You *want* the cases to be linked. You've got a taste for headlines now.'

The audacity of the accusation took her breath away. For an instant, she was speechless. Words stumbled angrily out of her mouth. 'That's absurd.'

'Is it? You've made it clear just how ambitious you are.'

Seth banged the table. 'Enough! Persis. I want you to carry on with your investigation. And you—' He pointed a finger at Oberoi. 'You can play devil's advocate. Just in case she's wrong.'

'I'm not wrong.'

But the SP had stopped listening.

25

The Dancing Stomach was packed with late afternoon diners, steam billowing from the open kitchen.

Unable to bear Oberoi's presence, she'd gone out to find something to eat.

She attacked a bowl of steaming noodles with the chopsticks that came with the order, and focused her mind on the case.

She knew that her priority had to be confirming the link between Stephen Renzi and Peter Grunewald. Neither the wooden dolls nor Safiya Mirza's testimony that Peter Grunewald had once visited the Renzi home were enough.

In spite of Seth and Oberoi's scepticism, she was convinced that the killer had not acted randomly.

He'd picked those men. Why?

A thought that had been squatting at the rear of her mind now eased its way to the front.

The dolls clearly held some meaning for the killer. Their very distinctiveness hinted at something personal.

She needed to find out more about them.

There was one place in the city that she could think of as a good place to start—

One of her chopsticks snapped.

She picked up the bowl, walked to the kitchen, and set it down in front of the proprietor, Mao Fung, a round man in an improbable toque.

'Your chopsticks keep snapping.'

He looked at her uncomprehendingly. His cheeks were aflame. His toque, more grey than white, sat on his head like a deflated soufflé.

She picked up the remaining chopstick and snapped it under his nose. He jumped.

'The next time this happens, I . . . I shall be displeased.'

She picked up the bowl, placed it in his hands, turned, and left.

The drive up to the Victoria and Albert Museum, through heavy traffic, took almost an hour. She chose a route up the city's western flank, along Nepeansea Road, past Kemp's Corner, then along Warden Road and the Breach Candy Hospital, where she'd been born almost twenty-eight years earlier.

Turning east at Haji Ali, she headed inwards along Dr E Moses Road, named after Bombay's first Jewish mayor.

Fifteen minutes later, she was parked inside the museum gates.

The V&A was almost eighty years old, a treasure house of the decorative and industrial arts. She'd visited on occasion, drawn by the museum's store of historical artefacts and its pleasing architectural oddities: the dimly lit entrance hall with its parquet flooring and vaulted ceiling, the scowling bust of Queen Victoria stationed by the doors.

She made her way swiftly to the museum director's office.

A quick conversation later and she was directed to the basement and a man named Victor Gomes.

Gomes, she quickly realised, was an Anglo-Indian. An English father and an Indian mother, she guessed, as was the usual way of such things. With the retreat of the British, men like Gomes had weathered a difficult few years. Not white enough to be classed as British, and not Indian enough to be given the accolade of patriot. Some had taken tramp steamers to England, to find a new life alien to the one they had known, a life, where, if the reports returning from Britain were to be believed, prejudice had already relegated them to the status of second-class citizens.

In the Old Country, a pukka accent and a sterling education meant little when set beside the colour of a man's skin.

He was a small man, in his fifties, with a head of curly grey hair, wearing a neat bow tie and a white shirt limp with sweat. Perched on a stool at a wooden workbench, sleeves rolled up to the elbows, he was examining the dissembled parts of a wooden toy, one with a clockwork mechanism.

Gomes, among other things, was the museum's resident plangonologist – a doll collector.

She explained the problem, then took the wooden dolls from her bag and set them on the workbench.

Gomes set a pair of spectacles on to his nose, and bent to examine the dolls under an Anglepoise lamp.

'They're certainly fashioned by the same hand,' he concluded, eventually. 'But these are not a child's dolls. What I mean is, they're not designed as playthings. Whoever made them has a strong affinity for the subject matter.'

'What *is* the subject matter?'

He seemed surprised. 'Well, I would have thought it was obvious.'

Normally such a comment would have raised her hackles, but Gomes did not seem to intend offence. 'These are regimental dolls. Or at least, someone's *idea* of a regimental doll.'

'You're saying they're toy soldiers?'

'No. Not the sort of toy soldier you're thinking about. If I had to guess, I'd say that whoever carved these was once a soldier, a low-ranking one – an infantryman, perhaps. These dolls might be his way of connecting to that time – a time fondly remembered, I suspect.'

She allowed the thought to settle in her mind.

In truth, she'd suspected that the dolls, with their distinctly soldierly bearing, might have a military connection. 'Can you narrow it down to a particular unit within the army?'

'I'm afraid I'm no military expert.'

26

By the time she made it back to Malabar House, it was past six and the office was as deserted as a cemetery, but with considerably less charm.

She locked the dolls away in a drawer, then sat back.

She saw that Birla had been his usual efficient self. Her old typewriter had vanished, replaced by a new model.

She inserted a sheet, and typed out a single line.

```
For truth is always strange; stranger than fiction.
```

Byron had long been her favourite poet. Of his many famous lines of verse, this had always seemed the most apt for the world she now inhabited.

She spent some time adding to her earlier report, detailing the visit with Gomes, typing up the findings from the past days.

Following this, she took out her notebook and summarised the three cases for her own benefit, attempting to untangle the various threads of her investigations:

ICE MAN
What was the Ice Man doing up in the Tsangchokla Pass?
Does notebook have any bearing on case?
Why are three pages torn out of the notebook?
What does *Caesar's Triumph holds the key* mean?
Why did Ice Man have paint and grease on his face and hands?

STEPHEN & LEELA RENZI

Murdered with hammer and knife, respectively. Why two
  weapons?

Leela Renzi not meant to be there that night.

Stephen once a soldier, but kept it a secret.

Stephen Renzi not real name.

Stephen kept safety deposit box with single sheet of paper.

What do characters on paper mean? Is it a code? Why was
  the sheet so valuable?

All staff at Renzi house have alibis.

Motive for killings unclear.

Wooden doll found at scene.

De Mello says Stephen agitated on day of killing. Why?

Ismail Siraj arrested by Oberoi. No apparent motive.
  Alibied by father.

PETER GRUNEWALD

Murdered in similar manner as Stephen Renzi.

Murdered day after Renzis.

Grunewald came to Renzi home months earlier. How did
  the two men know each other?

Like Renzi, Grunewald has a mysterious past – is
  Grunewald his real name?

Wooden doll found at scene – identical to doll found at Renzis'.

Grunewald agitated prior to murder. Why?

Ismail Siraj couldn't have killed Grunewald. He was
  certainly in village by then.

She sat there a moment, staring at the loops and whorls of her
own handwriting.

She opened the drawer and took out the sheet of paper that
Stephen Renzi had kept locked away, and smoothed it out on the

desk. The jumble of letters seemed to float off the page, shimmering before her eyes. Taunting.

She ran a finger along the ragged left-hand edge of the sheet, where it had been ripped out of—

A faint flicker of something, like the first whispers of the monsoon . . . It couldn't be.

She stood, went to the evidence cabinet, and returned with the notebook found on the Ice Man.

With trembling fingers, she turned to the back, and the three missing pages.

She picked up Stephen Renzi's note and held it against the torn edges of each of the pages. On the third try, she had a match.

The jagged edge aligned perfectly.

There was no doubt.

The page had come from the Ice Man's journal.

27

'What, precisely, are you looking for?'

The priest, Rebeiro, looked on anxiously as she lifted the mattress from Peter Grunewald's cot, and examined the seams. Slipping a switchblade from her pocket, she flicked out the knife, then slashed into the mattress.

'What are you doing!'

She ignored his cry, ripping open the mattress and releasing a storm of cotton fibres.

She searched in silence, quickly and thoroughly.

Nothing.

She finished with the mattress and began on the pillow.

Behind her, Rebeiro made whimpering noises.

There was nothing inside the pillow.

She stood back, a light sheen of sweat on her forehead and cheeks, and took in the room.

In the past hour, she'd examined every possibility, checked every hiding place the tiny room and Grunewald's meagre possessions had to offer. But there was nothing.

If the German had secreted a sheet of notepaper in here, she couldn't find it.

The notion had occurred to her back at Malabar House.

Discovering the connection between Stephen Renzi and the Ice Man had left her dazed and confused, the feeling that she'd turned a corner and walked into an alternate reality. The Ice Man had died years earlier, up in a frozen mountain pass. Stephen

Renzi had been murdered in his own bed just days ago. *How could the two men possibly be connected?*

But the evidence was irrefutable.

Stephen Renzi had been in possession of a page torn from the notebook discovered with the Ice Man, a page Renzi had kept securely hidden in a safety deposit box.

It beggared belief.

When she'd regained her bearings, she began to work the problem.

If Stephen Renzi and the Ice Man were connected, and Renzi and Peter Grunewald were connected – as the wooden dolls implied they were – then did it not also imply that Grunewald and the Ice Man were connected? Possibly by a second sheet torn from the latter's notebook?

After all, there were three pages missing. If Stephen Renzi had kept careful hold of one of them, then perhaps Grunewald had been in possession of another?

It was a leap, but one worth exploring.

As to the significance of the missing pages, *that* she hadn't yet figured out. What could be so important about a series of unintelligible characters?

She sat down on the cot, reached into the breast pocket of her shirt, and took out Renzi's sheet.

She held it out to Rebeiro. 'Did you ever see Grunewald with something like this?'

He examined the sheet, then handed it back to her with a shake of his head. 'No. Is that what you're looking for?'

'Is there anywhere else he might have hidden it?'

Rebeiro flashed a grim smile. 'All of Peter's earthly possessions are right here in this room. Frankly, the only material thing he ever valued was his crucifix. Because it brought him closer to our Lord and Saviour.'

She looked again at the sheet.

NIWMQ YA SICSMO

Instinctively, she suspected that it was a code. But what did the code conceal?

Finally, frustrated by her own inability to make any headway, she got up and left.

28

She arrived home into the midst of a storm.

Nussie was there, standing in the centre of the living room, scarlet-cheeked, wagging a finger at Sam as she harangued him. 'Have you lost your senses?'

Sam glared at her from his wheelchair. A vein throbbed at his temple. Aziz was standing between them, acting as a referee, the kind that suspected he might suffer a blow or two before the night was out.

She saw that Akbar was skulking under the piano, ears flattened.

Her aunt, it appeared, had got wind of Sam's new inamorata.

Nussie had always seemed to her a swanlike creature – beautiful, elegant, and utterly detached from reality. With her elder sister's passing, she had taken it upon herself to act as a surrogate mother to Persis, much to Sam's displeasure. The pair had never seen eye-to-eye, mainly because Nussie had always made it clear that, in her opinion, Sanaz had married well beneath her station. For years, she'd blamed him for her sister's untimely death.

As Persis had grown to adulthood, the pair had reached a fragile truce.

Sam knew, instinctively, that there were certain things a young woman needed, matters of feminine experience for which he was wholly unequipped. As a consequence, Nussie had become a regular feature in their lives, inviting herself around two, three times a week. If it hadn't been for her recent attempts to thrust Darius at her as a potential match, Persis would have more readily welcomed her aunt's presence.

'Have you finished?' said Sam, when her aunt finally stopped to take a breath. He glowered at her. 'First, it is none of your business who I do or do not see. Furthermore, this is *my* home. What makes you think you can turn up here and browbeat me?'

'This isn't about you!' Nussie marched over to Persis and placed an arm around her. 'Have you considered how Persis feels about this?'

'Persis is a grown woman,' growled Sam. 'Whatever she has to say, she can say to *me*.'

Persis disentangled herself from her aunt, took off her cap, and set it down on the dining table. A burst of static fluttered around her heart.

'It would be nice to know more about her. Meher, I mean.'

Her words were directed at Sam, but Nussie leaped in before he could speak. 'Let me tell you about her. She's a widower, twice over. The woman's already buried *two* husbands.'

A hiss of breath escaped Sam. 'She told me about her husbands. We have no secrets from each other.'

'And I suppose *you* told her you'd killed your wife in a car crash? I bet that gave you something to bond over!'

A shocked silence settled over the room.

Her father's knuckles whitened on the arms of his wheelchair.

Nussie, perhaps realising she'd overstepped the mark, fell silent, unsaid words bulging her jaw.

Persis suddenly realised what it was that was really bothering her aunt.

If Sam brought another woman into the house, Nussie's place in their lives would be fatally compromised. In that instant, she understood just how much Nussie had come to love her, and how she'd taken her aunt's presence for granted. She'd always weathered

Nussie's attentions as a necessary evil, often treating her as a figure of fun. How often had she lampooned her aunt's mannerisms to Jaya, Dinaz, and Emily?

Shame, as insidious as smoke, rose to engulf her.

She moved to her aunt's side and placed an arm around her shoulders. 'You'll always be a second mother to me.'

She was conscious that the words had a ring of formality, as if the cosmos had written lines for her, and she had uttered them on cue. And yet . . . there was truth there.

Nussie dissolved into tears, burying her head under her niece's chin.

When she had sobbed herself to a standstill, Persis led her gently to the door. 'Aziz will see you downstairs.'

When they'd left, she turned back to find her father pouring himself a whisky.

She joined him, helping herself to a decent measure, taking a gulp, then easing herself on to the sofa, where she closed her eyes for a brief moment, before facing him again.

'What if she's right? I mean, what do you really know about this woman?'

'I know enough.'

'Why now?'

'I've been alone a long time, Persis.'

'You're not alone. You have me.'

His face grew still and she knew that she had hurt him. It hadn't been her intent, but the conflict that raged inside her made it difficult to keep a steady hand on the tiller of her emotions. She couldn't imagine another woman in her mother's place, in Nussie's place.

Another woman in this home, the only home she had ever known.

The thought of it made her heart gallop.

'Look. I'm not a fool. You have every right to find yourself a companion. I want you to be happy. All I'm asking is that you take things slowly. Allow us both time to adjust to the idea.'

Something passed behind Sam's eyes – disappointment, anger, sadness. 'Too late,' he finally choked out. 'I've asked her to marry me.'

29

Breakfast had been a frosty affair.

Her father had hidden himself behind the *Times of India*, snapping the paper violently every now and again as he turned the pages.

For her part, Persis ate quickly and without any real hunger, the kedgeree turning quietly to ash in her mouth. She'd hoped the night might have given them both enough perspective to discuss the matter rationally, but her father seemed in no mood to offer an olive branch.

Was the fault hers? Was she being unreasonable? How could Sam have invited a stranger into their lives without consulting her first? Didn't he understand the cause of her anxiety? That it wasn't just concern for *him*? People were an unknown quantity. It took a long time to truly understand someone, and, more importantly, for them to understand *her*.

She had nothing against Meher Umrigar, but what if they didn't get along? Had her father thought about that? How would the three of them fare, trapped together, if they couldn't reach an understanding?

She'd never been good at compromise.

She reached Malabar House and discovered Seema Desai waiting for her in Roshan Seth's office.

'Why don't you give us a moment?' said Seth.

Seema left, not glancing backwards.

Seth drummed his fingers on the desk, the other hand cupped around his chin. 'Have you taken a vow to make my life difficult?'

'I'm sorry. You know how busy I've been.'

'Is that all it is?'

She said nothing.

'When they first sent you here, I cursed my luck. But I soon learned that I was wrong. *You* changed my mind.'

She hesitated. 'I'm not a teacher. She needs someone who knows what they're doing.'

'You're selling yourself short. I've watched you. You're a better woman than you give yourself credit for.'

His belief in her seemed a tangible thing. Was he right? Could she really act as a guide to someone like Seema? The girl had put her on a pedestal. The trouble with pedestals was that it was easy to be knocked from them.

'Fine,' she said, eventually. 'I'll find her something to do.'

'That's all I ask.' He shifted in his seat. 'Now bring me up to speed.'

She spent the next quarter of an hour detailing progress on the Renzi investigation, ending with her explosive revelation that the Renzi and Ice Man cases were linked.

For a moment, he said nothing, then: 'Show me the notebook.'

She went to her desk and returned with the Ice Man's notebook and Stephen Renzi's sheet. Putting them together, she demonstrated the connection that had led to her conjecture.

'Incredible.' His eyes were faraway.

'I haven't worked out what the characters mean, but I think it's some sort of code.'

He puffed out his cheeks. 'Even if you crack this . . . code, it doesn't mean you'll be any closer to proving Ismail Siraj innocent.' He dug a newspaper out from under his desk. The *Indian Chronicle*. 'Channa's doing a damned fine job stoking the mob.'

She picked up the notebook and waved it at him. 'This underlines the fact that it couldn't have been Siraj.'

His brow furrowed. 'How so?'

'This notebook links the Ice Man and Stephen Renzi. The wooden dolls link Renzi and Grunewald – and we know Siraj couldn't have been in Bombay when Grunewald was killed. The notebook and dolls together suggest that Grunewald is also, more likely than not, linked to the Ice Man, by way of Renzi. And *that* suggests that the same person that killed Renzi must have killed Grunewald. If that's the case, it's highly unlikely to be Siraj – he has no link to the Ice Man.'

'You're supposing a lot. You don't know for certain that Siraj has no association with the Ice Man. Or whether Grunewald really *is* linked to him. *If* he is, where's your evidence? Did you discover a sheet of notepaper in *his* possession?'

'No.'

'Then all you have is conjecture.'

Peter Grunewald remained at the forefront of her thoughts as she returned to her desk, where the girl, Seema, was waiting for her, holding a worn clutch bag to her chest.

Persis sat down and waved her into a chair.

'You're determined to do this?'

The girl nodded.

'Do you understand that the road will be long and difficult? They'll hate you for it.' She didn't need to spell out who she meant by 'they'.

Seema caught her lip between her teeth, then nodded.

'I have a task for you.' Persis wrote down an address on a slip of paper and handed it to the girl. 'Her name is Nussie. Tell her that I sent you. Ask her for the address of a woman named Meherzad Umrigar. Then tell her that I've tasked you to follow Umrigar around.'

Seema frowned, fingering a locket around her neck. It was in the shape of a small Ganesha, the elephant-headed god. 'Is she a criminal?'

Persis's eyes lingered on the locket. 'Let's just say that she's a person of interest.'

She reached into her drawer and handed Seema a blank notebook. 'Make notes. I want to know how Umrigar spends her day. Where she goes. Who she meets with. Do you understand?'

The girl nodded.

'And don't let yourself be seen.'

After the girl had left, Birla walked over.

'How did it go with Seth?'

She quickly brought him up to speed on developments.

He scratched his beard thoughtfully. 'Can you imagine the headlines when they find out the Ice Man is linked to these new murders?' He frowned. 'Do you think the same person killed *him*?'

The thought had occurred to her. But it seemed fantastical. The Ice Man had been murdered up in the Himalayan foothills years ago. It seemed a leap too far to suppose that the same killer had now set about collecting victims in Bombay.

Then again, if she could figure out precisely *how* Stephen Renzi and Peter Grunewald were linked to the Ice Man, it might crack all three cases wide open.

Her thoughts looped back to the torn page from the Ice Man's notebook. She needed to break the code . . . code.

A tumbler fell into place.

She opened the notebook, and turned to the page on which the Ice Man had left his enigmatic line of text: *Caesar's Triumph holds the key.*

Holds the key.

Excitement shivered along the base of her neck.

Somewhere in this line was the key to cracking the code set down on the pages torn from the notebook – she was now convinced that the three pages had been removed because they each held a section of a coded message, one that could only be deciphered with the help of this sentence.

The thought solidified her belief that Grunewald might have been in possession of one of those pages. And if that were the case, then it made sense that he would have hidden it as securely as Stephen Renzi had hidden *his* page. Not in a safety deposit box – that would hardly have been in keeping with Grunewald's fanatically pious demeanour – but somewhere closer to hand.

She'd searched the priest's room, to no avail—

Her zigzagging thoughts ground to a halt.

She leaped up, strode to the evidence cabinet, and returned with the bag containing Grunewald's personal artefacts.

She took out the Cross he had worn around his neck.

Examining it with a critical eye, she realised that there was a thin, barely visible line running around the central shaft just above the bottom. A crack in the metal. Looking underneath, she saw the head of a screw embedded into the base of the shaft.

Five minutes later, having scrabbled around for a screwdriver, she undid the screw.

A small section fell off the bottom of the shaft, revealing that it was hollow.

Something glimmered inside.

She grabbed a pair of tweezers and teased out the contents . . . a rolled-up piece of paper.

She unfurled it on to her desk, Birla peering curiously over her shoulder.

It was another torn page, scrawled with a meaningless sequence of alphabetical characters.

XQYWDMQ YA QIVI

She opened the Ice Man's notebook and set the page against the torn edges of the three pages at the rear.

All doubt evaporated.

Like Stephen Renzi's page, Grunewald's page had come from the notebook too.

Birla let out a long whistle. 'I guess you've made your point,' he said. 'We don't have three cases anymore. Just one very big, messy one.'

30

The revelations continued to swirl around her mind as she made her way to Bombay University for a lunchtime appointment with Augustus Silva, an old friend of her father's.

Silva was a tenured professor at the university, a well-known military historian who'd assisted her on previous cases. She'd called ahead, asking to speak with him about an urgent matter.

She found him out on the university's sports field, with a gaggle of students in costume gathered around a broken-down chariot.

A horse nibbled at the dry grass, looking distinctively out of place.

Silva spotted her and waved her over. He was a bear of a man – tall, round-shouldered, with a thick midriff. Curls of grey had infiltrated his dark hair.

His eyes crinkled warmly behind horn-rimmed glasses as he greeted her.

She noticed that his shirt, once powdery blue, had darkened with sweat.

She was suddenly conscious that her own shirt was sticking to her back. The heat had risen and came off the baking earth in waves. A bead of sweat trickled down from under her cap and along the side of her nose. She wiped it away.

'What's going on?' she said, nodding at the spectacle behind him.

'We're re-enacting the Kalinga War.'

She dredged her memory.

Indian military history was hardly her forte, but she knew that the Kalinga War had been fought between the Mauryan emperor, Ashoka the Great, and the eastern Indian kingdom of Kalinga. The conflict had been particularly bloody, so much so that Ashoka, surveying the carnage of the final battle, had promptly converted to Buddhism. He'd spent the remainder of his life practising ahimsa, the Hindu concept of non-violence, and extolling his own virtue via a succession of edicts inscribed on stone pillars, many still dotted around the subcontinent.

'I need your help,' she said.

He followed her to a covered section of the bleachers, where he eased himself on to the worn stone, took out a handkerchief, and wiped his face.

Persis sat down beside him, glad to be off her feet for a few minutes. Warmth penetrated her backside and worked its way up her spine.

Quickly, she explained the cases she was working on, then reached into her shoulder bag and took out the wooden dolls found at the Renzi and Grunewald scenes. 'I've been told these dolls might have a military connection.'

He turned the dolls over in his spade-like hands, then said, 'These are soldiers from a Gurkha regiment. The same soldier, judging by the facial features. A young hawaldar or sepoy. You can tell because there are no chevrons on the arms.' He pointed with a thick finger at the sleeve of one of the dolls. 'The Gurkhas wore distinctive slouch hats – they're called terais. And the knife: that's a traditional Gurkha machete – a kukri.'

'Are you saying these dolls might depict an *actual* soldier?'

'Possibly.'

'Is there any way to identify him?'

'If I'm correct about the regiment, it should narrow your search. But bear in mind that more than a million Indian soldiers fought for the British. The Gurkhas – mainly from Nepal – were particularly courageous in battle. Their regimental motto is "Better to die than be a coward". They won a hatful of VCs – Victoria Crosses. Used to terrify the hell out of the enemy with their battle cry: "Ayo Gurkhali!" The Gurkhas are upon you!' He paused. 'You also need to remember that such awards were often made posthumously. The man you're looking for might well have died in action. This might be someone's way of remembering a fallen soldier.'

She considered the possibility.

Could the killer be linked to an Indian soldier who had died in World War Two, a soldier who'd fought for the British Army? Might that be the source of the grudge against Stephen Renzi and Peter Grunewald, an Italian and a German?

The enemy.

Another idea pecked at her thoughts. According to the American, Trent Marlowe, Stephen Renzi had fought in the war. If Renzi had been a soldier, wasn't it likely that Grunewald, too, had served?

She explained the situation to Silva, adding that it was possible Renzi had changed his name.

'That'll make it difficult to trace him, I'm afraid. Trying to access Italian and German military records is no trivial matter. After the Nuremberg trials, no one wants to put their head on the chopping block.'

'Is there any way you could—?'

He put up a hand to stop her. 'I'll try my best,' he said. 'But no guarantees. If you have any photographs of the pair, send them to me.'

She reached into her pocket and presented him with an envelope.

He chuckled. 'Always prepared. Very good.'

'There's one other thing.'

Taking out the sheets torn from the Ice Man's notebook, she handed them to him.

His brow corrugated into a frown. 'I'm afraid these mean nothing to me.' He passed them back. 'Some sort of code or cipher, I presume. Soldiers used them extensively during the war to disguise the contents of military communiques in case they fell into the hands of the enemy.'

'Do you think the Ice Man might be a soldier?'

He looked thoughtful. 'Was he found in uniform?'

'No.'

'Is there anything to indicate that he might be a military man?'

'Only the connection to Renzi and Grunewald. I'm convinced they were both former soldiers. And now there's the fact that whoever killed them has a link to the Indian army, if we go by your analysis of the dolls.'

He considered the matter. 'The Ice Man was found in the Tsangchokla Pass, correct? That's in the vicinity of Dehra Dun. The Indian Military Academy is based there. A significant number of British personnel passed through the academy during the war years. You said the Ice Man has been up there for anything up to seven years? It's the right time frame . . .' He grimaced. 'I'm afraid the armed forces training programme isn't my area of expertise. What I do know is that the academy was in the papers recently, around the new year. I remember reading a piece about it in the *Indian Chronicle*. I'm not sure it will be of much help, but . . .' He paused. 'Let me make a few calls. Perhaps I can dig up an academy contact for you.'

She nodded her appreciation, then climbed to her feet, wiping the sweat from her palms on to her trousers.

'How's Sam, by the way? I haven't heard from him in a while.'

She hoped he might confuse the flush that had rushed to her cheeks with the effects of the heat.

'He's busy.'

'Busy? He sits behind a counter all day shouting at people. How busy can he be?'

31

The offices of the *Indian Chronicle* had moved three times in the past two decades, in short peristaltic hops along the bustling D.N. Road, until the paper's home was now barely a stone's throw from its arch-rival, the *Times of India*.

The two newspapers had been at loggerheads for half a century.

The *Times*, India's 'paper of record', had established a reputation for serious journalism, setting the bar for those who aspired to the same.

The *Chronicle* harboured no such ambitions.

From its inception, it had set its stall out for the masses. Its headlines were lurid, its reportage to be taken with a pinch of salt. It had found its niche early on and occupied it with the smug shrillness of a second wife.

With the coming of independence, the *Chronicle* had been sold by its British owners to an Indian industrialist with aspirations in the media arena. If the paper had been brash before, now it abandoned any pretence of sobriety, swiftly establishing itself as the city's preeminent bastion of muckraking journalism.

Persis nursed a particular hatred for the rag.

The *Chronicle* had made no bones about where it stood on the notion of women in the police service, making a special effort to undermine her own achievements.

She parked in a lane behind the offices, then walked back out front, and into a wave of foot traffic emerging from the Victoria Terminus station across the road. Jostled along by the Brownian motion of the crowd, she had to fight her way out to the covered arcade fronting the *Chronicle*'s building.

Ten minutes later, she had found her way to a senior editor, explained her mission, then followed him down into the bowels of the building where she was deposited into the care of a man in a long tunic and loose trousers with a head of flaming orange hair and a beard to match. His name was Adnan Shaikh and she recognised him as one of the Haj-returned pilgrims who displayed their piety by dying their hair in a manner that made them look like Scotsmen left out in the sun too long.

'How can I help?' asked Shaikh, sipping serenely from a steel teacup.

'I'm looking for editions around the turn of the year.'

He set down his cup. 'Follow me.'

As he led her into a badly lit labyrinth of steel shelves, weighed down with bound bundles of newspapers, she had to resist the urge to unfurl a string behind her. There were few markings on the shelves, yet Shaikh seemed to know exactly where he was going. 'It's lucky you're not looking for something a little earlier,' he said chattily. 'The rats have had a field day with the Twenties and Thirties.'

He finally stopped.

Looking around, he grabbed a wooden stool, clambered unsteadily atop it, and lifted down a bundle of newspapers from the topmost shelf. He threw the bundle on to the floor, raising a cloud of dust that tickled her nose.

She stepped back.

Shaikh brought down a second bundle, which he deposited next to the first.

'December 1949 and January 1950. Sixty-two editions.'

She took out her switchblade and cut off the strings binding the bundles. Then, crouched on her haunches, she began to go through each of the newspapers.

'Would you like a chair?'

She ignored him, quickly becoming engrossed in her task.

After a while, he left her to it, returning to his post at the front of the storeroom. She barely noticed.

Time ticked away.

Articles breezed past her eyes: India moving steadily towards Republic Day on January 26th, the day the country officially adopted its newly written constitution and became the world's most populous democratic republic. Political rhetoric filled the pages, interwoven with flashbacks to key moments in the struggle – the Jallianwalla Bagh atrocity in 1919, the sectarian violence of the Calcutta killings, Gandhi's assassination – and the sort of ribald stories that had made the *Chronicle*'s name.

The affairs of starlets, sordid accounts of corruption in municipal office, the occasional murder.

Low deeds in high places.

She found what she was looking for in the issue dated 2nd January, buried halfway inside the paper.

The headline read: *Indian Military Academy Adopts New Name.*

The article began by stating that, as of the first of January, the Indian Military Academy would be known as the National Defence Academy.

The piece went on to present a potted history of the place.

Instituted in 1932, with the express purpose of training Indian commissioned officers, the academy had been set up on the premises of the Indian Railway Staff College in Dehra Dun, a two-hundred-acre estate with room for a rifle range and obstacle course. Initially tasked to graduate forty officers a year, the campus had expanded considerably during the war years, with British officers joining their Indian counterparts.

This last fact gave her pause.

According to the article, some seven hundred British officers – both trainees and senior men – had passed through the academy between 1941 and 1946 ... *Could the Ice Man have been one of these men?* A British soldier who'd ventured into the mountains and become disoriented? Death by misadventure?

But if that were the case, surely the army would have come forward by now?

Then again, the British army was hardly known for admitting its mistakes. Until 1947, all the commandants of the academy had been British. Would they really publicise the fact that one of their officers had vanished?

She set down the paper, allowing the new information to settle in her mind.

If the Ice Man was indeed a British soldier, it might make it easier to trace him. The facility at Dehra Dun must hold records. No matter how deeply buried, there had to be reports of personnel who had died or gone missing.

It might also explain why they had been unable to find a missing persons report for the Ice Man. She doubted a wife would have been permitted to lodge such a report in the public domain with the army browbeating her into discretion.

But how *exactly* was the Ice Man linked to Stephen Renzi or Peter Grunewald, an Italian soldier and, possibly, a German one? And how were all three linked to a killer who had hinted at an association with a Gurkha regiment?

She continued picking her way through the newspapers until the end of January, on the off-chance that there was anything else of relevance ... Her eyes snagged on an article about the murder of Sir James Herriot, the case that had first thrust her into the national spotlight. The reporter, Aalam Channa, had been less than complimentary of her handling of the investigation. With a few vicious strokes of his pen,

Channa had reduced her to a caricature. A politically motivated mistake.

A fresh wave of anger pulsed through her.

'What an honour to have a celebrity grace us with her presence.'

Her head snapped around.

Her eyes widened as she recognised the figure standing by the nearest shelf.

Aalam Channa was a man fully aware of the dashing figure he cut. Tall and slim, he wore his trademark white Nehru suit lightly; it went well with the sardonic smile that had so often graced the pages of the very paper for which he reported.

A self-made celebrity who preyed on celebrities.

In the eyes of some, this made him the worst kind of cannibal.

His gaze fell to the heap of newspapers at her feet. 'I sense a story. Would you care to tell me what you're after? Perhaps I can help?'

She let loose a wild bray of laughter that cantered around the space before vanishing behind the shelves. '*You* would help *me*?'

He waved breezily at the newspaper in her hand. 'You mustn't take anything I write to heart, Inspector. I have an audience with certain . . . expectations.'

She lifted the paper, read from it. 'So you don't really believe that "in temperament, intelligence and moral fibre, the female of the species is, and always will be, inferior to the male".'

His smile stretched. He took another step forward, uncomfortably close now. 'There's no need for us to be enemies. Not when we could be friends.'

His breath smelled of aniseed; an aftershave strong enough to strip wallpaper wafted from him. 'I could make you a star,' he breathed. 'You're an attractive woman. My readership would embrace you with open arms . . . As would I.'

Another step and now he was practically breathing down on her, his dark hair glistening dully in the low light. Eyes as black as liquorice.

He stretched a hand towards her face … She dropped the newspaper, grabbed his fingers, and twisted, bending his wrist around until he was forced on to his knees with a grunt.

'Why don't you embrace yourself?'

She held him a moment longer, then let go and walked away, leaving him to clutch at his wrist, whimpering quietly in the semi-dark.

32

A note was waiting for her at Malabar House. The girl Seema had called.

She looked around. Only Haq was in the office, shuffling his walrus bulk around in his seat. 'When did the call come in?'

He spoke without turning around. 'About ten minutes ago.'

She snatched up the telephone and dialled the number scrawled on the note.

A high-pitched male voice: 'Hotel Ambassador Tea Room. How may I help?'

Momentarily nonplussed, she recovered quickly, and said, 'I'm looking for a Seema Desai.'

The voice dropped several degrees in welcome. 'Yes. She is here.'

A pause, and then Seema came on the line.

'What are you doing calling me from the Ambassador?'

'You asked me to follow Meherzad Umrigar. She's here. With a young man. I thought you would want to know.'

Her breath caught. A whistling sounded in her ears.

'I'll be there in ten minutes.'

The Ambassador was a relatively recent addition to the south Bombay skyline, built less than a decade earlier at the start of the Second World War. Its star had been eclipsed from the outset by its older rival, the Taj Palace Hotel, sitting pretty two kilometres away on the opposite flank of the city. While the Taj stared resolutely out into the Arabian Sea inlet, the Ambassador's upper floors overlooked Marine Drive and the Back Bay.

It took Persis longer to get there than she'd anticipated, honking her way through late afternoon traffic.

She parked out front, thrusting her keys at a bemused valet, and charged into the lobby, heading for the tea room on the ground floor.

As she barrelled in, she found her way barred by a maître d' in a penguin suit, a short man with a brisk moustache and a glistening pompadour that added much needed inches to his height. 'May I help you?'

'I'm looking for Seema Desai.'

He led her to a waiting area beside the reception counter, where Seema sprang up from a chair and greeted her nervously.

'Where are they?'

'Inside, madam.'

Minutes later, they were sat at a table to one side of the tea room, partly hidden behind a Grecian column.

'There,' said Seema pointing across the space towards an expansive painting of a Dionysian revel. Beneath the painting sat Meherzad Umrigar and a man who looked to Persis to be in his late twenties, good-looking in an angular way, with a prominent chin, a long nose, and a head of Brylcreemed hair. His smile seemed a permanent fixture beneath a rakish moustache.

The pair were bent low in conversation.

'May I take your order, madam?'

She jerked around. The waiter smiled pleasantly.

She glanced at Seema. 'What would you like?'

'I'm not hungry,' said the girl, quickly.

'Did you eat something during the day?'

The girl looked away. 'Yes.'

Persis could sense the lie. She was suddenly acutely aware that Seema was wearing smarter clothes than on the previous occasions they'd met, an embroidered tunic and a long skirt. An outfit reserved for special occasions, she guessed, carefully preserved over many years.

And yet, in the rarefied environment of the Ambassador, she remained demonstrably out of place. It occurred to her that it must have taken a particular resoluteness of will for her to set foot in a place like this. The girl was tenacious, if nothing else.

'We have to order something,' she said gently. 'Otherwise we'll draw attention. The force will pay.'

She regretted the words instantly as she saw the shadow that passed behind the girl's eyes. Seema, like many of her peers, suffered from the affliction of pride.

'There will be no charge, madam,' offered the waiter.

She knew the instruction would have come from the maître d'. It was an unwritten law of the city that a police officer *never* paid. A perk of the job, as most saw it. A man like Oberoi wouldn't have given it a second thought.

But she wasn't Oberoi, and Sam hadn't raised her that way.

'Bring me the bill,' she said.

He seemed confused, then nodded and scribbled down their order.

Twenty minutes later Meherzad and her companion settled their own bill and left, moving across the hotel's lobby at a leisurely pace to the grand staircase, Persis and her young ward following at a discreet distance.

Two flights up, the pair left the staircase and floated along a succession of carpeted corridors before stopping outside room 201.

Smiling seductively at each other, they unlocked the door, and entered.

Persis pulled back around a corner. She checked her watch.

She'd give them ten minutes, then catch them in flagrante delicto. She regretted the fact that Meherzad's betrayal would be hard on Sam, but it was better that he know now the sort of woman he'd pinned his hopes on.

Seema, standing beside her, looked on anxiously.

When Persis finally marched to the door, pounding on it with a fist, it swung back to reveal the young man, clad only in a towel. His lean greyhound frame was damp, as if he'd just stepped out of the shower.

'Yes?'

'Where is she?'

'Where is who?'

'You know who.'

He seemed nonplussed. His mouth opened . . .

'Persis?'

She spun around to find Meherzad walking along the corridor towards them.

'What are you doing here?' She seemed astonished. Her gaze drifted to Seema, standing behind the policewoman. 'That girl . . . I saw her earlier today . . .' Understanding dawned. 'Have you two been *following* me?'

Persis recovered swiftly. 'Yes. And now I know.'

'Know?' She seemed momentarily taken aback. 'What is it that you think you know?'

Persis waved at the half-naked man standing in the doorway. Exhibit A. There was no need to explain.

Meherzad looked between them. And then, astonishingly, she broke into a smile. 'Persis,' she said, gently. 'You've made a mistake.'

*　　*　　*

Back at Malabar House, Persis took a moment to settle herself.

The encounter with Meherzad had left her confused and angry – confused at the outcome, and angry with herself for falling prey to a rash impulse. The woman's reasonableness had only made matters worse.

Was it something within herself? With Indian society stacked against them, with men like Aalam Channa and Hemant Oberoi doing their worst to undermine them, didn't it make sense for women to hold on to some sense of kinship?

Then again, what if she wasn't made that way?

Finally, muddled by her own thoughts, she put the incident to the back of her mind and went to see Seth.

Quickly, she explained everything she'd learned about the Ice Man. 'I'll have to go to Dehra Dun.'

A protest shaped itself around his mouth, but then he seemed to change his mind. 'What makes you think the academy will cooperate? The army isn't known for their helpful attitude.'

'I thought solving the Ice Man case was a matter of national importance?'

He conceded the point. 'Fine. If you get stuck, give me a call. I'll see if Shukla can rattle a few cages in Delhi.' He stopped. 'I don't suppose you've mentioned any of this to Oberoi? About the link between the Renzi case and the Ice Man's?'

'No.'

'Don't. For now.'

33

The bookshop was open, though her father was not at his customary place behind the counter. A note by the telephone, scrawled in Sam's messy hand, read: *If you buy a book, leave the money in the jar.*

A single customer was in the shop, an elderly white woman in a floral summer dress and, perversely, gloves. The woman smiled at her, then went back to perusing the romance shelves.

Persis stood a moment, an odd sensation probing at the edges of her awareness. Her nose twitched. A curious smell in the air . . .

Paint. *Fresh* paint.

She swung her astonished gaze around the shop. Her senses had not deceived her. The shop's familiar beige walls had been transformed by a medley of bright colours: white, peach, and umber. The overall effect was of a mosaic, or the contents of a volatile stomach.

Amazement continued to hold her in place.

When it came to the store, her father had always lived by a set of unshakeable beliefs. First among these was that no one came into a bookshop for the décor, and second, that nothing truly bad could happen to a place of books. She'd spent many fruitless hours leading him through a history of bibliographical holocausts, from the burning of the Great Library of Alexandria to the recent Nazi-led book pogroms of the Third Reich.

She realised what it was that was truly bothering her.

The shop had been a constant in her life, changeless, ever-present, a fixed point among the upheavals that had marked the past two decades. Following her mother's death, it had remained in its own cocoon, a refuge from the ravages of memory, for both her and Sam. The shop had belonged to her grandfather, but it was Sanaz's enthusiasm that had persuaded Sam to make a go of it when old Dastoor Wadia had passed on; it was *her* love of the written word that had infected him.

He'd preserved the shop after she'd gone in the way some adults preserved a child's bedroom following a premature death.

The thought jerked her back to the present, and the reason she'd come into the shop.

She was now answerable to four sets of grieving parents, either living or deceased. The parents of Stephen Renzi, Peter Grunewald, the Ice Man . . . and Leela Sinha.

She recalled the way Priya Sinha had spoken of her daughter, the pain behind her eyes.

The dead demanded resolution. It didn't do to make them wait.

She moved behind the counter and into the interior of the store, making her way to a shelf at the back. Walking her fingers along the spines, she plucked out several books on codes and ciphers, then continued to the broken-down sofa at the very rear.

Setting the books on to the seat beside her, she began to go through them, one by one, her eyes alighting on familiar passages. She'd used the books during the recent investigation into the missing Dante manuscript. There was no way to be certain, but she believed that the enigmatic entry in the Ice Man's notebook – *Caesar's Triumph holds the key* – was a literal key to deciphering the pages that had been torn from it. She suspected that the Ice Man had left the entry there precisely for such an eventuality as this – namely, that in the event of his death, there would be a way to decipher the message coded on to those pages.

But what *was* the message? And how had two of the three pages ended up with Stephen Renzi and Peter Grunewald?

Presumably, this meant that a third page was out there somewhere, in the hands of another party. Who?

Why had Renzi and Grunewald considered the message important enough to safeguard for so long?

Most importantly: did the message have something to do with
their killing?

Augustus Silva, the military historian, had conjectured that the
message might be a military communique. The only way to find
out was to unravel the code.

Time ticked away.

She was beginning to despair, when she came across the answer
– or at least, what she felt *might* be the answer, in a volume entitled
A History of Codes and Ciphers.

In the second chapter, the author had outlined a cipher called
Caesar's shift – also known as Caesar's cipher. The cipher was one
of the oldest and most widely known, one of a class of encryption
techniques called substitution ciphers whereby each letter in a
message was coded by substituting it with another letter a speci-
fied number of places further along the alphabet. According to
Suetonius, Caesar had used a version of this technique, coding
his personal messages by shifting each letter three places to the
left.

Thus, using the cipher, D became A, and E became B. And so
on.

A simple word such as APPLE would thus become XMMIB.

According to the text, the cipher had enjoyed recent incarnations, lovers using it to send each other coy messages in English
newspapers, and the Russian army employing it during the First
World War in place of complex encryption methods that invariably left their troop commanders bemused.

She took out her notebook, and opened it.

Tucked into it were the Renzi and Grunewald sheets.

Unfolding the Renzi note, she began using the cipher to transpose the blocks of letters. If the characters NIWMQ YA SICSMO had been encrypted using the Caesar cipher, then all she needed to do to decrypt the message was shift each letter three places to the right on the alphabet.

After just a few moments, she knew she was on the wrong track.

Using the decryption, the characters NIWMQ YA SICSMO became QLZPT BD VLFVPR.

She went over it again, thinking that perhaps she'd made a mistake.

But there was no error. The Caesar cipher produced only gibberish.

With a sinking feeling, she applied the cipher to the Grunewald note, only to be met with further frustration.

The door to the shop jangled open, snapping her out of her contemplation.

Moments later: the sound of her father's wheelchair, with its squeaky right wheel, turning into the aisle. The aisle was narrow and he didn't quite make the turn, catching his left wheel on the edge of a bookshelf. He reversed, then tried again, clattering into the shelf. She heard him curse, then repeat the manoeuvre several more times before finally bursting into the aisle.

She could sense his anger; it billowed ahead of him like a wave of heat.

Climbing awkwardly to her feet, she steeled herself as he bore down on her, red-faced.

'Why did you do it?'

'I did what I thought was right.'

'You had her followed!' he hissed. 'Like a *criminal*.'

'She's going to be my stepmother. I have a right to know. *You* have a right to know.'

That stopped him in his tracks. She had known that it would. A momentary guilt twanged through her. She'd deliberately raised the ghost of Sanaz; her mother now hovered between them.

He seemed to deflate in his chair. 'That's unfair.' He looked away, aged in that instant by a dozen years. A beat of silence, in which she heard the woman shuffling around at the front of the shop.

'I've waited a long time, Persis. I promised myself I wouldn't bring another woman into our lives until you were ready. I put your needs before my own.'

She felt wretched. Everything he'd said was true. And yet ... was she really ready to give up Sanaz?

'I wasn't trying to upset you.'

'Did she tell you what she was doing at the Ambassador?'

'Yes.'

'He lives in Delhi,' said Sam. 'He's in town for a couple of days, staying at the Ambassador. Meher wanted me to meet him. Wanted us both to meet him. When we marry, he'll become your stepbrother.'

Not for the first time in the past hours, the thought brought her to a standstill. She took a deep breath. 'I – I don't think I'm ready for that.'

His face became dark. 'You're behaving like a child.'

She felt panic rising inside her. 'You don't understand.'

'Then explain it to me.'

'I have nothing against Meher. Or her son. But this is *our* home. Yours and mine. I – I'm not sure I'm ready to share it with another woman.'

His face swelled. She wanted to say so much more, but couldn't find the words. She wanted to tell him that it was more than just the dread of sharing a home with a stranger. It was about *him*.

The idea that he would no longer need her was terrifying.

She straightened her shoulders. 'Perhaps – perhaps it's time for me to leave? Stay somewhere else, I mean.'

She'd expected him to console her, but instead he turned away. 'It's my fault. I've coddled you. I've made you believe the world will bend to your every whim, no matter how unreasonable.' He sighed angrily. 'Perhaps you're right. Perhaps you *should* leave. At least until you can learn to behave like a decent human being.'

The words rooted her to the spot. She hadn't expected him to accept her offer, or to judge her so harshly.

For a moment, she stood there, her tall frame vibrating with shock.

And then she turned on her heel and headed for the door at the rear of the shop.

Back in her bedroom, she yanked out her suitcase from the wardrobe, threw it on to the bed – where it narrowly missed Akbar – and began hurling clothes into it, her earlier regret turning to anger.

Ten minutes later, she was done.

She closed the lid savagely, almost decapitating the curious cat, swung the case off the bed, and stormed into the living room.

Her father sat at the piano, plinking out a scale with the index finger of his right hand.

'I'm leaving.'

'I can see that.'

'I'm leaving *now*.'

'Don't let the door hit you on the way out.'

She resisted the urge to heave the suitcase at him.

Pirouetting on her heel, she slammed her way out of the apartment, banged her way down the stairs, and threw the case into the back of the jeep, then stood for a moment with her hands resting on the roof, the day's heat radiating into her palms.

A mewling sound drew her gaze downwards.

Akbar sat on his haunches by the rear tyre, staring up at her with his ghostly green eyes.

'Good boy,' she said, softly. 'I knew you wouldn't let me leave.'

The cat hissed at her, then turned and fled back the way he'd come.

She leaned against the jeep, her legs suddenly rubbery.

Looking up at the window above the shopfront, she wondered if her father was peering down at her from between the curtains.

A bicycle whizzed by, crunching over broken glass.

She closed her eyes, counted to ten, then got into the jeep and drove away.

34

'Persis! What are you doing here?'

Blackfinch stood in the doorway, staring at her in astonishment. His tall frame was cloaked in a pair of beetroot-coloured pyjamas, marked by stripes as if he'd recently escaped from prison. He held a tumbler in one hand.

'I need a place to stay.'

His lips framed themselves around a protest and then he thought better of it. 'Come in.'

She entered the apartment, dragging her suitcase behind her.

It was as she remembered. Maniacally neat – that odd kink in the Englishman's make-up meant that it would always be so – with a bookshelf that spoke to a disturbing penchant for alphabetical taxonomy.

'Have a seat,' he said, waving at the dining table. 'Have you eaten? I was making pasta.'

She lowered herself into a chair, registering the smell of basil from the tiny kitchen area. It mingled with the less savoury odour of fish from the nearby Sassoon docks floating in through the open window.

She stood up, walked to the window, and closed it.

'Probably a good idea,' said Blackfinch. 'Help yourself to a drink. There's gin, whisky, a bottle of red.'

She poured herself a White Horse, then sat back down, overcome by a feeling of infinite weariness.

Blackfinch surprised her by waiting her out.

In the short while she'd known him, he'd distinguished himself by his lack of tact. His sudden restraint was disconcerting.

'I've had a ... disagreement with my father.' This was all the explanation she could muster for the time being, and all the explanation he seemed to need. He didn't ask her why she hadn't gone to a friend or checked into a hotel.

The truth was she didn't know why.

Jaya would have taken her in, if only for the salacious gossip. Aunt Nussie would have fussed over her, offering a ready ear for her grievances.

But something inside her had *needed* Blackfinch. There was no point denying it. A primal instinct that had worn her down until all she wanted to do was open the door and let in the storm.

She showered while he finished dinner, closing her eyes and leaning into the feeling of being suspended, weightless.

They ate at the table, the radio tuned to the BBC Overseas Service.

A boy in the American state of New York had become the first subject for the prototype polio vaccine. Communist Chinese troops had marched into Kunming, overpowering the last forces of the Nationalist Chinese Party, the Kuomintang. Closer to home, Nehru continued to struggle with factions in his own party as he attempted to push through a bill dismantling the Byzantine feudal system that had held the country's lower classes in its grip since time immemorial.

Gradually, the story leaked from her.

He listened in silence, then shrugged and said, 'These things have a way of working themselves out. I remember when Susan and I divorced. I thought I'd never get past it. But, a few weeks later, there was a spring in my step and a song in my heart.' He grinned toothily. 'I'll wager you and your stepmother will soon be getting on like a house on fire.'

'Don't call her that.'

He waved a fork at her. 'Whether you like it or not, if Sam marries her, then that is precisely what she will be.'

'You think I'm being foolish, don't you?'

'Not at all. It's perfectly natural to feel trepidation at the idea of change.'

His words made sense, but did little to ease her bruised and battered heart. The last time she'd spent any length of time away from her father was when she'd boarded at the police academy. Even then, he'd telephoned her every night to make sure that Nussie's premonitions (of her being murdered in her bed and her honour being assaulted – in that order) hadn't come to pass.

She had to fight the urge not to pick up the telephone and call him. He would be worried. She didn't want him to go to bed fretting.

After dinner, Blackfinch seemed at a loose end. They sat on the sofa, drinking. She filled in the awkward silences by talking about the case, laying out for him the connections she had established between Renzi, Grunewald, and the Ice Man.

Her conjecture that the Ice Man might be a British soldier from the academy at Dehra Dun was met with a raised eyebrow.

'That seems quite a leap.'

'It's as likely as any other scenario,' she retorted. Blackfinch's tendency to make declarative statements gave him the air of a know-it-all caterpillar, a habit she found infuriating.

'You really think the army will talk to you?'

'I won't know until I get there.'

'When are you going?'

'Tomorrow morning. I've asked Birla to make the arrangements.'

He stared into his glass. 'It might help to have someone else along.'

It took her a moment to grasp his meaning.

Blood darkened her cheeks. The thought of the Englishman accompanying her was more welcome than she cared to admit.

When she didn't reply, he coughed, rose to his feet and went to a tabletop wind-up gramophone player. She was sure it hadn't been there the last time she'd visited. 'I find music helps me to sleep. Otherwise, heat and insomnia keep me up half the night. Not to mention the damned mosquitoes.'

He rummaged in a box beside the set-up, took out a record, removed it from its sleeve, blew on it, and set it on to the turntable.

It was a tune she recognised. 'Some Enchanted Evening'.

Blackfinch stood awkwardly by the gramophone, tapping his foot.

'I don't suppose you'd care to dance?'

The notion took her by surprise. She'd seen him dance once before, a sight for which she'd been unprepared. He was a man completely without rhythm. A three-legged bull trotting through a cratered field was as graceful as Nijinsky by comparison.

She understood that he was asking for more than just the dance. He'd made no secret of his attraction. It was she who'd backed away, afraid that a dalliance with an Englishman would jeopardise both her reputation and her career.

Afraid that she'd lose control of herself.

There had only been one other, before him. A man she'd fallen gracelessly in love with and who had betrayed her. A con artist who'd professed devotion, and then left with the bed sheets still warm to marry another.

He'd returned to Bombay after the collapse of his marriage, begging for a second chance. But she was no longer the ingénue he'd left behind. The academy had forged her into something formidable. A woman who'd retreated inside herself, raising the drawbridge behind her.

She'd vowed never again to let a man command her feelings.

Succumbing to a man like Blackfinch wasn't part of the plan. After all, where could it lead? She couldn't ever openly be with an Englishman. And even if she followed through and they ended up together, they couldn't marry. The Indian Police Service didn't allow married women to serve. Would she really be prepared to give up her career for a man, *any* man?

And yet . . . was it wrong to want it all? Love, desire, ambition? Didn't she have needs, like anyone else? Like her father?

She gulped her whisky and set it down.

To hell with it.

He seemed startled when she advanced on him. He hadn't expected her to say yes, she realised.

There was a moment of awkwardness while he set down his own glass and they worked out whose hand went where. She leaned into him, her hair still damp from the shower, inhaled the woody scent of his cologne.

He attempted to pull her into the dance, executing a judo-like manoeuvre that almost spilled them both to the floor. He seemed to have grown a second left foot in the past moments.

'Why don't you let me lead?' she suggested.

He nodded dumbly.

They danced, the music crackling around the small room, each wrapped in thought, stars crowding in at the window to watch them. She held herself to him, and he to her, two unlikely duellists.

Her heart rattled loosely inside her chest.

Finally, when she felt either they must stop or the floor would give way and they would be swallowed whole by the monster of their own desire, he looked down, and their eyes met.

In his gaze, she saw warmth, compassion, uncertainty.

'Yes,' she breathed.

He leaned down, and the music went away.

35

The roar of the engines drowned out the sound of her thumping heart.

Beside her, the priest shifted in his bucket seat, and gave her a sympathetic look. 'Is this your first time on an aeroplane?'

His accent was strange, lilting, not unpleasant. She remembered, with what little of her mind remained, that he had introduced himself as an Irishman.

She nodded, dumbly, her hands clamped like vices around the edges of her own seat.

It had all seemed straightforward when she'd asked Birla to organise transport for her up to Dehra Dun. The journey by train would have usually taken just over a day, but the line had been compromised between Delhi and Haridwar and the train company could offer no certainty as to when that leg of the route might be back up and running.

Birla had decided to use his initiative, a dubious proposition at the best of times.

He'd discovered that it was possible to fly north to Dehra Dun in around three hours.

What he hadn't mentioned was that there were no civil aviation routes up to the city, nor a permanent airport.

Instead, he'd booked her on to a mail flight aboard a tin bucket held together with steel rivets and embellished with wings and propellers. The plane, a decades-old Ford Trimotor, had been converted to postal duties by the simple expedient of ripping out most of the seats and replacing them with a steel cage. Inside the cage were boxes of mail, and, tied to a hook in the ceiling, a goat squatting on its hooves and examining her with the belligerent look of a martyr.

The priest had guessed correctly, of course.

Part of the mortal terror threatening to consume her stemmed from the fact that she'd never flown. There had never been any need. Bombay had been her whole life, and Sam was hardly the kind to drag himself on to a flying deathtrap for the dubious privilege of travelling to faraway destinations to consort with foreigners, a description he applied to anyone not born and bred within a hundred yards of his own birthplace.

She glanced out of the rectangular porthole window.

The aerodrome, India's first, had been around since the 1920s, home to the Bombay Flying Club. It was here that industrialist J.R.D. Tata had trained for the country's first pilot's licence. She knew the place had been the scene of frequent aviation disasters, particularly during the war when it had served as the city's premier airport. For years, the airstrip had had to be closed during the monsoon months because of waterlogging.

'These old buckets are very reliable,' the priest assured her. 'There's nothing to worry about.' He slipped a hand inside his cassock and emerged with a hip flask. 'Perhaps a drop of this might help?'

She grabbed it from him and tilted the flask into her mouth, greedily accepting the whisky. It burned her throat on the way down and she spluttered, spraying the seat in front.

But she felt better.

She knew that it wasn't just the flight. Heat rose to her cheeks as she recalled the previous night, with Archie Blackfinch. Her heart began to race . . . and then ran into a brick wall as she recalled the events of the morning.

Her mind shied away from the memory like a horse faced with a ditch.

Even now, hours later, it remained a blur. Everything that had happened – her reaction, the suddenness of it all.

She'd awoken to find Blackfinch fast asleep beside her, twitching in dreams.

Raising herself on to an elbow, she looked down at him, marvelling at his presence beside her with something akin to wonder.

Without his glasses, at rest, he seemed infinitely peaceful, no older than an adolescent. And yet . . . she had flushed, recalling the previous evening, how easily they'd fallen into each other, the simplicity of their movements, a dance that had waited too long and now took its own course without either of them having to direct their actions.

In that moment, gazing down at him, she'd felt a rush of naked terror, the understanding that she'd stepped across a line that might have been better left uncrossed.

She slipped out of bed, dressed while he mumbled in his sleep, then grabbed her suitcase and made her way to the front door. Seizing the handle, she opened it as quietly as she could . . . to find a pretty young blonde standing there with her fist raised, poised to knock.

They'd stared at each other in mutual incomprehension. The blonde lowered her fist. 'Well,' she finally breathed. 'Isn't *this* a turn-up?'

A beat.

'Who are you?' Persis managed to stammer out.

'Who are *you*?'

But there was no need for answers.

36

They landed on a makeshift bitumen airstrip twenty miles south of Dehra Dun at around two in the afternoon. The plane bumped and jarred along the poorly maintained track like a pebble skimmed across water, finally skidding to a halt just yards from a whitewashed cinderblock building that served as the airport's administrative hub.

Within twenty minutes of decamping from the plane, her fellow travellers had vanished. There had been three others, aside from the priest. A native couple who had chatted between them-selves for three straight hours and a big white man in a black hat who'd stepped on at the last second and then hadn't exchanged a word with anyone and slept the whole way through with his hat pulled over his face.

A man in a rattling flatbed truck had been waiting to pick up the goat – clearly the most important passenger on the flight. Other cars arrived for her fellow passengers, including a white Austin for the Irish priest driven by an earnest young Indian in a cassock whose look of wide-eyed stupefaction reminded her of the novices at the St Pius X College.

She had expected to be met at the airport.

Silva had found a contact for her in Dehra Dun, an academic colleague who, he had informed her on the phone that morning when she had called him from the Juhu aerodrome, would be able to arrange a meeting for her with a senior official inside the National Defence Academy.

It didn't bode well that the woman in question was already an hour late.

A man in a grubby uniform in the airport office gave her a bored look. 'No, madam, there are no taxis, nor buses, nor bullock carts. The postal service has its own pickup. Most passengers make their own arrangements or organise a hire car in advance.'

She looked through the grimy window into the surrounding jungle. She couldn't walk the distance to Dehra Dun, not with a suitcase in tow.

There was nothing to do but wait.

She used the hiatus to go over the events of the morning, stepping on to the memory like a cat on a hot tin roof.

The blonde's name had been Jane Davenport.

Blackfinch, who had followed her to the airport, breathlessly catching up with her just before she boarded her flight, had insisted that Davenport was nothing more than a friend. But it was obvious that his definition of friendship did not match her own.

'There's no need to explain,' Persis had said. 'It's my fault. I should never have come to your home. Last night was a mistake.'

'You don't mean that.'

She'd turned away from him.

'I'm coming with you.'

She turned back. 'No, Archie. You are not.' Anger vibrated through her. It was all she could do to hold back the rage that threatened to engulf her. *How could she have been so foolish?* To have been betrayed once was bad enough . . . 'Whatever is between you and Jane is none of my business. But, right now, I would prefer to be alone.'

'But—'

She raised a hand. 'This isn't open to debate. I'm sorry.'

He'd subsided. Her last glimpse of him was as she slipped through the doors leading to the tarmac, looking wretchedly after her, his suit dishevelled, his hair uncombed.

She'd felt a great roaring in her chest then, as if a dragon had been let loose inside her.

A distant honking turned her head.

She stepped back out on to the airfield. The temperature was cooler this far north, but heat still hazed from the pitted tarmac.

A car was snaking its way along the incoming road. As she watched, it tore down into the airport, roared across the asphalt, and screeched to a halt before her, raising a cloud of dust.

A flame-headed white woman waved to her from the driver's seat. 'Persis, is it? I'm Gillian. Augustus's friend. Apologies for being late. Time simply ran away with itself.' She laughed maniacally like a villain in a film with the heroine strapped to rail tracks and a train on the way.

Persis threw her suitcase into the rear seats of the open-top Rolls-Royce.

Five minutes later, they were sailing back up the road.

Her name was Gillian Fordyce, a Scotswoman who'd been in India for over a decade. She was currently writing a history of the Doon Valley.

'Augie was pretty mysterious about your mission,' said Fordyce as she careened around another blind curve. The car seemed to maintain only a passing acquaintance with the road, Persis couldn't help but notice. She was beginning to wonder if she'd make it to Dehra Dun in one piece.

'I'd prefer to keep it that way.'

Fordyce flashed her a curious look. 'Suit yourself. He warned me you were a bit prickly.'

She coloured, but the woman had already lost interest, honking madly at a small van blocking her headlong assault on the road.

They climbed up into the hills, slopes of Himalayan maple, litchi, and cherry trees.

Persis knew little enough about the Doon Valley to appreciate her companion's running commentary.

The valley, caught between the outer Himalayas and the Mussoorie range, was unusually wide and verdant, Dehra Dun the only population centre of note, a bucolic town nestled in the valley's palm, surrounded by eight-thousand-foot peaks, and fed by the Ganges and Yamuna rivers. Paddy fields had been hacked out of the jungle and a series of canals built that drained into the city, leading to its nickname 'the Venice of North India'.

Dotted around the hills were Buddhist temples. 'We've got quite a mix up here,' explained Fordyce. 'The Sikhs ruled for a brief period before the Nepalese took over. The British went to war with the Gurkhas in the early 1800s. There was only one way that was going to end: it wasn't long before the East India Company was running the whole damned show. All things considered, the place has managed to weather its changing fortunes rather well. There's a sense of timelessness here that makes it hard for anyone to work up a real head of steam about anything. It's probably what attracts us academics.'

Dehra Dun, Persis discovered, was home to various intellectual enterprises, including several of the country's elite boarding schools, the Survey of India, and the Forest Research Institute. It was at this latter establishment that Fordyce had arranged for her to be accommodated – Fordyce herself had been lodged there for a year.

'I would prefer to stay in a hotel.'

The woman stared at her, then nodded. 'Suit yourself.'

The Clive Hotel was located just a stone's throw from the city centre, a bland grey-brick building with a crow-stepped gable, a

stone thistle above the door, and myrtle growing thickly in planters on the porch.

A sun-bleached Union Jack was visible in one corner of a
ground-floor window.

Fordyce climbed out of the car. 'The owner's a bit of a stick, but
he's honest and doesn't have grabby hands, if you catch my drift.'
She beamed, the bobby pins in her wild hair, combined with
jaunty long boots and jodhpurs, giving her a faintly disreputable
air. 'I'll give you an hour to freshen up, then we'll go have a tilt at
the windmill.'

Inside the hotel, Persis found a small lobby in the style of a
Georgian drawing room, with ornate cornicing, cracked plaster,
walnut panelling, and curtained windows letting in a dribble of
weary light. A black Steinway sat in one corner like a neglected
child.

On one wall a blunderbuss hung above a wooden porpoise, the
juxtaposition of the two objects jarring.

At the reception counter – a chipped slab of brecciated marble
– she was forced to bang the bell three times before an elderly
white man, with a face like a pewter bulldog and a few desultory
wisps of hair neatly arranged over the top of his scalp, shuffled
into view. He looked at her disapprovingly, sniffing as if a noxious
odour had invaded the room. 'Yes? What do you want?'

Clearly, the man had trained at the same charm school as her
father.

'This *is* a hotel, isn't it?' she said, stiffly.

He scowled. 'What did you think it was? A cowshed?'

She coloured. 'I'd like a room.'

He squinted at her. 'On your own, are you?'

'Yes.'

He grunted, slipped a pince-nez on to his nose, and opened a
ledger.

Five minutes later, she trundled her suitcase into a room on the first floor.

It was small, with sickly-looking grey-green walls, a single bed, an empire armchair in faded stripes of blue and gold, heron's beak handles on the battered wardrobe, and a scarred rosewood desk on which sat a brass-necked lamp.

From the wall a portrait of George VI looked down at her with gormless benevolence.

A window overlooked a narrow alley where a malnourished man in a police uniform was urinating against the wall.

He caught her gaze and held it until she turned away.

37

By the time Fordyce returned, she'd showered, dressed – in a clean white blouse and beige slacks – and taken the opportunity to wander out of the hotel to find something to eat. She'd enquired at the desk but the surly proprietor had informed her that it was 'too late for lunch, and too early for dinner'.

Walking across cobbled streets, she soon found herself in a bazaar that might have been lifted out of an India some fifty years past. The whole town, she suspected, was one of those places where independence had failed to register in any meaningful way. Locked away inside its valley, Dehra Dun had more than a little in common with that other – albeit fictional – mountain redoubt, Shangri-La.

In the bazaar, she discovered a primordial chaos, as frantic as a seaport: cries of chaiwallahs and fruit sellers mingled with the shrieks of langurs and the baying of stray dogs; young women spun silk parasols in their hands as they flirted with handsome soldiers from the academy; an overturned bullock cart had instigated an argument, the cart owner's arms flailing in all directions as if directing traffic as he fought with an elderly man brandishing a cane like a fencing foil.

She found a Tibetan hole-in-the-wall restaurant, an oasis in the midst of the mercantile bedlam, and ate a plate of momos with a glass of lemonade.

Taking out her notebook, she went over the questions she'd jotted down, hoping that the man she was going to see would be as eager to answer them as she was to ask.

When she got back to the hotel, she found Fordyce waiting in her Rolls, the fan belt squealing as it idled. 'Admit it, you thought I was going to be late again, didn't you?'

Without waiting for an answer, she hurled the car into a three-point turn that nearly ran over a matronly woman in a sari. 'Come on,' she said, ignoring the woman's curses, 'let's get going.'

If Persis had thought the Scotswoman's approach to driving might be tempered by the confines of the town, she was wrong.

The ride to the academy lasted fifteen white-knuckled minutes. She got out of the car on shaky legs.

Fordyce exited from the other side and patted the hood. 'Used to belong to a local maharaja. He gifted it to the Forest Research Institute and the vice chancellor was kind enough to lend it to me. Between us girls, I think he's a tad sweet on me.'

They approached the entrance to the main campus of the academy, framed by mountains in the immediate background. The scene seemed better suited to a tourist postcard than a military setting.

Fordyce spoke to the uniformed guards on the gate, signed a ledger, and waited as the gate was swung back.

Persis followed her in and found herself in a parade ground, at the bottom of which was a striking, low-slung building in the colonial style with a portico, a gabled roof sporting black shingles, a central clock tower, and a painted façade in white and maroon.

'That's the Chetwode Building, the academy's administrative centre,' announced Fordyce. 'Named after Field Marshal Sir Philip Chetwode, the man responsible for this place.'

They moved across the drill square.

A company of cadets were being put through their paces, the shouts of their drill sergeant echoing loudly across the dusty ground. 'They call them Gentlemen Cadets,' Fordyce continued. 'Rather romantic, don't you think?'

Inside the building, they were met by a rake-thin adjutant sporting an unfeasibly large moustache, who led them along hushed corridors to an office at the centre of the building. Here he bade them wait, went inside, then returned to usher them in, closing the door behind him as he departed.

A tall man with a plough nose, receding hair, and a firm jawline rose from behind an expansive desk. His uniform was spotless. His boots gleamed in a way that hurt the eye. An aggressive moustache bristled beneath his nose.

'Persis, may I introduce you to Colonel Shyam Batra? He's been helping me with my research into the Doon Valley. Specifically, as it relates to the army's presence here in Dehra Dun.'

'You make us sound like an invading force,' said Batra, smiling. 'Please, take a seat. May I offer you refreshments?'

They waited as the colonel ordered tea, which duly arrived on a porcelain service imprinted with the academy's crest and motto: *Valour and Wisdom*. 'Now, how may I help you? Gillian was rather mysterious.' Batra's accent hinted at an English education. Persis suspected he was one of those Indians who'd benefited from stints at Harrow and Oxbridge.

She quickly introduced herself and her mission, leaving out details she felt the colonel had no need to know.

He steepled his hands and gazed at her. 'I thought I recognised you. You're the policewoman who headed up the Herriot murder case.'

'Yes.'

Batra's expression was inscrutable. 'Well, far be it from me to second-guess the IPS, but I don't think we'll be seeing women in the armed forces anytime soon.'

Persis stiffened.

'Not that I have anything against the idea myself,' added Batra hurriedly. 'It's just ... fighting on the front line is a little different to policing sleepy local neighbourhoods. We wouldn't want to put you girls in harm's way.' He smiled placatingly, not realising he'd just thrown a keg of kerosene on to the bonfire he'd lit.

She bit down hard on her tongue. She needed this man's help.

'Oh, come now, Colonel,' interjected Fordyce. 'I'm sure you wouldn't mind having *some* of us girls around.' She smiled winsomely.

Batra practically melted into his chair.

Persis took a deep breath and returned the conversation to the Ice Man. 'What I need is access to the records of the men who passed through here during the war. Specifically, Britishers. I want to find out if the Ice Man was a British soldier who went missing in the mountains.'

Batra set down his tea. 'I'm afraid that's impossible. The army does not share personnel records with civilians.'

'I'm here in my capacity as a police officer.'

'Your jurisdiction does not extend to the Indian military.'

She frowned. 'The Ice Man case is now a national matter. Delhi is taking a close interest. Our dead friend may have family abroad.'

The corners of his mouth stretched into the parody of a smile. 'If I didn't know better, I would say that was a threat.'

'Not a threat. Simply a statement of fact.'

She watched him press a thumb against a seam in his trousers. 'The man who set up this institution was an Englishman. A few miles from here is the Survey of India. Its most famous Surveyor General was also an Englishman, a military man by the name of Colonel Sir George Everest. He lives on now with the mountain that bears his name.' Batra leaned forward. 'Yet Sir George never set foot on Everest, nor did he have anything to do with determining that it was the world's highest peak. *That* calculation was carried out by an Indian named Radhanath Sikdar. History, alas, named no mountains after him ... I think it's high time we stopped worrying about appeasing foreigners, don't you?'

'I'm sorry about that. I was sure he'd be more helpful. Between us, I think he's a tad sweet on me.'

They were walking back across the drill square, Fordyce cheerfully leading the way as Persis followed, dwelling on the meeting. Batra's unhelpfulness meant that her trip to Dehra Dun was a wasted effort. She would return to Bombay no further forward in her efforts to confirm the identity of the Ice Man.

Disappointment stuck in her throat like a wishbone.

'The army and the civil service,' said Fordyce. 'The two places where due process can ensure that literally *nothing happens*.' She beamed. 'But all is not lost. There's someone else who might be able to help.'

'Let me guess,' muttered Persis. 'He's sweet on you.'

Fordyce stared at her. 'How did you guess?'

38

They drove to the eastern edge of town, to a neighbourhood of immaculate whitewashed bungalows built in the English style with trimmed lawns and nameplates on the gates. Houses straining for grandeur, with one eye on the lost horizons of the past.

Behind the homes, trees carpeted the slopes, a dense mat that rose to a sky of purest blue.

Fordyce brought the Rolls to a halt outside a flesh-coloured house with dormer windows and a handsome wreath on the front door. The nameplate said *Maple Lodge*.

A child – about four or five – was playing on a wooden swing on the front lawn. The boy squealed with laughter as a Labrador pup chased after the swing, barking madly. The child's burnished skin contrasted vividly with a shock of dirty blond hair and blue eyes.

They were led through the house by a native maid, out into a rear garden where a white man was engulfed by a deckchair, reading.

He rose awkwardly to greet them. 'Gillian. What a pleasant surprise.'

The pair embraced.

Fordyce turned to her companion. 'This is Persis. She's a policewoman up from Bombay, investigating the Ice Man, the one from the papers. She thinks he may have been at the military academy during the war. The academy, alas, has been less than forthcoming. I thought you might be able to help.'

He frowned. Taking Fordyce aside, they engaged in a brief, terse conversation.

Persis pegged his age around fifty, with the remnants of sandy hair edging a freckled scalp, eyes as blue as a swimming pool, and an emaciated physique that spoke of illness. He was dressed in a pair of beige trousers and a half-sleeved polo shirt that hung off his thin frame like a parachute.

Finally, they seemed to come to an understanding. He returned. 'Let's talk inside.'

His name was Andrew Cox, and he was the former commander in charge of the British POW camps at Dehra Dun. Prior to overseeing the construction and management of the camps, Cox had spent time in a senior role at the academy. After the war, he'd quit the army and decided to stay on in India, the decision, in large part, made for him by the fact that he had met and fallen in love with a native.

'There's a fair few of us here,' he said, waving a hand to take in the surrounding neighbourhood. 'Stayers-on. Mainly Brits, though we have the odd American and European. We've all bought land in India over the years, shares in tea plantations and the like. We live off the proceeds and our pensions. It's a comfortable life. To be frank, there isn't much waiting for me back home. Dreary Wednesday afternoons. Cribbage with the Joneses. At least here, I can get out into the hills. Sometimes I'll take a tourist out on the hunt. Plenty of deer up in those forests. No doubt time will thin the herd, but for now it's a splendid way to pass the time.'

She wasn't sure if he meant the deer or the community of former *burra sahibs* living out here on the edge of darkest India.

It was strange, she thought, how human beings learned to adapt.

For nigh on three centuries, men like Cox had called the shots in a country not their own, content that their right to do so was ordained by God, nation, and the colour of their skin. And then the world had changed, and the very ideals that had made conquest not only possible, but palatable, to the masses back home had lost their currency. It was one thing to claim the moral high ground while pretending that you were out in the wilderness civilising the uncivilised, quite another to make the same claim as millions rose up in non-violent protest against centuries of manifest tyranny.

That had been Gandhi's great achievement. To demonstrate to the world that you couldn't claim to be the arbiters of fair play while cheating your fellow man at every turn.

She explained her theory about the Ice Man. 'Can you remember an incident where a British officer from the academy went missing? Someone who went up into the mountains and never came back.'

He considered the question. 'No. That's the sort of thing I'd have heard about. We're a small military community. We wouldn't have left a man out there without a major search operation.'

She swallowed her disappointment.

Fordyce spoke. 'Persis, perhaps if you give Andrew some more details about this Ice Man, it might ring a bell?'

She thought about it and then decided to throw caution to the wind.

His expression abruptly changed when she mentioned the fact that the Ice Man's face might have been covered in brown paint and grease.

'Paint?' said Fordyce. 'Andrew, didn't you tell me a story once? About an escape?'

He seemed uncomfortable, but Fordyce was a terrier. 'Yes, I'm sure you did. You remember, don't you?'

Persis leaned forward. 'Does the reference to paint mean something to you?'

For a moment, the only sound in the room was the whir of the ceiling fan. The barking of the Labrador could be heard from the front of the house. Persis wondered where Cox's Indian wife was.

Finally, prodded by Fordyce, Cox spoke. 'We built two POW camps in Dehra Dun, out on the edge of town. One in the area called Clement Town, one in Premnagar. We kept the Italians in the Clement Town one, though some of the officers were lodged in the compound of a house on Old Survey Road. Once the Clement Town camp became too crowded, we had to move a few of them to the Premnagar one. That's where we kept the Germans, though we had Bulgarians, Hungarians, Rumanians and Finns there too. They called it the City of Despair, but that wasn't because of us. We treated them well. I dare say they didn't offer us the same courtesy over in Europe.' He paused. 'In all the years we ran the two camps, we only had one successful escape. April 1944. Four men. Two Germans, an Italian, and a Brit.'

'A Brit? What was a Britisher doing in the prison?'

'He was sent to us as a collaborator. His name was Bernard McNally. A civil servant from Bombay. His file was classified so we never knew exactly what it was he'd been found guilty of.'

'Why would a civilian be placed in a POW camp?'

'The camps at Dehra Dun were primarily intended for "enemy aliens". Civilians from countries fighting against the Allies who were living in India when war broke out.'

Persis had taken out her notebook. 'Who were the others? The escapees, I mean.'

'The two Germans were civilians too: Udo Kessler and Dieter Stuhlmacher. They were a pair of mountaineers.'

'And the Italian?'

'A man named Dino Orelli. He *was* a soldier, and had seen some action, though he hadn't exactly been on the front line.'

From the back of her notebook, Persis took out photographs of Stephen Renzi and Peter Grunewald.

Cox picked up the photograph of Stephen Renzi. She noticed that the small hairs on his arm had been bleached white by the sun.

'This is Dino Orelli. And that' – he indicated the other photograph – 'is Dieter Stuhlmacher.'

Persis sat back, resisting the urge to let out a savage yell. 'You're certain?'

He flashed a mirthless smile. 'I was the commander at Premnagar when they escaped. We tracked them up to the Tsangchokla Pass. That's where they vanished. I always thought they must have made it through to Tibet.'

'At least one of them didn't. Either Bernard McNally or Udo Kessler.'

He considered this. 'How tall is your Ice Man?'

She flipped through her notebook, to the notes she'd scribbled down during the autopsy. 'Five feet eight inches.'

'That's McNally. Kessler was a big man, well over six feet.'

Another flush of triumph. The Ice Man's identity was now confirmed. 'Do you have access to photographs of McNally and Kessler?'

He rubbed the side of his face. 'When we closed down the POW camps, all the records were transferred to the academy for storage until someone could work out where to send them. As far as I know they're still there.'

She looked at Fordyce. 'Do you think—'

'Not a chance. Batra isn't the type to change his mind.' Fordyce turned to Cox. 'Andrew. You still have friends at the academy.'

He squirmed in his seat, reluctance personified. But Fordyce was a human wrecking ball.

'Leave it with me.'

'Tell me about them,' asked Persis. 'The four men.'

His eyes seemed to shift into the past. 'They were an odd pair, the two Germans. Stuhlmacher and Kessler. Stuhlmacher was a gentle giant, a contemplative man, kept himself to himself. But Kessler ... he was cold; a hard, closed-off man. He had little time for anyone but Stuhlmacher. The pair of them were thick as thieves. I sometimes had the feeling they were ...' He didn't finish the thought. 'Kessler chafed in the camp. I think he probably persuaded Stuhlmacher to go along with McNally's crazy plan. He was like a wild dog caged for too long. Most of the inmates got along just fine, but Kessler was always getting into fights. He killed a man shortly before they escaped, a fellow inmate. Claimed it was self-defence. Had Stuhlmacher come forward as a witness. Without any evidence to the contrary we couldn't punish him. Frankly, it was almost a relief to have him gone from the camp.'

'What about Orelli?'

'Orelli was an odd one. A good-humoured man. Well liked. But, like Kessler, confinement didn't suit him at all. He'd tried to escape a couple of times, but he was useless at planning anything.'

'And McNally?'

'McNally blew hot and cold. He was a surly man, never gave a straight answer to a straight question. But there were times when I'd watch him and I'd see his mind working. He was smart, had a wealth of experience out here – in India, I mean – and the cunning of a rat.'

A thought circled back. 'The paint. Why did that jog your memory?'

He grimaced. 'They escaped by dressing up as locals. Disguised as a fence-repair crew. We had terrible problems with white ants eating away the posts for the barbed-wire fences. They put on native clothes, turbans, and darkened their hands and faces with a mixture of brown paint and grease. It was so simple that only a genius or a fool could have thought of it. But, like I said, McNally was a smart man.'

'It was McNally's plan?'

'Yes. He basically told me he was going to escape the day he arrived. He could be an arrogant bastard.' He stopped. 'He'd tried once before. Failed miserably.'

'Why did he take the others along? I mean, why let them in on his plan?'

'He needed them. The mountains are no place for an amateur. Kessler and Stuhlmacher were experienced mountaineers. And Orelli was a linguist. He spoke Hindi, and some of the local dialects. They'd have needed that, up in the hill towns. Of course, when you think about it, it was a ludicrous plan. Tibet was forbidden to foreigners. They were basically jumping from the frying pan into the fire. They had no guarantee that they wouldn't be executed or turned back the moment they set foot in the country. But that was McNally all over. A gambler.'

She pondered his words, mentally building up a picture of the man she'd been hunting.

'Of course, they still couldn't have done it without inside help.'

'What do you mean?'

'You can't trek through the mountains without provisions or the right equipment. How do you suppose they got them?'

She waited.

'One of the camp guards,' he explained. 'A native by the name of Bhadrasing Rai. He was a Gurkha, as were most of the guards.'

'Why would he help them?'

'That was something I never did find out.'

'Where is Rai now? I'd like to speak to him.'

'That's going to be rather difficult, I'm afraid. Rai is dead.'

39

An hour later, she was back outside the hotel. Fordyce had invited her to dine at the Forest Research Institute, but she'd declined.

She needed to think through Andrew Cox's revelations.

Eschewing the delights of the Clive Hotel, she decided to head towards the centre of town.

As she left, she was hailed by the proprietor. 'A man came in, looking for you.'

She was taken aback. Had Cox sent someone already? 'Who?'

'I'm not your secretary,' he said. 'He asked me if you were here and I said no.'

'He asked for me by name?'

'Yes.'

'Did he leave anything for me?'

'No.'

She paused. 'What did he look like?'

'He was a white man.'

White? Perhaps Cox had come himself. But then why hadn't he left a message?

Quickly, she described the Englishman to the surly proprietor.

'No,' he said, grudgingly. 'That wasn't him.' He said no more and shuffled back through a door behind the counter.

'Thank you, you've been incredibly helpful.'

Her sarcasm was lost on his retreating back.

* * *

As she navigated her way around the square, she considered the facts now at hand – in particular, that the Ice Man was a British civilian named Bernard McNally, sent to a POW camp at Dehra Dun for colluding with the enemy during the war. McNally had escaped the camp with three men. But something had happened during that escape and McNally had ended up dead in a cave in the Tsangchokla Pass.

Now, almost six years later, two of the men McNally had escaped with – Stephen Renzi and Peter Grunewald – real names Dino Orelli and Dieter Stuhlmacher – had been murdered in Bombay, within days of McNally's body being discovered.

That was no coincidence.

Someone knew. Someone knew of the connection between the three men and, for a reason she did not yet understand, had decided to murder McNally's former associates.

A thought shot out of the murk.

Might the killer be the fourth of the escapees? Udo Kessler?

But why? Why had Orelli and Stuhlmacher returned to India after the war? Why would Kessler murder them?

Did it have something to do with the pages torn out of McNally's notebook? Scraps containing a message written in code? If she could decipher the code, perhaps she might understand exactly what had transpired between the four men once they'd escaped from the POW camp.

Frustration pressed against the inside of her skull.

She found herself outside the post office.

A plaque held a roll call of Doonites who had fought and perished in the two world wars. Walking through the town, she'd once again had the impression that this was one of those places that aged only one year in ten, clinging to its past in a way that a city like Bombay – forever rushing headlong into the future

– could never do. Men like Andrew Cox had retired here because they thought they could escape the reality of a changing world that had displaced them.

Thinking about Cox brought her back to the POW camps that he'd overseen.

Cox had told her that the Premnagar camp had been built out beyond the edge of town where the jungle met the inhabited world. By all accounts, it had been left untouched since the war, neither the Indian army nor the municipal authorities having yet worked out what to do with it.

She was taken abruptly by the notion that she *needed* to visit the camp.

She knew there was little she might find there, but she wanted to get a feel for Bernard McNally and his confederates. In the past, standing at crime scenes, she'd felt the numen of such places, an intangible sense-impression that sometimes touched off new ideas.

It was a better alternative to kicking her heels around in a dusty hotel room waiting for the morning and a rattling flight back to Bombay.

She hailed a tonga from outside the Clive Hotel.

The driver, sporting a jaunty white turban and an obliging smile, took her to the edge of town, whereupon he refused to proceed a yard further. The Premnagar camp was still a half mile distant, and she found herself cursing her way through moonlit darkness, a torch in hand, the overgrown path shadowed by trees. A canal rushed by on one side, the musical gurgle of the water strangely soothing in the dark.

When she eventually emerged into a clearing, she was confronted by a barbed-wire-topped hurricane fence.

She swung the torch beam over the fence until she found a section that had been cut away.

Ducking, she wriggled through the gap, her blouse snagging on a rusted finger of wire. She cursed, then pushed through, ripping a hole in the fabric.

A hoopoe hooted in the darkness.

She stood, fingered the hole in the side of her blouse, then walked on.

The compound was shrouded in darkness, the shapes of nearby barracks looming out of the pitch as she made her way inwards.

Cox's words, his memories of the camp, circulated around her thoughts.

Premnagar had been divided into seven sections, each surrounded by double barbed-wire fences. In each section, a total of fourteen barracks had housed some five hundred men, grouped together by national identity. The German section had been named Campus Teutonicus, the Italian wing Campus Italicus. There had been a section for Indian political prisoners, and another for Italian priests, named Vatican City.

According to Cox, life in the camp was relatively idyllic.

The worst the prisoners had to contend with was the summer heat when the mercury would routinely touch forty degrees centigrade. In the winter, they were treated to views of snow-capped mountains, and satin nights when the lights from the nearby hill station of Mussoorie would spread along the slopes.

The prisoners passed their time in daily chores, sports, and musical concerts, and were even taken out to hike in the nearby foothills. With the benefit of hindsight, Cox had realised that those sanctioned excursions had helped McNally and his associates plan their escape.

A noise sounded behind her and she whirled around, the torch beam dancing in the dark.

Nothing.

She was suddenly aware of the pungent smell of her own sweat. Her heart was pounding.

What was she doing here? What could she possibly learn?

She kept on walking.

Cox had told her that Bernard McNally had planned his escape over a period of months, cutting through the fence that separated the various camp communities to liaise at night with Orelli, Stuhlmacher, and Kessler. He conjectured that McNally had recruited the two Germans first, once he'd discovered that they were experienced mountaineers, to help him plan the route up to Tibet. With Bhadrasing Rai's help, they'd smuggled in provisions, maps, compasses, shoes, and – as had later been discovered from some of McNally's barracks mates – two small mountain tents.

Once the plan was set, they'd brought in Dino Orelli – the man she knew as Stephen Renzi – perhaps realising that an interpreter would be a useful addition as they navigated the villages dotted along the route up to the Tsangchokla Pass.

But one question still bothered her: why had *Rai* chosen to help the four men?

A question for which Cox had no real answer, merely conjecturing that McNally had bribed the man. If so, Rai had not lived long enough to enjoy his ill-gotten spoils.

She passed an open drain and a row of latrines, almost engulfed by the gradual crawl of vegetation. Everywhere was the sense of slow ruin.

Another sound whirled her around. Something shook the branches of a tree overhanging a nearby section of fence. Langurs, perhaps. Or a leopard.

She stood in silence, the night humming around her.

What had happened between the four men that had led to McNally ending up dead in the mountains? An accident? Or, as she suspected, a falling-out?

It wouldn't have taken much. An Englishman, two Germans, and an Italian.

Enemies in war. Fair-weather friends during their escap—

A rush of footsteps behind her. Before she could turn, an arm had clamped itself around her throat, lifting her off the ground. The torch fell away. A gasp escaped her as she pulled at the vice-like forearm with her hands. Her feet flailed in the air, heels kicking against the body behind her.

She was slammed to her knees, a jolt of pain shooting through her legs and up her spine.

The cold muzzle of a pistol, set against her temple.

'Stop moving!'

A man's voice. Rasping, with a faint accent.

She willed herself to stillness, fighting the instinct to struggle.

'Did you find the sheets?'

Her breathing was ragged. She fought for calm. 'I don't know what you're talking about.'

The blow caught her unawares, the butt of the gun cracking against the side of her head, sprawling her to the floor in a daze.

She was pulled roughly back to her knees, darkness still swimming before her eyes.

'Lie to me again and it will be your last lie.'

She breathed hard through her nose. 'Which sheets do you mean?'

'The ones taken from McNally's notebook.'

She was silent. The muzzle poked roughly into her cheek again. 'Is it worth dying for?'

Bitterness consumed her. But the man was right. It wasn't worth dying for.

'In my room. At the Clive Hotel.'

'Wise decision,' rasped the voice, and then a blinding pain exploded inside her skull, and she whirled into darkness.

40

When she returned to the world, it was into a lightlessness so dark that, at first, she wasn't sure she had even opened her eyes.

She was sprawled on the floor, in what felt like an enclosed space.

As she limped to her feet, lightning bolts of pain crackled around her skull. She doubled over, a grunt escaping her.

Stumbling her way around, she realised that she was in a small, box-like enclosure, roughly six feet on a side and almost as high; her fingers brushed a flat metal ceiling.

She examined the walls with her fingers. They were solid, brick and mortar, the kicks that she aimed at them easily absorbed. She found a metal door, locked from the outside and just as resistant to her assault.

Finally, the beginnings of panic clutching at her throat, she yelled, 'Is anyone out there!'

Nothing. Not even an echo.

She shouted again, then again, and kept it up until she grew hoarse, collapsing at last into a corner, where she slid to the floor, knees pulled up, face clasped into her hands.

A sense of futility enveloped her, as pitch-black as her surroundings.

By the time she'd pulled herself together, her predicament had become vividly clear.

She was locked in some sort of solitary prison, in an abandoned internment camp, out beyond the edges of town.

No one knew that she was here.

By the time someone thought to search the internment camp, she might have passed into a stupor, dazed by hunger, thirst, and heat. Would she even hear a search party pass by? Would they bother to examine every single building in the camp, every enclosure?

She could die here. Out in the middle of nowhere, surrounded by jungle and the ghosts of men once held against their will, buzzing like fireflies in the night.

A fist of rage erupted inside her, fuelled by a primal sense of terror.

She scrambled to her feet and attacked the door again, punching and kicking it until her knuckles bled, screaming obscenities at the top of her lungs.

Finally, exhausted, drained of emotion, she stepped back, breathing hard.

In the silence, a sound.

She tensed.

Footsteps. She was sure of it.

Fear brushed the walls of her chest. Had her attacker returned to finish the job?

And then, a voice: 'Persis, is that you in there?'

41

'How did you find me?'

Blackfinch dipped the handkerchief in a bowl, then dabbed at her forehead. The smell of mercurochrome twitched her nostrils.

They were back in her room at the Clive Hotel, Blackfinch performing a passable imitation of Florence Nightingale.

The overwhelming relief she had felt when he'd turned up outside her makeshift prison was giving way to a rage that had settled at the centre of her chest.

Her room had been searched, that much was evident. The pages from McNally's notebook were gone, lifted from inside her own notebook, which had been discarded, thrown into a corner together with the contents of her wardrobe.

'It wasn't that difficult. After you boarded your flight this morning, I spent an hour sitting in a café thinking about things. And then I decided I couldn't simply let it lie. I needed to talk to you and I didn't want to wait until you got back.

'You'd already told me you were going to meet with a Gillian Fordyce in Dehra Dun. You'd mentioned you'd been put in touch with her via your military historian friend, Augustus Silva. I called the university, spoke to him, and he gave me a phone number for Fordyce.

'I took the afternoon postal flight up from Bombay, and contacted Fordyce once I got into town. She sent me to your hotel. When I didn't find you here, I stepped outside, checked out the local area, came back, discovered a trio of tongas outside the hotel, and interrogated the drivers until I found the chap who'd taken you to the edge of town. I asked him what else was out there and he told me there was only jungle and the old POW camp. I took a chance . . . Any idea who attacked you?'

She'd been considering the question ever since he'd unbolted the door to her prison.

She hadn't got a look at her attacker, but he'd been a tall man, big and strong. And his accent . . . 'He was German.'

'What would a German be doing up here? And why would he want to attack *you*?'

She explained her theory, the theory that had come to her in the past half an hour. Namely, that her attacker was Udo Kessler, the fourth man to have escaped from the Premnagar camp in 1944.

She conjectured that Kessler had been in Bombay, tracking her investigation of the Ice Man – Bernard McNally – and the murders of his former associates. She strongly suspected that Kessler might have been behind those killings too. He'd guessed – or hoped – that she'd discovered the sheets torn from McNally's notebook, and had followed her up to Dehra Dun to retrieve them.

She knew that there were blind spots in her assumptions, but if she was right, then it made sense that Kessler was in possession of the third sheet.

Now that he had all three of them, would he be able to decipher the code?

The question was: *what did the code reveal?* What had been so important that Bernard McNally had seen fit to encode it in his notebook? Was this the reason he'd died in the mountains?

A scenario sprang into her mind, fully formed.

McNally's confederates had conspired to murder him after their escape. They'd then taken the pages from his notebook. But why had they split the pages between them? Was the plan to reunite at some point in the future? After the war, perhaps? That would explain why Renzi and Grunewald had been living in Bombay.

But it was now more than four years after the war.

Why had they still been there?

She followed the winding path of her conjecture.

If Udo Kessler was indeed the man who'd attacked her *and* the murderer of Orelli and Stuhlmacher – Stephen Renzi and Peter Grunewald – *why* had he killed them? If it was solely to retrieve the sheets of notepaper, why had he waited till now?

The answer, she suspected, was linked to the discovery of the Ice Man. Kessler must have realised that the corpse discovered in the Tsangchokla Pass was that of Bernard McNally – for some reason, this had triggered him to violence.

And then there were the wooden dolls. What did *they* have to do with all this? Why would Kessler leave them behind at the murder scenes?

There was a twisted logic here that she couldn't fathom. Not yet. But the shape of the problem was gradually emerging from the murk, like a sunken wreck slowly winched up to the light—

'Ow!' She flinched as Blackfinch dabbed at the bruise on the back of her skull.

'Sorry.'

She stood up, and turned to face him.

He stood there, green eyes blinking in the room's dim light, dark hair dishevelled, dressed in a sky-blue shirt and trousers, as handsome as the day she'd first met him.

A silence fell and she realised he'd been desperately filling the awkwardness between them with words.

It came out of nowhere. The terrible gravity of her desire for him, flowing over her like an ocean wave, capsizing the boat of her equanimity. Memories returned, savage and painful, from that same morning, the woman at his door . . .

'You have to go.'

'Persis—'

'Go.'

He took a deep breath. 'No. Not until you've heard me out.'

She stared at him. He'd rarely been so forceful, one of those Englishmen who'd rather shoot themselves in the face than speak out of turn.

'What happened between us last night was . . . unexpected. Don't get me wrong. It was everything I could have hoped for. And more. But you'd led me to believe that nothing of that sort *could* happen between us. The woman you saw this morning . . . Jane . . . I met her a few weeks ago. She's an art purchaser, here on a mission to evaluate Indian art. She doesn't know many Brits out here, and so she asked me if I'd accompany her to a viewing. I was feeling rather miserable – about us, I mean – and so, in a moment of weakness, I said yes. That's how it started.' He paused. 'I admit, we've stepped out a few times. No man is an island, Persis.'

She turned away, not wanting to look at him.

'It's not Jane that I want. It's you.'

'I know,' she said, softly. 'Archie . . . you're a good man. But let's play this out. Where can it possibly lead between us?'

'Does it have to lead somewhere? Why can't we simply enjoy the journey?'

'Because I'm an Indian and you're an Englishman.'

'Why should that make a difference?'

'If you don't know the answer to that, there's nothing I can say to explain.'

'The world has changed, Persis. The rules have changed.'

'Maybe for you. But for someone like me . . . I have to answer to the world *I* live in.'

'That's ridiculous. To deny what we feel because of ... what? Fear of what others might think?' His face squirmed in frustration. 'Persis ... I think I may be in love with you.'

She said nothing, his words clutching at her heart.

'Do you love *me*?'

She wanted to answer him, but to do so would only prolong her anguish. 'Archie ... please. Go.'

He seemed set to protest, then dipped his head, disappointment evident in the slump of his shoulders as he set down the handkerchief and walked out.

42

She awoke with a stiff headache, made worse by a cacophony of crows outside her window, a noise to wake the dead and then send them running for cover.

The throbbing only worsened under a cold shower.

Back in the bedroom, wrapped in a bathrobe, she stared at herself in a hand-held mirror. She felt years older. Was this how it would be? Each investigation adding an extra weight to her mind and body?

A knock at the door.

She took another look in the mirror, adjusted her bathrobe, walked to the door, took a deep breath, and opened it, expecting Blackfinch to be standing there, blinking at her like a buffalo in a field.

It wasn't Blackfinch.

Instead, a messenger in a khaki uniform stood there, impatiently tapping at his teeth with a pen. He thrust a large manila envelope into her hand. 'Please sign.'

She accepted the delivery, then closed the door. Walking to the room's ancient desk, she tore open the package and pulled out several slim folders accompanied by a note.

The note was from Andrew Cox: *There isn't much here. Paperwork for the prisoners that arrived at the camps was haphazard at best.*

She sat down at the desk, pushed aside the lamp, and set down the five slim folders.

She picked up the topmost one and opened it.

Inside, on the opening page, was a ghostly, stamped photograph of the man who had called himself Peter Grunewald, real name Dieter Stuhlmacher. A grey card labelled *Prisoner of War History Sheet*, inserted at the back of the file, stated that in August 1939, Stuhlmacher had been arrested by British soldiers in the city of Karachi, in the company of Udo Kessler.

According to their own testimony, the two men had been planning an ascent of the Diamir Face of Nanga Parbat.

Two days later, war had been declared, and their status as 'enemy aliens' in India was confirmed; a week after that they found themselves transferred to the POW camp in Dehra Dun.

In the next file, she found a photograph of Udo Kessler, a boyishly handsome man with light eyes and swept-back, jet-black hair. A slight curve to the mouth, almost of amusement. Persis's eyes rested briefly on the image, wondering if this was, indeed, the man who'd attacked her the previous evening.

In the third file, she found Stephen Renzi – Dino Orelli – staring out at her.

The moment was jarring, having come face to face with the man's corpse less than a week earlier.

Orelli's military record was sparse.

Following his capture in early 1941 during the disastrous Italian North Africa campaign, he'd initially been held at a POW camp in Ceylon, then transferred to Bangalore, and later to Dehra Dun. A note in *his* Prisoner of War History Sheet suggested that, for a while, he'd been a model prisoner, and had shown a talent for painting – so much so that he had been let out on occasion to paint frescoes at a church in the town. But then the rot had set in, and he'd attempted to escape, unsuccessfully, on several occasions.

Inside the next file, she found a photograph of Bernard McNally – a blunt-faced man with a thick moustache, short, wiry hair, and intense, dark eyes – but little else in the way of tangible background information.

Her gaze hovered over the photo. It felt strange to finally put a face to the Ice Man.

The accompanying Prisoner of War History Sheet stated that McNally had entered the camp in August 1943, but there was nothing listed next to Rank or Prior Containments. Neither was any reason given for his transfer to a POW camp designed for Allied enemies.

A simple note at the foot of the sheet read: *Bernard McNally. Transferred to Group IV, Premnagar, Dehra Dun, under the auspices of the India War Office.*

Cox had told her the truth.

McNally's presence at the camp was a mystery.

She set down the file and picked up the last folder.

Here she discovered the military record of Bhadrasing Rai, the camp guard at Premnagar who had helped the Europeans escape. The record detailed Rai's brief time in Burma, noting that his active service had been cut short by a wound sustained in battle – shrapnel had embedded itself in his knee, incapacitating him for a lengthy period and resulting in his return to the village of Nagar Koti, just outside Dehra Dun.

A faded photograph showed a very young Rai, clean-shaven and fresh-faced, in uniform.

A signed death certificate was tucked into the back of the folder.

Rai had perished just days after McNally and his associates had escaped.

She wondered again why the camp guard had helped them. Why put his own career in jeopardy for Europeans, especially a Britisher?

Frustration gnawed away at her.

The files had raised more mysteries than they had solved.

She was no further forward in understanding why McNally had been killed or how to unlock the enigmatic code he had left behind in his notebook.

She picked up Udo Kessler's file and stared again at the photograph.

Her instincts told her that she was looking at the murderer of Stephen Renzi and Peter Grunewald. But why had he killed them? Why *now*?

Most importantly: was she also looking at the man who had killed Bernard McNally after the four of them had escaped from Dehra Dun?

43

Having dressed, she made her way downstairs to the morning room, where she found Blackfinch perusing a copy of the *Times of India*, and engaged in conversation with the hotel's proprietor.

She was astonished to notice the transformation in the man's demeanour. A complaisant smile lit up his mealy features, and he was leaning into whatever it was that Blackfinch was saying as if he'd never heard anything so fascinating.

She dropped into the chair opposite her colleague, bringing the bonhomie to a crashing halt.

'Good morning,' said Blackfinch, carefully. He set down the paper. 'Persis, I presume you've met the proprietor of our establishment, Harold Whitman?'

'Yes,' said Persis, curtly.

She saw that Whitman's expression had curdled. 'You two ... you're together?'

'Yes,' said Blackfinch.

'No,' said Persis, firmly. 'We're colleagues. Here on official business.'

Whitman looked from one to the other with yellow eyeballs. His desire to all but adopt Blackfinch had vanished. She'd seen such reactions before. It was exactly the sort of thing she'd tried to explain to Blackfinch. Post-independence India may have prided itself as a bastion of liberal, free-thinking democracy, but few were willing to accept the union of a white man and a native woman.

It wasn't just relics such as Whitman that thought this way.

She tried to imagine what Aunt Nussie would say if she knew her only niece had spent the night in an Englishman's bed.

'How are you feeling?' asked the man himself, as Whitman walked stiffly away.

'I've been better.'

The memory of their shared night – and everything that had happened since – lingered, making it difficult for her to meet his eyes. Everything about him seemed to both attract and repel her: his antiquated manners, his oft-times boorish charm, his obliviousness to matters of fact.

'Persis, about last night—'

'Archie ... I'm sorry. I'm sorry for speaking so directly. But everything I said ... it's for the best. For us both.'

'I disagree.'

'Nevertheless. Can we agree to be rational? I value you greatly as a colleague; I don't want to lose that.'

'A colleague?' he said, hollowly.

'Yes,' she said, firmly.

He opened his mouth, but then closed it again. It pained her to see him in such distress. But it was better this way. A clear understanding. A clean break.

Finally, he nodded. 'If that's what you wish for, then colleagues it is.' He took a deep breath, then reached for the teapot with shaky hands.

She sensed that this wasn't the end of the matter, that he'd merely backed away so that he could regroup. It would have to do for now.

She watched him pour tea, handling the teapot as if it were a rare and precious object.

She told him about the courier, then took out the files from her bag and showed them to him, watching as he went through them.

'Curiouser and curiouser,' he said eventually. 'Four men, thrown together by the tides of fate. An Englishman, an Italian, and two Germans.' He smiled grimly. 'Sounds like the opening to a bad joke.'

She picked up her teacup. 'I think it must have driven Stuhlmacher and Kessler mad, to be confined to the POW camp, able to see the Himalayas every day, but not be able to climb.'

'You think that's why they agreed to help McNally?'

'Not the only reason. They'd been in the camp for over four years. Escape might have seemed a good idea by then. Cox told me that Kessler pushed Stuhlmacher pretty hard to go along. The two of them were very . . . close.'

'What about Orelli?'

'On the face of it, his involvement makes less sense. The life of the inmates at Premnagar was hardly arduous. All he had to do was wait out the war. Why take such a risk, trekking through the mountains to a country where foreigners might be shot on sight? But Cox said he'd tried to escape before. I think he simply went stir-crazy. Not everyone is built for prison.'

Blackfinch tapped McNally's file. 'It's a shame there's not much here about our Ice Man. I sense a story.'

She nodded in agreement. 'What I still can't understand is why Bhadrasing Rai, the camp guard, agreed to help them.'

'I'd have thought it was obvious.' The Englishman picked up a piece of toast and scraped off the burned edges with a butter knife. 'McNally must have bribed him.'

It was the same reason Andrew Cox, the camp commander, had conjectured. Yet, it still seemed to her an incredible risk for Rai to take.

'Of course,' Blackfinch continued, crunching into his toast, 'you could always ask those who knew him. His colleagues. His nearest and dearest.'

The thought had occurred to her. She had no hope of tracking down Rai's former colleagues, but the file Cox had sent her stated that Rai hailed from a village just north of Dehra Dun.

She came to a decision. Bhadrasing Rai's family – if any remained – might be able to shed light on why he'd helped Bernard McNally and his associates escape from the Premnagar POW camp.

A detour to Rai's village seemed warranted.

Blackfinch agreed to accompany her, though he was pessimistic of their chances of discovering anything useful.

She had half thought he might refuse, and was glad when he said yes. At the back of her mind was the suspicion that the man who'd attacked her was still somewhere in the vicinity.

They hired a jeep with a driver, and took the Rajpur Road out of town.

Within the hour, they were climbing into the hills, the jeep's engine straining against the gradient as they zigzagged up forest-covered slopes, a sheer drop on one side. Here and there Persis spotted a vehicle that had tumbled over the edge and lodged in the branches of a tree. She wondered if the bodies had been left to rot inside, just as the rusted hulks had been left to the elements.

Cool, crisp air whipped into the jeep, a welcome relief after the sunken humidity of the town.

They arrived in Nagar Koti, a sleepy hamlet of less than five hundred souls, shortly after eleven. The village was one of dozens nestled in the hills some twenty miles north-east of Dehra Dun. Many of them had become home to communities of Gurkhas and other immigrants from nearby Nepal.

It didn't take long to ask the way to the village sarpanch – an elder serving in the capacity of informal mayor – and from thence to be guided to the childhood home of Bhadrasing Rai. It appeared that Rai was a man of relative fame in the region, his story now a part of local folklore.

The Rai home was situated at the top of a rise, a single-storey drystone dwelling with a sloping roof of rough slate tiles and a green-painted door and shutters, framed by a vault of cerulean sky.

Inside they found an elderly couple, Bhadrasing Rai's parents.

Rai's father, Delsing Rai, was smoking a hookah on the rear porch, the fragrant smoke carried by a gentle breeze towards a collection of houses, seemingly built on top of each other, some hundred yards distant. Surrounding hills rose on all sides, dotted with more houses and the occasional white-painted temple.

From their vantage point, they could see labourers – men and women – hacking with pickaxes at a barren field, and a group of schoolchildren walking behind a man and a donkey along a bridle path dotted with mounds of dried dung.

A trio of goats grazed near the porch.

Persis explained the reason for their visit, watching carefully for the old man's reaction. The dialect of the region was Garhwali, but the majority of locals also spoke Hindi, a fact for which she was thankful.

Delsing took the hookah from his mouth, and stared at her. He was a small man, thin, with a lugubrious face, grey hair, and a few wisps of white clinging to his chin. His eyes were grey, contrasting with the creased darkness of his skin.

'Bhadra was a patriot,' he said. 'He didn't deserve the things they said about him.'

'Is it true that he helped the westerners escape?'

'Yes.'

'Why?'

He puffed on the hookah, the liquid bubbling in the bowl. 'Bhadra had been a soldier himself. He fought in the war, out east,

239

in Burma. He was wounded. They gave him a medal and sent him home. He needed work. He found it at the Premnagar camp when the British began hiring locals as guards.'

'Did he ever mention Bernard McNally to you?'

'Yes. Many times.' He held her with his ghostly eyes. 'McNally saved his life.'

She suppressed an intake of breath. 'I don't understand.'

'They were out on one of their excursions. In the hills around the camp. The weather turned wet. They should have gone back, but they didn't. Something went wrong, and Bhadra slipped and fell into a lake. Bhadra cannot swim, nor could the other guard he was with that day. He would have drowned, but for McNally. The Englishman dived in and saved him.'

Persis sat back. Finally, a ray of illumination.

A tug on her arm. She leaned into Blackfinch and translated for him.

'Well, I guess we know why Rai felt duty-bound to help McNally. But what happened to *him*?'

She posed the question to Rai's father. She'd heard one version of the story from Andrew Cox, but she wanted to hear it from those who had been closest to the man.

Behind her, she heard Rai's mother begin to softly weep.

'They came looking for him,' rasped Delsing. 'After the escape. The British quickly worked out that he'd helped McNally and his friends. Bhadra ran back home. He was afraid; he didn't know what he should do. He'd fought for the British and now he'd betrayed them.

'When they came for him, he panicked. He fled into the hills. They chased him up to Hunter's Falls. I went with them. I hoped to convince Bhadra to surrender. I hoped I could stop anything bad from happening to him. I failed.'

'The British killed him?'

He nodded. 'He ended up on the cliff, with nowhere to go. I begged him to give himself up, but he wouldn't. He fired at them. They fired back. I saw him go down, clutching his chest. He fell into the ravine. His body was swept away by the river.' Tears had gathered in the corners of his eyes. 'It took me a day to find his corpse. We cremated him and spread his ashes into the river that killed him. Can you imagine that, Inspector? Seeing your only son killed? Lighting his funeral pyre?'

Bitterness choked his words.

Persis allowed a moment to pass, and then, 'Is there anything you can tell me about McNally or his associates? Anything your son might have said that might help me understand what is happening now?'

He set the hookah aside. 'Bhadra idolised McNally, but he never trusted the others. McNally didn't either. He was certain the two Germans would betray him the first chance they got. But he needed them to get through the mountains, and they needed him to escape from the camp. According to Bhadra, he was the cleverest of them.' He stopped. 'There was something else. Bhadra said that McNally had some sort of hold over the others, something that bound them to him. He told me he didn't know what it was, but it must have been powerful.'

'Do you have any idea why the others returned to India after the war?'

He shook his head.

'There's one other thing.' She reached into her bag. 'When the German and the Italian were killed, the murderer left these behind.' She held out the wooden dolls.

It was as if she had held out a cobra. The old man stiffened, his eyes starting from his head. Behind her, Bhadrasing Rai's mother gasped.

'You recognise them,' Persis whispered.

He seemed to bring himself under control, murmuring a prayer under his breath.

Finally, he nodded, and reached out, taking one of the dolls from her and running his fingers over it in seeming wonder. 'Bhadra used to carve dolls like this. They were reminders of his time in the army. It was a hobby. He used to teach the soldiers in the camp. It helped them pass the time.'

Her mind was leaping ahead. 'Did he teach McNally and his associates?'

'I don't know. Possibly. What I know is that I saw him carving dolls like these just before they escaped. He told me they were good luck charms.'

'Did you know he was planning to help them? Why didn't you stop him?'

'My son owed Bernard McNally his life. There was a debt to be repaid. A debt of honour. For a Gurkha, such a debt means something. I couldn't possibly explain it to you.'

She sat back. It was all beginning to fit together.

Four men had escaped from Dehra Dun. One had died in the surrounding mountains. Years later, the remaining three had returned to India.

And now, Udo Kessler had murdered Dino Orelli and Dieter Stuhlmacher – the men she knew as Stephen Renzi and Peter Grunewald. He'd then followed Persis to Dehra Dun and stolen the sheets ripped from Bernard McNally's notebook, the sheets that had been in the possession of Orelli and Stuhlmacher.

Her mind flashed back to the big man who'd boarded her flight up from Bombay at the last second and had then kept his face hidden beneath his hat, pretending to be asleep. Could that have been Udo Kessler?

She felt sure it must have been.

How else could he have known that she had chosen to stay at

the Clive Hotel? He must have waited for her and Gillian Fordyce after he'd left the airport in a hired car, and then followed them.

She further conjectured that Kessler had carved and left the dolls at the scenes of the killings. Either that, or he'd left behind dolls that Bhadrasing Rai might have given them when they'd escaped from Dehra Dun.

Why?

Was it some perverse means of marking the connection between the men, a reminder of their time in the POW camp?

She frowned.

The explanation made little sense. Then again, how often did a murderer's actions conform to the tenets of logic?

There was also the question of why he'd acted *now*. What had triggered his actions?

It had to be the discovery of McNally's body. Nothing else made sense.

She suspected that Kessler had already been in contact with Orelli and Stuhlmacher in Bombay. He'd been forced to act once news of the Ice Man hit the headlines. Perhaps he'd suspected the pair might flee the city, fearing implication in McNally's murder, and he would miss his opportunity to retrieve the coded sheets.

It was becoming clear to her that those sheets lay at the centre of the mystery. A secret that McNally had held close to his chest, and that he clung to even now, from beyond the grave.

If she was to unravel that secret, she needed to find out more about the man, and why he had ended up in a prison in Dehra Dun.

44

'Explain it to me as if I were a small child.'

Seth looked at her from behind his desk with red-rimmed eyes. In one hand, he clutched a tumbler of Scotch, in the other a cigarette. He looked as if he hadn't slept since she'd left Bombay two days earlier.

She'd returned the previous day, taking the evening flight back with Archie Blackfinch.

There'd been an awkward moment at the aerodrome, but she'd quickly put an end to it by hailing a taxi and asking the driver to take her to Jaya's home. Blackfinch's disappointment had been evident, but there was little to be done about it.

Sooner or later, they had to accept the reality of the situation.

Besides, Blackfinch would be better off with Jane Davenport. A white woman, with none of the complications that their own equation entailed.

Jaya, of course, had been thrilled to receive her, and even more thrilled to get the inside track on the situation at Persis's home. She'd already caught a whiff of Sam's affair at the dinner with Dinaz, and felt duty-bound to add her own unwanted opinion to the matter.

'It's shocking,' she said, leading Persis to a guest bedroom on the second floor of her three-storey bungalow in Cuffe Parade. 'At his age, he should be thinking of retiring and planting vegetables, not planting his own vegetable in some old widow.'

Persis had dwelt on her friend's words as she'd unpacked and readied herself for bed.

Sitting in front of the dresser mirror, she'd looked at her reflection and found an unexpected feeling steal over her. Guilt. Jaya's opinion of her father's dalliance with Meherzad had been ... cruel. There was no other word for it. An instinctive desire to leap to his defence had bubbled up inside her, yet she'd said nothing.

Didn't Sam deserve better from her?

She recalled innumerable instances when he'd gone out to bat for her. To hell with the world, he'd told her. You are your own woman. Live your life as you see fit.

If only it were that easy.

She considered phoning him, but in the end she turned out the light and pulled the sheets up to her chin, to spend hours wrestling with her thoughts before the arrival of a fitful sleep.

The sound of a commotion returned her to Seth's office.

The door opened behind them and Amit Shukla, Additional Deputy Commissioner of Police, strode in. Seth gaped at him, as if a corpse had sprung to life and walked into his office, and then he shot to his feet, threw the cigarette into his Scotch, and threw the Scotch into a waste bin under his desk.

'Sir. This is a ... surprise.'

'Not an unpleasant one, I trust,' said Shukla briskly, walking to a seat and dropping into it. He nodded at Persis. 'I hope you're well, Inspector. I had hoped to catch you here. My understanding is that your investigation has recently taken you out of the city. Perhaps you might enlighten me as to your progress?'

Her shoulders straightened.

Shukla, a small man with the sleepy-eyed charm of a Buddhist monk, and a reputation for civility matched only by his reputation for shooting dead the careers of those who displeased him, had always struck her as one of the new breed of senior Indian officials who revelled in keeping their underlings off-balance. Perhaps that marked an important difference between the current administration and the British. The British ruled with the iron certainty of self-belief. They had no need to play games.

Quickly, she brought the ADC up to speed, detailing her findings in Dehra Dun, and the links between the three murders she'd been tasked to investigate.

Shukla listened without interrupting.

When she'd finished, he ran a finger over his upper lip and stared off into the distance. Finally, he spoke. 'So your contention is that our Ice Man is a disgraced British civilian who, for reasons you have not yet uncovered, was sent to a POW camp in Dehra Dun, subsequently escaped, and was then murdered by his fellow escapees?'

'Yes, sir.'

'The remaining men, again for reasons unknown, returned to India years later. And now one them has taken it upon himself to murder the others, all in pursuit of scraps of paper harbouring a coded message that you cannot decipher?'

'Yes, sir.'

'A message that you have now lost.'

She stiffened, flushing. The idea of appearing incompetent in Shukla's eyes distressed her in a way she would have found hard to put into words.

He continued to examine her, then looked at Seth. 'I suppose you can imagine the reaction should such a story become public?'

Seth's head creaked forward. In Shukla's presence, he appeared to have all the animation of a taxidermist's dummy.

The senior officer sprang to his feet. 'Inspector, from this moment on, nothing is to be released into the public domain without my express approval. Is that clear?'

She blinked. 'I don't understand.'

'It is time to bring this matter to a conclusion. As far as the world needs to know, we have identified the Ice Man. An unfortunate British civilian who ventured into the Himalayas and perished there. Details of his time at the POW camp are irrelevant.'

She stifled the urge to shout. 'We can't keep something like that hidden. It will come out eventually.'

'We'll deal with that eventuality when it arises. Don't underestimate the power of denial, Persis. I'm certain the army will back my judgement in this respect.'

'What about the murders of Stephen Renzi and Peter Grunewald?'

'Completely unrelated.'

She gaped at him. 'But, sir, that's— that's not the *truth*.'

His mouth stretched into the thinnest of smiles. 'Come now, Persis, we've discussed the nature of truth before. Wasn't it Gandhi who said that truth will stand even in the absence of support? Be content that you've discovered a *version* of the truth.'

'Are you saying I should let the killer get away with it?' Her voice had risen; she couldn't hold herself back.

Shukla's gaze hardened. 'You said it yourself. There were four escapees and now three are dead. There is no one left for your murderer to pursue. He has what he wanted and much good may it do him.'

'And who will answer for the dead?' She was almost shouting now. 'What will I say to Pramod Sinha when he asks about his daughter's killer?'

'I suggest you leave Sinha to me.'

She threw a helpless look at Seth, who drew his chin into his neck and retreated into a passable imitation of a lamp post.

Shukla paused at the door. 'The most expedient course of action isn't always the most palatable. Be patient. Persevere.'

As the door closed behind him, Seth flopped bonelessly into his seat. 'That man—' He stopped, passed a hand over his eyes, and reached for the packet of cigarettes in his breast pocket. 'I suppose it's too much to expect that you can see the sense in what he says? Let sleeping dogs lie, Persis. They have a nasty habit of biting both of us in the rear.'

Back at her desk, she sat in front of her typewriter, jaw working in fury.

Birla wandered over. 'I'm guessing from your expression that Shukla had nothing good to say.'

She recounted her conversation with Seth and the ADC.

'I don't see the problem,' he remarked. 'Shukla has basically given us licence to drop all three cases.'

She glared at him. Birla weathered her irritation nonchalantly, chewing on a rod of sugarcane, the juice dribbling down his chin and on to his collar.

After he'd wandered away, she spent a moment considering her next course of action.

Regardless of Shukla's edict, she wasn't about to abandon her investigation. Perhaps, on some level, he knew that, had anticipated it. She wouldn't put it past him.

The man was as Machiavellian as any politician, and in the new India that was saying something.

If nothing else, there was the simple fact that Ismail Siraj, the Renzis' security guard, was still imprisoned, accused of murder. Should she stop now, there was little doubt that he would be convicted of the crime.

She picked up the phone and dialled Augustus Silva.

'Persis, I'm just heading off to a lecture ... I'm afraid I haven't made much headway with your deceased friends. They're proving as hard to trace as I'd suspected.'

'I may be able to shed some light,' she said.

She gave him Renzi and Grunewald's real names, adding the names of Bernard McNally and Udo Kessler, and the scant details she had of the time the four men had spent together at the Dehra Dun POW camp.

She heard him whistle down the line. 'That's quite a story. Well, it explains why I haven't met with much success. If Stuhlmacher, Kessler and McNally are civilians, they're a little outside of my purview. I'll try again, but I wouldn't hold my breath.'

She set down the phone, then left her seat to visit the washroom on the ground floor.

As she was finishing up, bent over the sink, two young women entered, chattering loudly. They spotted her and the chatter died. They eyed her warily, as if they'd come face to face with a tiger. She pegged them as secretaries, of the kind the corporation seemed to employ by the dozen, as if there was a factory somewhere churning out young Indian women, dressed as Europeans, sharp-witted and keen to embrace the opportunities presented by the new India.

What did they make of her, a police*woman*, wandering around their building in her khaki uniform? She had never thought of herself as an inspiration to others, and the truth was that few women considered her as such. Conditioned by millennia of patriarchy, she was often painted as an evil influence, corrupting a generation of demure daughters-in-law.

These two were making their way in the world; in their own small way, they too were forging a path that others might follow. The battle with India's colonisers was over, but the battle for women to take their place in the new society Nehru was fashioning was just beginning.

One day a trickle, the next a flood.

She nodded at the two girls – who nodded back – and left the bathroom.

Back in the office, she pulled forward her typewriter, and settled down to work.

She heard Seth's door open and close behind her.

Moments later, she sensed a shadow hovering at her shoulder.

She turned, expecting to see the SP, and instead found herself looking up at Seema Desai.

The girl's expression was drawn.

'Seema. What are you doing here?'

'Superintendent Seth asked to see me. He—' She paused, then plunged on. 'He has dismissed me from the mentee programme.'

The girl was on the verge of tears, holding herself together by sheer force of will.

Persis stood. 'Wait here.'

She charged into Seth's office like the German tanks entering Czechoslovakia. 'You can't dismiss her.'

Seth looked at her calmly. 'Why not? You told me yourself you have no time for her.'

She hesitated. 'I was wrong.'

'Is that why you tasked her to follow a civilian around?'

The air went out of her lungs.

'What were you thinking, Persis? Have you any idea how much trouble you could have landed us both in if that woman had lodged a complaint?'

'You can't blame Seema for my actions.'

Seth stood slowly, and glared at her. 'When are you going to realise that rashness has its consequences? You caused this and you'll have to live with it.'

Back in the office, she discovered that the girl had left.

She turned on Birla. 'Why did you let her go?'

He shrugged. 'What did you want me to do? Tie her to a chair?'

She fell into her seat, upset in a way she would not have thought possible just days earlier. Strange feelings swam around her stomach.

Guilt. Distress.

Yet, it *wasn't* her fault.

Perhaps if she repeated that enough times, it would become the truth, or at least a lie she could live with.

45

The Bombay Secretariat, a four-hundred-foot-long building designed in the Venetian Gothic style, with a façade of arcaded verandas in Porbander stone and a tower as imposing as the top hat of an Englishman out on the town, stood a short ten-minute walk from her father's bookshop, on the eastern side of the Oval Maidan.

The Secretariat had sprung up, like many of its sister buildings of colonial enterprise, as a direct result of Bombay's burgeoning maritime trade in the latter half of the nineteenth century, a trade that had transformed the city into the 'gateway to India'. The striking edifice had been built to house the seat of administration for the Bombay Presidency – the Bombay arm of that monolith bureaucracy once known as the Imperial Civil Service, then the Indian Civil Service, and now, under Nehru, as the Indian Administrative Service.

Persis arrived at the building with her emotions still churning.

Seth's dismissal of Seema Desai weighed on her mind. Guilt sucked at her feet, threatening to drag her into the murk.

In the end, she'd retreated back to her investigation. The simplicity of pursuing a case invariably returned her to her sense of mission. It was why she'd always chosen to follow her own light, never beholden to anyone, never needing anyone.

She'd come to the Secretariat in pursuit of an earlier thought.

Andrew Cox had told her that Bernard McNally had been a civil servant and that he'd been transferred to the Dehra Dun

POW camp from Bombay. If that was the case, then the chances were that he'd worked for the Bombay arm of the Indian Civil Service, and that meant a record of his employment would exist at the Secretariat.

At least, that was her theory.

Experience told her that nothing was straightforward where the ICS was concerned.

Stalin had once mused as to how so few Britishers had managed to rule a country of three hundred million. The answer was not in force of arms or even the machinations of *divide et impera*. It was the dead hand clutched at the throat of every native via the Indian Civil Service that had brought the country to heel. With forms required in triplicate for matters as simple as recording the death of a water buffalo, was it any wonder that generations of bewildered Indians had found themselves entrapped by the so-called steel frame underpinning Britain's colonial enterprise?

She entered the cool of the old building.

On all sides, suited and booted Indians in buttoned-down collars and ties scurried along, the inheritors of empire, glancing importantly at watches and swinging leather satchels like miniature wrecking balls.

No one paid her a second glance.

She made her way to the reception counter, a monolithic slab of Italian marble that could have doubled as a runway for light aircraft, and spoke tersely to one of the women sat behind it, whose expression of helpful receptivity quickly vanished.

A phone was picked up and a call made.

On the first floor, past the Council Hall and Committee Rooms, she located the offices of the Revenue Department. Enquiries led her to the door of the head of the department, whose dominion was heralded by a brass plaque engraved with the name Ajay Chatterjee.

Inside the office, she discovered a short, slender individual in wire-framed spectacles sat behind an imposing desk of Bombay blackwood like a child perched on a high chair. There was something similarly childlike about his round, smoothly shaven face, a sense of gleeful bewilderment, perhaps, at the lofty position he found himself in.

He would not be alone.

For the greater part of its existence, the Indian Civil Service had been run by white men, Oxbridge alumni lured to the subcontinent and its manifest perils with outrageous salaries and the heady promise of power. The natives had been relegated to the lowest ranks, little better than pen-pushing coolies. But with the advent of independence, the majority of Brits had departed, leaving a void quickly filled by those already barnacled to the system.

Chatterjee's dress was immaculate – a white shirt, tie, and herringbone trousers. He'd eschewed the jacket, and rolled up his sleeves. A plate of rasgullahs sat on the desk, next to regimented piles of paper and string-bound folders.

A ceiling fan stirred the dead air, doing little to alleviate the heat.

He waved her into a seat. 'Inspector, your query is a curious one. May I ask why you happen to be interested in this man?'

She debated with herself how far to trust him, and then decided that it would be only a matter of time before McNally's identity was released to the newspapers by ADC Shukla.

Quickly, she explained.

'The Ice Man!' Chatterjee was practically bouncing on his seat. 'To think, he may have been an ICS man! Of course, we shall be delighted to assist.'

*　　*　　*

It took over an hour for the relevant paperwork to be dug up and delivered to Chatterjee's office, an hour that she passed by taking lunch with the man – at his invitation – in the Secretariat's lavishly appointed retiring rooms.

She discovered, contrary to her initial impression, that far from the 'pink chitty Napoleon' she had supposed, Chatterjee was an astute man, and – all things considered – a charming one.

'They say we're gumming up the works with our "licence Raj",' said Chatterjee, picking at a grilled hilsa, 'but the truth is that running a nation as large and as divided as India would be impossible without a framework of rules. The British knew it. Just because they've left, it doesn't mean we should allow ourselves to descend into anarchy.'

'I'm not sure my father would agree. He thinks the ICS is run by babus, aping their former British masters, and pining for a country they've never seen. No offence intended.'

'None taken. It's true that I studied at Wren's and Oxford. In many respects, my outlook might be considered more British than Indian. But the blood in my veins is as Indian as yours. I participated in the revolution. I marched in the streets. One doesn't have to wear a dhoti and spin cotton to prove one's love for one's country.'

Back in his office, Chatterjee scanned through the files on his desk, and then gave her a summary.

'Your guess was correct. Bernard McNally did work for the ICS. His personnel file states that he came out to India in 1930 at the age of twenty-two. He was employed by the ICS in the Bombay Presidency's Revenue Office and swiftly rose to the position of Additional Collector. Remember, the bulk of British revenue was generated through taxation, primarily land revenues. But anything that *could* be taxed was taxed. Given the chance, the

British would have taxed the last breath out of a donkey.' He gave a small smile, more a grimace. 'It was the job of the District Collector – and his officers – to ensure the smooth flow of such revenue.

'In January 1943, McNally was deputed to the Deccan States Agency, the arm of the Bombay Presidency that controlled relations with various princely states in the region. He was sent out to the wealthiest of those states, the Kingdom of Badlapore. He was there for some six months, and then something happened. He was arrested, tried behind closed doors, and sent north to Dehra Dun.'

She stared at him. 'What did he do?'

He pulled off his spectacles and rubbed the lenses with a handkerchief. 'That's just it. It doesn't say. Or rather, the report has been redacted. Here, see for yourself.'

She took the file and scanned the report, or what little of it was visible between the blacked-out paragraphs.

Chatterjee had not exaggerated.

McNally had been arrested in July 1943. No details of the reason for his arrest and subsequent trial were left discernible in the report.

A month later, he'd been transferred to the Dehra Dun POW camp.

Incredible.

What could the man have done to have occasioned such a veil of secrecy? More importantly, how difficult would it be for her to pierce that veil?

Chatterjee took her silence as an invitation to conjecture. 'I suspect he was discovered to have stuck his hand in the till.'

'Why would he do that? I thought ICS officers were well rewarded – the British ones, at any rate.'

He smiled. 'The life of a middle-ranking ICS officer consigned to the sticks isn't as glamorous as the legends would have you believe. Men like McNally weren't riding around the countryside shooting tigers and settling land disputes for grateful locals like latter-day King Solomons. It was a hard life. And with the arrival of the Quit India movement, it often became a dangerous one. In spite of Gandhi's best intentions, more than one ICS officer met a violent end out in the hinterlands.' He stopped to replace his spectacles, pushing them up the bridge of his nose. 'Contrary to popular opinion, the ICS has always maintained rigid standards of integrity. The men of the service have traditionally been considered impossible to bribe. It's one of the earliest lessons inculcated in us.'

'So if McNally *had* taken a bribe it might have brought the ICS into disrepute?'

'Quite possibly. Remember, a war was on, and the British were currying favour with an increasingly antagonistic Indian legislature, endeavouring to raise troops and revenue. Corruption among senior ICS officers might jeopardise the smooth flow of men and funds. They couldn't afford a scandal.'

The explanation made sense. But without the facts, it did little to help progress her own investigations into the murders of McNally, Stuhlmacher, and Orelli.

She returned to scanning the file. A detail caught her eye. 'It states here that McNally was married.' She recalled now the note in McNally's journal about getting it to his wife in the event of his death.

He lifted a finger, bidding her wait, then scrambled through the other files. 'Here. McNally married in Bombay. To one of those women who came out as part of the fishing fleet – that's what we used to call British women who came to India to seek ICS husbands. The old joke was that men like McNally were worth a thousand pounds, dead or alive – because of their enormous pensions.'

She took the file and scanned it.

McNally had been married to a woman named Catherine Huthwaite, the ceremony conducted at Bombay Cathedral on the 16th of August 1935. There was no indication as to how Huthwaite had fared after McNally's arrest.

A Bombay address for the couple was in the file, as well as a permanent address in the county of Cornwall in England.

Persis transferred the details to her notebook, thanked Chatterjee, and left.

46

Back at Malabar House, she picked up the phone, dialled the switchboard and asked to be connected to the McNallys' Bombay address. An Indian voice greeted her, and moments later informed her that no one by the name of Catherine Huthwaite had been resident at that address for at least five years.

She returned to the switchboard and asked for a trunk call to be made to the McNally residence in England.

Minutes later, she heard the tinny sound of a ringing phone.

'Hello?' A female voice. English.

'Am I speaking with Catherine Huthwaite?'

A pause. 'It's Kitty, not Catherine . . . Who is this?'

'My name is Inspector Persis Wadia. I work for the Indian Police Service in Bombay. I have some news about your husband.'

An intake of breath. 'You've found him, haven't you?'

'I'm afraid so.'

Quickly, she explained the circumstances of her call.

Her words fell into a hollow silence, and then she heard the sound of weeping.

'Madam?'

The silence stretched until finally Huthwaite spoke. 'I suppose I knew in my heart that he was gone. It's been so long since I've had any contact with him. If he'd been alive he'd have found a way to get in touch.'

'When *was* the last time you were in contact with him?'

'Just after his trial. They allowed us to meet before they took him away. He warned me they might not allow him to send or receive mail. But he said he'd find a way to get in touch once it was safe to do so.'

'I've read his file. It's been heavily redacted. What exactly was your husband convicted of?'

'That's just it. I don't know. He refused to tell me. Said that he didn't want me in their cross hairs.'

'Their?'

'His superiors. The people behind his arrest.'

'You must have some idea?'

Huthwaite sighed. A dog barked in the background. 'Look. The truth is that I've built a new life. I tried to wait for him, but after six months without contact, I spoke to my parents and moved back to England. I was pregnant, you see. The prospect of trying to raise a child out there, on my own . . . I couldn't face it. And so I came back. It was the right decision. For me and for my son.' She hesitated. 'I've met someone. We've been together a while now. We couldn't marry because I didn't know where Bernie was, whether he was dead or alive. I couldn't ask for a divorce. I suppose it's redundant now.'

Persis imagined the woman slowly coming to terms with the situation, the bad news and the good. True love was a myth. Nothing lasted for ever, not even promises of everlasting adoration.

'Bernie told me they'd accused him of collaborating with the enemy. The Germans, I mean. He told me it was nonsense, but by then I didn't know what to believe. He said they wanted something from him and he wouldn't cooperate. Sending him to Dehra Dun was their way of intimidating him. But they didn't know Bernie. He was as stubborn as the devil. He told me that even if he gave them what they wanted, they'd destroy him anyway.'

'How can you be certain there was nothing to the accusation?'

She bristled. 'Whatever his faults, my husband was no traitor. He didn't much care for the war, but he wasn't a collaborator or a spy.'

'Is there anything you *can* tell me, anything about his behaviour in those last months?'

Seconds ticked away. 'Something happened out in Badlapore. Bernie hated the posting, but the DC left him with no choice. The District Collector, I mean. Bernie's immediate superior. A month into his time out there, something changed. I don't know how to describe it. He was filled with a sudden *excitement*. You have to understand, my husband was an intemperate man. An unhappy cynic. He felt hard done by. He'd been passed over for promotion, felt slighted by his colleagues. They made fun of the fact that he wasn't an Oxbridge man. Not a *gentleman*.' She spat the word. 'Whatever he'd achieved, he'd achieved off his own back. But he told me they'd never let him go higher than Additional Collector, always answerable to some inbred fool from the Home Counties a decade his junior. It left him with a chip on his shoulder the size of Wales.'

'What was he doing in Badlapore?'

'His job. Administering the collection of land revenue, tax revenue, resolving property matters, inspecting district offices.'

'Did you go with him?'

'No. I can't stand the interior. I'd had a bout of dengue fever the year before and we both agreed it would be better for me to stay in Bombay. Besides, I had a job of my own. I was teaching English at the Sophia College. Unlike a lot of the ICS wives, I've never been the type to sit at home twiddling my thumbs or throwing kitty parties.

'Bernie would visit every weekend. Badlapore is only a five-hour drive from the city.' She hesitated. 'There *was* one thing ... That last month before his arrest, he spent a lot of time visiting the ASI. The Archaeological Survey of India office, here in Bombay. Almost every weekend. He told me it was something to do with his work in Badlapore, but he was hazy on the details. I don't know if it's relevant, but there was something about the way he spoke that now seems to me to be at one with that strange change in his demeanour. Or it could just be my imagination.'

Persis noted down the details of a man Huthwaite remembered her husband mentioning at the ASI, then asked, 'A notebook was found on your husband's person. In it, he indicated that it should be returned to you. There were several pages with coded messages. Does that mean anything to you?'

'No.'

'There was also a statement. *Caesar's Triumph holds the key.*'

A choking sound. 'Caesar,' she repeated. 'That was the nickname his colleagues at the ICS gave him. It was meant to be unkind. They didn't like the fact that Bernie would gripe about how he was due more from the service, how the Indians should treat him with more respect than they did, how they should pay their dues to the empire without complaint.'

'I don't see the relevance.'

'Render unto Caesar that which is Caesar's.'

Persis understood. The quote attributed to Jesus in the New Testament. *Render unto Caesar that which is Caesar's, and unto God that which is God's.* Meaning that Christians of the time should submit to earthly authorities – namely, the Roman Empire – when obliged to do so, but save their soul and devotion for God.

Many Englishman had thought the same way about India.

'Does the sentence mean anything to you?'

'No. But then, very little of what Bernie was doing by the end made any sense to me.'

47

Having put down the phone, she picked it up again and asked to be put through to the Archaeological Survey of India, Bombay Circle.

Here she tracked down the man Kitty Huthwaite had suggested her husband had met with prior to his arrest, a Professor William Meadows. She was told by Meadow's secretary that the professor was unavailable, presently working on a site on Elephanta Island, and not expected to return to the mainland until the following day.

As she set the receiver back in its cradle, Oberoi wandered in, threw her a poisonous glance, then spent the next thirty minutes making calls at his desk, his voice uncharacteristically hushed.

She strained to hear what he was saying, but could make out little.

And then, just as abruptly as he had arrived, he set down the phone and scraped back his chair. He approached, looming over her desk. 'I've spoken with a judge of my acquaintance. A date for Siraj to appear in court will be expedited.'

Before she could reply, he turned and stalked out of the office.

She breathed a sigh of relief. She was in no mood for another sparring session.

Birla turned up, plucking at his collar, sweat shimmering on his forehead.

She brought him up to speed, then asked him to go to the Arthur Road Jail to check on Siraj. With Oberoi doing his damnedest to see the man convicted, she was concerned for his welfare.

After Birla had left, muttering under his breath, she found herself returning to the conversation with Kitty Huthwaite.

Bernard McNally had been sent out to the princely state of Badlapore in early 1943. In his capacity as Additional Collector, he had been one of the men responsible for ensuring the smooth flow of revenue from the state. But then something had happened there that had caused a change in him, a change significant enough for his wife to notice.

He'd also begun liaising with a senior man at the Archaeological Survey of India. Why?

And then, out of the blue, he'd been arrested for conspiring with the enemy.

McNally's wife claimed the arrest and trial had been a sham, designed to apply pressure on her husband. But to what end?

Impatience gnawed at her, until finally, she stood up, grabbed her cap and made for the door.

Sometimes, the illusion of forward momentum was as important as the destination.

48

Elephanta Island: a lonely stub of tide-tormented rock lying ten kilometres out in the city's harbour, dominated by undulating hills covered in fragrant swathes of mango and tamarind trees. Named by the Portuguese for a colossal stone elephant found there in the early sixteenth century, the island had gained international fame for the enigmatic cave temples cut into its hills.

It had been years since she had last ventured here. The previous occasion had been with Sam, a birthday outing. It wasn't the easiest place to get to for a man in a wheelchair.

The thought brought with it a savage memory: Sam barking at the bemused boat crew like a rampant Captain Bligh.

The journey took just over an hour.

She'd been forced to board one of the tourist launches that clogged the jetty at the Gateway of India monument. A rate card set out the costs for the transportation of various animals to the island: five rupees for a donkey; ten rupees for a bullock.

She wondered how much the rate was for a policewoman.

Leaning over the starboard railing, placing as much distance between herself and the clutch of daytime romantics, tourists, and caterwauling families as she could without actually leaping into the sea, she watched the late afternoon sun shimmer on the bottle-green water as the mainland dwindled away.

They landed at the island's western jetty.

Enquiries with a local tour guide led her to the island's

principal cave temple complex, where she discovered an archaeological team hard at work, supervised by a balding white man with
a pipe clamped between his jaws and saddle stains of sweat under
the arms of his beige-coloured cotton shirt. The gentleman was
directing a young Indian perched on a bamboo scaffold as he
worked on a twenty-foot-high bust of Shiva, a Trimurti, Shiva
depicted with three heads, representing his traditional roles of
destroyer, preserver, and creator.

A lantern swung by the native's elbow as he patiently ministered to a crumbling spot beside one of Lord Shiva's ears.

'Professor Meadows?'

He turned to squint at her in the gloom.

She introduced herself and explained her mission.

He plucked the pipe from his mouth. 'As you can see, I'm a
little preoccupied.' He pointed the pipe at the colossal statue. 'The
Portuguese used them for target practice. The British ignored
them. And now your government has seen fit to allow tourists to
tramp through here without the slightest regard.'

'It won't take long,' she persisted. 'I've come a long way.'

He pouted, then said, 'Carry on, Rahul. I'll be back soon.'

They stepped out into the sun. 'Let's walk up the hill,' he
suggested. 'I need to stretch my legs.'

They talked as they climbed.

'What can you tell me about Bernard McNally?'

'An odd sort of fellow,' replied Meadows. 'I've never had much
time for ICS men. Puffed-up martinets, for the most part.
McNally came to me back in, oh, spring of '43, I should think.
He'd been sent out to Badlapore. He'd taken an interest in the
temples out there, and wanted to know a little about them.'

'Was this in his official capacity?'

'Yes and no. Temple revenue was indirectly taxable during
the Raj. I say indirectly because the initial British policy on the

subcontinent was largely one of non-interference in native religious affairs. They were loath to get the plebs riled up, and the easiest way to do that was to encroach upon their relationship with their gods. And the interlocutors in that relationship were the temples and their priests.

'Of course, with such a steady stream of cash finding its way into temple coffers, it was only a matter of time. A Pilgrim Tax became a short-lived experiment in several states. Following that, various Religious Endowment Acts have, ostensibly, empowered the temples to manage their own revenue. The fine print, however, allows for trustees and agents to aid in that management. That's where men like McNally came in. The District Collectors and their officers invariably promoted themselves to local temples as agents or trustees, thus ensuring that the British government took its pound of flesh. A tithe by any other name …' He grimaced. 'Having said that, I think McNally was cut from a different cloth. I think he became genuinely interested in the history of these magnificent edifices. In that respect, he was no different from me, I suppose. It gets under your skin, the idea that Indians were out here fashioning these incredible monuments thousands of years before Christ showed up. It's the reason I stayed on after the last trump sounded on the Raj. My life's work is out here, not back in some dusty office in London.'

They'd reached the top of the hill.

Perched there were two seventeenth-century cannons, each mounted on a circular iron dais. On one side of the cannons, the hill fell away sharply from a stone ledge.

'Was there anything specifically that McNally wanted to know?'

'He was intrigued by the temple relics he was cataloguing – part of his role was to log all temple assets in the state. He told me he'd carried out a similar role during his stint in Bombay. It's one of the reasons they sent him out to Badlapore. He'd spent quite a bit of time just before his posting looking at the old temples around the Banganga Tank. Do you know the ones I mean?'

She nodded. The tank was an ancient feature of the city, not far from the Malabar House station. An eight-hundred-year-old rectangular pool, fed by an underground spring, around which several temples had accreted.

'At any rate, some of the relics he was examining in Badlapore sounded incredible. He kept promising to take me down there, but we never got around to arranging it. And then it was too late. He vanished. It was most strange.'

She considered his words.

What could McNally's interest in Badlapore's temples possibly have to do with his arrest and confinement to a POW camp in Dehra Dun?

A brace of langurs shrieked in a tree overhanging the twin cannons.

She was struck by a sudden clarity of thought.

The only way to find the answers to her questions was to retrace McNally's footsteps.

She would have to go to Badlapore.

49

It was past seven when she arrived back at Malabar House.

A note in Birla's untidy scrawl informed her that Ismail Siraj was faring as well as could be expected at the Arthur Road Jail. As a postscript, he'd noted that a call had come in from Augustus Silva.

The military historian had requested that she call him back at his office.

He picked up almost immediately.

'What have you got for me?'

'I'm afraid I've found no trace of any of your missing escapees. After their flight from Dehra Dun, they seem to have kept their heads down, until resurfacing in Bombay. The military authorities may well have tried to locate them, but to no avail.'

Disappointment churned inside her, but she'd expected as much.

She thanked Silva for his efforts, and set down the phone.

Getting to her feet, she walked the short distance to Seth's office. The SP usually worked late – if work is what you could call a day spent drinking, smoking, and reflecting bitterly on the past.

'Come.'

Inside, she found him – to her surprise – reading. He'd picked up one of the books on ancient Rome she'd brought in when trying to unravel the line about Caesar in McNally's notebook.

'Did you know that Seneca was compelled to commit suicide by Nero?' He peered at her over the top of his spectacles. 'I suspect such a fate awaits me one day . . . You have something to tell me.'

She summarised everything she'd discovered, finishing with her desire to travel to Badlapore.

He set down the book. 'Shukla called. He plans to announce the Ice Man's identity in the next forty-eight hours. A press conference at which the commissioner will also be present.'

'Will he be telling the world that McNally was a suspected collaborator who went missing from a POW camp in Dehra Dun?'

'No. What he *will* be doing is drawing a line under the investigation.'

'And the murders of Stephen Renzi and Peter Grunewald? How does he plan to brush those under the carpet?'

'He doesn't. They're separate investigations. McNally died years ago. The link between him and the others is irrelevant.'

'He didn't die. He was murdered. And now his killer is loose in the city. I think it's Udo Kessler.'

He sighed. 'Why would Kessler – assuming he's even in Bombay – suddenly decide to go on a killing spree?'

'Isn't it obvious? The finding of McNally's body has triggered him.'

'Yes, but why?'

She grasped for an answer, but the truth was that this was one of the many unanswered questions still plaguing the investigation. 'I think it's tied up with the pages they ripped out of McNally's notebook. There's something we don't know yet, something that ties everything together.'

'And you think you can find the answer in Badlapore?'

'I think it's worth a shot.'

He rubbed his chin. 'Fine. When were you planning on going?'

'I'll leave in the morning.'

'On your own?'

'Who else do you suggest I take?'

He considered this. 'Technically, the Renzi case is still Oberoi's—' He raised a hand to stifle her protest. 'Fine. Fine. Birla and Haq, on the other hand, are tied up.'

She frowned. 'What could be more important than this?'

'It may surprise you to learn that this office does not revolve around you. There are other cases that require attention.' He tapped a finger on the desk. 'Perhaps you could ask that friend of yours? The Englishman.'

A warmth rose to her cheeks. 'No.'

He stared at her. 'Fine. Well, if you go up there alone, be careful. Badlapore isn't Bombay. They have some antiquated thoughts about women in positions of authority.'

She slid the jeep to a halt at the top of a narrow alley. A pair of beggars chatting by a handcart laid out with dried pomfret turned to stare at her. She saw that one of them was a leper, a rag tied around his hand, his eyes the milky-white of the partially blind.

She walked past them, into the alley, gradually working her way through the maze of shanty dwellings. Every so often, she would stop and ask directions. There were no road signs here, no markers. The slum, like many in Bombay, hovered in that strange limbo between transient and semi-permanent, too established for the government to simply bulldoze away, yet lacking the legitimacy to enjoy any sense of security.

She'd heard it said that Bombay made men feel small, but that didn't seem to stop them from pouring in in their multitudes.

Flies to the dung-heap, as her father had drily put it.

She found herself outside a low door cut from a sheet of corrugated tin. She hesitated, then rapped on it, the sound echoing loudly along the alley.

Moments later, the door swung back.

Seema Desai stood there, looking out curiously, before astonishment took hold.

'May I come in?'

The girl blinked in the gloom, then nodded and stepped aside.

It was as small as Persis had supposed – a bare room, the walls painted sky blue, with a single cot, on which lay a stick-thin old woman, asleep. Beside the bed was a short steel almirah, atop it a selection of idols – she recognised blue-skinned Krishna and elephant-headed Ganesha – and a lit diya. One corner was given over to a kitchen: a stove, a floor mat, shelves lined with a selection of steel pots and pans.

On the other side of the room: a round-topped wooden table and a single chair. A young girl – pigtailed, no more than six or seven – sat there writing in a schoolbook.

She looked up at Persis with round eyes.

'My sister, Geeta,' said Seema, waving at the girl. She pointed at the bed. 'My mother.'

'I need to talk to you.'

They stepped back out into the night. A hurricane lamp hung from the side of the kutcha house across the alley, moths roiling around it. A man stood a few doors down, smoking a bidi.

'Why are you here?' A suppressed anger, barely concealed.

'I'm travelling to a place called Badlapore tomorrow, in pursuit of an investigation. Would you like to accompany me?'

The girl stared at her in astonishment.

Persis said nothing.

Finally, Seema breathed in. 'Is this your way of making amends? If so, it's too late.'

Persis glanced at her sharply. But the girl was not easily cowed. Persis spoke stiffly. 'I thought you'd appreciate a second chance.'

'Is it me or you who needs the second chance?'

A radio blared in the sudden silence. She slipped her cap back on. 'Fine.' She began to walk away.

'What time are you leaving?'

She turned back. 'Seven a.m.'

'I'll be ready.'

50

Leaving Bombay for the second time in the space of a few days, she was acutely aware of the feeling of fleeing a battlefield, one where the terrain marked the vagaries of her own emotions.

She'd spent another night at Jaya's, simultaneously fretting over and annoyed at her father. Not only had Sam failed to call, but his intransigence in refusing to send an emissary in the form of Aziz or even Nussie had struck her as particularly truculent.

She'd telephoned her aunt, who had reassured her that she'd spoken to Sam and informed him of his daughter's whereabouts. The man had simply grunted and put down the phone.

And then there was Archie Blackfinch.

She'd been glad of his intervention in Dehra Dun, glad of his company, but his continued presence served only to scramble her internal compass. The wretchedness of their situation made it difficult to concentrate on anything else.

In Dehra Dun, he'd told her that he loved her. But if that were truly so, why had he stepped out with Jane Davenport? Were all men thus? If the object of their infatuation failed to reciprocate immediately, they simply picked the next horse in the stable?

It was grotesque, as was her own thrashing anguish every time she thought of him.

She picked up Seema at the agreed time.

Smartly dressed in an embroidered white kurta and navy slacks, the girl had folded herself into the jeep with barely a word. The awkwardness of their silence had persisted until they were an hour out of the city, and stopped at a roadside dhaba to eat a hurried breakfast.

They'd attracted a great deal of attention at the eatery, sitting in the sun on rope charpoys as omelettes and parathas sizzled on the griddle, a row of crows eyeing them beadily from the branches of a gnarled banyan. A group of boisterous truck drivers in dusty turbans joked among themselves on a nearby charpoy, occasionally glancing at Persis's uniform with undisguised curiosity.

She was glad that she'd chosen to wear it.

The undercurrent of hostility was unmistakable.

A man poured chai into steel cups and set them down on a rickety wooden table.

'Why did you really ask me to come with you?'

The sudden question, after such a long silence, caught her off guard.

She bought herself a few seconds by sipping at her tea. 'What is it that you want to hear?'

'Some acknowledgement that the way you treated me was . . . wrong.'

'And what good would that do you?'

The girl gave her a belligerent look, then raised her own tea to her lips.

'You introduced your mother and a sister,' Persis continued. 'Where's your father?'

'He left us a few years ago. We haven't seen him since.' Another silence. 'Who is in *your* family?'

She felt strangely uncomfortable answering the question. 'Just me and Sam – my father. My mother passed when I was a child.'

'And the woman you sent me to follow?'

'She – she's someone my father has met recently.'

'He's going to marry her?' The girl was sharp.

'Yes.'

'And you don't like it.'

She hesitated. 'I don't know. I just— I wasn't prepared for it. I suppose I'll get used to the idea. In time.'

Seema said nothing and they ate in silence for a while, the clatter of the dhaba rising and falling around them.

'This case that you're investigating in Badlapore . . .?'

Persis outlined the contours of her investigation, beginning with the Ice Man, and leaving out details she felt the girl had no need to know.

'Isn't it strange?' Seema said. 'The English always seemed so obvious when they were here. And now this man leaves behind a mystery that has intrigued the nation.'

Persis stared at her, but the girl simply sipped at her tea, the mid-morning sun flashing from her spectacles.

They crossed into Badlapore just before noon.

Persis mentally reviewed the little she'd learned about the region.

Prior to independence, the Deccan States Agency had overseen some forty princely states and *jageers* – feudal vassal states – to the east of Bombay, with Badlapore being the largest. Though barely eight thousand square kilometres in size, the state had enjoyed a long history of relative prosperity, inevitably attracting the interest of the East India Company. A short-lived rebellion in the mid-nineteenth century had been brutally put down, and a docile regent installed, handled by a political agent at court whose ruthlessness had been matched only by his avarice.

In due course, Badlapore had been awarded the status of *salute state* and granted the privilege of a nineteen-gun-salute protocol for its rulers, a succession of Hindu Maratha maharajas of a dynasty that had survived the Mughal empire and would go on to survive the Raj.

In the last decades of the colonial era, Badlapore had joined the Chamber of Princes, a forum instituted by King-Emperor George V to permit the rulers of India's princely states the illusion of a voice in their own governance, and the even greater illusion of national unity among the noble classes.

She recalled her father's scathing assessment of the Chamber. 'The princes have barely a brain between them. Their only concern is that we don't set our sights on *their* fiefdoms after we've evicted the British. You can accuse the British of divide and rule, but the truth is we were divided long before the white man showed up. Noble against peasant. High caste against low. And the ringleaders of this circus: our benighted princes.'

Following independence, Badlapore had ceded to the Dominion of India, retaining a titular monarch, the maharaja Shivaji Rajaram, a twenty-four-year-old with a reputation for wild parties and fast cars, several of which he had wrapped around lamp posts dotted around the state. That he had survived relatively unscathed only reinforced the long-held belief of the local citizenry that an element of divinity tempered the royal bloodline.

The population of the state numbered half a million, with some fifty thousand residents in the state capital, the town of Vijaynagar. It was here that Bernard McNally had been based during his time as the region's Additional Collector.

51

The offices of the District Collector hadn't changed with the changing of the guard. The building – a sprawling red-brick structure fronted by an arched gateway that resembled the entrance to a fort – exuded a faded imperial grandeur, as if pining for days of old.

A cow squatted in front of the entrance, the guards at the gate making no effort to move it along.

Persis navigated her way around the animal, and presented herself to the two somnolent sentries. The pair looked at each other as if she'd tasked them to work out the meaning of life, then ushered her vehicle through, unwilling to tangle with such an exotic creature as a woman in uniform.

She drove into a dusty courtyard from the centre of which sprouted a round ornamental flower bed, sporting only the burned tops of dried grass. Sliding the jeep in between several other vehicles, she disembarked, then, with Seema trailing behind, made her way into the building.

A short while later they were ushered into the office of the Additional Collector for the region, a man named Kishore Ambekar.

Avuncular, with a round, sagging face, tired eyes, and a peppery moustache, Ambekar listened politely as she explained their mission.

The ceiling fan, in concert with a pair of standing punkahs, ruffled his short hair and the stacks of paperwork lined up along the edges of his desk.

He looked like a man in a trench, hiding behind sandbags.

Crooking his finger at a heat-dazed peon slumped on a stool in the corner, he ordered refreshments.

'I remember McNally,' he said eventually. 'I worked for him as a deputy collector. At the time, Indians could not achieve the rank of Additional Collector, let alone District Collector. With independence, all that changed, and I was finally promoted to AC.' He waved a hand at the office, with its marbled white floor and whitewashed walls. 'This was McNally's office. He was an odd man. Sharp, but also a very private individual. Unlike most of the British I became acquainted with, he liked to do things for himself.' He pointed at a small desk in the corner. A typewriter sat on it, beside a lamp. 'That's his typewriter. He brought it with him from Bombay. Occasionally, he would type his own memoranda. I'd never seen an Englishman do that before. I once asked him why he didn't just use the secretaries. He told me there were some things he preferred to keep close to his chest.' He gave a tired smile. 'The British spent three hundred years here, but still couldn't bring themselves to trust us. I can't help but think that *that's* where they really failed. A failure of the imagination.'

'Have you any idea why McNally was arrested? What he was tried for?'

He shook his head. 'Frankly, it was a shock to us all. It was so rare for a Britisher to be held accountable for any sort of misdeed. All I know is that police officers came here one day to tell us he'd been arrested and to search his office. They wouldn't allow anyone to visit him, nor did the truth filter back to us.'

'There must have been speculation?'

'Rumours, yes,' he said, nodding. 'I thought he might have upset the District Collector, a notoriously unforgiving man. But it wasn't that. Some said he'd bungled a particularly sensitive administrative matter, but that didn't sound like the McNally I knew. Whatever else he was, the man was no fool. He couldn't abide incompetence.'

She pondered his words. 'I've been told that he spent the latter part of his time here working with the local temples?'

Ambekar paused as the peon returned with a steel tray bearing three glasses.

He picked up his cane juice and sipped at it. 'Yes. Temple revenue is an important source of income in Badlapore. The priests don't like it, but, then, they don't like anyone wetting their beaks at their well.'

'Was there anything about his interaction with the temples that might have led to his arrest?'

'I can't think what he might have done to upset them. Or why the British would have cared. We saw no dip in our income from the temples, and that was all that mattered to the DC.'

Seema spoke up. 'Was he a religious man?'

The question surprised him. He'd largely ignored the young girl but now gave her a second look. 'Not that I saw. It's not unheard of, of course. Britishers being drawn to *our* religion, our way of life. But McNally wasn't even a practising Christian. I doubt that he suddenly chose to "go native".'

'Were there any temples he was particularly interested in?' Persis asked.

He smiled as if she'd asked a foolish question. 'Surely you must know why Badlapore attracts so many visitors?'

She blinked, searching for an answer.

Seema spoke up again. 'The Karishma Mandir.'

He smiled. 'Yes. The Temple of Miracles.'

Before leaving, Persis walked over to McNally's typewriter. 'Why have you kept it?'

'My secretary uses it. She's unwell today.' He glanced at his watch. 'I suppose it's a reminder too. That all things crumble eventually. In the last years of the Raj, the DCs became increasingly desperate men. Once, they had been as omnipotent as gods; like gods, they could do no wrong. But, by the end, with open rebellion in the streets, all they prayed for was to not be the last man standing when the music stopped.'

Persis brushed her fingers over the typewriter's keys.

Something about the instrument seemed oddly familiar. This sensation was overtaken immediately by another, one that came upon her unawares, an instinctive notion that *here* lay the answer to the mystery . . .

Ambekar continued to speak. 'I saw a lot of things in those last days. The avarice of men with nothing to lose. Sometimes, I wonder what we might have built had the British chosen to treat us as equals instead of inferiors, as a nation to be developed, instead of merely plundered. The great civilising mission they spoke about was a comforting lie, a tale to help them sleep better at night. They came here for bounty, and when they left, they were like schoolboys fleeing a ransacked sweetshop, pockets loaded down with all they could carry.'

52

They drove through the centre of town, a series of congested lanes and squares with a surprisingly modern feel, and a preponderance of small hotels and guest houses. Persis guessed that the influx of pilgrims visiting the state's temples had given rise to a lucrative tourist industry.

Continuing eastwards, they finally came to the Karishma Mandir – the Temple of Miracles – sitting on the banks of a sluggish river.

She found herself unprepared for the scale of the building.

The temple rose at least five storeys into the sky, a mighty edifice built as a quincunx of four sandstone towers with a fifth rising from the centre. Each tower was in the form of a *shikara*, an ornately carved pyramid, along the sides of which danced gods and goddesses of the Hindu pantheon, and athletically copulating princes and princesses.

She'd seen such temples before, of course, but none as imposing.

As a non-Hindu, she harboured little interest in Vedic architecture. Her own religious leanings were limited to occasional visits to the fire temple with her father or even rarer trips to Bombay's Towers of Silence, as another of Sam's friends was laid to rest inside the stone structures, to be duly consumed by vultures.

An enormous causeway led up to the temple, heaving with bodies.

On either side were shops selling everything from coconuts and sticks of incense to white dhotis. Indeed, many of the male visitors were clad in these, with the women almost universally dressed in saris. Some of the pilgrims were all but naked; some crawled towards the temple on their bellies, watched by round-eyed children.

She realised that Seema was mouthing a prayer beside her.

It was impossible to take the jeep any further through the press of bodies.

Abandoning it at the top of the causeway, they moved through the crowds towards the temple, then turned right and walked a further three hundred yards along the riverbank to a squat concrete building.

Here, at the complex's administrative offices, Ambekar had arranged for them to meet a temple functionary.

Ten minutes later, they were sat in a stone-walled office, over-looking the river where cranes cawed incessantly and wheeled above the water. Bathers could be seen at the water's edge, dipping ritually into the water, heads bobbing up and down like aquatic penitents.

The door opened and a man walked in.

He was of medium height, wearing a wide-collared, white sports shirt rolled up to the elbows and grey trousers.

He was also, Persis couldn't help but notice, astonishingly handsome.

A matinee idol out of context.

Clean-shaven, his thick black hair had been parted to one side with geometric precision, and his brown eyes twinkled with warmth.

'My name is Aakash Kumar. I serve as the official liaison for the temple. I understand that you require some help with an investigation?'

He slipped into a seat behind a small but beautifully tooled desk, then listened intently as Persis explained the reason for their visit.

His face slackened. 'Bernard McNally. Now there's a name I haven't heard in a few years ... Do you really think you've found him?' The eagerness in his tone set alarm bells ringing.

'You knew him?'

'I know *of* him.' He seemed to weigh his next words. 'Was ... anything discovered with McNally's body?' He looked down, taking a sudden interest in a piece of paper on the desk.

'What do you mean?'

He hesitated. 'Nothing.'

She stared at him. 'Why was McNally arrested? At the time, he was working closely with the Karishma Mandir. What did he do here that led to his imprisonment?'

He frowned. 'It was before my time. McNally's role was to document our annual revenue so that the British could take their share. I have no idea why he was arrested.'

'I don't believe you.'

She felt Seema startle beside her. The young man's eyes widened. 'That was most ... direct.'

She said nothing.

He ran a hand through his lush hair. 'There are certain matters I'm not authorised to discuss.'

'Then who is?'

'Well, the temple's senior priests, I suppose.'

'Then why am I wasting my time with you?'

He blinked rapidly. She suspected he had rarely been spoken to in this way. 'Inspector, I appreciate you have a job to do, but please understand. The Karishma Mandir is thousands of years old. We have a certain way of doing things. Empires have come and gone – the Mughals, the British – but the temple and its priests persist. We won't be bullied into cooperation.'

'Perhaps you'll change your mind when the full force of the Centre descends on you.'

He grimaced. 'Nehru's government is no threat to us. They've been trying to take away control of the temple's income since independence. The matter is lodged in the Supreme Court and no doubt will remain there until both you and I are dust.'

Persis glared at him.

'Please, sir. It's very important.'

They both turned to look at Seema. The girl became dumbstruck under the handsome young man's scrutiny.

'I don't doubt that it is,' he muttered. He seemed to think the matter over. 'Very well. I will ask the priests.'

He led them out of the building and back towards the temple.

As they reached it, he stopped at the top of the causeway where an open-fronted shop selling women's clothing was doing a brisk trade. Turning to Persis, he said, 'Non-Hindus are not permitted inside the complex. But, if you don't tell anyone, neither will I. One thing that we cannot disguise, however, is your uniform.' He waved at a rack of saris. 'Take your pick.'

'You can't be serious.'

'Oh, but I am, Inspector.'

53

He led them into the temple complex, stopping only so that they could remove their shoes.

The sari rustled as Persis walked. She felt intensely uncomfortable, having rarely worn such a garment, as if all eyes had turned to scrutinise her.

The inner courtyard, a wide expanse of white marble, was thick with bodies, the scents of sandalwood and incense in the air. The courtyard was embraced on three sides by a continuous porch made up of an arched colonnade, creating a series of shaded passageways.

A dais at the front of the space was set with a series of marble idols from the Hindu pantheon.

Kumar led them around the roiling crowd, through a teakwood door, and up a flight of marbled steps to a balcony overhanging the courtyard.

'You've caught us at a bad time. Today is the visit of the royal family. The puja may take a while.'

The middle of the courtyard blazed with heat, direct sunlight falling on to the heads of the gathered worshippers. They seemed neither to notice nor care.

Persis estimated that there must have been several hundred of them, packed in like cattle.

A conch echoed around the confined space.

A series of uniformed men – armed – entered the courtyard and beat back the crowd, clearing a pathway to the dais. They were followed by a tall, paunchy man in a gold-trimmed dhoti, sporting a handlebar moustache and a necklace of emeralds, with a central stone the size of a duck egg. In his right hand, he held a curved sword, the tip pointed rigidly up at the heavens. He marched stiffly forward like a clockwork soldier.

Behind him trailed two young boys, similarly dressed and wielding miniature swords.

The younger could not have been more than four and was struggling to prevent his dhoti from falling to his ankles.

'The maharaja of Badlapore, Shivaji Rajaram,' said Kumar.

'Does he do this often?' asked Persis.

'The Badlapore royal family built this temple three thousand years ago. For fifty generations, they have served the Karishma Mandir.' He glanced at her. 'The British never understood the connection between faith and power on the subcontinent. The temple was so named because, in ancient times, this land was beset by an unending drought. The royal family at that time built the temple as a plea to the gods – and the gods responded. Within a year of the temple's inauguration, the monsoon returned.'

The maharaja stopped before the dais.

An expectant silence fell over the crowd. Seconds ticked away, and then, from the shadows behind the dais, the priests of the temple emerged one by one, dressed in saffron robes, sacred threads around their necks, white and red lines of ash smeared across their foreheads.

When the last two emerged, a sigh rose from the crowd. Many fell to their knees and prostrated themselves.

Persis saw that the brace of priests held between them a wooden plinth on which was sat another idol. The statue, about two feet from tip to tail, was of a god reclining on what looked like a multi-headed cobra.

Fashioned from gold and set with a blaze of jewels, it shone brilliantly in the sunlight.

Beside her, she realised that Seema had joined her palms together and was praying fervently.

'The Sheshnaga,' said Kumar. 'As the king of the nagas, the Sheshnaga is a primal being in the creation mythology of Hinduism, half snake, half god. He is a devotee of Lord Vishnu, hence why Vishnu is depicted with him.' He leaned over the balcony as if drawn to the glittering object. 'The Vishnu Sheshnaga is one of the holiest idols in the country, almost three thousand years old. To Hindus, its value is incalculable.'

'Let me guess,' said Persis. 'Bernard McNally tried to calculate its value anyway and tax the temple.'

He smiled ruefully. 'No, Inspector, he did much worse than that.'

She expected him to elaborate, but he'd turned back to the ritual taking place below.

She looked on as the priests led the maharaja through the prayer service, a selection of euphonious orisons, taken up by the crowd, followed by a long list of blessings bestowed by the priests upon the royal family.

As the service drew to a close, the maharaja and his sons placed flower garlands on to the idol, and made a votive offering of a rectangular tin box.

One of the priests opened the box and displayed it to the audience.

Cash.

Finally, with a ringing of small bells, the service ended.

The two priests who had brought in the Vishnu Sheshnaga carefully hoisted it aloft and vanished back the way they had come. They were followed by the remaining anchorites, until only one remained, a scrawny, hollow-eyed elderly man with a straggly white beard that trailed down to his navel.

He picked up a steel tray and handed it to the maharaja.

On it was the prasad, the food that had just been blessed by the prayer. The maharaja now proceeded to hand out morsels to the crowd, inciting a tidal surge that was brutally beaten back by his guards.

With order restored, the distribution of the prasad continued apace until the tray was empty.

With that, the maharaja took his leave, and the elderly priest vanished into the inner temple.

The crowd began to disperse.

'What did you mean?' said Persis. 'When you said that McNally had done much worse?'

Words hovered on his lips. 'You'll have to be patient, Inspector. Allow me to speak with the priests. May I suggest that you return in three hours?'

'It can't take you that long to speak with them.'

'No. But it will take me that long to convince them, if I can do so at all.'

54

They walked back up the causeway, bundled along by the departing crowd.

At the top of the road, a community of cafés and roadside eateries had sprung up, catering to famished pilgrims. They found themselves in a small restaurant serving vegetarian fare, a clatter of noise and steel utensils.

They ordered quickly, though Persis had lost her appetite.

She knew the answers were within her grasp, but the idea that the priests of the Karishma Mandir might choose not to cooperate filled her with an anxiety bordering on dread. *What could Bernard McNally possibly have done here that had led to his arrest and imprisonment?* How did it tie in with the murders that were taking place now, years later?

'You're not a person of faith, are you?' Seema's voice broke into her thoughts.

'Faith in god? Gods? No. Not really.'

'I suspect you don't have much faith in people either.'

Once again, the girl had surprised her. 'I noticed that *you* seemed quite taken with the performance.'

'Prayer is not a performance. It's how we commune with the divine.'

'I bet your mother has been praying since the day you were born. What good has it done her?'

The girl's face hardened. 'She draws comfort from her faith. If not for this life, then the next.'

'I don't believe in resurrection. Reincarnation. Whatever you want to call it. We have one life. And then it ends. No one really knows what awaits us.'

'What awaits us is the Absolute. Our atman – our souls – will merge with the Ultimate Reality.'

'I suppose you have to have faith to believe *that*.'

'Faith is about letting go of individuality. Of the ego.'

'Is that why you're here? I thought it was because you were *ambitious*.'

Seema blushed. 'I didn't say it was easy,' she muttered, and went back to her plate.

They arrived back at the temple at the allotted time. Darkness had fallen and thousands of diyas lit up the causeway like a landing strip. Lights placed on the temple's *shikaras* illuminated it for miles around, the sandstone glowing as if transmuted into gold.

Kumar had asked them to meet him at a side entrance, an arched marble doorway guarded by a brace of men bearing rifles and sporting fanned turbans.

When the door swung open, they were surprised to see that the handsome young man had shed his shirt and trousers for a saffron robe. His chest was bare and broad, a tilak of two white lines – enclosing a vertical red line – prominent on his forehead.

The mark of Vishnu.

'Please, come with me.'

They followed him into the temple, where he led them to a spiral staircase and down several floors.

'I hadn't realised you were a priest,' Persis said.

'I'm not,' he said, over his shoulder. 'But I am a qualified pandit. I've studied Vedic scriptures and Hindu law. The temple paid for my schooling. I've worked for them ever since.'

'Indentured servitude?'

'Not at all. I'm free to leave whenever I wish. Someone like you may find it incomprehensible, Inspector, but I draw great satisfaction from my work here. I've always believed in faith as a force for good.'

'Religion has been the cause of more death and pain in the history of the world than any other human endeavour. That's a fact.'

'I disagree. It's only when faith is misused that it leads to such outcomes. For millions, it remains a source of inspiration.'

They arrived in a dimly lit chamber where a pair of guards sat outside a broad iron door.

At Kumar's signal, the door was unlocked, and they entered. As soon as they had passed through, the door was locked behind them.

They travelled along stone corridors, and then down a flight of stone steps leading into another chamber, lit by torches held in sconces lining the walls.

Sweat cooled from the ancient brickwork.

Before them was an enormous arched door, the surround ornately carved with images of gods and goddesses. At the apex of the carving was the multi-hooded head of the Sheshnaga. On the surface of the door were engraved two serpents, facing each other, fangs bared.

Sat beside the door, legs crossed, beard curled into his lap, was the elderly priest from the earlier prayer service. He seemed lost in a meditative trance, and they were forced to wait until his eyes flickered open, and he clambered slowly to his feet.

Kumar joined his hands in greeting, bowing his head. Seema did the same.

The old man waited for Persis to imitate the gesture. She duly obliged, and he nodded his head in acknowledgement.

'May I present Shree Satyanarayan Shastri, the head priest of the Karishma Mandir complex. I have informed him that you have made great progress into the investigation of the events leading up to the disappearance of Bernard McNally six years ago. Shree Shastri has agreed to share information with you, in the hope that you will be able to bring that investigation to a positive conclusion.'

She frowned. The obvious question was: why did Shastri care? But she sensed that the moment was delicately balanced. One wrong word and her audience with the priest would be terminated.

'What I need to know is exactly what McNally did here. What led to his arrest and how is it tied up with the temple?'

She waited as Kumar translated. She had spoken in Hindi, but the aide relayed her words in a formal Sanskrit that she found impossible to follow.

Shastri listened, and then nodded. He turned to the dark door before them, closed his eyes, muttered what sounded like a mantra, then reached into his robe and took out a long iron key.

With Kumar's help, the door was opened, releasing a breath of cool air from the space within.

They entered a large chamber bathed in flickering torchlight. A narrow passageway bisected the chamber. On either side, open doorways led into further chambers.

Kumar plucked a torch from the wall and led them along the passageway, stopping at each chamber to show them what lay inside.

What lay inside was treasure.

That was the word that sprang to Persis's mind. It was as if they'd walked into a cave from the *Arabian Nights*.

Wooden boxes overflowed with rings, bangles, lockets, chains, and precious gemstones. Some of the crates had disintegrated with time and the contents lay in haphazard heaps on the stone floor. In the corner of one chamber stood a golden throne; in another, golden idols of gods and goddesses, golden miniatures of elephants and coconuts, and stacks of gold and silver bars.

Persis reached out a hand towards a box brimming with gold coins.

Picking one up, she saw that it was Roman.

'What you see here has been seen by very few people,' breathed Kumar. 'This is the accumulation of three thousand years of offerings, as well as centuries of trade with empires from all over the world.' His voice seemed to echo in the flickering dark.

She shivered. There was meaning here beyond the eye's reach, ancient and unfathomable.

Kumar led them onwards to a chamber at the end of the passageway.

Here, in contrast to the other rooms, there was only one object.

The Vishnu Sheshnaga, resting on a stone mount.

Kumar held the torch above the idol. The light flickered from myriad encrusted gemstones: rubies, diamonds, emeralds. The gold shone with a lustre that seemed to blaze in the dim chamber, like the radiance of a captive sun.

'You wanted to know why Bernard McNally was arrested? Here is your answer.'

55

'I don't believe it.'

Seth stared at her, sagging in his chair. In the sudden silence, the radio continued, playing a popular ditty from a film she recognised but whose name escaped her.

It was just before nine a.m., and the fragile calm she'd discovered upon entering the basement of Malabar House had been shattered by her revelation.

'What you mean is you don't *want* to believe it.'

In truth, the steadiness of her response belied her feelings.

Time seemed to have speeded up.

They'd returned from Badlapore the previous night, shortly after midnight, a tiring drive that nevertheless passed in a blur. Her mind had been aflame, working out the permutations of her discovery.

She now knew why Bernard McNally had been arrested, why he had been imprisoned.

Before making her way to Jaya's, she'd dropped Seema to her home.

The troubled look in the girl's eyes had stayed with her as she drove on towards Cuffe Parade.

At Jaya's home, she'd found Nussie waiting for her in a state of agitation. 'Where have you been?'

She explained quickly, in terse sentences.

'Badlapore? You went out of the city and didn't even think to tell me?'

'It was official business.'

'That's beside the point. You should have told me.'

She bristled. 'I know you mean well, but I'm not a child. I'm a police officer. Where or how I discharge my duty is no concern of yours.'

Nussie seemed taken aback and Persis immediately regretted her tone. She relented. 'Look. I'm fine. Jaya has been looking after me. And your concern *is* appreciated. Truly.'

Slightly mollified, her aunt sank back into the zebra-striped coach and picked up her martini glass. 'Your father and his bride-to-be were spotted at the fire temple. Things are moving rapidly.'

Persis said nothing. All she wanted was to take a shower and to be left with her thoughts.

Nussie took another slug, then, 'Sam rang me today. Asked me if we'd be attending the wedding. By "we", he meant you, of course ... I – I suppose we have no choice but to accept the situation. Salome has ensnared her Herod.' She drew herself up, a martyr with a martini. 'We must think of Sanaz. What *she* would have wanted.'

Persis knew that her aunt was right. But she couldn't think of this now. Exhaustion had begun to play its insidious song.

For a moment, her thoughts hovered on her mother.

What *would* Sanaz have wanted? Surely she would have wanted Sam to find happiness. And not just Sam. What would her mother have made of the mess her only child had made of her own romantic endeavours? How wonderful it would have been to have her here now, to talk to, to help her sift through her emotions.

'I'll have to inform Shukla,' said Seth, wrenching her back to the present.

She hesitated.

She'd spent a restless night wrestling with the pieces of the puzzle. Though much of the jigsaw was now in place, there were still gaps. 'Is that wise?'

'I don't know. But it's prudent. This isn't something we can sit on.'

'Why not? Clearly, there are many who already know and they've managed to do a pretty good job of keeping a lid on it.'

He considered the situation, then shook his head in wonder. 'When I was a child, my father took me to the Karishma Mandir. There have always been rumours of an enormous treasure hidden under the temple. My father told me there were caves full of diamonds as big as your fist. So many that it looked as if the stars had been plucked from the sky and handed to the temple priests. And it's not the only one. Many temples around the country are sitting on the sort of wealth that would make Midas look like a pauper.' He paused. 'How did McNally do it?'

It was the same question she'd posed to Kumar when he'd finally revealed the truth: Bernard McNally had stolen the Vishnu Sheshnaga.

Stolen it and then hidden it, refusing to reveal its whereabouts even when arrested, even when imprisoned. A secret he may have taken to his icy grave up in the Tsangchokla Pass.

'He compromised one of the guards while he was there assessing the temple's income. A combination of bribery and threats. He concocted a revenue case against the man's son. Threatened to imprison him. On the other hand, the guard could choose to look the other way while McNally helped himself to a small measure of the loot. So small that no one would notice. A few gold coins. A necklace.'

'And he believed that?'

'Desperate people believe what they want to believe. I've been inside those chambers. If McNally had taken anything other than the idol, he might never have been discovered. The priests say they have a record of everything in there, but no one knows for sure.'

'Then why take the idol? Why do something so foolish?'

'I think he fell in love with it. He'd spent some time working with the temples around the Banganga Tank, here in Bombay. It piqued his interest in ancient Vedic relics. I think he simply had to possess it.'

'He must have known they'd catch up with him.'

'Yes. That's why he hid it where no one could find it. That's why he refused to speak when they arrested him, even when they sent him to Dehra Dun. I believe he thought he would always find a way to escape, a way out, and when he did, the idol would be waiting for him.'

Seth shook his head. 'Such arrogance.' He looked up. 'I suppose I can understand why the authorities – those who knew, I mean – wanted to keep it a secret. A Britisher making off with one of the holiest relics in the country at the height of the Quit India movement? All while the British were trying to recruit Indians to fight their war for them. But tell me, why did the priests go along with the conspiracy of silence?'

'The masses are fickle. How would they have reacted to the revelation that their priests – entrusted to safeguard their spiritual well-being – had lost a god? They also did something very foolish. They replaced the Sheshnaga with a replica. And they didn't tell the maharaja. Once they'd ordained the lie, there was no going back. If their deception ever comes to light, they're finished.'

'So in the end, it boils down to human weakness. Greed. Fear. Self-preservation. All for the sake of a golden idol . . .' For an instant his eyes glittered, and then, just as abruptly, dimmed. 'What's the point? You can't take it with you.'

She refrained from comment. She'd learned to weather Seth's occasional philosophical outbursts. She watched him now as he poured out a whisky and sipped at it.

'But how does this all tie in with the murders of Stephen Renzi and Peter Grunewald?'

'I think McNally used the idol to convince them to help him escape from the POW camp. Promised them a share of the bounty. But something went wrong up in the mountains and they killed him. Later, after the war, they returned to India to try to find it.'

'Presumably, they failed.'

'Yes. I think McNally set down the location in his notebook. The three pages that were torn out. He did that as a precaution. In the event that he didn't make it through the mountains, he hoped the notebook would be returned to his wife and *she* might be able to unravel the code and find the Sheshnaga. A fortune to sustain her and his soon-to-be-born child.

'At the same time, by setting down the location – albeit in code – he thought he might better convince his confederates that his story was genuine – the fact that he was willing to share information – without giving the actual location away.' She stopped. 'Once they killed him, they tore out the three pages and each man kept one. That way no one man could work out the answer and cut out the others. My guess is they made a pact to reunite after the war.'

'How can you be sure none of them found the idol?'

'Because each man still had his torn page. We found the ones in Renzi and Grunewald's possession. Orelli and Stuhlmacher, I mean.'

'Found and then lost.'

She coloured. 'Yes.'

He sipped at his glass, watching her squirm. 'And you now think the fourth man – this Udo Kessler – is our killer?'

'Yes. I think the discovery of McNally's body triggered him to action. He couldn't risk an investigation that might have led back to Dehra Dun and then eventually to himself, Orelli and Stuhlmacher.'

'If Kessler has all three pages, perhaps he's already worked it out,' continued Seth. 'Perhaps he's found the idol and left the country. He's probably sitting in some Bavarian forest, drinking schnapps and laughing at us.' He sighed. 'What next?'

The question to which she had no answer.

She was convinced that both Kessler and the missing idol were still in the country. Perhaps it was wishful thinking, but what else did she have to cling to? The trouble was that there were no threads left for her to pull on, no leads that might take her further.

She'd hit a brick wall.

'There's one more thing . . . Ismail Siraj. We need to clear him. He had nothing to do with the Renzi murders.'

Seth looked as if he intended to argue, then nodded. 'Let me speak with Shukla. For what it's worth, I have no more wish to see an innocent man in jail than you do.'

56

Revelations, when they came thick and fast, had a way of enervating the senses.

Back at her desk, she took a moment to rest her eyes, and then sent the peon for a lime water.

After almost two weeks of pursuing three separate cases, she was struck by a sense of exhaustion so profound that it was all she could do not to curl up under her desk and pass into a dreamless stupor.

Yet it was too soon for self-congratulations.

She had woven the three cases into one, and now knew precisely why the Ice Man had ended up in a POW camp in Dehra Dun. She marvelled at Bernard McNally's audacity. How had he possibly thought he would get away with stealing the Sheshnaga?

More importantly: where had he hidden it? And where was Udo Kessler?

Gopal returned with her lime water. A suspicious froth floated atop the murky liquid. She ventured a sip and almost gagged, wondering if he'd simply stuck a glass in the nearest latrine.

If nothing else, the foul concoction proved a tonic for her senses, like being clubbed around the head with a polo mallet.

She settled her typewriter in front of her and began to write up her notes. Even as she did so, she realised that she would have to omit any reference to the stolen idol. But habits were hard to break and so she continued, detailing as much of her efforts as she thought might escape ADC Shukla's censorship.

An hour passed, and the silence seemed to gather around her like the quiet just before dawn. She felt something nudge against the back of her brain. The feeling became persistent, a rushing sound like the roar of an oncoming train hurtling towards her in the dark.

She paused, fingers poised over the keyboard of her typewriter.

Was it something she'd scribbled in her notes?

She scanned the last paragraph, but could find nothing there.

And then her eye fell to the typewriter's name, engraved in gold font on the ornate paper rest at the top of the instrument.

Triumph. The model that Birla had replaced her old Remington with.

A blaze of light flared inside her skull.

Triumph. Caesar's *Triumph* holds the key.

Excitement trembled through her.

Bernard McNally's wife had stated that her husband had been given the nickname Caesar by his colleagues. And in McNally's old office in Badlapore, his one-time underling had mentioned the Englishman's penchant for typing up his own notes. She remembered walking over to the machine, brushing her fingers over it. Something had struck her then, but she hadn't been able to pin down the thought.

The typewriter had been a Triumph.

She was certain of that. The image blazed in her mind with perfect clarity.

McNally had been directing them to that fact. Why?

The answer came hot on the heels of her own question.

This was the key to decoding the pages torn from his notebook.

Earlier, she had supposed that he'd used the Caesar cipher. But McNally had been cleverer than that. He'd modified the cipher to use not the *regular* alphabet but the alphabet employed by a type-writer – the QWERTY alphabet.

With shaking hands, she took a piece of paper and wrote out the keys in the order they appeared on the Triumph.

QWERTYUIOPASDFGHJKLZXCVBNM.

Thus, applying the Caesar cipher – where each letter was shifted three places to the left – would mean that, for instance, M became V, and P became U.

She was certain she had the answer. With this realisation came another, one that burst the balloon of her elation.

She'd discovered McNally's key but no longer had anything to apply it to.

She'd lost the sheets from the Englishman's notebook.

No. Not lost. They'd been taken from her. By Udo Kessler.

Bitterness gathered in her throat like bile.

She stared, glassy-eyed, at the typewriter, at her half-written notes—

She jerked upright.

Her notes.

She scraped back her chair and all but sprinted to the steel almirah in the corner of the room. Yanking open the door, she plucked out the case files she'd prepared for the murders of Dino Orelli and Dieter Stuhlmacher – Stephen Renzi and Peter Grunewald – returned with them to her desk, then searched fever-ishly inside them ... *There.*

In each file, she found her own hand-typed notes recreating the torn pages that had been discovered inside Dino Orelli's safety deposit box and Dieter Stuhlmacher's crucifix.

How could she have missed this? How could she have forgotten?

She sat down, took a moment to calm herself, then worked her way through the two sets of alphabetic characters, applying the modified Caesar cipher.

She started with the note found in Stephen Renzi's bank locker.

NIWMQ YA SICSMO

Employing the QWERTY version of the cipher, shifting the letters back three to the right, N became W, I became A, W became T ... and so on.

When she'd finished, she had the following:

WATER OF GANGES

Applying the same method to the line from the note found in Peter Grunewald's crucifix – XQYWDMQ YA QIVI– she came up with:

BROTHER OF RAMA

She sat back and stared at the two lines.

Water of Ganges. Brother of Rama.

Disappointment gradually smothered her sense of triumph.

What could McNally possibly have meant by these lines?

She was certain that he'd hidden the idol somewhere in Bombay. The temple aide, Kumar, had told her that McNally had been arrested early in the morning the day after he'd stolen the Sheshnaga. The guard who'd helped him had suffered a crisis of conscience shortly after the Englishman had left the temple and had informed the temple priests.

McNally had barely had time to get from Badlapore back to Bombay before the police had been knocking at his door.

They'd endlessly gone over his route between the two locations, but there was no realistic place where he might have secreted such a valuable treasure.

And yet, if these two lines were hinting at a hiding place for the idol in Bombay, they were of little help.

The Ganges, fifteen hundred miles in length, flowed past countless settlements as it swept across the Deccan plateau from its source in the Himalayas.

But Bombay was not one of them.

Might McNally have passed the idol to a friend to later stash in a village or town on the banks of the Ganges?

No. According to his own wife, the man *had* no friends.

Brother of Rama.

The god Rama – if that was who McNally meant – had three brothers: Lakshman, Bharata, and Shatrughna. Her grasp of Hindu mythology was shaky, but she recalled that Rama was considered an avatar of Lord Vishnu while his brothers were considered incarnations of Sheshnaga, the cobra-headed lord of the half human, half serpent semi-deities known as the nagas.

Was this an oblique reference to the Sheshnaga? If so, what possible help was that in marking its current location?

She ground her teeth in frustration.

Could it be that the third note – presumably in the possession of Udo Kessler – would somehow render these two lines comprehensible? She couldn't see how.

The thought temporarily lifted her spirits.

Kessler had all three notes. But there was a good chance he'd got no further in working out the answer than herself. She now felt certain that *that* was why all three men had still been in possession of their sheets, years after they'd returned to India.

They hadn't realised the importance of that fourth page when they'd torn the others out of McNally's notebook. *Caesar's Triumph holds the key.*

Unless McNally had told them, they could not have known his nickname had been Caesar. Or that he routinely used a Triumph typewriter.

But one person *would* have known. His wife.

And if Kessler's efforts to decode the pages had met with frustration, then it was a good bet the man was still in Bombay. Which meant—

A noise lifted her head. Moments later, the door was swung almost off its hinges, and Hemant Oberoi walked in. He seemed primed to explode.

He braked to a halt before her desk. 'I've just come from the Arthur Road Jail. A call came through to say that Ismail Siraj is to be released tomorrow.'

'Yes.'

What else was there to say? She was glad Seth had followed through on his promise. It amazed her that Shukla had so readily acquiesced to the request and acted with such swiftness. Vacating a man's confession of murder was no simple matter.

Perhaps she'd misjudged the ADC, after all.

'You had no right!' His voice was a hiss. 'This was *my* case. My—'

He stopped, overcome. His fists pulsed at his sides, eyes ablaze with a rage that was palpable. She realised then what a small man he was, in spite of his broad shoulders, his good looks. A man of such limited vision that even the slightest challenge could crumble the foundations of his world.

A Narcissus whose self-love would eventually destroy him.

In that moment, she felt not anger but pity. Pity for a man who could have been so much more, but was doomed, by the sum of his own weaknesses, to fall short.

'Am I interrupting anything?'

They both turned.

Archie Blackfinch stood by the door, glancing between them.

Oberoi blinked rapidly, then turned and stalked out of the room.

The Englishman approached. 'He seemed a little put out.'

She nodded, gathering her notes.

'I – uh – called yesterday. They told me you'd ventured out of the city.'

'Yes.'

'The last time you left Bombay I had to rescue you from inside a locked cell.'

She looked at him sharply. 'I would have found a way out eventually.'

'Yes. Of course.' He coughed. 'Still. It might have been prudent to have invited me along. Just in case your attacker is still enamoured of you.'

She didn't give him the comfort of telling him that she'd had the same thought not moments earlier.

'What did you find in Badlapore?'

She hesitated. Should she tell him? She decided against it. Instinctively, she sensed that the fewer people who knew about the Sheshnaga, the better. For now, at any rate. 'Nothing of importance.'

He nodded uncertainly. 'Well, you'll be pleased to know that *I* may be of help. This morning I had a flash of inspiration.' His green eyes became animated behind his spectacles. 'You told me that you suspected that your attacker in Dehra Dun was on the same flight as you. *I* came up on the afternoon flight. To purchase a ticket, I was forced to show some form of identification. It's a postal route, so they're careful about who they let on board.'

She was struck by the preciseness of his conjecture. So simple, so logical. Why hadn't *she* thought of it?

'You think this man was careless enough to use his real name?'

'I think he was acting in haste. He couldn't have known in advance you were travelling to Dehra Dun. He was simply following you. When people hurry, they make mistakes.'

57

The Juhu aerodrome was a twenty-kilometre drive up the city's western flank.

She arrived to find a significant police presence, both inside and outside of the airport.

She was alone, Blackfinch having left Malabar House for a meeting with the Chief Minister and the Crime Branch.

'I can't miss it,' he'd explained. 'We're discussing the future of the lab. Promise me you won't do anything rash if you find out anything at the airport. If this is the man we're looking for, he's already proven that he's willing to resort to violence.'

She'd mumbled some words to the effect that she'd wait for him before taking action. He seemed mollified and had left with a spring in his step.

She was stopped at the entrance to the airport and her identification checked.

'What's going on?'

The constable handed back her identity card and said, 'An important dignitary arriving from Beijing, madam.'

Inside the airport, she was directed to an administrative building, a low, whitewashed structure out on its own at the far side of the airfield.

As she walked across the concrete, she saw a gaggle of cameramen and flunkies converge on a military aircraft glinting in the sun. An elderly Chinese gentleman emerged from the plane's door, and made his way slowly down the steel steps, accompanied by a retinue of his own. As he reached the bottom, an Indian from the welcoming party sprinted forward with a garland of flowers, tripped in his haste, and landed in a heap at the Chinese man's feet.

The visitor conferred with a colleague, then set a hand on the concussed Indian's head. Clearly, he'd been informed that the Indian was performing a pranāma, a touching of the feet as a mark of respect for an elder.

She arrived at the administrative building, entering into the sort of controlled chaos she associated with disturbed ant heaps. Eventually, she found herself in the office of a round-shouldered man with an outsized moustache and bottle-bottomed glasses, sweating so profusely that he appeared to have been deluged by a passing shower.

She listened to him shout at someone on the phone.

Finally, he banged the instrument down, closed his eyes, took a deep breath, and faced her. 'Who are you and what are you doing in my airport?'

Ignoring his tone, she explained the reason for her visit.

He gaped at her. 'Have you any idea what I'm dealing with today? Not only do I have a visiting politico from Beijing, but I've had two flights cancelled, one of them because a nest of scorpions was discovered on board, and the other because a man died on the way from Calcutta.'

She took a deep breath. 'I need your help,' she said. 'It's impor-tant. Lives may be at stake.'

'Welcome to *my* world,' muttered the man.

In the end, he sent an underling to help her.

The young man led her to an airless room at the back of the building. Here folders were racked into steel shelves stretching the length of the space.

In short order, he dug out the passenger manifest for the afternoon flight to Dehra Dun on the day Persis had flown.

He set the folder down before her and ran a calloused thumb down the page.

'There were five passengers aboard that flight. Two were foreigners. One was a Father Malcolm Gill. The other was a man named Erich Brückner.'

Excitement flared inside her. Brückner. That had to be *him*. The man who'd followed her, assaulted her, and left her to die in that locked prison box in Dehra Dun.

Udo Kessler.

'Do you have an address?'

'He purchased the ticket in the name of a company. Indo-Germanic Exports Limited.' He showed her the address and she copied it down.

'What did he look like?' she asked.

'I'm afraid I wouldn't know. Frankly, it's unlikely that anyone here will remember one passenger on a minor flight such as this.'

Back outside the airport, she climbed into her jeep.

She understood Blackfinch's desire to act as some sort of knight in shining armour, but if the Englishman had seriously thought she would wait, he was out of his mind.

A memory struck her, of a voice rasping in her ear, an arm like an iron bar around her throat ... She got out of the jeep, walked back inside the airport building, and telephoned Malabar House.

To her frustration, Birla was nowhere to be found.

She left a message with the peon, asking him to note down the address to which she was headed, then went back to her jeep.

Adrenalin shivered through her as she turned the key in the ignition and drew the jeep out into traffic. These were the moments when she felt truly alive. When life's vagaries fell away and all that was left was the purity of her mission.

58

The route to Erich Brückner's office took her up past Jacob Circle, along Haines Road, past the Mahalaxmi race course and the old Hindu burial ground where, back at the turn of the century, the municipal authorities had interred thousands of bodies during the plague outbreak.

She remembered her late grandfather, Dastoor Wadia, telling her about the epidemic, how it had ravaged the city's poor, and the efforts of the British and Indian armies to control the outbreak. Dastoor had not hesitated in describing the symptoms of the disease to the seven-year-old Persis, the fever, the horrific swellings in the groin and armpit, the terrible death toll. The old man had always had a matter-of-fact way about him that stayed with Persis long after he'd made his own way into the fire, passing silently in the night just a year after her mother's death.

'None of us are entitled to a long life or even a good one,' he'd told her. 'Make the most of every moment.'

She arrived at the location of Brückner's office.

A stench hovered over the row of rundown buildings, emanating from a nearby sewage works.

She parked the jeep at the top of the narrow road, and approached on foot, staying close to the overhanging walls. The stench deepened, took on a texture that turned her stomach.

She arrived at the building she'd come looking for. With a cracked and stained façade of pink stucco, it looked as if it was being held up by the crumbling edifices on either side. A dog was asleep on its paws beside the door.

On the road, a milky-eyed handcartwallah watched her, smoking.

Behind him, an elephant hauling timber lumbered down the road.

She slipped her revolver from her holster and stepped into the building.

Walking up two flights of creaking steps, she became aware of the fact that her heart had begun to thud. Her fingers felt slippery on the butt of the gun.

On the second floor, she found an open door inset with frosted glass. On the glass, in black font: *Indo-Germanic Exports Limited.*

Peering inside, she saw an elderly peon so deeply asleep on a stool she thought he might have died there. Behind him was a clutter of packing crates, steel filing cabinets, and a battered wooden desk on which was set a small fan, pointed at the old man.

A second door to one side of the anteroom was closed.

She saw a dim shadow moving behind the opaque glass.

Tightening her grip on the revolver, she grasped the doorknob, then thrust the door back and charged inside, raising her weapon.

A woman stood frozen behind a desk, holding a piece of paper and staring at her in mute astonishment.

She was Indian, in her thirties, wearing a sensible skirt and blouse, with fashionably styled hair, red lipstick and pointy-framed witch's spectacles. Sweat shimmered on her neck and clavicles. Strands of damp hair had escaped from the top of her head and lay plastered to her forehead, giving her a somewhat dishevelled look.

Her eyes were focused on the revolver.

'Where is he?'

'Where is who?'

'Brückner.'

The woman took a deep breath. 'Mr Brückner is away on business.'

Persis looked around the room. It was small, with two desks, a ceiling fan, and a large canvas on the wall of Kali, goddess of death.

'Can I put my hands down?'

She realised the woman had been holding up her hands, sweat stains prominent under her arms, the sheet of paper still in one hand.

Persis lowered the revolver.

The woman sagged. 'Who are you and why are you looking for Erich?'

'I – I wish to speak to him.'

'Is that why you charged in here waving a revolver around? Because you want to *speak* with him?' Her tone was withering.

'He's a dangerous man.'

'Erich? You can't be serious.'

Persis paused. 'Who are you?'

Her name was Rosa Santos and she was Brückner's secretary, one of only two employees of Indo-Germanic Exports, the other being the ancient peon still asleep on his stool in the reception.

She'd worked for Brückner since the inception of the company in mid-1946.

'What does the company do?'

'Exactly what it says. We export Indian products to Germany.'

'What sort of products?'

'Anything, really. Mangoes. Coconuts. Wooden elephants. Erich says it doesn't matter as long as someone on the other end is willing to pay for them.'

'Is the company successful?'

She gave a dry laugh. 'Take a look around. If this is what success looks like to you, I'd hate to see your definition of failure.' She sniffed. 'I suppose I shouldn't complain. We make enough to get by. And Erich treats us well.'

'Tell me about him.'

'Do you mind if I smoke?'

She watched as the woman slumped into her chair, fished out a packet of cigarettes, lit one, then leaned back and blew smoke up towards the ceiling fan. Sweat glistened on her long throat.

'There's not much to tell. He's an intensely private man. Rarely talks about himself. Rarely talks about anything, for that matter. Trying to have a conversation with Erich is like trying to talk to a camel.'

'Did he know a man called Stephen Renzi?'

She frowned. 'The name sounds familiar. I think he may have mentioned him. Yes, I'm sure of it. I believe he came here a couple of times. Erich called him a friend which always struck me as strange. Erich doesn't have *friends*.'

'What about a man named Peter Grunewald? Very tall. Blond. He'd have been dressed as a priest.'

She nodded, recognising the description. 'Yes. He's been in a few times too. He and Erich had some very intense conversations, though he wouldn't tell me what they were about.'

She absorbed this. 'Does he have family? Is he married?'

Santos burst out laughing. 'Erich is one of those men too preoccupied with their own concerns to pay attention to a woman. At least, I've never seen him pay attention to *me* . . . I suppose he has needs, like the rest of us. But how he scratches that particular itch . . . It's not something I've ever asked.'

'Did he ever speak about his past?'

'No. Never. That was the one taboo subject. I learned that early on.' She pulled at the top of her blouse, uncomfortable in the room's sticky heat. 'What sort of trouble is he in?'

'The worst kind.'

She seemed suddenly weary. 'That's a shame. I always pegged him as a decent man. Underneath it all, I mean.'

'Do you have a recent picture of him?'

Santos opened a drawer, rummaged inside, and came up with a scrapbook.

Inside, a series of news articles detailed events in the life of the company, beginning with a fanfare and quickly petering out. The last article was almost two years in the past. 'I suppose I thought we'd grow, become one of those success stories you hear about . . . I guess I should be grateful I have a job. Though I wonder for how much longer.' It was a question more than a statement, but Persis was staring at a photograph inserted between the cuttings.

It showed a tall man, thick around the torso, with deep-set eyes, a square forehead, and a brooding expression. The face was clean-shaven, but marked by deep vertical grooves on either side of a tight-lipped mouth. She couldn't imagine that such a mouth had ever smiled. She compared this image of Udo Kessler to the youthful photo she'd seen in his POW camp file. They could have been of different men.

Kessler's experiences had clearly taken their toll.

'He isn't a handsome man,' said Santos. 'But he's civil. Up to a point. Cross him and he'll let you know about it. I remember once one of our buyers tried to stiff us. Had the gall to turn up here with some inane excuse. Erich almost throttled the man.'

'Where can I find him?'

Santos puffed on her cigarette. 'He really isn't a bad man. Please don't tell me he's some sort of war criminal on the run.'

'Tell me where he is.'

She shuddered, then took a deep breath and told her.

59

The house at the end of the row was shrouded in darkness by the time she arrived.

The address Santos had given her lay on a narrow alley near Ballard Road in Fort.

Just ten minutes from the home of Stephen Renzi.

She parked the jeep around the corner and approached on foot. A bicycle zipped by her, startling her with its bell, the boy atop it looking back, partly in curiosity, partly in annoyance. A couple strolled along the road, pausing beneath a lamp as the man took out a packet of Capstans and lit one.

They glanced at her, then turned back to their conversation.

Brückner's home was a tiny Victorian-era bungalow, with a narrow, whitewashed front and sash windows, a relic of a bygone age. As Bombay's population exploded, such homes were being bulldozed aside for apartment towers, high-rise prisons where the burgeoning middle class could hover above the teeming masses.

Old Bombay was vanishing, chewed up in the meshing gears of the future.

Her heart pounded in her ears. A feeling of recklessness flew wild in her blood. She knew that what she was doing was fool-hardy. She felt Blackfinch stumbling around inside her head, his hot breath whispering along her inner ear.

But it was too late.

She could no more stop her own momentum than she could the incoming tide.

An image of Sam flashed into her thoughts, and she was forced to clamp down on an instinctive rush of emotion. She cleared her mind and focused on the moment.

Taking out her revolver, she knocked on the door, then stepped back and to the side.

An eternity passed.

She knocked again.

Nothing.

The windows above her remained dark.

She considered attempting to kick down the door, but decided against it.

A small side door fronted a narrow alley leading to the back of the home. She clambered over the door, dropped silently to the other side, and followed the path to the rear. Here she found a tiny, untended space, and a flimsy porch door inset with a small rectangular window.

She broke the window with the butt of her revolver, reached in carefully, and opened the door.

Darkness spilled out into the sweltering night.

She walked through a cramped rear room, and into a larger space.

Inside, she found a light switch.

The room was spartan. Whitewashed walls, a two-seater sofa, a sideboard with a radio and a folded newspaper. A small table.

She walked down a corridor with her revolver held out before her and entered a kitchen, another narrow space with the minimalist trappings of the confirmed bachelor. There seemed to be no sign of recent activity, no half-eaten meal on the wooden table or dishes in the sink.

Turning back into the corridor, she padded upstairs.

Sweat trickled down her temple and along her jaw.

There was only one bedroom and it was as devoid of personality as the rest of the house. If Erich Brückner – Udo Kessler – lived here, he touched the earth lightly, a gossamer presence.

The bed was neatly made. In the wardrobe, she found clothing that was dark and unimaginative. Shirts, trousers, suits. Sensible colours; inexpensive, hard-wearing.

A search of a set of bedside drawers turned up nothing.

She sat down on the bed and allowed her mind to expand around the empty home.

Kessler was gone. She felt the certainty of it like a cannonball rolling around in her gut.

The German must have worked out the answer to the riddle, found the idol, and left the city with his treasure.

But *how* had he worked out the answer? How had he known to apply the modified Caesar cipher to the torn pages?

Frustration fell on her like a shroud; she almost wept at the thought of it, of coming so close and ending up with nothing. Neither the killer of Stephen and Leela Renzi, Peter Grunewald, and, most probably, Bernard McNally, nor the priceless artefact that McNally had stolen and hidden.

She had failed and there was little she could do to change that fact.

After an age, she stood, took one last look around the room, then walked back downstairs.

As she hovered at the bottom of the steps, her eye fell on something.

A brass doorknob attached to a panel under the stairs.

She walked to it, grasped it, and pulled the panel back, revealing an opening and a staircase leading steeply down into darkness.

The presence of the cellar was unusual. Bombay's architects tended to eschew basements because of the risk of flooding during the monsoon and the sweltering heat during the summer.

She listened for signs of life, but the only sound was that of her own breathing.

She descended the stairs; they creaked underfoot, accompanying the renewed thumping of her heart.

At the bottom, she found a thin cord hanging from the ceiling.

Pulling it activated a single dim bulb that threw shadows around the space. A bare concrete floor, whitewashed walls, a long workbench set against one wall, and bracket shelves against another.

Concrete columns bisected the space at haphazard intervals.

An open toolbox lay under the workbench, a selection of tools on the floor beside it.

She approached and squatted beside it.

A rat squealed somewhere in the darkened corners, startling her.

The sound of rushing feet.

She whirled around, rising from her squat . . . and then a starburst of pain as something thudded into her forehead. The revolver went off, an explosive sound in the confined space.

She fell back, her head cracking against the concrete floor. A low moan escaped her.

The last thing she saw, as she faded into blackness, was a dark shape looming over her, a face blurring into black.

60

She became aware of the ticking of a clock.

As she climbed back to consciousness, she realised that it was the sound of a moth batting against the naked light bulb. Its movement turned the light into a chiaroscuro of shadow playing along the walls and floor.

Pain arced around her skull, and she winced, instinctively attempting to raise her hands to her head, only to find that she could not do so.

She was trussed to a wooden chair, with thickly corded rope.

A man – Erich Brüchner – *Udo Kessler* – stood to one side, watching her impassively.

He was bigger in the small space than she had supposed from his photograph; squat, with the build of a dockworker or a thug in a gangster flick. He wore a pair of black trousers and a white shirt with the sleeves ominously rolled up. The flickering dark lent a hint of villainy to his sombre features, a monster made flesh.

'You shouldn't have followed me.'

'I thought *you* were following *me*.'

The corners of his mouth twitched.

He reached into the pocket of his trousers and pulled out a thin bundle of folded papers. 'I can't figure it out,' he said. 'The code McNally used.' He stepped towards her. 'Have you worked it out?'

She stared at him. 'What happened in Dehra Dun?'

He seemed to contemplate the question. 'McNally asked us to help him escape. He knew he couldn't get through the mountains without us. At first, we refused. Or rather Dieter refused. He had no appetite to risk our lives. But then McNally told us about the idol; he was desperate and thought if he promised to share, we'd help him. He was right. I knew that after the war, the idol could set us up for life.'

'You trusted him?'

'Of course not. We wanted some guarantee that he wasn't lying to us. I asked him to tell us where he'd hidden the idol *before* we left. But McNally was no fool. He knew if he told us, we'd have no reason to help him. And so he set down the location of the idol on the pages of his notebook, using a code. If we wanted to get our hands on it, we'd have to get him safely through. We agreed on a plan to meet up after the war and recover the idol together.'

'What would have stopped him from betraying you once you were through the mountains?'

Kessler smiled mirthlessly. 'I gave him a convincing reason not to. I told him that if he tried to run, I'd hunt him down, no matter where he went, no matter how long it took. And when I found him, I promised to kill his wife and child first. To prove to him that I meant it, I killed a man in the camp. After that, there was no chance McNally would betray us. He was an administrator. He'd never encountered a man like me.'

She remembered the story Cox had told her about Kessler murdering another inmate at the camp. Kessler had claimed self-defence, but he'd now confessed to having murdered the man simply to prove a point to McNally. A shudder moved through her.

'How did McNally die?'

Kessler's face glistened. 'He panicked. We were up in that cave where his body was found, riding out a storm. But McNally didn't want to wait. He thought the authorities were close on our heels.

We were so near to Tibet, he wanted us to make a run for it. But he had no experience in the mountains. He didn't understand how the weather could put us all in danger. I told him we were going to spend the night in the cave and he would just have to deal with it.' He stopped. 'I woke up in the night to find him trying to suffocate Dieter. Afterwards, Dieter told me a noise had awoken him. McNally had been trying to creep past him to the mouth of the cave, holding his pack. I suppose McNally sensed Dieter had awoken and was trying to stop him from calling out. He had his pack over Dieter's mouth. Something snapped inside me. I picked up a rock . . . When I recovered myself, McNally was dead.'

It was said so matter-of-factly that he might have been describing the putting down of a rabid dog. She watched him return the papers to his pocket.

'If that's true why did you kill Dieter Stuhlmacher? Why did you kill Dino Orelli?'

He stared at her. 'I didn't.'

'You expect me to believe that?'

'Does it matter what you believe?'

'If not you, then who?'

'I don't know. After I killed McNally, we stripped him of his clothes, took whatever else we might need, and left him there. We made a pact. We tore the pages from his notebook and split them between us. We agreed to go our separate ways, then meet again after the war, as we'd originally planned, and work out the answer together.' He seemed to have a sudden desire to talk, as if a switch had been flicked inside him. She guessed that he'd never had the chance to say these things out loud. A confession, of sorts. 'I returned to Bombay in December 1945. We'd all agreed to meet there, even before escaping from the camp. It was the only clue McNally had been willing to give us. He'd told us that the idol was hidden somewhere in the city. He'd suggested we meet beneath the clock tower at Victoria station at twelve o'clock on New Year's Day, the first New Year's Day after the war ended.

'That first year, Orelli and I both showed up; Dieter turned up a year later.

'At first Orelli was keen to find the idol, but then things changed. He met a woman, married. He'd started a business, as a cover, but then it began to prosper. He built a *life*.'

'What about Peter Grunewald – Stuhlmacher?'

Kessler hesitated. Something passed across the big man's face and she remembered Andrew Cox's conjecture that the two Germans had been closer than mere friends. Was that why he'd reacted with such rage when he'd seen McNally trying to suffocate Stuhlmacher? 'Dieter discovered God on the road to Damascus. He came back to India not for the treasure, but for penance. To convince the three of us to tell the truth. He lacked the courage to do it alone. He had a vision of us walking into a police station and confessing to McNally's murder.' His voice was flat. 'They refused to cooperate, refused to show me their pages. I had no idea where they'd kept the sheets. Even if I'd forced them to tell me, none of us had managed to work out how to decode them. And so I waited, hoping they'd change their minds, hoping they'd come to their senses and we'd solve the puzzle together.' He stepped forward. 'But I suspect you've beaten us to it.' Another step. 'I don't want to hurt you, but I will.'

The words came with such an absence of emotion that it was all she could do to stop herself from shivering.

'Even if you find the idol, what then? What would a man like you do with it?'

The question seemed to confuse him, as if he'd never considered it. She suspected that there was a hollow inside him, one that would never be filled. Like Alexander, in the wake of each conquest came only emptiness.

Perhaps that's why he'd been driven to climb mountains.

His gaze flattened. He walked past her, dropped into a crouch beside the toolbox, and returned with the hammer.

He held her wrist down where it was tied to the chair's armrest, then raised the hammer. The smell of his sweat and a suggestion of cologne forced its way into her nostrils.

She squirmed, suddenly maddened by terror. 'No!'

The hammer arced down, slammed into her left hand, crushing the two smallest fingers.

White-hot pain. She screamed, an unbridled yell of anguish torn from the deepest part of her. The cry echoed endlessly in the narrow room, before vanishing into the walls.

When conscious thought returned, she realised that her head was lolling on her chest, drool escaping from her lower lip on to her shirt.

Pain throbbed along the length of her arm.

She couldn't bear to look at her hand.

Instead, she focused on him. He didn't smile. He didn't gloat. He seemed, in some ways, infinitely saddened. Yet, another part of him hinted at a bottomless reservoir of patience. He could do this, inflict such agony, for as long as it took.

'Tell me what I want to know.' His dark face wavered above her.

Her mouth was full of rocks. The words refused to come.

He leaned in, grabbed her wrist, and raised the hammer.

She bucked, rocking the chair wildly on its legs, a scream gathering in her throat.

A dull knocking sound, seeping in from above.

He hesitated, then stepped back.

The knocking sounded again, persistent. The knock of someone who had no intention of going away.

He walked to the workbench, set down the hammer, and picked up her revolver.

Returning, he pulled a handkerchief from his pocket and tied it around her mouth. Stepping back, he examined his handiwork, then turned and walked towards the stairs.

61

Pain clouded her thoughts. Her left hand throbbed.

She knew she had only minutes to act. *Think!*

She blinked sweat out of her eyes, then tested her bonds. They were securely fastened, by a man who knew exactly what he was doing.

Think!

She looked around the room, but the shadows were of no help. Panic threatened to overwhelm her.

You're going to die here.

Her wildly thrashing mind latched on to a single thought. The toolbox.

From above, she heard the sound of muffled voices. There was something familiar in the rhythm of the new voice—

No time to think about that now.

She forced air into her lungs via her nostrils, then began to use her body to rock the chair.

Slowly, but surely, she built up momentum, until the chair was rocking back and forth on the tips of its legs. With a final backwards lunge, she tipped it over and fell back, crashing to the hard ground, sending a jolt through her spine, and another flash of pain as the back of her skull met the concrete.

She held her breath, fear constricting her chest. Had Kessler heard?

But the voices from above continued.

She now began to rock the chair from side to side until finally she tipped over on to her right-hand side, her right arm and leg pinned against the floor. Another blinding flash of pain flared from her left hand.

Using what little purchase she could find with her foot, and contorting her body into a series of contractions and thrusts, she began to scrape along the floor, a few inches at a time.

It seemed to take an eternity to move the few feet to the toolbox.

Her uniform was soaked in sweat. Her breath came in hard gasps.

She reached the toolbox. Her right hand had just enough freedom to scrabble on the floor among the tools scattered there . . .

Had the voices stopped? Was Kessler on his way back?

Another wild burst of panic speared through her chest. Her heart threatened to burst from her ribs.

Her grasping fingers closed around a toothed blade.

A hacksaw. Or rather, the blade of a hacksaw.

She worked it around in her fingers, and began sawing away at the rope holding her right wrist to the arm of the chair.

It seemed to take for ever, but eventually the rope frayed enough for her to release her arm.

She wasted no time, moving on to her other hand. She dared not examine it too closely. The pain had flattened to a dull crashing at the back of her mind.

With both hands free, she sawed away the ropes from her legs, and clambered to her feet, pulling away her gag.

A moment to gather herself.

She looked around for a weapon, alighted on the hammer, hefted it with her right hand, and turned towards the stairs.

There were two of them, two voices, floating from the room at the back of the house.

She walked towards the voices in a daze.

As she entered the room, she saw Kessler standing with his back to her, blocking her view of the second man.

The voice was familiar . . .

Kessler moved aside.

Hemant Oberoi stood there, in uniform, a belligerent expression on his handsome features. That expression broadened into shock as he saw her standing there, a hammer held in one hand.

A moment of perfect stillness. And then everything happened at once.

Kessler reached behind him, grasping for the revolver tucked into the back of his trousers.

Her voice jerked to a start. 'He has a gun!'

Oberoi seemed frozen to the spot, and then he reacted, reaching for his own holstered weapon.

But he was too late. Kessler's arm whipped around . . . Persis threw the hammer, operating on instinct. It hit him on the crook of his elbow, deflecting his aim so that the bullet fired harmlessly into the wall behind Oberoi.

The policeman dropped to one knee, finally struggled loose his own weapon, and fired.

Kessler fell back against the far wall, the revolver dropping from his grasp, then slid downwards, hands clutching his stomach.

The sound of the shot lingered in the room.

The strength went out of her legs and she leaned against the door frame.

Oberoi rose to his feet. He took a deep breath, moved towards Kessler, kicked away the revolver, then turned to her.

His gaze took in her exhausted state, the rope burns on her wrists, then fell to her left hand.

His eyes widened, but he said nothing.

She pushed herself away from the door, stumbled towards

Kessler, then dropped to her haunches. Reaching out with her right hand, she plucked the sheets of notepaper from the pocket of his trousers.

Kessler didn't react. His gaze was fastened to the space between his splayed legs, almost contemplative. Blood, dark red, seeped from between his fingers.

'Will you live?' she croaked.

His eyes flickered and he finally raised them to meet her own. He seemed about to reply, but then didn't.

'Why did you kill Orelli and Stuhlmacher?'

The silence stretched, warping into something dark and velvety, a sliver of night that flew from the eyes of the dying man and gradually enshrouded the room.

62

'It might seem odd to hear right now, but you've been relatively fortunate.'

The doctor was short, jowly, and as bald as a billiard ball. His narrow shoulders gave way to an ample stomach, propped up by fistulous legs. The combination was disconcerting, as were his words.

'I've seen hammer blows that have shattered bones into a dozen pieces. You've managed to get away with oblique fractures to the shafts of the fourth and fifth metacarpals. We've splinted the injury and we'll put you in a sling for a few weeks. The bruises on your skull will heal in due course.'

She nodded, a little stunned. She'd expected much worse.

The last of the adrenalin drained from her. She leaned against the backrest of the chair. The bright lights of the hospital room stabbed into her eyes and she closed them, enjoying a moment's relief.

The events of the evening were finally catching up with her.

She marvelled that she hadn't fallen into a stupor. Pain throbbed from her hand, but it seemed distant, like sound heard through a door. The painkillers were beginning to kick in.

'You have quite an audience waiting to see you,' continued the doctor. 'Several policemen, and an old man in a wheelchair threatening my staff with bodily harm should anything happen to you. I tried to explain to him that it was just a hammer blow to the fingers. He asked me if I'd like to be hit with a hammer. By him.'

She opened her eyes and stared at him. The man was unsmiling.

'Please. Send him in.'

'And the policemen?'

'They can wait.'

Sam came rolling into the room as if driving a tank.

He stared at her splinted hand, curled up in her lap, then said, 'I suppose you find this gratifying?'

She said nothing.

'From what I've been told, you could have been killed tonight. You were fortunate your colleague showed up when he did.'

She grimaced. She had no need to be reminded of the debt she now owed Hemant Oberoi. In some ways, death might have been preferable.

As they'd waited for the ambulance to arrive at Kessler's home, they'd had a brief, stilted exchange.

Oberoi had admitted that he'd tracked her down in a rage. He was still convinced that she'd deliberately sabotaged his efforts on the Renzi investigation, undermining him with ADC Shukla by securing the release of Ismail Siraj. He'd returned to Malabar House to have it out with her, to see if he could salvage his case, and discovered that she'd left the address of Indo-Germanic Exports with the peon.

Arriving there, he'd met with Rosa Santos, Erich Brückner's secretary, who had explained the exchange she'd had with Persis just a short while earlier. The encounter had left him confused. Santos had mentioned that Persis had asked about Stephen Renzi.

Who was this Erich Brückner and how did he fit into the Renzi investigation?

Stepping outside, he'd allowed his anger to cool and, for the first time, had wondered if perhaps his colleague had stumbled on to something. He was loath to admit that he'd been wrong about

Siraj, but at the same time, he was curious to find out exactly who this German was and how he might be connected to the case, the case that he was still notionally in charge of.

In the end, he'd driven to Brückner's – *Kessler's* – home and knocked on the door.

To his surprise, the German had answered, and then attempted to drive him away. Something about the man's demeanour had instantly raised his suspicions.

He'd batted Kessler's objections away, and practically forced his way into the home.

Moments later, Persis had arrived and everything had gone to hell.

The awkwardness of their conversation had led to a significant revelation.

This was the first time that Oberoi had ever killed a man, the first time that he had fired his weapon in the line of duty. In spite of his bravado, he'd hitherto skated through his police career, a wealthy dilettante playing at being an officer of the law.

She was astonished by the change in him. It was as if a whole other man, vulnerable, bewildered, lay hidden inside the boorish oaf that she'd known.

Not for the first time, she wondered if she'd been too quick to judge.

Oberoi was a product of his time, his upbringing. Could he ever have seen her as anything more than a woman? Would he ever be able to get past the monument of himself so that he might become a better man?

They'd parted on an uncomfortable note. She'd thanked him. For saving her life.

He hadn't known what to say and had departed still weighed down by his own confusion.

'How did you find out?' she said, returning to the hospital room.

'Your friend, the Englishman. He called me. Thought I should know. He's out there too.' His tone was searching, but for once he confined himself to merely examining her with an inquisitive gaze. She said nothing.

He seemed to steel himself. 'Look ... I know you're disappointed with my decision to marry Meher. But try to understand. One day, you're going to leave. You'll marry and have a home of your own. Where will I be then? An old man in a wheelchair, trundling around in an empty space with nothing but a cat for company.'

'He's *my* cat,' she said automatically.

He frowned. 'It may seem a joke to you, but the fact is that I find the prospect ... terrifying. I don't need a lot of people, Persis. But everyone needs someone. I've chosen Meher because we understand each other. We're not teenagers. We're like a pair of crabs. All hard shells and claws. Life has been no kinder to her than it has to me. But we know that we can make each other happy. All I ask is that you respect our decision.'

She found it hard to meet his eyes. Shame grasped her by the throat, and she understood now how childish she'd been. In two decades, her father had never once expressed himself so openly. He'd been her rock, and a rock shows no fear, no pain. A rock cannot experience loneliness. But a flesh and blood man ... ? It was she who was at fault, not Sam. She, who'd denied him the right to *choose*.

'I'm not disappointed. I could never be disappointed in you. I just ... it's always been you and me against the world ... I'm afraid. Afraid that you won't need me in the same way. I'm afraid of losing my place in your life.'

He seemed astonished. 'Persis. How could you possibly think that? You *are* my life and have been since the day your mother died. Nothing can change that.'

Tears blurred her vision. Words stuck in her throat and she was forced to march them out at gunpoint. 'You're an impossible old man and I love you.'

By the time her father left, to be replaced by Roshan Seth and Archie Blackfinch, it was nearing midnight. Exhaustion threatened to overwhelm her.

'Why didn't you wait?' said Blackfinch, softly.

There was no anger in his voice. Merely sadness and concern.

Seth, on the other hand, made little attempt to disguise his annoyance. 'I've never met an officer so willing to hurl themselves into harm's way.' He glared at her and then, as if sensing her weariness, relented. 'Tell me everything.'

It unfurled as a disjointed narrative, delivered piecemeal – everything she'd discovered, everything that Udo Kessler had told her in his basement confession.

When she'd finished, Seth perched himself on a hospital bed opposite her chair, feet braced against the floor as if he expected the bed to fly out from under him at any moment.

'So Bernard McNally stole the idol and they sent him to Dehra Dun because he wouldn't return it. He used the idol to bribe three fellow inmates to help him escape – which they duly did – except he tried to run out on them and so they killed him. And then they went their separate ways, came back here after the war, and have been at loggerheads ever since. No one has found the idol, and now all three of them are as dead as McNally.'

The summary was more for his own benefit than anyone else's. He was a man who preferred to do his thinking out loud. 'I suppose you were right. Finding McNally's body was the catalyst for Kessler murdering the other two. He probably thought that sooner or later someone would put together the pieces and come looking for the three of them. He'd waited long enough for the others to cooperate, and now time had run out.'

She shook her head. 'Kessler denied any hand in the killings.'

'And you believe him? The man was out of his mind.'

She hesitated, unwilling to contradict him. Kessler had been a murderous sociopath, that she did not doubt. But she recalled his seeming bemusement when she'd accused him of killing his colleagues. He had had no cause to lie.

But if not Kessler, then who?

Seth wearily got to his feet. 'I'll have to inform Shukla. God knows what he'll make of it.' He hesitated. 'I suggest you take a few days off. Give that hand a chance to heal. Let things work themselves out.'

'What if Kessler was telling the truth? There's a killer still out there.'

'And he'll *stay* out there, with or without your help. Besides, no other foreigners have been killed in the past week. Aside, of course, from the one you and Oberoi dispatched this evening.' His smile was devoid of humour. 'Kessler is the most likely suspect for the murders of Renzi and Grunewald. As far as I'm concerned, the case is closed. I'll wager a small horse that Shukla will agree with me.'

'And when the next body turns up?'

He grimaced. 'One body at a time, Persis. One body at a time.'

After he'd left, an uncomfortable silence descended on the room.

She could hear the sounds of the hospital seeping in from under the door – raised voices, the squeak of a bed being wheeled along the corridor.

She found it hard to meet Blackfinch's steady gaze.

'It's difficult to know what to say—' he began, but she cut him off.

'Try not saying anything.'

He stiffened, and she instantly regretted the outburst.

They sat in silence, until he summoned up the courage to speak again. 'When I was young, my father took us – Thad and I – to the country estate of his employer. The man was fabulously wealthy, and a peer to boot, so you can imagine my father's delight at receiving an invitation to a weekend of grouse shooting. He was an ambitious man and suspected that his employer was grooming him for a senior post.

'Thad and I found the whole thing terribly exciting: the estate was one of those old piles that seemed like a castle out of a fairy tale. With our father occupied, we had the run of the place.

'Thad had brought a torch with him and convinced me to go exploring in the woods late at night. He was younger than me, but I was always the more reticent, the more straight-laced. Galahad to his Arthur.

'The forest wasn't enchanted. Far from it. It was cold, and dark, and full of odd noises. Thad seemed in his element, but after an hour, I'd had enough, and so I turned back. It was at that point that the ground vanished from under me.' He paused. 'I'd fallen into a poacher's pit. Seven feet deep and almost as wide. I'd twisted my ankle badly and was in agony.

'When my father arrived, he looked down at me for the longest time without saying a word. Finally, he told me that I could spend the night in the pit. As a salutary lesson on the perils of misadventure.' He sighed. 'I'm not suggesting you change who you are. But a modicum of caution wouldn't go amiss, don't you think?'

They said nothing, allowed the silence to stretch, neither willing to raise the hoary topic of their own complicated equation. More than anything she wanted to talk to him, to explain how he made her feel, but she knew that it would do no good.

Finally, Blackfinch stirred. 'Would you like a cup of tea?'

She nodded. He smiled weakly, and left the room.

She leaned back in her chair. The need for a moment of respite, to be alone, became overwhelming. But blankness eluded her. Thoughts kept intruding, about the case, about the evening's events, about Blackfinch.

Her eye fell on a painting hung on the wall. A mythological scene depicting Rama and his brother Lakshman on the field of battle, bows raised.

The image returned her instantly to the notepapers she'd taken from Udo Kessler.

In the hours since, she'd been given no opportunity to examine them. Now, she reached up and plucked the papers from the breast pocket of her sweat-stained khaki dress shirt. Smoothing out the last of the sheets – Kessler's sheet – she fished a pen and her notebook from her trouser pocket, then wrote out the QWERTY alphabet on the back of the paper. She now added under each letter the letter corresponding to the Caesar key – namely, the alphabetical character three letters to the left.

She used this to decode Kessler's sheet.

When she'd finished, she had a third clue:

ARROW OF GOD

She wrote this beneath the other two sentences from Orelli and Stuhlmacher's sheets.

Water of Ganges.

Brother of Rama.

Arrow of God.

What could McNally have possibly meant? That it was a cryptic message leading onwards towards the hidden idol, she did not doubt. But how to begin deciphering it?

Revelation quivered just over the horizon.

She closed her eyes and allowed her mind to wander back over everything she'd discovered, about McNally, about the case. She was certain that he'd hidden the idol in Bombay. He'd have wanted it somewhere his wife could easily have retrieved it, in the event that he found himself incapable of doing so. Somewhere that it might be hidden with little chance of accidental discovery. A location that his wife might work out by the nature of his riddle, possibly a place that she would associate with him.

A thought nudged the back of her brain.

Something about McNally, about his work in Bombay.

She opened her eyes. Her gaze fell on the painting of Rama and Lakshman.

Lakshman, the most famous of Rama's brothers. Lakshman, a god renowned for the prowess of his archery. And there was something else, a story related to Lakshman, his arrow, and the Ganges . . .

It came in a burst of illumination.

She had it.

She knew where McNally had hidden the Vishnu Sheshnaga.

63

'What are we doing here?'

The road was deserted. Blackfinch had parked his Austin beside a handcart. Underneath the cart, its owner dozed fitfully.

She said nothing, merely grabbed the door handle and climbed out of the car. Her left hand throbbed inside its sling; she set the pain to one side and took stock of her surroundings.

She'd never visited the Banganga Tank before, never felt the need to. As a Parsee, Hindu shrines held little attraction for her. Now, with the smell of the nearby sea thick in the air, she led Blackfinch from the main road and into a narrow alley which she hoped led up to the tank. The porter they'd asked directions from at the hospital had been precise, and for that she was thankful.

A full moon lit the way as they climbed up the steep lane. She noticed that the walls on either side were covered in colourful murals depicting scenes from Hindu mythology.

At the top of the alley, a narrow opening led through to the tank.

They passed through and came out into a surprisingly large space, stone steps leading down to a rectangular pool of dark water at least a hundred metres on its longest side.

On the far side, a temple complex lay quiescent in the night, seemingly deserted, its outline reflected in the water. A pair of ducks were curled up near her feet. The smell of incense lingered in the air, mingling with the smell of excrement.

'Are you going to tell me what this is about?' Blackfinch seemed mystified.

She was grateful that he'd come this far. She doubted she could do this without him, not with one arm incapacitated.

'This is the Banganga Tank. It's been a holy site for Hindus for centuries. As a consequence, many temples have built up in the vicinity. One of McNally's roles as a revenue officer was to account for temple income, so that it might be taxed; before he was sent to Badlapore, he spent some time looking at the temples around the tank.' She stopped. 'After he'd stolen the Sheshnaga, he needed somewhere to hide it, somewhere in Bombay that he or his wife could easily get to, a hiding place it would be difficult for others to stumble across . . . I believe he came *here*. I think he hid the idol in the tank.'

'You think because he once worked here, he chose this as his hiding place?' His tone was sceptical.

'Not just because he worked here. Because his clues lead *here*. In his notebook, he wrote out hints. Kessler and the others thought he was writing them for their sake, but the truth is that McNally was writing them for his wife. So that if anything happened to him, *she* could use his notebook to locate the idol. Those clues, once decoded, read: *Water of Ganges. Brother of Rama. Arrow of God.*'

Puzzlement settled on the Englishman's features. 'We're nowhere near the Ganges. Even I know that.'

'No. But according to Hindu mythology, the Banganga Tank was created when the god Rama stopped here while searching for his wife Sita. It's the story of the *Ramayana*. Rama was overcome with fatigue and thirst and asked his brother Lakshman to fetch him water. Lakshman shot an arrow into the ground and water began to flow from that spot – that water is deemed by the faithful to be a tributary of the Ganges. In fact, the word "baan" means arrow; the literal meaning of Banganga is "the Ganges created by an arrow". The arrow of a god – Lakshman. The brother of Rama.'

He weighed her words, then looked around. 'So you're suggesting he came here, having stolen the idol, and ... did what? Threw it in? That pool is at least a hundred metres in length, and God only knows how deep.'

'I don't think he just threw it in. He would have wanted to be able to retrieve it without too much difficulty. He'd have known that during the day devotees congregate by the side of the tank, venturing in near the steps to bathe.' She pointed to the centre of the tank, where a metal pole could be seen rising from the water, glinting in the moonlight. 'That pole marks the exact spot Lakshman's arrow is said to have pierced the earth. If I had to guess, I'd say *that's* where McNally would have chosen. It's the holiest place here; aside from the temple priests, no one is permitted near it.'

He looked at her, and then understanding dawned. 'That's why you brought me here, isn't it? You want me to swim out there and take a look.'

'My arm is in a sling,' she said. 'If you won't do it, I'll take off the sling and do it myself.'

He stared at her. 'I'll bet you would too,' he murmured.

She was suddenly discomfited by the way he continued to look at her.

'Persis—'

'This isn't the time.'

He hesitated, then said, 'When *will* be the time?'

A question to which she had no answer.

The silence stretched around them, and then, finally, he stirred to life. 'Fine ... I guess you're fortunate that I was a champion swimmer at school.'

She watched as he took off his jacket and tie, and then pulled off his shoes and socks. He folded them neatly and set them on the ground. He took off his spectacles and handed them to her, then ran a nervous hand through his thick dark hair. In the moonlight, his outline seemed to shine with a ghostly phosphorescence.

'I suppose you have no idea how deep it is?'

'No.'

He looked out at the pool, muttered something under his breath, then walked down the stone steps and waded into the water, his tall form leaving long ripples in his wake.

She watched him swim out to the metal pole, his stroke strong and even.

Reaching the pole, he held on to it for a moment, and then dove, flipping up his legs and scissoring down into the dark.

Seconds ticked away, and a sudden anxiety grabbed at her.

Moments later, he broke the surface, and began paddling back to the shore with one hand, the other clutched around something she couldn't make out.

He waded out, water falling from his eaves in great cascades, and made his way back up the steps, his bare feet leaving footprints on the stone.

Standing before her, hair plastered to his scalp, his eyes shone.

He set down the burlap sack he'd recovered, then fell to his knees, undid a knot at the top of the sack, pulled it open, and reached inside.

64

Glory is in the attempt to reach one's goal and not in reaching it.

She'd read somewhere that Gandhi had once said that.

She'd never understood the sentiment. What possible glory could there be in failure? To strive for the summit and fall agonisingly short? To live with the knowledge of what might have been?

With the recovery of the Sheshnaga, she'd achieved all that might have been expected of her, if not more. And yet, sitting in Roshan Seth's office the following morning, she couldn't help the disappointment crowding her thoughts.

She watched Seth as he paced his office animatedly like a cheetah in a cage. He'd taken one look at the idol, and almost keeled over with shock. She realised that he'd only partly believed her. Perhaps that was the way with fabled treasures. They held currency only as long as they remained in the realm of myth and legend. Made real, they lost much of their potency.

Or, at any rate, their meaning became something altogether different.

Seth's agitation stemmed not from the priceless nature of the artefact, but from his anxiety at being temporarily responsible for its safekeeping.

'How many others know about this?'

The night had passed in a blur.

She'd returned from the Banganga Tank to her home, to Sam.

He'd taken one look at the idol – and the bedraggled, drenched figure of Archie Blackfinch gently steaming in his living room

345

– and immediately ordered the Englishman home – much to Blackfinch's chagrin – and his daughter to bed.

'What about the idol?' she'd said, plaintively.

'What about it?' he'd retorted. 'It's just a lump of shiny metal. Any meaning it has, *we've* given it. It'll still be here in the morning. Unless you think *I'm* going to make off with it?'

In truth, she'd been glad that he'd taken charge, glad that they'd slipped back into their old roles, as if the preceding days, their rift, had been a figment of her imagination.

By the time she'd peeled off her uniform and stood under the shower, her feet had transformed into cement blocks. She barely made it to the bed, where she all but collapsed on top of the waiting Akbar. Sleep came instantly, a dark, dreamless void from which she awoke with a clarity of purpose that had stayed with her as she'd dressed, and sat for a hurried breakfast with her father, listening with only half an ear as he described the ongoing preparations for his wedding.

Now, facing Roshan Seth, she focused on the matter at hand. 'No one,' she said. The SP had no need to know that she'd told Sam everything.

He looked at her disbelievingly, and then his expression softened. 'How are you feeling?' His concern seemed genuine.

'I'll live.'

The door to the office swung open and ADC Shukla walked in. His eyes swept the room, taking in the burlap sack on Seth's desk, the sweating superintendent, and Persis.

His gaze rested for a moment on her arm, encased in its sling, and then, without waiting for an invitation, he walked around the desk, opened the sack, and looked inside.

His expression remained neutral, but Persis saw a quickening in his eyes.

Finally, he let go of the sack and stepped back to take Seth's seat behind the desk. He placed his palms together and stared at

Persis over the top of them. 'You continue to amaze me.' He stopped. She could almost see him mentally change gears. 'I hope you understand that none of this can ever be made public?'

Her brow furrowed. 'I understand why the temple priests wouldn't wish it to be known that their congregation has been praying to a fake idol these past years, but why does the Bombay police care?'

Shukla's round eyes became thoughtful. 'Did you ever study Chanakya, the Mauryan philosopher? He once wrote that a man should never live in a place where people are unafraid of the law. Well, Persis, India is such a place. Our struggle to rid ourselves of the British has convinced the average citizen that *any* authority might be overturned, by the simple expedient of disobedience. The one authority to which this rule doesn't seem to apply is one none of us can see or touch or hear, at least not directly.'

She looked at him blankly.

'God, Persis. God is the ultimate authority, the ultimate lawmaker. And his intermediaries don't wear khaki; they wear saffron robes.'

She began to understand the shape of his argument. 'You want to return the idol and use it to exert influence over the priests?'

'The priests of Badlapore are connected to temples across the state. They are respected and revered. Their word is all but law. A single edict from the Temple of Miracles will work wonders for how the public perceive us and our role. Wouldn't *that* be a miracle worth something?' He smiled humourlessly, then rose to his feet. 'The idol will be returned.'

'No.'

He frowned. Seth's eyes bulged.

'No?'

She straightened her shoulders. 'What I mean is that I'd like permission to return the idol personally. Sir.'

He continued to stare at her. She wondered what it must be like inside his mind; all shiny levers and ball bearings moving in complicated orbits. 'Very well. I suppose you've earned that privilege. But you'll be accompanied by a retinue of my men. As a precaution, you understand?'

She understood. The Vishnu Sheshnaga had vanished once. It would never be allowed to disappear again.

She realised that Shukla was still examining her. 'There are many kinds of evil in this world, Inspector. Some would argue that systematically stripping a nation of its cultural heritage is the highest form of iniquity. Consider the facts. For three hundred years, the British asserted a moral superiority over us, a mendacity that licensed them to act with impunity, the lowliest man believing himself entitled to behave in the manner of a robber baron. Yet, our way of life, the religious iconography that underpins that way of life, is thousands of years older than their own.

'The Sheshnaga is priceless in a way no Englishman can fathom. It is a symbol. During our darkest moments, man turns not to friend or foe, but to god. If god can be stolen, it undermines the very foundations of that belief.' He paused. 'Shed no tears for Bernard McNally, Inspector. The time of Britishers looting our most sacred artefacts is at an end.'

It occurred to her then that Shukla was a Hindu, a Brahmin.

Perhaps there was more to his machinations than political expediency. In his veins moved the spiritual sap that galvanised the priests of the Karishma Mandir. In his own way, he was a servant of Vishnu, a man for whom worldly chattel meant little before the beneficence of the divine.

65

The meeting with Shukla and the euphoria of his agreeing to allow her to escort the idol home lasted only as long as it took to return to her desk.

The spectre of Udo Kessler kept returning to her; his looming face, the pulpy sound of the hammer connecting with her hand, the proximity to her own death, so close that, for an instant, she had glimpsed the afterlife.

But none of that had truly stayed with her.

What *had* stayed was Kessler's confession – or rather, the lack of it.

He'd denied killing Stephen Renzi and Peter Grunewald – the men he'd once known as Dino Orelli and Dieter Stuhlmacher. Why? He'd been in complete command, so why lie to her?

It made no sense.

She pulled out her notebook and began to go over everything she'd learned since the beginning of the case.

If Kessler hadn't killed the others, then who?

The likelihood suggested that it had to be someone who had known all of them. She dismissed the idea that the murders were unrelated, or a random coincidence.

But the four men had only met at Dehra Dun.

It stood to reason, then, that it could only have been someone from the camp.

Who had known the men well enough to serve as the final piece in an already complicated puzzle?

Andrew Cox.

She toyed with the idea a moment.

Might Cox have been involved from the outset? Perhaps, during McNally's time at the POW camp, he'd found out about the Sheshnaga, and the plan to escape and meet up in Bombay after the war.

Perhaps he'd found out too late to stop the four men escaping.

But now, with McNally's body retrieved from its icy cave, perhaps Cox had seen an opportunity to capitalise on his knowledge. Perhaps he'd employed an intermediary in Bombay to seek out the men he knew as Orelli, Kessler, and Stuhlmacher. And thus, ultimately, acquire the Sheshnaga.

Wouldn't that be a prize worth killing for?

No.

Such a scenario was based on wishful thinking, not logic.

If Cox had been involved, he wouldn't have helped her in Dehra Dun. Without his help, her investigation might have ended there and then.

She dismissed the Englishman as a likely suspect.

Her thoughts continued to spiral outwards.

To be able to murder Orelli and Stuhlmacher in quick succession, the killer must have known where both could be found. He must have known that Orelli and Stuhlmacher – Renzi and Grunewald – were in touch with each other in Bombay.

How would he have known that? Had he been following them around?

No.

The killer *knew* the two men.

A boulder crashed through her thoughts.

What if the person she was looking for had been in front of her all along? Hidden in plain sight?

An image of the wooden dolls flashed into her mind.

Udo Kessler had had nothing to do with the dolls, of that she was now certain. The dolls had been a hobby of the guard, a Gurkha, Bhadrasing Rai, who'd helped the Europeans escape, and who'd subsequently been shot and fallen to his death in a ravine, his body found the next day and cremated by his father, Delsing Rai. Delsing had told her that his son had taught soldiers at the POW camp how to carve. She'd conjectured that perhaps Kessler had carved the dolls and left them behind at the murder scenes. Or perhaps he'd used dolls given to the escapees by Bhadrasing Rai. Either way, his reason for placing the dolls at the scenes had escaped her.

But if Kessler wasn't the killer, then what were the dolls doing there?

Unless . . .

She closed her eyes and tried to remember the meeting with Bhadrasing Rai's father. His manner, the way he'd avoided her eyes when he'd described his son's fate.

Her pulse quickened as she allowed her thoughts to close around a wild hypothesis.

She recalled, now, Delsing Rai telling her *why* her son had helped Bernard McNally escape . . .

A debt of honour. A debt the Gurkhas took as seriously as a blood oath.

She took out her notebook, flicked through it, then picked up the phone and asked for a trunk call to be placed to Dehra Dun.

Three hours later, Gillian Fordyce called back, having completed the errand that Persis had asked her to undertake.

The Scotswoman had confirmed Persis's theory.

Everything fell into place.

She now knew who had killed Dino Orelli, Leela Sinha, and Dieter Stuhlmacher.

*　　*　　*

The home was set on the very edge of a patch of waste ground crowded with an assortment of kutcha dwellings. Pigs rooted around in a mound of filth, and a pair of wild dogs watched her with keen interest as she dismounted from the jeep.

Birla aimed a boot at the dogs. They avoided his clumsy foot with ease, then began barking loud enough to wake the dead.

Approaching the door, she rapped on it with the knuckles of her good hand.

She'd been here a week ago, to confirm an alibi.

Moments later, the door swung back to reveal a boy – no more than three or four years old – staring up at her with round-eyed trepidation.

The boy hadn't been present during her last visit.

Before he could speak, a man appeared behind him.

'Inspector?' said Manas Ojah, Stephen Renzi's former driver. His gaze was curious.

'I'd like to talk with you. Perhaps it would be better to do it outside.'

He stood there a moment, face impassive, then nodded.

Reaching down, he pushed the child gently back inside, then stepped over the threshold, closing the door behind him.

'Is your wife inside?'

'No. She's at the bazaar.'

They walked towards the jeep. 'What is this about?'

She dug into her pocket and took out the wooden doll she'd found at Stephen Renzi's home. Holding it out, she said, 'I thought you might like this back.'

He froze mid-step. For a while, he simply stared at the object and then his shoulders relaxed and he took it into his hands. The ghost of a smile played across his lips.

She recalled now that he'd told her that he was from Assam. Another lie.

But he'd known that Assam was home to a large Gurkha community, many of whom had arrived there as members of the armed forces during the British administration. Perhaps that's why she hadn't immediately suspected him, even after discovering that Bhadrasing Rai was a Gurkha. Beneath his beard, he seemed much older than Rai had any right to be. He looked nothing like the fresh-faced young man she'd seen in the military file Andrew Cox had sent her in Dehra Dun.

His experiences had aged him beyond his years.

'You were Stephen Renzi's driver – in another life, you knew him as Dino Orelli. Your real name is Bhadrasing Rai. You were a camp guard at the Premnagar POW camp in Dehra Dun. That's where you first got to know Orelli, Bernard McNally, Dieter Stuhlmacher and Udo Kessler. You helped them escape.

'When the British came for you, you were shot and fell into a ravine. Your father claimed to have found your body a day later and cremated you. He lied. My colleague in Dehra Dun has just spoken with him.

'You weren't killed by the bullet or the fall. Your father arranged a fake cremation and asked the local doctor, a close family friend, to sign a false death certificate. The doctor was a Gurkha too. He knew that you'd helped McNally and the others escape because of a debt of honour. He understood.' Her eyes held his face. 'How did you survive the fall? How did you know the others were in Bombay?'

The silence stretched, broken by the squabbling of the rooting pigs. 'I have a wife,' he murmured, finally. 'A child.'

'You also have a bullet-wound scar on your chest, and another one on your right knee from the wound you sustained while serving in Burma. It won't take much to prove that you are Bhadrasing Rai. Or would you prefer that we arrest your father and bring him here to identify you?'

He stared at her with startled eyes.

'How did you survive the fall?' she repeated.

His shoulders seemed to collapse. 'I fell into the water and the torrent carried me downriver. I thought I would drown, but, for a reason only the gods know, I was thrown a lifeline. A tree had fallen into the river. I became caught up in its branches and gained enough purchase to pull myself on to a mudbank.

'Once I'd recovered, I knew that I was seriously wounded. I returned to my home, late in the night, barely making it there before I collapsed. My father fetched the doctor. He removed the bullet lodged in my chest. *He* saved my life.' He stopped. 'My father knew that if the British discovered I was still alive they'd arrest me. I would be shot for helping prisoners of war escape. And so he persuaded the doctor – and several close friends – to attend a fake cremation. The doctor certified death and Bhadrasing Rai ceased to exist.

'I stayed hidden until I was strong enough to leave Nagar Koti. I clambered atop a goods train headed south, ending up in Bhopal. I spent a few months there, working as a coolie, begging, stealing, anything to survive. And then I made the decision to go to Bombay. It seemed the best place to hide.

'I adopted a new name, a new past for myself. I found work, as a labourer down by the docks. In time, I established a life, of sorts.'

'How did you find the others?'

'After the war ended, I remembered something I'd overheard them discussing when they'd been planning their escape. Something about meeting up after the war on New Year's Day at Victoria Terminus. I didn't understand why they would want to meet again. I asked McNally, but he wouldn't tell me. I knew he had some great secret he was holding over the others, something he wouldn't share with me.'

She wondered if the note of bitterness in his voice was real or something she was imagining.

'After the war, I went to Victoria Terminus, just on the chance that they might be there. I was lucky. I spotted Dino Orelli and Udo Kessler. Orelli was astonished to see me – he was calling himself Stephen Renzi by then. Kessler was displeased that I had recognised them. He didn't trust me, didn't want anything to do with me.

'I begged Orelli to take me in. I suppose I gave him no choice. He couldn't leave me out there, knowing what I knew. He gave me a job, as his driver. A year later, Dieter Stuhlmacher was waiting at the railway station. He too had a new name: Peter Grunewald.'

She held his gaze. 'I know that you took Stephen Renzi – Orelli – to meet with the others over the past few years. Udo Kessler's secretary remembers you. I called her before coming here. Described you to her. She remembers that you came looking for Kessler after Renzi was murdered. She thought it strange that you'd come without Stephen. She didn't know that you'd already killed Stephen the night before.'

She waited, but he said nothing.

'Did they meet regularly? The three of them?'

'No. Once Stephen settled into a new life, it was as if the past faded away. But Kessler was persistent. He would call at the house on occasion. Stephen would beg him to stay away, tell him that he'd visit him at his offices instead. He didn't want Leela asking questions.'

'And Peter Grunewald? Dieter Stuhlmacher, I mean?'

'He'd found religion. I don't think Stephen knew how to act around him. He stayed clear of him. Though that didn't stop Stuhlmacher coming to visit now and again.'

'And they never told you what it was they were meeting about?'

'No. I knew it was something to do with their time together at Dehra Dun, but Stephen wouldn't tell me. Neither would he explain why McNally hadn't shown up in Bombay after the war, like the rest of them. That always troubled me. I suppose I always had my suspicions, but Stephen assured me they'd all made it safely to Tibet and then parted company. He said he had no idea where McNally was now, but he was certain that he was safe and sound.' His lips twisted with distaste. She imagined him choking on the lie, when he'd first discovered that McNally had been murdered by his colleagues. 'McNally saved my life. That day in the mountains, we were out on an excursion. He tried to escape. He might have made it too, but while chasing him, I fell into a lake. He could have kept running, but for a reason I still can't fathom, he stopped and leaped in to save me. We recaptured him. From that moment on, I was his man.'

She paused a moment, unexpectedly bewitched by this portrait of Bernard McNally.

She dwelt again on the unpredictability of the human condition, the way a single individual might be made up of contradictory traits and impulses. McNally was no angel. But perhaps he was no devil either. 'How did you know the man we'd found in the cave *was* McNally? It might have been anyone.'

'I knew,' he said. 'The route they picked led up into the Tsangchokla Pass. And when I saw the image in the newspaper, the description, the sandy hair, the shirt he was wearing, I just knew. Even without his face, I knew it was him.'

She said nothing. Whether by luck or good judgement, he'd been right, and that leap of faith had set off his murderous rampage.

'Bernard McNally saved your life. You owed him a debt. By helping him escape you thought you'd repaid that debt. But when you realised that he'd been murdered by the men he'd escaped with, you decided that the debt remained unpaid. You couldn't let them go on unpunished. And so you killed Stephen Renzi and

Peter Grunewald – the men you knew as Dino Orelli and Dieter Stuhlmacher. Why didn't you kill Udo Kessler?'

For a moment, he resembled a statue, like those independence martyrs made of stone, gathering dust in town squares up and down the country. 'I tried, but I couldn't find him.'

She realised she'd been holding her breath. A part of her wondered whether Kessler had suspected that Rai had been behind the killings. That would explain why he'd temporarily gone underground until resurfacing at his home. He must have realised that the only man who could possibly have connected both Stephen Renzi and Peter Grunewald had to be their one-time camp guard.

Renzi's driver.

'Why did your wife give you an alibi for the night of Stephen's murder?'

He gave a sad smile. 'I gave her sleeping pills that evening. I took them from Leela Madam's room. I was only gone an hour. As far as my wife knew, I never left her side that night.'

'You murdered Leela too. She had nothing to do with Bernard McNally's death.'

His expression became pained. 'I had no intention of harming her. I had no idea that she'd be home that night. She was not supposed to be there. It was only when I climbed into their room, and drew back the bed curtains, that I saw her. What could I do? If I had let her live, she would have awoken. I had no choice. I – I tried my best to ease her into the next life.'

His eyes fell to the floor. Persis continued to look at him. What use was remorse in a cold-blooded murderer?

'Tell me about Peter Grunewald – Dieter Stuhlmacher.'

'Dieter was a good man. When I came for him, he did not resist. He asked to be allowed to pray one last time. I believe he was glad to be free of his guilt.'

She suspected there was a grain of truth to this.

She recalled the priest Rebeiro telling her that Stuhlmacher practised mortification of the flesh. Clearly, the man had been consumed by guilt, even if he'd assumed much of that guilt for a crime he hadn't actually committed.

'Stuhlmacher didn't murder McNally. Neither did Stephen Renzi. It was Udo Kessler who killed him.'

He blinked, momentarily uncertain. 'It doesn't matter. They were all complicit. They had years to tell the truth, but they lied. To me, to themselves.'

'And Ismail Siraj? Was he complicit too? He might have hanged for their murders.'

He shook his head. 'No. Ismail is my friend. Had they not released him, I would have come forward once I'd found Kessler. I would not have let him pay for my crime.'

Did she believe him? There was something utterly sincere about the man, in spite of the fact that he was a killer. 'Why the dolls?'

'McNally loved them. He told me that his father had been a carpenter. He'd make wooden toys for McNally when he was a boy. Perhaps that's why he saved me that day. I don't know.

'He asked me to make one of myself so that he could take it with him as a good luck charm through the mountains. That's what he called me: his good luck charm. Because he'd come up with his escape plan on the day I almost drowned and he saved my life. A plan to walk through the mountain passes to Tibet, and from there to China.' He paused, his eyes like glass. 'I suppose I wasn't the talisman he needed, after all.'

She wondered what had happened to the doll McNally had taken with him. Stolen, no doubt, along with his backpack, by the men who'd killed him. 'Udo Kessler is dead.'

His eyes flared, but he said nothing.

Did he need to know *why* McNally had been killed, the secret that had cost him his life?

No. What possible good would it do him to learn about the stolen idol?

She wondered at the strength of purpose it took for a man to commit the crimes Rai had. There was no doubt that he'd hang. A small part of her felt a measure of desolation that this would be so; and then she thought of Leela Sinha, and her resolve hardened.

In Rai's own warped mind, he had righted a great wrong. She remembered something Sam had once said, only half in jest: 'The only sure-fire cure for madness is death.'

She reached behind her and unclipped handcuffs from her belt.

Holding them out, she said, 'It's over. You've avenged him. But at what cost?'

He smiled sadly. 'Sometimes, justice demands a sacrifice.'

66

'Religion and politics make terrible bedfellows.'

Blackfinch had leaned in to whisper these words, but his poorly modulated voice had been picked up and amplified by the closeness of their surroundings. Like a flock of starlings poised for flight, the temple priests shuffled in place, nervously cocking their heads at one another; an anxious murmur passed through those that understood English.

Aakash Kumar, the temple liaison, flashed Blackfinch the sort of look reserved for drunks at weddings, and then swung his gaze towards Persis.

It was a wonder the Englishman had been allowed in at all, she thought.

It was only when she'd explained his role in helping recover the Sheshnaga that Kumar had been able to convince the temple guardians, who continued to regard her companion with a mixture of suspicion and alarm.

She couldn't blame them.

The last Britisher who'd managed to find his way in here had betrayed their trust.

Now, she watched as the twelve priests, robed in saffron, regarded the metal trunk the way one might an explosive device. Faith had its limits. At the eleventh hour, belief had deserted them. They'd been told the Sheshnaga had been recovered, but until they saw the evidence with their own eyes, they could not accept it.

The journey from Bombay had taken over six hours, escorted by ADC Shukla's armed retinue. The guards had not been allowed to set foot in the temple. Down here, in the torch-lit dark, it was now left to her and Archie Blackfinch to bring the matter to a close.

She saw that the white-bearded head priest was looking at her with a bird-bright gaze.

Stepping forward, she unlocked the trunk, then moved back towards Blackfinch.

At a nod from the elderly priest, two others took her place, opened the trunk, reached into it, and lifted out the idol, placing it gently on its dais with a soft scrape of metal on stone.

For a long moment, nothing happened. They seemed entranced, these twelve men who claimed oneness with the cosmic mysteries, keepers of the faith and the flame, bewitched by an idol made by men, an idol of gold and precious minerals, holding in its form the ineffable spirit of god. And then their voices rose in unison, a prayer amplified by the cave until it seemed to be coming from the very walls, a song of such power and beauty that even she couldn't help but be affected by the extraordinary pull of their mystery.

Religion, faith, such things had always seemed too esoteric, too lacking in the certainties that ruled her life for her to ever truly *believe*. But here, now, in this place of stone and unearthly resonance, she could understand the need for men to shoot arrows into the darkness of their own incomprehension. Call it god, or the creator, or a higher power, but deep in the human soul was a kernel of recognition that there had to be *something* out there responsible for the cosmos, responsible for the infinities that lay so far beyond the reach of human comprehension.

She felt strangely empowered.

Here, in this domain of men, she could almost imagine herself a goddess.

The prayer ended. The twelve priests closed around the idol, blocking it from view.

Kumar turned and nodded towards the entrance to the cavern.

They followed him out, as the priests' voices rose again in the strange half-light of their subterranean world.

They emerged from the temple into the piercing brightness of afternoon.

A mass of people trooped along the causeway leading to the temple, an invading army of the pious, the vain, the penitent, the fickle, and the hopeful. How many truly believed, she wondered? How many had been trained *into* belief?

'I could use a drink,' said Blackfinch, shattering the moment. He turned to Kumar. 'I don't suppose you'd care to join us?'

Kumar shook his head. 'I have duties to attend to.'

The two men shook hands.

Kumar turned towards Persis. 'Should you ever feel the need for spiritual guidance, feel free to get in touch.' He paused. 'You are a most remarkable woman, Inspector.'

She was suddenly unnerved by his gaze.

He smiled, then turned and wandered back into the temple.

'Is it my imagination or was he flirting with you?'

She raised an eyebrow. Blackfinch rarely noticed such things; the fact that he'd commented on it spoke volumes. She felt heat rising along her throat. Finding herself alone with the Englishman, she found herself discomforted. They'd barely spoken on the journey over. One of Shukla's men had been posted to their jeep, stifling any chance to clear the air.

Where did they go from here?

The truth was she didn't know. She couldn't deny her feelings, yet, at the same time, she could not give in to them. She knew herself. She could never accept a life as the echo of another's music; nor could she surrender her career to the fleeting raptures of passion.

And what of Blackfinch? What did he really want? Did he truly believe they could have a life together? Or was she just an exotic adventure before he inevitably returned to England and found himself a more suitable life partner?

A woman like Jane Davenport.

'He's a pandit,' she said. 'I believe they're sworn to a life of celibacy.'

'Really?' He seemed to brighten. 'Can't say it sounds like my cup of tea, but more power to him.'

She saw that he was examining her curiously. He waved at the temple. 'All this . . . you don't believe in any of it, do you?'

'I believe – I believe in reason,' she said. 'And I believe that we're all here *for* a reason.'

This seemed to take him by surprise.

She knew that he'd been raised a Christian, but she knew, too, that, like her, the vicissitudes of life had eroded his faith.

'How many angels can dance on the head of a pin?' he muttered, and then, after another silence, he burst into a grin, disarming her. 'To hell with it. Let's go get that drink.'

She nodded. A feeling of relief washed through her.

Whatever happened next between them could wait.

For now, the sky was blue, the heart was strong, and the mind was clear. There were battles to fight.

But today, here and now, only the moment mattered.

END

Author's Note

Although this is a work of fiction, many of the ingredients have been culled from fact:

- The POW camps at Dehra Dun were home to over a thousand prisoners during the war, mainly 'enemy aliens', civilians from Axis countries unfortunate enough to be caught in India when World War Two broke out.
- The characters of Dieter Stuhlmacher and Udo Kessler are very loosely based on Heinrich Harrer and Peter Aufschnaiter, two famous mountaineers who were captured in Karachi in 1939 while planning an ascent of Nanga Parbat.
- Harrer and Aufschnaiter spent five years in the Dehra Dun camp, before escaping, climbing the mountain passes into Tibet. Their escape and subsequent years living in Tibet – and Harrer's interactions with the then young Dalai Lama – are captured in the Brad Pitt film *Seven Years in Tibet*, based on Harrer's book of the same name. (To be clear, neither Harrer nor Aufschnaiter were murderers!)
- The Caesar cipher is as described, though the QWERTY version of the cipher is my own invention, inspired by another cipher known as the 'QWERTY or Keyboard cipher'.
- The Banganga Tank is a real feature of Bombay and its origin myth is as described in the book.
- Sheshnaga – or Shesha – is a primal being in Hindu mythology, the king of the nagas, semi-divine deities that are half human, half serpent.

- The Hindu god, Lord Vishnu, is often depicted reclining on Sheshnaga.
- The Karishma Mandir is based on various temples around India, but particularly the Padmanabhaswamy temple in Thiruvananthapuram, the state capital of Kerala, in southern India. It is often cited as the richest place of worship in the world.
- In 2015, an article in *Forbes* stated that treasure estimated to be worth one trillion dollars lay beneath the temple. What is known for certain is that in 2011, five vaults were opened by a team approved by the Supreme Court of India and fabulous riches discovered therein, much as I have described the treasures in the vaults beneath the Karishma Mandir.
- An audit conducted in 2016 into the assets of the Padmanabhaswamy temple suggested that a great deal of the treasure had mysteriously vanished. One can only speculate how much of the priceless wealth collected by the temple over the millennia of its existence has been plundered down the ages, and by whom.
- The issue of antiquities taken from sovereign nations by colonial powers around the world remains a thorny one, with arguments presented on both sides as to why such items should or should not be returned to their country of origin. With respect to Britain and India, the debate last reared its head in recent years over the fate of the Kohinoor Diamond, currently housed in the Tower of London as part of the British Crown Jewels. At present, there appears to be no appetite in the British government – or the British monarchy – to send the great diamond back to the subcontinent.

Acknowledgements

If I seem to be having a great deal of fun writing these books, it is because many others are helping to make the series possible.

So, thank you to my agent Euan Thorneycroft at A.M. Heath, my editor Jo Dickinson, my publicist Steven Cooper, Helen Flood in marketing, and assistant editor Sorcha Rose.

I would also like to thank the others involved at Hodder, namely, Juliette Winter in production and Dom Gribben in audiobooks. Similar thanks go to Euan's assistant Jessica Lee. And thank you once again to Jack Smyth for another terrific cover.

My gratitude also to my colleagues at the UCL Jill Dando Institute of Security and Crime Science: Dr Hervé Borrion – for acting as French translator; and Dr Jyoti Belur, whose former life as an intrepid policewoman in India serves, in part, as an inspiration for the character of Persis.

Finally, a grateful nod, as ever to the Red Hot Chilli Writers, Abir Mukherjee, Ayisha Malik, Amit Dhand, Imran Mahmood and Alex Caan … I'm not sure what for, but I'll think of something.

READ MORE OF THE HIGHLY ACCLAIMED
MALABAR HOUSE SERIES

'A hugely enjoyable book'
ANN CLEEVES

'The Da Vinci Code meets post-
Independence India. I'd be surprised
if I read a better book this year'
M.W. CRAVEN

And the fun never stops ... Listen to bestselling crime authors Vaseem Khan and Abir Mukherjee on the Red Hot Chilli Writers podcast

A podcast that discusses books and writing, as well as the creative arts, pop culture, risqué humour and Big Fat Asian weddings. The podcast features big name interviews, alongside offering advice, on-air therapy and lashings of cultural anarchy. Listen in on iTunes, Spotify, Spreaker or visit WWW.REDHOTCHILLIWRITERS.COM

You can also keep up to date with Vaseem's work by joining his newsletter. It goes out quarterly and includes:

*Extracts from Vaseem's next book *Exclusive short stories and articles *News of forthcoming events and signings *Competitions – win signed copies of books *Writing advice *Latest forensic and crime science articles *Vaseem's reading recommendations

You can join the newsletter in just a few seconds at Vaseem's website:

WWW. VASEEMKHAN.COM

THRILLINGLY GOOD BOOKS FROM CRIMINALLY GOOD WRITERS

CRIME FILES BRINGS YOU THE LATEST RELEASES FROM TOP CRIME AND THRILLER AUTHORS.

SIGN UP ONLINE FOR OUR MONTHLY NEWSLETTER AND BE THE FIRST TO KNOW ABOUT OUR COMPETITIONS, NEW BOOKS AND MORE.